Other Books by Alan Cheuse

FICTION

Candace & Other Stories
The Bohemians: John Reed and His Friends Who Shook the World
The Grandmothers' Club
The Tennessee Waltz
The Light Possessed
Lost and Old Rivers
The Fires

NONFICTION

The Sound of Writing (Edited, with Caroline Marshall)
Listening to Ourselves (Edited, with Caroline Marshall)
Fall Out of Heaven
Listening to the Page: Adventures in Reading and Writing
Talking Horse: Bernard Malamud on Life and Work (Edited, with
    Nicholas Delbanco)
Writers Workshop in a Book: The Squaw Valley Community of
    Writers on The Art of Fiction (Edited, with Lisa Alvarez)
Seeing Ourselves: Great Stories from America's Past (Edited)

Library of Congress, Prints & Photographs Division, Edward S. Curtis Collection, LC-USZc4-11256

A novel of american dreaming

To Catch the Lightning

Alan Cheuse

SOURCEBOOKS LANDMARK™
AN IMPRINT OF SOURCEBOOKS, INC.®
NAPERVILLE, ILLINOIS

Published by Sourcebooks Landmark, an imprint of Sourcebooks, Inc.

P.O. Box 4410, Naperville, Illinois 60567–4410

(630) 961–3900

Fax: (630) 961–2168

www.sourcebooks.com

Cheuse, Alan.
  To catch the lightning : a novel of American dreaming / Alan Cheuse.
      p. cm.
  1. Journalists—Fiction. 2. Washington (State)—Fiction. 3. Psychological fiction. I. Title.
  PS3553.H436T6 2008
  813'.54—dc22

                        2008014780

        Printed and bound in the United States of America.
            BG 10 9 8 7 6 5 4 3 2 1

For Kris, days, years, life...

acknowledgments

My deepest thanks and appreciation to Dominique Raccah and Shana Drehs...

And to Gibbs Smith and Betsy Burton, for their kindness along the way...

That which in the lightning flashes forth, makes one blink,
and say, "Ah!"—
(Kena Upanishad)

WATCHMAN

I pray the gods will give me some relief
and end this weary job. One long full year
I've been lying here, on this rooftop,
the palace of the sons of Atreus,
resting on my arms, just like a dog.
I've come to know the night sky, every star,
the powers we see glittering in the sky,
bringing winter and summer to us all,
as the constellations rise and sink.
I'm still looking for that signal flare
the fiery blaze from Troy…How I wish
my watching could end happily tonight,
with good news brought by fire blazing
through this darkness.

*[The signal fire the Watchman has been waiting for
suddenly appears. The Watchman springs to his feet]*

Fire gleaming in the night!
What a welcome sight! Light of a new day—
you'll bring on many dancing choruses
right here in Argos….

(Aeschylus, *Agamemnon*)

In Honor of William E. Myers

prologue

the assistant

UNTIL SOMEONE TELLS YOU, you never know in whose dreams you appear. So it was quite a surprise to me in my twenty-ninth year, when I was just settling in to my job as a reporter in Seattle and looking forward, in my youthful delusion, to the prospect of marriage with a sweet young woman I had met while covering a story about a fire, that life took for me such an unsuspected turn.

Midwesterners, and I was born one of them, don't love surprises. But my studies in Greek literature at Northwestern had given some glimpse into a life that was nothing but, even with the gods supposedly overseeing everything. It's an odd picture of life you get when you look at it this way. All the surprises, in hindsight, seem perfectly planned, and all our planning—such as the certainty that a man can find complete satisfaction in the classics, or that he would never be happy writing for a vulgar newspaper, or that he would never dare to take a leap into the unknown canons or traverse the plains where vast tribes of people lived in a time that could never be known within his own time—even the least of it, when it comes to pass, seems like great good luck.

Lately, Washington State, with its coastline offering a view onto the eternity of the Pacific, had trained my eye into looking longer and harder than ever before toward a future that I could not quite envision. Such was life then near the turn of the new century in our American country, a land large enough to hold past and future in a single moment. Michigan, Washington, lake and ocean, tragedy and optimism, all this was so mixed in my mind back then that I could hardly compose myself in order to do my job, which was to write about politics and mayhem, two subjects that in this time and place were, for the local newspaper, sometimes difficult to separate.

(Oh, America, where someone steeped in Homer and the tragedians could turn what little talent he had toward the trivialities of the present and hope to find in them some longer and deeper meaning! But then I took up the classics not so much for the poetry as the adventure, and this is where it got me, covering fires and petty crime in a city on the edge of the vast country we call ours.)

That was who I was and what I was doing, when, on a Sunday in a dry month with the sun brilliant overhead and Mount Rainier standing out against the southeastern sky so close as to convince any dreamer that he might reach out and touch the snowy peak as though poking at the icing on a holiday cake, my sweet young woman—a schoolteacher (since childhood I have always been sweet on schoolteachers)—and I went for a stroll along my adopted city's uneven streets where much was new among the storefronts after a terrible blaze some years before my arrival. At college I had learned that, at least when it began for the Greeks, the stage was a world. Living in Seattle, and having met and courted this local girl, whose name I will keep out of this account out of respect for her shyness and honor, I discovered soon enough that all the world was a stage.

"Oh, William, look!" said she, who, at the time, I imagined would be my wife. I glanced up to see the fateful sign—

EDWARD CURTIS
PHOTOGRAPHER

Interesting name, I thought. Do I know that name? What's in that name? Gathering my courage (for what young man, seeing himself footloose and free, doesn't admit to the fear of a moment such as this), I said, "We'll have our engagement portrait made there one day."

She melted into me, and though we walked past the shop, the sign lingered in my mind. We had strolled nearly all the way to the next street corner—which I remember well, because an old Indian man wrapped in a sodden brown blanket sat at the curbside, hands outstretched in what might have been a plea for assistance from passersby, or from his God—when I felt such a pulsing in my legs as to stop. My fiancée (for what else was she?) stopped with me, in perfect harmony with my momentous indecision.

And I turned and led her back along the sidewalk.

"Where are we going?" she said.

A small bell with a big clapper clanged as we entered the storefront. Inside it was dim, until our eyes grew accustomed, and then it became a brighter space, decorated with photographs of grim couples, some much older than the two of us, others much younger, none of them great advertisements for the marriage that must have spurred the occasion of the pose.

"Good morning." A tall, slender long-jawed man with sandy brown hair and piercing eyes stepped out of the back room and spoke to us.

I liked the fellow immediately. There was a certain mixture of strength and softness about him that put me at ease.

I said, "We would like a portrait."

My girl squeezed my arm in excitement.

"Oh, William," she said, showing me the bluest part of her eyes.

"Well," the photographer—Edward Curtis, according to the sign—cleared his throat and beamed at us. "This seems to be quite an occasion."

"I—" my girl said.

"She—" I said.

"Let me guess. You hadn't yet told her?" Curtis showed us a big smile, one that you never see in photographs of him. "Do you like surprises, Miss?" he said to her.

My girl could scarcely speak.

"Y-yes," she said in a voice just above a whisper. "Surprises like this."

"Marriage will hold many surprises for you," Curtis said. "I have found."

It was my turn to clear my throat.

"And I have offered up the first one," I said.

"Have you set the date?" Curtis said this with the ease of a man hoping to figure out the situation before him.

"It will be soon," I said, "this lovely creature willing."

My beloved was a smart girl, but she could also be coy, and now she played more the coquette than the scholar.

"Will it?" she said. "Oh, William…." And she feigned to swoon in my arms.

Curtis was a busy man with a booming business. He was, as I soon discovered, becoming the photographer whom everyone in Seattle society sought out for their family portraits. It was because of work that he excused himself, saying he would have his wife come out and make the appointment with us—adding that that was how they themselves had become reacquainted, when her family had come in for a portrait some years after their first meeting when he and she were much younger—

I looked at my new fiancée, and she looked at me, blissfully, full of hope—as Mrs. Curtis stepped into the front of the store.

I wouldn't have imagined this puffy-faced, red-haired woman as the mate of such a handsome man as the photographer. But then he had a special eye, and who was to know what he saw when he looked at her—at least I was not to know that, not yet, not then.

No smile on her face. In fact, she seemed quite put out to be called to duty.

"The children stay with my mother-in-law," she said, as if she believed we were immediately about to inquire.

"We, of course, have none," I said, a silly remark, which I was embarrassed about as soon as the words left my lips.

"They'll come soon," Mrs. Curtis said in a flat voice, the accent of which I could not place.

"We first have to marry," I said.

"That is the order of things," Mrs. Curtis said, as if recalling something she had heard in a sermon. "Marriage portraits, children, and a newer portrait."

"Which must make this such a thriving business," I said.

"We are doing well," she said, "though we have a lot of mouths to feed."

"It is one of the great new inventions of the modern world, isn't it?" I said.

"The portrait?" Mrs. Curtis said.

"Yes, the photographic portrait," I said. "Though I prefer words."

At which point my fiancée got my attention by squeezing my arm.

"Well," I said, "we must make an appointment."

"When is the wedding?" Mrs. Curtis asked.

I looked at my fiancée and she looked at me. I named a date and she squeezed me even harder.

"Clara!" Curtis called from the back room.

"Just a moment," she answered, taking up a large black appointment book and turning to the date I had named.

"Myers," I said, "Mr. and Mrs. William Myers."

"Soon to be," said my fiancée, a light sibilance on her lips, and no ability to predict the future, "very soon...."

⁓

However, events came between us and our desired goal—whims, wills, money, hopes, the stuff of usual drama, which is not the subject of my story here. Let me just say that a few years passed before this dear (and as it turned out, long-suffering woman) and I set a date. By then I had forgotten my vow to have Curtis make our portrait. It was for another reason that I eventually reencountered the straight-backed, sandy-haired photographer. Born a Midwesterner like myself but having lived a long time close to the Pacific, he had become by then a man with an urgent way of carrying himself, who saw himself as someone with vision though with some difficulty expressing it. When a client of his who taught at the university referred him to a former reporter with a facility for languages who was teaching Greek part time, he sought me out and offered me a job.

"I didn't know this when we first met. You're a reader and a writer," he said in that paradoxical way he had of making his sometimes nearly overbearing presence almost quite unassuming. "I'll make the pictures to go along with that."

That's what we did, this great New World dreamer and

myself. And now decades later, after hundreds and hundreds and hundreds of nights together on the plains working on the great project of our lives, I am only just completing his part of the story, which is in many ways not simply the story itself but the story of the story. From beginning to end, it seemed to me—as a protagonist trained in tragedy—a new sort of tale, a peculiarly American form, with trials and obstacles, and triumphs and failures that made and tested character, all of it in a race against that villain time to capture a way of life that was dying just as another was being born.

one

the clamdigger

So, SING IN ME, O Muse! (if you are still listening to pleas such as mine)....

Sing in me of Edward Sheriff Curtis...of his great quest and adventures, of his heroic yearnings to make known the faces and songs and souls of the First Americans before they faded into Time, and of the cost to his marriage, to his family, to his spirit, and to his life. Sing in me, first, of the echoes in his name, Curtiz, Cortez, which carries us back to the story of the man who conquered the New World, and then sing in me how our Curtis tried to turn the flow of time in the other direction, from conquered to conquering, from unknown to known, from now to then.

Sing how Edward Sheriff Curtis first arrived in Seattle when he was still a gawky boy, all arms and elbows, attending to his ailing father, a Civil War veteran and preacher; how they traveled by train all the way from the family home in Wisconsin, across the prairie where once buffalo by the millions grazed; and how young Edward in his day dreaming populated the empty landscape with all these absent herds. His father read the Bible and dozed—his heart was wearing —and Edward, after the prairie faded behind them and they had climbed into the mountains, gazed at slide after slide in the stereopticon given to him as a gift by a photographer for whom he had worked after school and in summers. A tall boy, he could muster a long reach when he tried, and adults liked that. He had a future, they all decided, the nature of which was not yet clear.

His older brother, Raphael, a Seattle resident of some years now who had prompted the family relocation, liked that. As soon as Edward arrived in town—and settled across the Sound where his father rented a small wooden house and prepared to bring out his wife, daughter, and youngest son who had remained behind in Wisconsin—Ray gave him a job in his livery stable. Within a few years Edward had saved some money, and with his brother's help he bought a partnership in a small photography business downtown. (A partner in a business at such an early age! Oh, America! Oh, commerce!)

Seattle—my Muse, help me to conjure its watery-blue skies, the Sound, its lake, its hilly streets, the distant snow-capped mountains—had suffered a major fire and the city was slowly recovering from the ordeal. Though not a single life was lost, family portraits went up in smoke, and photographers such as Edward were helping to restore the images to the walls, images of the new families if not the old. And in the midst of this he lost his own father. Soon after his business partner retired, he, now sole owner, moved across the water and started a family of his own, marrying red-haired, pale-skinned Clara, whose portrait he had made a few years before.

~~~~~

CLARA, IN HER WORDS

And she? Oh, she! She plunged into this infatuation she called by the name—in a diary that she kept for a while but abandoned after her children came along (but not to get too far ahead of things here)—of first and only love.

I feel, she wrote, *like the child my parents always treated me as being. I am lost, and I need a hand to hold in order to stay on the path. He seems ten feet tall to me, I look up to him so far.*

And yet he does not look down on me. He talks to me, the only man who has ever talked to me, as an equal. He tells me about his work, about his past, his family, his dreams for the future. Perhaps the cause of this goes back into the time in his adolescent years when, injured in a fall in the warehouse where he was working to bring home some needed money to his family, my father and I, who happened to be on an errand in that same place, gave him aid and brought him to a doctor who wrapped his aching back.

Though Edward did not remember me the day my family and I came into his studio for our portrait, I believe that we were destined to come together. I was more than a plain girl, my Papa told me. I think he was right. Look into the eyes of that portrait Edward himself made of me (and the others) on that fated day we met again in the studio, and anyone who sees deeply enough will see more than they might have bargained for in me. At first sight, plain—and, clearly, unmemorable. The second time, and thereafter, see my depth. My own mother often told me that, and from her I learned I had a history myself, a family history that began to the north and east and extended westward (a word Edward liked to say).

Canada, the home of both my father and mother, was just a word to me. As was Pennsylvania, the state where I was born. I loved where I lived when I first awoke to being alive, here on the shores of the Sound.

I kept dolls, my first loves. Edward courted me as though I was one of them, and I enjoyed it.

He was very sweet. He would sit with me in the parlor on my mother's best red chairs and talk about his life, telling me about a birdcall in the night that first woke him to himself when he was a boy, about his mother, his father, about his stereopticon, and his first photography lessons. He told me about the great train ride he and his father had made, and how he had imagined vast herds of buffalo racing alongside his window. All of this made me see he was a sensitive young man, someone who would care for me with affection and feeling.

I told him about my dolls. I couldn't tell him how I hoped for a good husband and children.

We walked along the shoreline, side by side but never touching, looking west to the mountains. It was always west, west, west that he talked about.

"One day," he said, "I would like to sail to Hawaii."

Never a word, never a notion about returning again to the mountains to the east of us, or scouting the snowy country to the north, or returning to cross the Great Plains, which he had traveled a while ago.

We gazed out over the Sound, the wind whipping up white-topped waves that looked as dangerous as ice. I don't understand why I have always been afraid of the water.

Children began to arrive, first a son and then a daughter. At the time of the event, which I will in a moment describe, Harold—young Hal—had just turned four and their new daughter Beth, a long and lithe young thing, was just thirteen months, and Edward's mother-in-law had become a familiar fixture in the brick house on Eighth Street to help Edward's own mother with the care of the children. Clara's sister moved in as well. All that help freed Edward to think about his work and his life. And yet thoughts of the latter made him restless, because he had little idea about what the future held for him beyond the next day's portrait making. And so, in this uneasy and unsatisfied state he would pick up his camera and tripod, leave the crowded house, and wander along the beach.

On this particular morning, with the women talking over the breakfast table and the children bickering, he felt unusually anxious and put upon, and he felt driven, or pulled, to leave the house as soon as he could—early in the day, low clouds overhead, low tide, the powerful reek of seaweed and fish in the air, gulls calling—he, a young fellow of impressive height, walked this morning with a slight stoop because of his burden as he scoured the gray sand for artifacts of he knew not what—his mind filled with shards of family life, children's outcries, requests, demands, dreams, nonsense.

And at the particularly loud and raucous cry of a soaring gull he glanced up and saw a small, dark thing at the water's edge far along on the sand. It seemed like nothing, just a clump of something, old clothes, seaweed, nothing; he didn't know. But he felt an odd curiosity, almost as if he were being pulled toward it. Subject for a photograph, perhaps? He noticed a lot of things but made few of them into pictures. But this...whatever it was, child, stranger, wayfarer, who knew? He strode heroically forward and when he was close enough, he could see the woman crouched above the sand just at the waterline, swaddled in a blanket and digging with a stick—digging for clams.

"Good morning," he called out to her.

She looked up at his approach.

Their eyes met.

Deep and deep and deeper—he saw far into her foreign soul.

They negotiated. He gave her some coins. She told him, in a voice he could scarcely hear beneath the noise of wind and lapping water, that her father had been the chief of all this land. He gave her more coins and set about his work, feeling a brief wave of nausea and drawing back for fear that if he lingered too long she might pull his own spirit into hers and never let him go.

He hurried up the steep streets to his studio, with beach sand still in his shoes, his equipment seeming lighter than air, and rushed through the door and into the back. Pushing aside all other business, he made the photograph, watching carefully as the woman's mud-colored face—nearly a blur with sweat and determination that covered the cracks and fissures made by time—floated up out of the dark. The sway of her arm, reaching down as she dug in the muck, connected to the necessity of her body and the receding tide and all the muted light behind her—

Here she was!

He tapped the photograph into a simple frame and gave it a prominent place on the wall of the studio.

He spent some time gazing at the picture, more real to him now than the memory of having seen the woman along the sandy strand.

With this chilling thought imprinting itself in gooseflesh on his neck and arms—that life might disappear but his picture of it could remain—he had started down a path of no return.

His first Indian: this was how he thought about it when his reason returned. As if he had had a plan.

His.

It took him years to understand that it might have been the other way around.

two

the climb

THE CENTURY WAS GETTING old, but time was young, and he had plenty of it. One year went by, and then another; his reputation grew. Some customers came to him off the street, as we know, after seeing his sign. Others came by recommendation and word of mouth.

And then one afternoon in the offices of the *Seattle Times,* my employer at the time (though I was probably off to cover a fire or a prank where some boys hauled a rowboat up a tree), where Edward had come to place an advertisement, in a large room that rang with the noise of typing machines and the clang of typesetting in the background, and shouts and calls and sneezes and coughs and moans and even the noise of someone far in the distant corner of the room weeping, weeping, weeping, a major turn in his life took place.

"Curtis!"

A man hailed him as he sauntered through the room, soaking up the sounds of this hectic life. This was a fellow just a few years older than Edward, wearing a striped blazer and a straw hat that seemed somewhat out of place—a bit too jocular—in this busy setting.

"Yes, sir," Edward said in his best commercial voice. He was twenty-four years old, his business was on the ascent.

"The name's Mecklinburg." The man offered Edward his hand.

"Edward Curtis. I don't believe we've met."

"I know who you are. A friend of mine over there"—he jerked a thumb toward the clutch of reporters and editors who sat at a distant desk hovering over some manuscript or other (perhaps even some story of mine that would become tomorrow's news)—"he recommended you. I came in looking for a photographer and he told me that you did fine portraits."

"I try," Edward said.

"I'd like to come by your studio and talk to you," he said.

The man offered him a sharply delivered smile—that was the look of business of the time—and they parted at the door. Edward went up to the proper desk and placed his advertisement, cheerful with the thought that his name was getting known and that his clientele was growing by the month. In that youthful fashion of having discovered that he was a magnificent person in his own right, he took pleasure in staring and staring at his name in the newspaper.

Edward S. Curtis
Portrait Photographer

A few days later this same Mecklinburg did drop by the studio. It happened to be an afternoon in which Clara had stayed home with the children—as Edward had begun to see, she was a woman torn between her duty to her children and her desire to work in the world, in other words, to be a modern woman. Edward's younger brother, Asahel, whom Edward had engaged as a portrait assistant, much against his better judgment, was absent, too, having impulsively headed off to the Yukon to search for gold. A silly impetuous boy was how Edward regarded him, a boy who flopped around in circles, like a bird with a bent wing.

Edward, of course, saw himself as a modern man, with a dream about what he must make of his life that he could not yet put into words, and so from time to time, at night, when he would awaken in the dark and wonder, terrible doubts overtook him, and he sometimes got out of bed, careful not to wake the sleeping Clara, and stood at the window, and on nights without clouds he caught a fleeting glimpse of the passing reflection of the moon on the Sound. In one of those fits of sleeplessness that mingled with the dread of failing, at what he did not know, but failing nonetheless, he recalled a night, which he had recounted to Clara when they had first met, when he was a boy, lying in bed, only to be awakened by a bird call outside his window, and feeling his blood freeze, sure that the house was surrounded by wild Indians.

Ah, Edward, portrait of the photographer as a boy turned man, and now and then still doubting!

As it turned out, Mecklinburg had a proposition for him that would send him well on his way toward dispelling these doubts.

Mecklinburg was an officer in a mountain climbing club called the Mazamas, and the membership was preparing to celebrate its third anniversary with a three-day excursion to Paradise Valley near the summit of Mount Rainier. He and some of the other forward-thinking men in the group wanted Edward to climb with them and make some photographs of the occasion.

"And bring your wife, man, bring your wife."

Edward talked it over with Clara.

"They are all those rich folk, aren't they?" she said. Her green eyes flickered like a gas lamp in the middle of a wind storm. Yes, she had her ambitions. She wasn't afraid of mountains, or at least she didn't admit to this until later.

"Every sunny morning of my life here I have seen that mountain. I think it will be quite a holiday to climb the slopes."

"The mothers will watch the children?"

"Of course, Edward. The mothers and the sisters. They'll be happy to splash about on the beach without me telling them to be careful."

He reached out and took her in his arms.

"We will have a glorious time. It will be like being rich for a little while. It's a commission. The best I've ever had."

Her eyes still flashed a mysterious green fire. Unlike the cool and distant gaze of the clamdigging Indian woman—which he thought about now and then, especially since he placed that photograph in his studio—Clara's look came from a source he recognized even if he did not fully understand it. Oh, married life! They had produced two children, and he was certain that he knew less about her than when they had first met.

But for all of that, they had, at first, a fine time on the mountain climbing adventure, beginning with their departure from the city. The club members had put the money together to rent or buy a number of newly manufactured motorcars to transport everyone from Seattle to the base of the mountain in only a few hours, a trip that would have taken much longer by carriage. No one felt more thoroughly modern than Edward and Clara as the trees fell behind them and they moved at a speed of about twenty miles per hour.

"What do you think?" Mecklinburg called out over the wind of their passage.

"Fine," Edward said, nodding his approval. "Very fine. The ride is so much smoother than a carriage that we might as well be sailing along on water."

"Good," his patron called back, holding up his straw hat in a gesture of triumph and laughing when the wind tore it from his hand.

"Stop the car," Edward said.

Mecklinburg coughed up another laugh. "Let it go, let it go, let it all go!"

That to Edward summed up the spirit of the Mazamas crowd.

Soon they went vertical, climbing toward the camp at the foot of the glaciers on the southern slope of Rainier. Many birds flew up around them, with pine siskins and rosy finches among others he recognized.

"There's mountain goldenrod," Mecklinburg pointed out to him when he inquired about some of the plants. "And lupines—"

"Those I know," Edward said.

"—well, and purple fireweed, is that new?"

"It is."

"Asters you've seen. And gentian. But look; see, there are what we call avalanche lilies."

"New to me," Edward said. "Avalanche lilies, Clara. Have you ever heard the name?"

She said no. Edward took her hand. "We must make some photographs of these flowers while we're here."

Below them lay hazy valleys to the south and to the west the bluer than blue sky, suggestive of the Sound that lay beneath it. Above in the bright sun of a summer morning, the glaciers fairly glowed with their own whiteness, as if drawing in light from the sun and turning it up to a higher intensity. "And a wonderful mixture of heat and cool," Edward added. "The wind up here is so refreshing, yet the sun still warms us."

"That's nothing compared to what you'll find up there," Mecklinburg said, with a nod toward the glaciers. "And now...." He made a theatrical sweep of his arm.

"And now," Edward said after him as they reached the environs of the camp.

"Now?" Clara said. There was a newer look in her eye, and he wasn't certain he could define it.

But here was a world above the world, which he was only just discovering. There were many folks on the mountain, not only the Mazamas folks. However, the club members held his attention as they prepared for their own climb set for the next day. "Now" was the time, as it turned out, to set up his equipment and make the portraits, some of groups and some of individuals. Edward and Clara worked in a large tent the Mazamas had erected for them, a breezy shelter from the rising glare of stone and ice.

Before too long, Mecklinburg and a few other members offered to take Edward and Clara on a short hike that would lead to some unexpected thrills. So Clara consulted with some of the other women at the camp and the next thing Edward knew she had ducked behind a curtain someone had put up under the roof and reappeared wearing a pretty set of white bloomers with red frills at the ankles and waist, several layers of blouses, and a broad-brimmed hat, which she tied under her chin. If they had only had the time just then he would have taken her picture.

But there was no time. Along with Mecklinburg and two other couples, they struck up along a trail north of the camp and hiked about a half mile or so until they had entered under the shadows of a ledge made of large overhanging rocks. It was much cooler under here, with an even colder breeze blowing out from under the rocks, and though Edward assumed that they had stopped only to rest out of the glare of the bright sun, Mecklinburg and the others kept on walking along under the ledge directly into the force of that cooler stream of air. The small loose rocks underfoot soon became covered with a thin veneer of ice and only the loose gravelly residue that covered the ice made it possible to walk without slipping.

Clara gripped his arm. "Where are they leading us? I'm frightened."

Edward told her not to worry and glanced back along the way they had come, where the underside of the huge rock ledge now seemed to be lowering close enough to the path that it gave the appearance of shutting like some horizontal aperture in his camera lens. The air had grown much colder around them, with that cold breeze blowing directly in their faces, so that their progress felt almost like a walk in a waist-high stream or small river where the rush of the current can push you back.

A child's hand could have restrained him at this point, he was so weakened by the altitude and the difficult business of walking across the ice. Yet Clara, despite her declaration of fear, seemed quite at home. He admired her large strides forward. Perhaps childbirth had strengthened her lungs while the chemical fumes in Edward's workroom had made his weak. In any case it didn't take long for her to disappear around a bend in the path, leaving him alone and huffing and puffing, feeling the chill of the narrow ice-bound route as a strange sort of burning sensation on his forehead, cheeks, and chin. Fortunately Mecklinburg had mentioned that they ought to bring gloves and these, which Edward had been carrying in his jacket pocket, he now slipped on his hands, sorry that he had not paid better attention to the man's other suggestions about putting on layers of clothing against the wind.

"Ed…ward?" Clara's voice echoed along the frozen rock.

"Com…ing!" he returned the call.

The trail took a slight downward turn and he followed it as the wind increased. Coming around the corner of the next large mass of ice-coated rock, he found his companions gathered at the front of a large, dark, open space beneath another rock ledge, the cave mouth from which all that cold air had been flowing. *Was* flowing, for it poured up from out of that dark tunnel like a river cascading horizontally—if such a thing is possible—over the lip of a falls. And all of them stood there, buffeted by its force, making a real effort to stand their ground.

"Once we get inside the wind will drop off," Mecklinburg said, motioning for them to move forward.

Clara looked back for Edward and seeing him bringing up the rear nodded and moved along with the others.

"Feeling a little better about this?" he asked when he caught up with her.

"It's fascinating," she said.

The smooth ice took on an eerie blue color as they walked into this mammoth cave, and it lay along the walls in an undulating, rippling pattern as though it had only moments before been submerged beneath the ocean and then frozen suddenly in the very midst of its own liquid insinuations. How strange to make these associations with the ocean so high above the sea! But he did feel somewhat fish-like, walking in these high, broad corridors in this odd blue icy light that seemed nearly to turn the thin air to water.

Removing a glove he touched the side of the wall, feeling the cold as a sting of fire on his fingertips. There was something about the thickness of the freeze and the way that it appeared to have been shaped and arranged, almost as if by a sculptor's hand, that kept his attention. He stared down into it, trying to see through to the wall of rock itself, but the light was intense;

yet at the same time it was quite opaque. Edward had the distinct awareness that someone had been here long before him and had stared at this wall, and then, after the ice had formed, had tried to penetrate the frozen blue wall with eyes ferociously fixed in order to view that same spot that he had seen at the beginning of things, when he had taken his first look. Was he first or last? Was he looking back in time, or forward? Edward couldn't say.

Early that night they took to their beds—or their bedrolls, to be exact—in preparation for an early start up the glacier the next morning. Edward and Clara had their tent to themselves, and he rolled the flaps down against the wind and the prying eyes of any of their Mazamas neighbors, though these jolly and mostly red-faced Seattleans were a rather cheerful and accommodating bunch who left them to themselves, not out of snobbery but out of politeness.

"Clara," he said after they had arranged themselves next to each other in their thick bedclothes on their respective pallets. "I want to talk but I don't know how to explain."

"I'm worn out from climbing, Edward. We can talk in the morning."

"We'll be in a crowd. As we usually are at home or in the studio. Alone, here with you, without the children, or customers," he said, "I enjoy it. I enjoy being here with you."

The wind sang a brisk song outside their tent.

She made a long sigh and turned her head away.

"I miss the children."

"I miss them, too, Clara. But think; many of these other couples surely must have children."

"I'm sorry," she said. "I'm tired." She leaned toward him and gave him a peck on the cheek. "We need our rest because we'll need our strength."

"Clara, we could say that about just about every day of our lives."

She became silent, and he thought she had gone to sleep, but while he was lost in a jumble of thoughts and pictures in his mind—faces, eyes, water, waves, ice, more eyes—she spoke up again.

"Edward?"

"Yes, my dear?"

"I'm frightened, Edward."

"Of what, Clara? There's nothing to worry about. These climbers know what they're doing. They are more than amateurs." (As he said that, he thought to himself, "As I am, in my business, more than an amateur.")

"No, no," she said, and he could feel her tossing one way and then another alongside him. "Not of this climb. Of the climb of...*life*...."

"How melodramatic!" Edward thought. But beneath that he was thinking, "Yes, it has been a climb, of sorts, but what did we know about marriage before marrying? How could we have anticipated any of it?"

"Are you worried about our life together?" he said.

"Not of our life together, but of my life alone. Sometimes I have such strange thoughts. Do you think I'm being foolish?"

"No, no, I would never think of you that way. But tell me, dear Clara, what precisely is troubling you?"

"I don't know; I can't say. It's just a feeling of nervousness about things."

"Nervousness."

"I don't know a better word to describe it."

"Nervousness. It may be our modern way of living," he said. "We've gone from horses to motorcars, from drawing to photography. There's bound to be many more changes in our lives, more than we can imagine. The world is moving forward, Clara. We've got to move with it."

In the dark of the tent Edward could barely see her, but he knew by the sound of her voice that she was disagreeing.

"Edward, those are all big changes. I'm not interested in those. I want to make a good life for us and the children. Perhaps these are small things to you. I think you dream bigger than you tell me."

"If I don't tell you much, Clara, it's because I don't know, because I don't have anything more than an inkling. But up here on this mountain, I have a grander sense of what I might do. It's just...."

"Just what, Edward?" She spoke sympathetically; he could hear that in her voice. But there was also—was he imagining it?—a touch of dissent, of regret, perhaps even scorn, as if she were unhappy that he could not be satisfied with the things that satisfied her. He used the word *grand*, and perhaps she objected to that, perhaps even thought he was being grandiose. But he felt it; he felt as though he were on the verge of something quite larger than himself.

"I don't know. I can't say."

After this conversation, it was a good while before Edward could find his way to sleep. He could have told himself it had to do with the altitude. They were some eight or nine thousand feet above sea level at this camp. The usually long and deep breaths he took just before sleep seemed shorter than normal, and now and then he would find himself gasping inadvertently as though he might have suddenly found himself under water.

Finally, darkness settled over him, and he slept hard but dreamed a little, too, which he was sure, at least at first, must have accounted for what he saw—the face of the clamdigger, the old chief's daughter, blurred and smeared with night. She was both young and old, shifting back and forth from maiden to hag, and in one of her incarnations as dream-hag, she spit out words that he understood in the dream but not when he awoke.

Except for: "We meet again." (Years later—on one of those dark nights in the field when after a long day of work we took our minds off our labors by talking, talking, talking—he said, "I'm a rationalist, a kind of scientist as much as artist; all photographers have to be both, I think. So if you had told me this story I wouldn't have believed it, the apparition of the clamdigging Indian woman I met on the beach. I would not have believed you, but it happened to me....") Though he was certain that she must have told him to leave his sleeping wife, get up, go out of the tent, and listen.

And he did; he did. Snow crunched underfoot—an odd sound to hear in the beginning of summer—and the light, cool wind played about his ears. He walked and walked, gazing up into the star path, thinking back to his dream.

"Are you there?" he called in his mind to the Indian hag who had appeared to him. No answer. And then an urge came over him, and he stopped. He gave a bold shout but heard nothing in reply but his own echo, at first fluttering and then torn to pieces on the wind.

"Hello?" he tried again, to no avail.

"Stupid, Curtis," he told himself and took a step back toward camp. "Oh, the tricks and demands of a man's mind!" he lamented. "The mind like a jibbering animal, dithering here and there."

Trying to calm himself, he focused on the stars, the distant stars. Cool, bright points in the sky, sailors steered by them. And men like Edward Curtis? They gazed at them, hoping for a glimpse of some meaning beyond them, beyond their own lives, for the world around them, for the universe that encapsulated them. Staring, neck getting stiff, longing, wondering—oh, to question the nature of things and receive only a stiff neck in return! He gave his head a shake, like an old horse standing too long in a stall. This was another of those moments!

He heard a sound high and away on the wind, a halloo too late to be an echo of his own voice, carried along some distance by the tenuous nature of the drifting air. A shard of a noise far above, then blasted away by fast-running currents of wind. Then silence. Or was it just an echo?

He called out again, waiting in the starry dark, this time to no response. He turned and walked back toward camp. He lay down on his bedroll under a few heavy blankets—in spring, mind you, up there in another season, another point of the compass!—and remained awake a while wondering about that echoed call under the stars and who it might have been if it had been anyone at all except his own imagination calling out within his own mind. And then, alongside the slumbering Clara, he fell into a deep sleep, from which he did not awaken even once until first light.

That light came early up there on the slopes of Mount Rainier, and dawn found him with plenty of time to ruminate about his mixed appetites, understandings, and foolish longings while he moved in and out of sleep. What was that call he heard?

By the time they made their departure, he wasn't sure which part of the night was real and which was dream. But it was in the bitter, cold air just after full sunrise when they made their way up the glacier. Because much of their trail was composed of ice bridges over the crevasses, they had to climb before the heat of the day grew so intense that the ice would begin to melt.

There were a dozen of them, led by Mecklinburg and his wife, Seattleans all. They climbed up this vast pink slab of snow and ice at an angle of about thirty degrees. The sun rose at their backs while Clara trudged in front of him, too sharply focused on her task to turn and give him a smile. Behind him walked a couple whose names he had already forgotten (though, as it turned out, the man was an acquaintance of his brother Ray and owned a feed and grain warehouse down in the city).

"That...color?" he asked, catching a breath at each word.

"Algae," the man behind him said. "A little bug that lives up here in the snow, if you can imagine it—"

"I don't have to...imagine," Edward said over his shoulder. "I can see it."

"And it's got an odor, too," the man said. "Can you smell it?"

Edward took another breath. "Watermelon!"

"That's right," the man said. "Watermelon. Delightful!"

"Clara!" Edward called to her to explain.

At last she looked at him over her shoulder, without pausing in her step. "I heard it," she said. "I heard it." And she breathed deeply herself.

Along with his wife in bloomers and the scent of watermelon drifting over the ice, many other things distracted Edward: tiny fleas that hopped about their boots when they stopped to rest and a little farther along, a half-mile-wide swathe of writhing worms just below the surface of the flow. And on the other side of a broad causeway of solid ice that carried them high above a deep crevasse, they made a promenade into a strange field of seracs that rose up out of the glacier like slender frozen trees.

Wonders here were many, and he had only seen the beginning of them. After another half hour of climbing they paused to rest beneath the large outcropping of a glacial slab, and though the sun now had risen to slant at an angle on their shoulders and necks, they also felt a wall of heat in the shade beneath the ice that slanted out overhead.

"Come," the feed and grain man said (Guterson was his name, as Edward recalled), leading him farther under the ice. A small deep hole appeared just before them. "Wait...." He held up a hand, making Edward pause. A blast of boiling wind shot up just before them, sending them jumping back into the cool air behind.

"Whoa!" Edward said, shaking off his fright. "What is that?"

"Hot vent," Guterson said. "Rainier is a volcano, neighbor. And it's alive and breathing, breathing fire like a dragon." With a loud rush of sound another shot of fiery wind blew up past their feet.

"That's how we can climb it so easily," Guterson said. "Some time ago it blew its stack and leveled out a shallow crater at the top. Therefore, there are no tall rocks for us to scale up here, just this incline."

"Tough enough for me," Edward said, watching longingly as Clara walked along ahead him.

"If you love it, you'll master it," Guterson said.

After another hour Edward understood what he meant, though he spent most of this time putting one foot in front of the other and looking up only now and then to see his surprisingly agile Clara climbing just ahead of him. One foot before the other, up and up, up and up, head and neck bent to his task, watching the heels of Clara's boots, listening to the crunch of the dry snow underfoot. Above and all around—he sneaked a look now and then—a vast scrim of pale blue sky rose up in every direction. Not a cloud to mar the azure perfection. And it was far too high for birds, even eagles. A little further down he might have asked himself, "Why are we climbing?" But the closer they got to the summit, the clearer the answer became. They climbed because they wanted to go as high as they could. They climbed because the peak of this mountain, so close to

home, towered above everything else they could see. And so
they needed to get the best of it and look down from its mighty
height. Was that enough of an answer? It was for Edward at the
time. He longed for Clara to see it the same way.

Soon they reached the crest and looked into the shallow crater
of Mount Rainier, up from which great fire and rocks had burst
who knew how many thousands of years ago, lifting the top of
an entire mountain and raining it down the slopes they had just
mastered, cutting ledges and forming caves, and poking holes
through which the still volatile mountain breathed its fiery
breath. To contemplate the power and force of the mountain
was almost more than Edward could muster. Better to turn and
look out from the rim, out across the vast expanse of air to the
west and north all the way to the Pacific, where silver clusters of
cloud appeared as large as model sailing ships on a pond, and
over to the Sound and the Strait, which glimmered in the light
of the early summer afternoon.

He anticipated a quiet night of good sleep after their exertions
that day. But just as soon as he closed his eyes, listening to
Clara's sleep-breathing, it happened again. The shape-shifting,
clamdigging Indian hag! This time, upon awakening, he
remembered what she had said. Edward lay there a while,
wondering about his sanity, wondering about his life. The
tugging at his sleeve put his mind on something else, something
quite wonderful.

"Hurry," Clara said.

"Are you serious about this?" he said.

"Quickly," she said, "before everyone wakes."

He was surprised, shocked, and pleased, and after a few
moments, ready to fulfill his duty and take his pleasure—a
married man with a house full of children and relatives could

not let an opportunity like this pass by. (Obviously, a married woman couldn't either.)

"You're not still frightened, are you?" he asked her afterward in a quiet voice.

"No, no, I'm not."

So it was that on a lovely sunlit morning, while their fellow climbers lazily assembled for a jaunt up the glacier, Edward, camera in one hand, led Clara off across the snow-splashed slope to look at flowers—large patches of blue lupines and orange asters lent beautiful contrast to the white all around and above—and when he at one point looked up at the call of a rosy finch he caught a glimpse of movement up on the ice. Mountain goats, he surmised. Or another party of climbers. At this time of year, he had learned, climbers from all around the West and across the country began their ascent of Mount Rainier. It amused—and amazed—him to consider that all the while he was working down below in the city, each year climbers had made their way up, up, across the glacier and higher still, to the crest of Mount Rainier and gazed down upon the living map below.

"It must be the air up here," he mused, that he should be caught in such mental meandering as this, wondering as he did now about who climbed the mountain when he was a child. Or, farther back yet, who climbed it first, in the days when the Russian sailors ran their schooners up and down the coast. Some seaman must have spied the crested white dome at some great distance from the Sound and said to himself, "That peak I must climb so that I may look down upon the place where now I look up." Isn't that the way our species thinks? It's there, so we'll do it.

"And you slept well?" he asked Clara.

"Fitfully," she said. She pulled at a loose strand of hair. In her climbing costume of blouse and bloomers she seemed quite fetching, especially as she made toward him a mock curtsey. Someone called to them to return—Mecklinburg, assembling his forces, stood now in the midst of them, waving his arms like an orchestra master.

When the sun rose and painted them with light, men who had started up the trail in jackets shed them and packed them in their kits or tied them around their waists. Women did the same with shawls and sweaters. It was as if none of them, however experienced they might be, could reconcile the season with the surroundings and come to terms quickly with this odd mixture of sun, heat, ice, and cold.

One foot after another, their efforts made them sweat despite their icy surroundings. Above them in the pale blue sweep of the sky the sun had swung around to the south, where in the valleys below fog still clung to the base of the mountains, cottony and ruffled. To the north, oh, the north, it remained the same for an hour of their climb, the steep cliffs of the Kautz glacier blocking their view of the crest.

"How are you, miss?" he asked of Clara, enjoying the mock-flirtation. Each of them was carrying equipment, though hers was, of course, the light part of the load.

"I'm well," she said, flinging him a smile. Small beads of water had broken out in a line across her smooth forehead and her already-red cheeks reddened even more. Edward could not help but notice the small, dark stains spreading out beneath the arms of her blouse. His own face must have turned a bit red at the memory of their early morning encounter.

"Let's leave the main trail in a few hundred yards," he said, glancing at the line of climbers they were following.

"Do you know where we're going?" she asked.

"Oh, just to see if we can find more flowers," he said. But his heart was beating hard, in anticipation of something else.

The main group climbed upward, as Edward kept Clara walking along a narrow trail near the lip of the glacier, and then over a wide ice-bridge above a chasm that, though only about a hundred feet deep, if they fell, would be enough to trap them until what would be the end of their very short lives. The trail then sloped down and turned them farther to the east. A faint screeching rose to their ears, and they could see below, a thousand feet and more beyond the edge of the ice fields, a pair of eagles spiraling up and then turning in the air and swooping down, down far past where their eyes could follow into the clouds and mist that gathered where the mountain met the forests sweeping up from the distant edge of the horizon.

"You see?" he said to Clara as they paused on the trail, their backs against a smooth sheet of ice thinned out by constant exposure to the morning sun, so that it revealed the dark rock beneath.

"All the while I was living below," she said, "I never imagined this. I'd look up at the mountain and just see its whiteness, like one big mound of snow, the clouds sometimes blocking it from view. When that happened it just faded from my thoughts."

"But it's always here," Edward said. "We live, we work...we...raise our family; the mountain is always here."

Clara tore her eyes from the view and fixed her stare on Edward. "But shouldn't we catch up with the group now?"

"I...want to walk this way a little farther."

He motioned for her to follow as he edged along the trail. Just a short way ahead it narrowed, and they had to concentrate to keep their balance because of the equipment they had in tow. As the way grew slightly wider and turned up and around a large outcropping of ice and rock, his chest loosened and he found himself breathing a little easier.

"Come along," he said, stepping in front of Clara—the trail had widened just enough for that—and as if she were his daughter and he were helping her along the path up to the glacier, he reached behind him. She reached out and found his groping hand with her own. He tugged at her and she came up alongside him as the trail became a path leading directly before the gaping mouth of a dark ice cave slashed in the side of the glacier, one of the many such caves carved by the surging vents of heat from the bowels of the petulant volcano beneath the ice.

"In there," he said in the voice of a man who knew where he stood.

"What?" She seemed genuinely surprised, though she did not let go of his hand.

"We'll step in there," he said. "The cave. Warmer. The heat vents."

"Heat vents?"

"Good, at night," he said, seeing how ridiculous was his statement in the face of the warm sun spilling its heat down on them.

"Oh," she said.

"Put these down," he said, setting the tripod and the camera onto the ice before the lip of the cave.

"Alright," she said, taking her hand from him in order to gently place her burden down alongside his own.

"We'll look for flowers," Edward said.

"In there?"

"There may be," he said, reaching for her hand again.

"You know better than I," she said, taking his hand.

"I don't know much," he said.

"Still, more than I," she said.

"I don't know," he said.

They stepped together into the dark cave and paused there, his face inclined toward hers and hers toward his. The air within this hideaway gave off a strange mixture of the sulphurous and the delectable, as though the vents of steam had carried it a long way up, all the distance from the green fields in the lowest valleys, and from the boiling cauldrons of volcanic flow below the strata where they lived, mixing it, swirling it about as it surged up through one of the many mile-high chimneys that lay hidden behind the ice and rock. Even as they stood there, a warm blast of steam blew past them from the inner recesses of the cave, bathing them in a mix of stink and perfume.

"Halllooo!" a voice from deep within the cave.

Edward started, as though from a blow to the ear. Clara pulled free of him, her eyes wide, both of them spinning around to stare into the bruise-blue dark of this aperture in the mountainside.

A stocky fellow wearing a parka and large gloves came stumbling out of the back of the cave, his hand extended toward them.

"So glad to see you, never thought we'd find our way out."

"What, ho?" "Look, look!" Several other men staggered up behind him, their eyes blinking against the bright light at the entrance to the cave.

"We thought you were angels," the man in the parka said, "the way the light from the opening in the cave splashed out all around you! We thought *we* were dead, wandering two days lost and last night all night in the dark of that hole, and the only thing that kept us warm was the hot steam that nearly cooked us!"

Library of Congress, Prints & Photographs Division, Edward S. Curtis Collection, LC-USZ62-60986

three

yukon!

THREE DAYS LATER AND the men from the cave were expected for dinner at the Curtis house.

"Who are they, again?" Clara asked Edward to explain before the guests arrived.

"Grinnell is the editor of *Forest and Stream* magazine," Edward said. "Very influential nature editor."

"And the little man?"

"That's Pinchot, head of the Federal Forestry Division. And the other is Merriam, head of the United States Biological Survey. One counts trees and the other counts birds and foxes, I suppose."

"We made quite a rescue then, didn't we?"

"I believe we did. They know a lot about a lot of things," Edward said. "The country would have been at a loss without them."

"They wouldn't have died up there in the cave, do you think?" Clara regarded him with new, knowing eyes.

"Died? No, I don't think so. But cooked, maybe. Yes, cooked, indeed!"

Edward laughed and waited for her to laugh with him, but she remained stony-faced.

"If we had gone any farther into the cave, would we have been cooked, too?"

"Yes," he said. "Cooked. Yes, definitely." They looked at each other as though promising silently not to speak about what might have transpired if those men hadn't found shelter in that cave. Had the mountain air addled their minds? Even the Mazamas must know you can't live at sea level the same way you do at the mountain top.

At dinner, Grinnell went on at length about how he and his fellow climbers, Merriam and Pinchot, had come up on the mountain to reconnoiter, had gotten lost, and finally had stumbled into the cave to keep as warm as they could.

"But what," Edward said aloud after dinner, "if Clara and I hadn't ducked in there?"

Grinnell, somewhat of an authority, he told them, on the Indians of the Great Plains—having recently lived among them for a year or so—punched up the fire in his pipe and announced, "There's an old Indian legend, Blackfeet or Blood, can't recall which, that says if you save a man, then you're responsible for keeping his soul alive after that. So I suppose the least we can expect is that tomorrow you'll give us a tour of your city."

Edward stood and bowed toward him. "I'll show you my studio, sir…and perhaps sometime you can show me around New York City."

"And Washington," said Pinchot, a short, plain-faced fellow with hair brushed back and nearly glued to his skull.

"And Washington," Edward said.

"And Blackfeet country," Grinnell said. "Wouldn't you like to meet some real Indians?"

"Sounds quite exotic," Edward said. "But so does Washington."

"Never been East, have you?" Merriam said.

Edward nodded his head. "I was born in the East."

"Where was that?" Merriam asked.

"Wisconsin. And we then moved to Minnesota."

The men had a good laugh. "Your East is our Middle West."

In fact, they had quite a fine time all around. Clara mostly listened. She was a good listener. Edward could see in her eyes that she was taking it all in. And she had cooked a good fish and poured cream on some berries for dessert. It was an enjoyable evening.

The next morning, as the light rose from behind the distant but sharply outlined summit of Mount Rainier, true to their word (They were so decent and polite! Edward had never known men like these before!), they were waiting for him outside the studio. Usually by this time he would find his younger brother already hard at work. But Asahel—or Asa, as they called him—was still in the Yukon digging for gold, and so the door was locked. Once inside the studio, Edward mentioned this, and Grinnell, who had been admiring Edward's portraits, particularly that of the Indian clamdigger, laughed at his reaction to his brother's departure.

"Would you consider coming up to the Yukon yourself?" he asked.

"To dig for gold? I'll leave that to my brother."

Grinnell guffawed. "There's all manner of things golden up there," he said. "Everything that's gold doesn't actually glitter. And, sir," he said, "that photograph of yours." He pointed to the clamdigging woman. "It has a certain quality."

Yukon gold—Edward had forgotten all about that conversation when a few months later a letter from Asahel arrived saying

that he was on his way home. That letter still lay crumpled on
the counter at the studio when Asahel himself, bags in hand, his
clothing ragged, appeared forlornly in the doorway. "Hello,
Edward," he said. "Did you receive my letter?"

Edward snatched up the letter and waved it like a baton. "Just
in time not to be entirely surprised," he said. "Set down your
bags. Open them. Show us the gold."

Clara, hearing the talk, came out from the back room and
said, "Asa, we missed you."

"Thank you," said Asahel, with the same sad face.

"And the *gold*?" Edward said.

"Edward, please," said Clara. "He's a tired fellow." She always
took up for the younger man, whereas Edward never gave his
brother a minute to recover.

Asa did appear exhausted. He smiled sheepishly and said, "All
the gold was gone by the time I arrived."

Edward, giving in to some of the meaner impulses that young
men feel but don't understand, tossed the letter down onto the
counter and walked past his brother and charged out onto the
street. He wandered the downtown, railing in his mind against
Asahel without really knowing why. Was it something out of
boyhood? Something their parents had done to pit them each
against the other? Well, there wasn't time in this world to wonder
about such things. That was just the way it was. Anger still ruled
Edward as he walked. When a ragged, dark-faced Indian man,
small enough to be a boy and reeking of fish and alcohol, bumped
against him, Edward's first instinct was to strike out at him.
Sensing something, the man darted away. Edward kept himself
under control and dug in his pockets for a few coins.

"Wait!" he called out, following the man down the street. But
the Indian ducked into an alley and disappeared. Edward
jangled the coins in his hand and then stuffed them back into

his pocket. What might he have done if he had caught up with the man? Handed him the coins, yes. And perhaps offered to make his portrait?

At last he felt settled enough to return to the studio and get back to work, ignoring his brother through the rest of the day. Yukon! What kind of fools chased such illusions?

Edward settled deeper into his life of portrait making, saying to himself now and then that he would become the best portrait maker in the West, if not the entire country. He kept these thoughts private, as some dreaming young men often do when they are afraid to jinx their aspirations. But one night, in the private darkness of their bedroom, he went so far as to allow Clara a glimpse into his dreams for the future.

"I've been hoping for that, too," she said. "That would be wonderful. We could make a good life."

"Yet it is good enough now, isn't it?" Edward moved toward her, and she inched away, before apparently changing her mind and moving toward him. He clasped her to him and began to make love to her. She seemed a little apprehensive at first, and then demurred. It was as if their encounter on the mountain had never taken place. Edward drove hard against her, his mind shut, until in the middle of things he thought he heard a cry—one of the children?—and desisted.

He could have sworn he had heard a sound in the dark, and when a fleeting image of the clamdigging hag flashed before him, he felt a shiver in his spine. He quickly built up his courage and resumed loving his wife.

In this fashion—domestic, with only a slight tinge of worry—life drifted along, filled with family, the children especially, and a number of customers who posed for portraits. A season passing, the sky changing over the Sound from pearl to opaline white and then to blue, with some not unexpected rain from time to time. This was the happy life lived by millions of fortunate people, under the same sky as the other many more millions who had less and needed more, some only in some ways and others in every way.

A few months later a letter arrived from Grinnell, asking Edward if he would, of all things, participate in an expedition to the Yukon that Harriman the Eastern railroad man was sponsoring. Yukon! But this was not a search for gold. Harriman, from what Edward knew of him from reading the newspapers, certainly had gold enough! No, he gathered from the letter that this would constitute the first major attempt on the part of the U.S. government, together with private sources, to investigate the wildlife and land in that region. Grinnell stated that they wanted him to serve as the expedition photographer, an immensely flattering proposition.

Edward wrote back immediately, without consulting Clara, saying it would take some preparation, but that he would join them. He then spoke to his wife, hoping she would agree with this plan. "Do you see what an important opportunity this? And how many events had to fall into place for it to happen? Our climb up Rainier with the Mazamas and stumbling upon the lost men huddled in the ice cave?"

"The Yukon?" Clara asked. "Isn't that comical? You railed against it when Asa went. Your work is in our studio, you said. And you want to abandon it to take a trip with some rich Easterners who do nothing but look at birds?"

"It may be a way to advertise my work among these rich Easterners. It may be a way to find good new clients." He had feared that she might respond like this, and so he pushed all the more. "It will be an opportunity for you to run the studio with Asa while I'm away."

"Edward?" She sat up attentively. "Really? Do you think I can?"

"Of course you can, Clara," he said. "You are a very smart woman." She leaned toward him, staring, though he couldn't tell if she was assessing him or considering his estimate of her.

The night before Edward left Clara cooked a wonderful meal, fish from the Sound and vegetables from the garden at the Port Orchard house, and the children, almost as if they knew something important was going to take place, behaved fairly well, and they talked and sang, and by bedtime all of them felt quite cheerful.

"Thank you for the lovely dinner," Edward said after they excused the children from the table.

"You're welcome," Clara said. "In fact, you're quite welcome. In fact, so welcome that I wish you wouldn't leave." She turned momentarily tearful, and he came around the table to kneel and hold her around the waist.

"Oh, Clara, I don't want to go, but I feel I must."

He sighed and wondered how it was that he knew so little about himself. "I am hungry for what I don't know."

"That is the difference between us, isn't it, Edward? Men hunger. Women feed people." Her tears had stopped.

"Clara," he said, "I don't know—"

"No, you don't, do you?" She breathed deeply and pressed her palms to her forehead.

In the quietest voice above a whisper, she said, "Do you think I can manage the business?"

Edward was quick to assure her. "Of course you can. Of course."

She turned quieter than quiet, breathing only, not speaking.

"Are you all right?" he said.

"No," she said. "I am not."

"Is it—?"

She dropped her hands and curled her lips into a nasty smile. "Edward, stop talking. Put the children to bed."

"I will, but first—"

"That *is* first," she said.

And so he sent the children off with a few nursery rhymes, which he pronounced in a quiet voice and a little song or two hovering just above his breath.

"Going to Yukon, Papa?" Beth said.

"I am," Edward said, "and perhaps one day I'll take you along with me. Would you like that?"

"Will Mama come?"

"If she likes," Edward said.

"Then I'll go," Beth said. (How could it be possible? Grown enough to speak!)

"Perhaps one day," Edward said. He took up her small beautiful hands and kissed them. "We shall do that."

She smiled up at him and fell asleep almost immediately.

Hal remained awake, asking for a story. Edward found himself telling him a tale he hadn't known he'd known, about a fairy ship in a sea as cold as ice and as beautifully sparkling as jewels in a crown. There was a magic seal and a good witch who presided over the entire enterprise

"Will you live on the ship, Papa?" Hal asked him.

"On the fairy ship?"

"On the one you'll sail in."

"Ah, yes, yes, of course, I will. And a grand old ship it is."

"Will you make a picture of it for me?"

"I will, son. I will."

CLARA, IN HER WORDS

I was leaning over the washboard in the kitchen, finishing the laundry, while my mother-in-law sat at the table bouncing little Beth on her lap and Hal was out digging for treasure in the back yard, when I heard the sound of the front door opening. I went to see who was there, thinking, perhaps hope against hope, that it might be Edward. Could he have come home from the Yukon so soon? But instead of Edward, here stood Asahel, squinting at me—he had a particular squint that must have begun when he was a child—and nearly out of breath.

"Asa," I said. "Is there something wrong?"

"No, Clara," he said.

"Then why aren't you at the studio?"

He remained silent. Beth asked her grandmother to stop the bouncing. "Unka Ace," she said, in that adorable way she had of mangling his name.

"Hello, little girl," Asahel said, leaning toward her. She danced away, Edward's mother following her out of the kitchen.

"Why, Asa," I said.

He looked over at the wall.

"Asa?" I said.

"Oh...yes," he said, giving me a look like a bad little boy. "I closed the studio. I'm going to take my own pictures for the rest of the day."

I felt a rush of heat along my shoulders and neck. "But that's what Edward is doing," I said, "and you are supposed to be taking care of the studio."

He made a disagreeable noise in his throat. "He's not the only one in the family with an interest in making pictures."

"No, I know, but you agreed...."

*He giggled, a nervous sound. "He doesn't always have to tell me
what to do. He might ask me."*

"I suppose he might," I said.

*"He shouldn't take advantage of you," said his mother from the
doorway where she been listening intently, "just because you are the
youngest."*

"That's right," Asahel said. "Thank you, Mama."

That was when it came to me. "The studio is now closed?" I said.

Asahel nodded, mischievous, child-like. "I locked the door."

"And you won't go back?"

*"Not t-t-today," Asahel said with a boyish little stutter. "I have
my freedom. I will make my own pictures of the shore and things."
He did everything but stamp his foot in glee.*

*Wiping my soapy hands on my apron, I turned to my mother-in-
law and said, "If you stay here with the children, I will reopen the
studio for the day." And that was how I first became a practical
mother and a businesswoman.*

The *George W. Elder*, the ship Mr. Harriman hired for the
expedition, sailed north along the Pacific coast in the summer
of 1899 with about a hundred and thirty men aboard and a
few children. Working with Edward was a smart fellow from
Seattle named Dean Inverarity, who knew his photography.
Among the other folks on the expedition were some of the
most unique and fascinating Americans whom Edward had
ever met at that time: Louis Agassiz, the Harvard biologist;
John Muir, who wrote about the wilderness; and Grinnell and
Merriam themselves, without whom he would not have been
here.

If he and Clara hadn't stopped at the entrance to that snow cave, if he hadn't climbed with the Mazamas, if he hadn't made his portraits, if he hadn't made that portrait of the clamdigging Indian princess, which had caught Grinnell's eye, if his Pap hadn't taken him west, if, if, if…. He pondered these "ifs" as he leaned on the ship's mid-deck railing and stared off into the pearly light hovering above the Pacific seascape. If, if, if, and yet a man had to be ready to take advantage of such turns of fate and opportunities.

On the port side, the jade-green ocean pulsed. Edward crossed to the starboard rail and found himself standing with the long-bearded Muir, gazing at the passing shoreline and the glorious purple-mauve mountains rising behind the forests that came down like a vast green carpet all the way to the sea.

"Even by our Puget Sound standard," Edward said, "this, sir, is monumental."

Muir stroked his dark brown beard and kept on staring off into the distance. "Each mile that goes by," he said, "is like turning the page in some marvelous picture book."

"God's book," said a voice from behind them, and they turned to see Harriman himself, strolling along the deck with his children in tow and Merriam at his side. (It never occurred to Edward, until he saw them, that a man could bring small children along on such an expedition. He had a flickering thought of Clara, troubled already by his departure, listening to him tell her that one day he was going to take their tiny Beth on a journey north.) "God wrote these pages for us to read."

"Very medieval of you, old chap," said Merriam. "Medieval concept. The world as a book, which we human beings must learn to read if we're to understand God's purposes."

"Emerson put it that way in his essay on nature," Muir said. "A fine piece of work that I highly recommend to all of you."

"Can the children read it?" Harriman inquired. He touched the head of his oldest child.

"With a little help," Muir said. "But absolutely, yes. Emerson works a style that can speak to readers at many levels."

"Well, I may read it with them. I presume that we have it in the library we've got on board."

"There's little that's pertinent to scientific inquiry and philosophical discourse that you don't have in the library," Merriam said.

"My intention, exactly," Harriman said. In a greatcoat, his usually close-pressed hair blowing in the cool offshore wind, he appeared to be just another passenger on the voyage rather than the financial force behind it all. The children clung to each of his hands as if they might at any instant sail off the deck in the wind.

"What a way to live," Edward reported to his new companion, Inverarity, that night when they took a stroll around the deck. "We were discussing the medieval approach to nature, the theory that one should read the world around us the way one reads a book. And I had the thought, while Harriman stood there in the wind, that in fact nature *was* like a book to him, a collection that he's purchased for his own edification. Amazing, to be so wealthy and yet retain such curiosity. Some of those other robber barons would just as soon burn the books as read them."

Inverarity, a cool Seattle character and a Mazama, lighted a pipe, or attempted to, and didn't make much of a success of it until they stopped and he ducked behind a bulkhead. "The world is opening up to us," he said. "I predict that the twentieth century is going to be a time to behold." Sparks flew up out of the bowl of his pipe as soon as he stepped back out into the wind.

Beyond those small bits of light, instantly devoured by the night, lay darkness, oblivion, a moonless strait separated from the Alaskan ocean by a small string of islands. What God wanted them to read in this invisible landscape in the dark, Edward couldn't have said, unless it was to inform them that there was a time for reading and a time for closing their eyes and turning their vision inward. If, when he had stood in the dark on the slopes of Mount Rainier and listened to the sounds on the wind, he had the first inkling of what life in the field could be like, here was his next lesson in what it was like to have your mind turned inside out.

"It's like a dream, this trip, for me," Edward said. "One moment, it seems, I was working in my studio, living daily life with the family, and now we are on board this ship, chugging northward, ever northward. Amazing!"

"I'm all out of breath about it myself," Inverarity said. "Before this I imagined that climbing Rainier was as close to adventure as I would ever come." He sucked on his pipe and Edward watched the bowl glow ever so faintly as the wind scooped out more sparks and whirled them away into the dark. The deck suddenly heaved beneath them and he reached for the railing. Salt spray blew back in their faces. Edward breathed in the salt and the iodine taste of fear that had backed up in the valves of his heart.

"Sailing north into the frozen night and still every day taking us closer to the twentieth century turns out to be a bit rough," he said. Inverarity laughed at Edward's feeble attempt at humor, and they walked and talked until they had toured the deck enough times to tire them out.

Edward went to the library the next morning and sure enough there was a listing for Emerson's essay on nature. Except that someone had already signed it out—Inverarity! Over dinner that night (after Edward had borrowed the volume from him and read the essay), they had a good talk about this philosopher-poet and the way he viewed things.

"He's a Deist, as I see him," Inverarity said. "Someone who believes that God exists in everything."

"Emerson? I believe he's a Pantheist," said Merriam, a regular at their table.

Grinnell had been standing alongside the table, listening to the talk. He sat down next to Edward and said, "Odd, but I think that he's a straight-down-the-line believer. It's not that God is everywhere, but everywhere shows the marks of God's creation." He glanced over at Edward. "What do you think, Curtis?"

"It's certainly true of where we are now," Edward said, gesturing toward the window. Mountains rose to the horizon clotted with thick white clouds. He couldn't help himself. As mature a man as he took himself to be at age thirty-one, he had the strangest sudden notion that he should scan the air for a glimpse of his dear, late father whom in that instant he imagined might be soaring along above their ship toward the northern ice. Wouldn't he be looking out for me? The odd question flitted into his mind and then out again unanswered. Oh, he felt as certain of himself as anyone his age might feel—and yet he knew in his heart that he needed a guide, someone to help him find his future.

"You think it's so then?" Merriam called him back to the issue at hand.

"There's some higher force made these mountains and this ocean," Edward said. "I'm not a church-goer, though my father was a minister. Whatever's done it, call it Nature or call it God, it's made a mark on things."

"And keeps on making a mark?" Grinnell spoke up again.

"Emerson writes in a way that stays in my mind," Inverarity said. "'I become a Transparent Eye-ball.'"

"You do?" This was Harriman, who had gotten up from his table and come over just in time to catch the last of the discussion.

"I have become a blinking eyeball," Edward said. "I don't know what to believe. Except that...."

"What?" Dean asked.

"Yes?" Merriam looked on with interest.

"Except that I do have the feeling that I *can* believe. When I was a boy, I listened to my father's sermons, and I believed what he believed. But now...."

Harriman hovered over them, a sort of god himself, for their journey at least. "Yes?" he said.

"But now I live in a certain confusion, sometimes believing, sometimes wavering in my belief...."

"And sometimes knowing nothing at all except that you do not know?" Harriman stared down at him, and in that instant it was possible to imagine that he was a philosopher, whatever philosophers looked like, rather than a railroad magnate.

"That, too," Edward said.

"A modern man," Merriam said with a large smile on his lips.

"Very modern, yes," Grinnell added his assent.

"Curtis is our hero, then, is he?" said Harriman, his host.

"Absolutely," Inverarity said.

"If I'm the hero, God help us all," Edward said. "I'm just an ordinary fellow with some mechanical ability."

"And we are as gods," Merriam said.

"I am not," Edward said.

That night, at Harriman's urging, the steward broke out several extra bottles of wine. By midnight, Edward was woozy with alcohol. In his cabin, he stripped off his clothes, flung himself down on the bed, feeling the roll and pitch of the ship as it drove onward into the dark. He lay there a while under the sway of the wine, wondering about Clara and the children, seeing them in their sleep back home, missing them, and yet feeling the freedom of being apart. They had other inlets to explore the following day and only a few more weeks in which to see as much as they could see. And what if life—what if *his* life—were like this voyage? he asked himself. What if? And what if?

The visages of bird, seal, and bear loomed up near the tree line. They could see the totem poles as they sailed slowly into the natural cove at Cape Fox Island two weeks later. But no smoke rose from the houses. Almost everyone on the expedition came out on deck and attempted to scout the horizon, while the crew lowered boats and as many of them as could fit in the small vessels set out for the beach. Grinnell could hardly contain himself, leaping from the boat into the shallow water and hurrying onto the shore. And he was followed by Merriam and Edward, who wasn't going to allow these chaps to get the jump on him.

It seemed odd that no natives came out to meet them, though the others didn't seem to take this as a fact worthy of consideration, walking immediately to the nearest house and opening the door—not knocking, mind you, but walking right up and opening it, as though they knew that no one was inside. And how right they were. As they went from house to house it soon became apparent that the entire village was deserted, though the faint odor of fish oil and old smoke lingered in the houses. Clothing lay scattered about, as well as some cooking pots and wooden utensils. It amused Edward to find a row of small photographs in cheap tin frames of people he assumed to be the former residents—a wide-faced man and woman with their heads covered with hats of fox fur, and a much older woman holding a small child in her arms. These last two were wearing clothes that would not have seemed out of the ordinary on the streets of Seattle.

Who are these people? Edward wondered to himself. *Some sort of Indians? Or should I ask, Who were they?* For whatever reason everyone who lived here had picked up and departed some while ago. The coals in the fires were cold and birds nested in some of the chimney holes. The dog that crawled out of a corner of one of the houses had so many starkly revealed ribs that it was clear no one had fed him in days.

"Perhaps weeks," Grinnell said, over their little outdoor supper that evening. "Hard to figure. Weeks, a month or so…. Everybody must have just picked up and left."

One of the men from the Harriman staff asked a question. "Some sickness here, you think?"

Grinnell appeared to disagree. "Possibly, but really I don't think so. They would have left some signs to warn others away from here. To these people, sickness comes as a curse from the gods. I suppose…." He paused and chewed on his food.

"What's that?" Edward said.

"Well, I don't pretend to know anything at all about these Eskimos up here. I lived with Blackfeet only, and those are the ways I know something about. But these people don't just abandon their village for no reason. Could be they were fleeing from a curse of some sort."

"A curse?"

"A demon come out of the woods to frighten them," Grinnell said. "Or tried to steal their children. Or put a blight on their fishing. My guess is that it has to do with fishing."

"My father was a preacher," Edward said, "but I've never believed in *demons*."

"There's a logical answer to every question," Muir said. "Fish stopped coming here, perhaps," said Muir. "Could be they didn't take care of the fishing grounds, took too much out of the water."

"Wouldn't they know better than to do that?" Edward spoke up on instinct

"I suppose," Muir said. "I just don't know enough about them."

"Nobody does," Grinnell said. "And if they're gone, it's going to be difficult, if not nigh well impossible, ever to know anything about them."

The fire sparked and caught Edward's attention. Up there among the tall totems, shadows seemed liquid and playful, dancing as the fire commanded, over and above the bizarre carvings of animal faces and human limbs. They decided to make camp on shore. It was not unpleasant to sleep out here in the lee of the calm waters, with the perfume of the big pines wafting over them, and when Edward climbed into his bedroll he had the comforting sensation that he had become a small child again and that his long-lost Pap might step out into the clearing at any moment holding a string of trout or a band of bright feathers, which he had collected along the shoreline where the eagles swooped to catch their daily prey.

Pap, he said to him in his thoughts, *I hope you're not too angry that I've left your old religion behind.*

He could imagine Pap saying, "Well, Ed-Sir," (which was what he had called Edward throughout most of his childhood) "I'll only be angry if you don't find a new religion some time ahead."

The surf whispered a reassuring chorus. Seabirds called out as first light spilled across the waters. Edward lay there a while, trying to figure how he might capture the essence of that view with a camera. "But damn!" he said to himself. "It's people you make portraits of, not some landscape without people. And what are portraits but the agreed upon public place where two inner lives, that of the subject and that of the photographer, meet?"

Still, he wondered if he could do it.

As the light increased, the crew searched among the houses, and Edward was busy talking to Merriam and his crew about their intention to take pieces of the place back aboard the ship.

"How can we do this?" he pointed to the men who were throwing ropes around the outstretched wings of the eagle at the top of the tallest totem.

"With care, that's how," Merriam said. "Listen, Curtis, how do you think we know so much about our native birds? Because Audubon drew them. And in order to draw them accurately he had to shoot them first. Difficult to draw a bird on the wing, wouldn't you say?"

"I'm not going to get into a schoolboy debate about this," Edward said. "But we don't know if these people are coming back to their village. And if they do, what are they going to come back to? Their sacred poles gone? Stolen?"

"Think of us as borrowing them for scientific purposes." A shout came from the men just then, and Merriam walked over to help with the roping of the poles. Edward wandered over after him, watching them ease the long, ornate carving down onto the pebbly ground so that one of the eagle wings at the top became a kind of prop on which the entire sculpture rested at an angle. And then they walked on to the next pole, this one decorated with a leering frog and a snarling bear at the top. It came down with less work, but lay there more pathetically, the strangely vital animal visages pointing nearly facedown. A stage without actors—that was how this struck him. And he tried to imagine the people, painted and dressed in their skins and animal bone, walking through their daily lives in this setting. What did they speak and sing, know and believe? He knew what faces and noises flashed through his own nighttime outings. What did *they* see when *they* dreamed?

Within the next hour all of the exterior carvings that stood around the village had been catalogued, tagged, and towed out to the *George W. Elder*. Meanwhile some of the investigators began to remove things from the houses themselves.

"Their cooking pots?" Edward said in disbelief.

"Listen, Edward," Grinnell said, "commiserate with Muir over there if you don't like our practices. But as I told you, this is the way we do it."

"You went into your Blackfeet camps and removed their cooking pots?"

"They were still cooking with them," he said. "But if they had disappeared the way these folks have, why then, yes, we'd have taken their pots."

Edward drifted over to where Muir was standing, and by the look on his face he was no happier about the procedure than Edward was. "Rape in the name of science," Muir said. "Do you agree?"

Edward thought of the example of Audubon, which Grinnell had cited, and he had to admit that it confused him. Finally, he said, "But if these people have gone…."

"Gone where? And who are they in the first place? How do we know any of this? And what gives us the right to take anything we please from their houses?"

Edward held his empty palms to the sky; his mouth tasted bitter. He reached down into his pack and took out his notebook. And then went to fetch his tripod and camera.

"What if," he said to Grinnell, "you delay this for just a short while so that I can take some photographs of the houses in their original state?"

"Fine with me," Grinnell said. "I only wish you'd thought of that before we'd pulled down the totem poles."

"I wish I had, too. I've got only one shot that I took from the deck when we first approached."

"Attention, you!" Grinnell called out to the men. "Hold off just a while so that Curtis can take his pictures!" And they did.

＿＿＿＿＿＿＿＿

That night around the fire, Grinnell said, "Some trading must have gone on between these folks and distant tribes. Look at this...." He held up a small carved object that caught the fire-light. "...this amber amulet I found in one of the houses.... It's certainly not local.

"What trees are here? And which drip sap? No, someone put this in a pouch in a warmer climate and headed—well, I don't know in what direction, west? Because, if east, they must have come on boats, yes? But could these tribes come across from Siberia in small boats? There's some speculation about a land bridge that connected Alaska to the other side, but I don't know much about that. But say they paddled, or even walked, and you can figure how long that would have taken, carrying their goods for trading and hoping to bring back—more questions—what? More of the same whalebone and walrus tusk? That's why I believe some traders must have come from the east or south. And long ago, long before our people arrived here from Europe, before the Spaniards came. I suppose we and the Spaniards look pretty much the same to the Eskimos, if they've ever seen a Spaniard. This amber must have come from a region of lost forests, forests long ago disintegrated, dissolved, and ground to dust, and the sap preserved under deep heat and pressure."

"And the traders?" Edward said.

"I've read articles by a man named Boas. He and some others in his field are trying to look at these matters scientifically.

Which Arctic tribe came from where, and such. But where our own red men came from and how they live—let alone how they *lived*—is as much a mystery to the red men themselves as it is to us. When I gaze upon this amber, that's what I see—a mystery, plain and simple."

Staring into the sparking fire, Edward tried to picture it: a trading party from the land with big trees that oozed this golden sap, and how they harvested these beautiful frozen globules, counted them, arranged them by size, and decided which to take on what route. Say it was a group of landlocked natives who had heard of a great river, so wide you could not see the other shore, which lay to the far west over the great mountains. These people must have tasted in their nostrils salt and seaweed for the first time when they came down out of the mountains—near present-day Sacramento, say—and caught a hint of the delta and the waters beyond. Well, not as strong as this, not anywhere near as strong as this, but a touch of it, and to their pure powers of scent, it might have been a hundred times, yea, a thousand times more powerful than to our poor noses doused in horse dung and gas-light fumes and motor oils.

"How can a man know even a part of this?" Edward spoke aloud, but it was a philosophical question that he posed to himself. Nothing before had ever snared his mind like this.

"Read and make site visits, and study," Grinnell said.

Muir tamped his pipe tobacco down in the bowl of his long smoker and nodded. "Walk with open eyes. Talk in a quiet way to these people where you find them. I hear that it works."

"But you need to know something before you visit them," Grinnell said. "If you just listen it can be quite confusing. When with the Blackfeet, I heard, say, a story about the origins of marriage. I'd then think I knew what they believed about it. But two weeks later someone would tell me another story, and I'd say, how can you have two such myths as this, and I'd get a big Red-shrug. I went to an old man, known to be wise among the Blackfeet elders, and put my question to him. He looked at me as though I were a stupid block of wood. 'Do you mean,' he said, 'we cannot have two ways of looking at it? One story to believe before marriage, and another one after?'"

They laughed at this, and someone took out a silver flask and passed it around.

"What would a man do?" Edward asked.

And now as they spoke, Grinnell stood and looked into the darkness over the water. The wind whipped up sparks up in spirals around his feet.

"To find out about them?"

"Yes. You lived with the Blackfeet, what, two years?"

"About that," he said. "Just about. Yes."

"And you learned a lot about them."

"Somewhat," Grinnell said. "A half-educated man sounds like a sage among the ignorant. Not that I'm making a judgment about you, Curtis, you understand."

"Of course, of course. Two years. And that's only one tribe."

Muir coughed and pointed his pipe at the dark. "Of, how many? A hundred? Two hundred? Five hundred tribes?"

"North American tribes?" Grinnell gave a little laugh. "I suppose that's correct. No one has done a count. At that rate, it would take a thousand years before anyone could truly become an expert on these red men and how they live."

"They'd all be dead or turned into white men by then," Muir said. "Or both."

A pair of seabirds swooped nearby and then veered off, and Edward followed their flight up and away into the dark. "It's intriguing," he said. "It certainly intrigues me."

"Of course it does," Grinnell said. "It's rather like being an ornithologist and discovering that your parlor's full of rare, winged creatures, even some that sing. Here we are, nearly in our own backyard, well, you down in Seattle, and they're all right here, and there's all this great mystery to decipher. That Schliemann fellow over in Turkey went to dig up Troy and found wonders, didn't he? But here we are at home and can just take a shovel out back and dig. We don't even have to dig, do we? It's all there. Out in the open. Waiting for us."

"Yes," Edward said, "I see. We only have to open a window. Or go out onto the back porch, and sit there and take notes." Edward stood up, filled suddenly with a zeal he had never ever felt before.

Grinnell stepped close to him. "Might you consider doing it?

"I'd make more photographs than notes," Edward said.

"Of course, of course. Now wouldn't that be something! A pictorial record!" Grinnell got so excited that he began to pound his fist in the air. "That's it, isn't it? Curtis, you've got to do it! That's it, that's it! A careful and methodical pictorial record of all the tribes on the continent!" The two men now stood so close that Edward could taste Grinnell's breath on the air. Suddenly out of the dark a swooping seabird changed direction and hovered just above them, and as they looked up, the bird let drop a large gobbet into the wind.

"For luck," Edward said, as the guano splattered on the beach, some of it spattering on his shoe.

Grinnell nodded his head in agreement. "Yes, yes, if we are at all serious about this, you'll need it."

⟳

Of course Edward couldn't have known just how soon he would need it. On the following afternoon the *George W. Elder* put into a small natural harbor at Glacier Bay, and Dean Inverarity and Edward, in a fit of foolhardiness, paddled out in a small canoe toward the edge of a nearby glacier. Seabirds followed their passage.

The surf pounded against the ice at the shoreline just below where the glacier pushed its head toward the sea. As they rowed toward it, the birds swooped down and away from them, as if to suggest some other route. But what did the two men know? They kept on pulling the oars through the briny water, which was littered with bits of debris, some no larger than a hand, others as large as the canoe.

"What do you read in that, old boy?" Inverarity called to him over the noise of water and birds.

"Read?"

"Yes, what in our old Emersonian way would you read into the shouts of the birds?"

"They're hungry," Edward said. "Looking for fish. Or telling us to stay out of their fishing grounds."

"I suppose...." Inverarity heaved his strength into the oars. "I suppose they don't know that all you want to do is take some pictures?"

"I'll explain," Edward said. "But I'm not sure I'll make my message clear to them." He took a deep breath. "You birds!" he shouted at the nearest gull. "Listen to me! We're here only to take pictures!"

But the birds skimmed away, leaving them alone with the boat, the water, and the light. Even Inverarity's presence seemed to fade as Edward stared up at the glacier. They approached its towering face, the broad sweep of it stippled with amazing variations of light (despite the general overcast sky)—stripes of dark blue and almost emerald and near-white. All of this pouring down the complex crystal structure as though some painter had overturned barrels of these delicate colors at the top of the flow. It overwhelmed Edward's eye even as it entranced him—all this shade, cast, and variation—and he gazed upward, nearly hypnotized, the berg itself one giant jewel set out on the dark velvet of a jeweler's cloth.

Except the cloth was white, whiter than white, all this snowy whiteness surrounding this subtle near-rainbow of color, which at a distance seemed no less white, and no more, than the land and sky that bordered it. Only the water lapped dark, and darker, against the base of the ice, as if the fullness of color—all colors at once steeped in this heaving surf—were waging war. Words from his father's old Sunday sermons drifted through his mind. Was this the writing of God, or whatever deity, put into the stuff of earth? Emerson would say so, he thought. Yet if true, it seemed a cold and terrible signature, which only the foolish or the brave—and he counted himself in that former category— might look upon and read.

"Ready?" Inverarity swung their little vessel around and held it as steady as he could so that Edward could pick up his camera and focus on the berg without the possible obstruction of a figure between Edward's eye and the ice. And as they turned he took a quick look back at the ship and saw several hands on deck waving, waving to them.

"Cheering us on?" Edward asked, as he took up his instrument and squinted into the viewfinder.

"What?" Inverarity's voice sounded distracted, sleepy almost, over the sound of the lapping waves.

"Cheering," Edward said, as he peered into the narrow focusing glass.

"Look," Inverarity said.

"I am," Edward said, holding himself steady as the boat rose beneath him. The white, the blue-white, the blue-green-white, the blue-white-green, now sapphiric glow of the ice held his eye to a magnetic point.

Suddenly came a crack like a rifle shot and his body jerked.

"Go!" Inverarity called.

"What?"

A blast from the ship's horn echoed across the inlet. Edward looked up to see more hands on deck waving, waving, tiny pips of sound—shouts across the gulf—while seabirds squawked and squealed overhead.

"Go!" Inverarity shouted.

And as he sat down, his camera in his lap, and picked up the paddle, Edward glanced up the length of the glacier, the height rather. Oh, he was shocked and confused as it happened, stood again, and then fell back into his seat with a bang, managing somehow to hold onto his camera with one hand. Inverarity spun them around and began to paddle furiously, furiously, furiously, even as Edward could see the ice sliding over the edge of the glacier, the edge of the glacier pushing out in extension from itself. It seemed, as he looked back, as though time had slowed like molasses, gathering at the lip of an overturned jar and slowly getting ready to spill. The ice slid out over the edge of the glacier, poised above the inlet—while Inverarity rowed furiously, furiously—and then slipped into the air between the rim and the water—falling, falling—

"Whoaa!" Edward cried out when the vast chunk of ice smashed against the surface of the water, sending up an explosive spume of water and cloud.

Another blast of the ship's horn.

"Hurry!" he said to his companion in a matter-of-fact way, surprising himself with his calm.

"Unh," Inverarity made a grunt.

"Hurry," Edward said.

"Unh," Inverarity repeated each time he pulled the paddle through the water. With his back to Edward, the man watched the ice hit and settle and then saw the wave of water moving steadily toward them across the surface of the inlet.

"Move," Edward said.

"Unh," Inverarity grunted.

"Move," Edward said again.

"Unh! Unh!" And the wave rolled toward them with the speed of a herd of panicked buffalo.

"Ho!" The water rose under them, and they humped into the air and then down again.

"Whoa!" And up again, just barely able to keep themselves from capsizing.

"Unh," Inverarity made the noise again, and with another roll of the concussive waves, Edward fell and banged his back against the wood of the stern.

He supposed they hadn't truly understood how close they had come to dying until, dripping with salt water and soaked with the sweat of their own fear, they reboarded the *Elder*, and their shipmates slapped them on the back and congratulated them on the narrowness of their escape. Edward gasped for air, and he thought for a moment that after having just escaped death by falling ice, he would die on the spot of a bursting chest. How odd it seemed at the time, as his fireside conversation with Grinnell the night before flooded into his mind, and in the heart of a great calmness, he saw now what he wanted to do with the life he had just preserved.

four

the end of some things, the beginning of others

AFTER EDWARD LEFT FOR the Yukon, Clara took complete charge of the business: ordering the chemicals and equipment, writing the advertisements, setting up the appointments, everything. Clara, she discovered about herself, was the kind of woman for whom marriage was not enough to fill her life—she enjoyed the day-to-day affairs of her work.

"Stay out of this," she said. "Men are business; women are home. Care for your children. Let Edward do the other work. And if he is away then have his brother take care of the studio. Otherwise you will feel only sorrow. Could I have helped your father with his timber work? No better than he could have helped me. Think of your duty to the home and the children."

But Clara found that she was good at what she did, and so while Edward had his wide world of ships and glaciers, and who knew what else, she directed the daily round at the studio. Now and then, in a quiet moment, she might marvel at the distance she had traveled since walking through the studio door and seeing Edward. But mostly she spent her days

engrossed in the hour-to-hour management of this small
company.

Still, Clara, despite the new life she so enjoyed in his absence,
had not lost her wifely sense of duty. She even felt a certain
amount of good cheer upon seeing him. When he returned
from his new world, he came in through the door carrying his
bag and wearing a sheepish grin, and it cried out to her for affection. To Edward, the house seemed smaller, more confining
than he had remembered it, but somehow at the same time it
felt rather comfortable and comforting.

"I'm so happy that you're back in one piece," she said, giving
him a peck on the cheek. His clothes gave off a smoky odor, as
though he had hovered close to too many pagan campfires for
too many nights in a row.

He set down his bag. "Whatever did you think might happen
to me?" He pretended to be mystified, but laughed to himself,
recalling his close encounter with the falling ice.

"I worried, Edward," Clara said, taking his coat from him.

"And I did, too," came his mother's voice drifting down from
the stairway.

The children came running. "Daddy, Daddy!" Beth cried out
as she wrapped her little arms around his legs, while Florence,
the gift of their climb together up Mount Rainier, crawled about
the floor, oblivious to his arrival.

"Happy to see you, darlings," he said, taking them up in his
arms. "Where's young Hal?"

"Carousing with boys in the yard," Clara said.

"Little Flo," he said, touching a finger to the nose of the
youngest, "little flower."

"Am I a flower, too?" Beth asked.

"You are always my flower," Edward said.

"Even when I'm not a baby?"

"Even then."

Hal came running through the doorway. "Ho!" Edward called to him. "Come here, son."

He stood there, hair dark, frowning.

"Fetch my small bag," Edward said.

Hal just stood there.

"Something in it for you, son," Edward said.

Then Hal went to the front door, found the bag, and delivered it to his father.

"I was thinking of you, son," Edward said, opening the latch and reaching inside. He couldn't help but think of his own Pap as he found the carving and handed it to Hal.

"Oh," Hal said.

"Do you like it?"

"Oh," Hal said again, holding up the small ivory bear that Edward had found lying in the doorway of one of the houses at Cape Fox Island.

"I think it brings good luck," father said to son.

Hal looked at the bear and then at his father, and he smiled.

"Me, me," said Beth. Edward gave her a small bird carved out of walrus ivory, which he had also carried from Cape Fox. Without hesitating, she swung it through the air as though to make it fly.

"And me?" Clara came over and sat on the chaise next to him. A smile flickered across her face. It pleased her that the children seemed pleased.

"My love," Edward said, reaching into the bag once more, "I have something for you as well." And he held it out to her, a nearly rectangular piece of amber, and inside, a tiny silver-winged insect nearly perfectly preserved.

"It's so beautiful," she said. "But how on earth...?"

"I found it up there," he said.

"In the snow?"

"No snow where we anchored that night. It was a small Eskimo village, completely deserted, people had recently lived there, but they had all disappeared, faded away."

Clara held her gift up to the light from the window. The late summer day gave off beautiful light, not a rain cloud in the sky. The amber in her hand glowed with a soft caramel-like suffusion. "A sad story." She stared at the amber. "And pretty remains."

The children ran a circle around them.

"There's more to the story than pretty. I just don't know what that is."

"Will you go back to find out?" She seemed, in fact, both curious and upset. Listen to her, talking about his leaving again when he had only just arrived! It made Edward feel a bit down in spirit.

"It's a long, hard trip north, but I might return some day. Something about those missing people calls out to me," Edward said. He took her hand and with this gesture, he changed the mood. "Thank you for taking charge of the studio while I was gone. Did my brother pitch in at all?"

"Your brother did a fine job keeping up with the trade."

"Did?"

Yes, his brother was gone when he got to the studio, decamped for some other horizon, and taking one of the business's cameras along with him.

"Don't be angry with him, Edward," Clara said, when Edward returned to the house. "He's a good person and he wants to be like you."

"You mean he wants to become a man nearly choleric with the thought of his brother leaving the business without notice?"

"He mentioned to me that he was leaving. I have hired a new man."

Edward stared at her incredulously. "You hired a new man?"

"That is what I do, when you're away chasing vanishing pagans," Clara said. "And I have become quite good at it, if I may say so myself."

The next week, the new man—a talented fellow as it turned out, named Adolph Muhr—showed up for work. Within a month he proved to Edward that he was quite capable enough to run the business alone, even with frivolous Asahel gone his merry way. The portraiture business continued to flourish; the seasons changed; the rains came and went; Mount Rainier went in and out; and the Easterner Grinnell returned to Seattle.

Into the studio he came and without fanfare asked Edward, "Have you been making plans for your field trip?"

"My field trip?"

"You haven't begun to make plans?"

"The time isn't right. I've just taken in a new fellow at the studio—"

"The time is never right for such things, old boy," Grinnell said. "But time is running out. Remember the deserted village? These tribes, all the many hundreds of them, are fast losing all of their old ways. They need men to meet them on their own ground and record their customs before they vanish from the earth. They need you to do their *portraits*." Or had he said, as Edward remembered it many years later while recounting it to me, "They need *you* to do their portraits...," singling out Edward for this difficult mission.

Whichever the intonation, Grinnell looked at Edward in his winning way, and for a moment the photographer tried to imagine a Blackfeet chieftain sitting before a fire with a fellow like Grinnell and talking about the old ways of the tribe. Edward laughed to himself. He didn't even know what a Blackfeet chieftain looked like! Or what it meant to be a "chief."

Did he lead a tribe? Did he look on as Indians all went their own ways?

"What is so amusing?" Grinnell wanted to know.

Edward told him his thoughts.

"All the more reason to begin as soon as you can. Time is flying past. The years are rushing by at a headlong pace. Every day that goes past, another of the old ways falls by the wayside and another chief dies."

Edward turned a long face toward his would-be mentor. "That's a hard thought to consider for a fellow like me, standing knee-deep in small children in Seattle at what seems like the opposite of a headlong pace."

"Curtis," he said, taking Edward by the shoulders, "you've got to take the plunge."

Edward laughed again, out of embarrassment, and with a little touch of wonder and a certain dash of fear. "Yes, yes, I must plunge."

A week went by. Grinnell left for the East and Edward struggled to explain his plan to Clara—and to himself—in conversations usually, and uneasily, conducted in the middle of the night.

"The business is flourishing."

"It is," Clara said.

"In large part to you, because of your devotion to it."

"Thank you, Edward."

"And so if I left again for a month or so, you would be perfectly capable of keeping things running, especially with Muhr now in place."

"Of course, I could do that. Though people would miss your personal touch, Edward. And the children would miss you terribly. As would I."

"Ah, Clara, I know. I know."

Some nights and days later he made his decision—which didn't turn out to be as terrible as he had thought it might be—and went to see his brother Ray, who by now had made quite a success for himself in the livery business.

"Tell me," Ray said as soon as they stepped into his office, a smoky den that smelled of animals, leather, and the residue of the cigars he loved to puff on.

"Tell you?"

"Why you haven't come to see me before this. It's been a long while."

"The years race along," Edward said.

"Which is good for me," Ray said. "People dashing here and there, they need horses; they need wagons and carriages. Those motor cars are for the rich only." He smiled and picked up a cigar box from his desk, holding it toward Edward. Edward demurred.

Ray said, "If you don't need a smoke then what do you need?" With all of the care that the photographer put into setting up a subject, the liveryman lighted a cigar and puffed out great gobs of sweet-smelling smoke.

"I need...." Edward felt quite shy as he explained what he needed, how much and when, but he got it out.

"All for Indians?"

"That's right."

"I don't have much of an opinion about them," Ray said. "They're dying like flies, passing out on the pavement, killing each other, fading away."

"That's an opinion," Edward said.

"It's a fact."

"That's why I need to do this," Edward said.

"Who put you up to this? Some of those rich Easterners I've heard you've been traveling with?"

"Who told you about them?"

"Our wives talk," Ray said.

"What did she say—?"

"Not important. What do you think Pap would say?"

"He would approve, don't you think?"

Ray smiled and more smoke flew out of mouth. "I do. That's why I'll help out. But one thing I can't help you with is Clara. I suggest you try to smooth things out with her."

"I didn't know her feathers were ruffled."

"As I said, wives talk."

"She doesn't understand...."

"Women don't," Ray said. "They hate cigar smoke, sometimes I'm afraid they hate our dreams." He pursed his lips. "Modern women.... Maybe you'd be better off finding yourself a squaw. But maybe one a little younger than that woman whose picture you got in your studio."

"Do you know she's a princess, Ray?"

"Princesses or paupers, I hear they make good wives, do nothing except for you, and when you need to ride off to war, they help you pack your bags."

"I don't think warriors have bags to pack."

"Don't they have quivers with arrows?"

"Ray, I have to admit, I don't know very much about them."

Ray puffed out a great big cloud of smoke. "I'm willing to put up some money so you can learn."

~~~

Edward, quite aware of his deficiencies when it came to the project he had in mind, made some inquiries over at the university about how to find a writer who also had some skills with old languages. Thus, he arranged to meet a highly recommended, recently hired former newspaper man named William Myers—

yours truly.

He walked into the room at the university club and looked at me. I looked back at him, and we both quickly recalled our first encounter.

"And the girl?" he said. "Have you married her?"

"We have set a date," I said. "But I always seem to find a reason to push it back further into the future."

"If you delay too much, she will never let you forget that," Edward said.

After he had explained what he wanted us to do, I decided that I would set the wedding date for immediately upon our return from the trip that Edward proposed. Yes, that was my plan.

That meeting changed my life forever, which was what I had hoped would happen when I left Chicago for Seattle. For a while I was certain that the newspaper business would shock me out of my classical caste of mind. Not that the Greek historians didn't record murders, rapes, and mayhem galore—not to mention what we find in Homer—but I always had my father's voice ringing in my ears, saying, "Be practical, son. If you want to write, write something that people will want to read."

Shortly after taking my degree from Northwestern, I wrote my last classical elegy—O Chicago! O Stockyards! The stench of Thy loins rises skyward to the questioning nostrils of the gods!—and hopped on the train west. The endless plains, like an ocean, the clouds like mountains—my first views of the territory beyond our grand Midwest was quite like that of young Edward's some years before. Though, by the time I entrained, the buffalo had been lost so, so long ago that I couldn't even imagine them, and telegraph poles rose where tepees once stood all along the way.

All these things started pouring out of me when he asked me a simple question about myself. "You write poetry," he said. "Are you good at languages?"

"I have a knack," I said.

He gave me a look—a sharp look, the look of a man who gauges people and situations through a certain lens. "We won't be working with any tribes that speak Greek."

"My knack connects my ear to my brain," I said. "I think I can help."

"Even with languages you've never heard before?"

"If you give me a chance, I'll show you," I said, amazed at my own audacity, because I had no idea whether or not I would be good at the job. However, I knew I wanted it. Oh, yes, I did. Travel on horseback along canyon rims? Nights on the plains? It called out to me; it called out much louder than any plans I might have had for marriage and a family, at least at the time. There is the direction I call West in the spirit, and even if you stop at the Pacific you can keep on traveling there.

"Well, sir," Edward said, giving me another long sharp look, "I don't know that I'm prepared for this work myself, but perhaps the two of us can do it well together."

A cold little shock ran through my body. I knew it. I could tell. I wasn't dreaming. I *had* just changed my life! Though I was still unaware how the West had changed forever my naive attempts to make a classical style.

My fiancée, my dear schoolteacher, took the news rather tearfully, but vowed that she would wait for me.

Clara Curtis's response was much more complex. The moment came just after a quiet supper with the children. Through the kitchen window you could see a thin ray of sunlight above the rim of the mountains, even as the rest of the slopes were lost behind a curtain of steadily falling rain. After the children had left the table and gone upstairs to do homework or play, he told her what he had decided. Clara gave him a questioning stare and turned her back on him, as if looking out the window at the rain had suddenly taken on the utmost importance.

He took this to be a sign of disapproval. Oh, if he could only have read her mind! She was suffering but did not want to reveal it to him. She wanted success for him, for all of them, but she wanted him to embrace the family and their life together as well. How could she express this pain? Nothing in her life had prepared her for this. Marriage, family, making her nest and staying put in it—that was how her mother raised her. And add to that her latest accomplishments, working in the studio. Despite her own competence in his absence, she did not want to live with a wayfarer, a wanderer.

"Again?" was all she said.

"Again?" he said.

"You're leaving us again?"

He couldn't see her face, but he could hear the trouble in her voice. "My darling," he said, moving to take her in his arms. But she pulled away, holding to herself by the window. He stood up and felt something spring loose in his chest.

"Very well then, I won't go," he said. "I'll stay with you and the children, build up the studio, and give up all this talk about going into the field and opening up my lens to the various tribes that Grinnell and I envisioned. All this palaver about turning my business into an art and my art into an instrument of history, why it was just talk. I am not going anywhere." He said all this, nearly shouted it, to her unmoving back.

"Now and then," he continued, "I might wander down to the harbor or take the ferry over to one of the islands, and find some old Indian meandering along the waterside and make pictures that I'd then put up on the wall of the studio as a way of showing that I had a broader view of things than just the families of the city's bankers and judges. And you and I and the children—and mothers and sisters and cousins—we'll make the grandest family outings on the weekends in good weather, taking the ferry over to the island and taking picnics at Port Orchard, and our happiness will multiply. And if from time to time we notice some darkness around the fringes of things, some misery beyond the borders of our particular family portrait, why then we will do the charitable thing and hope that our few dollars can bring some of those downtrodden natives a bit of temporary hope. What if the Indians fade away into eternity unnoticed and unmemorialized? Other civilizations have gone quietly that way. Perhaps ours will too, if all our photographs go up in smoke."

Clara had pressed her hands to her eyes and was crying. "Please don't be cruel."

"I am not cruel. I am telling you the truth. Perhaps the truth is cruel."

"Please," she said. "Just go. Go."

"Clara, you can come with me," he said.

"You're not planning a mountain picnic of a few days, are you? You know I can't leave the children."

"We'll find a way. We've got Mother here, for heaven's sake, Clara."

"How long do you plan to be away?"

He wanted to keep silent. But she pressed him with a look. "I…don't know. I'm going to try this just one time. I promise you."

"Go," she said. "Go and do what you have to do."

"I think I have found a project, Clara," he said.

"Those rich men from Washington—"

"They're not rich. Grinnell, Merriam, they are government servants, Clara, for heaven's sake."

"They work for the government because they can afford to," Clara said.

"Listen to me," he said. "I've found someone right here in town who'll help with the money for my little expedition," he told her. "It's just a test, Clara. An experiment."

"And what rich man is that?"

"Someone you know," Edward said.

"Who is that?"

"Someone very close to you," he said.

Clara's curiosity got the best of her as she puckered her face into a question and leaned closer to him. "And who is it, Edward?"

"My brother Ray," he said. "We discussed it together," he said.

"Without me," Clara said.

"It so happened that...you weren't present, dear, when I thought it was appropriate to discuss."

"I wasn't there. You knew that if I were, I would have made him see the truth."

"The truth?"

She raised her chin a mark and glanced out the window at the rain. "The cruel truth is that you're fast becoming a big fool, Edward Curtis," she said without looking back at him. "I thought the trip to the Yukon would help to get such thoughts as all this out of your system. But it's only made things worse."

It stung him, the way she spoke. "Is that so?" he said.

"What else am I to make of you?" Now Clara turned her gaze on him again and what a strange gaze it was, a mix of anger, sympathy, jealousy, and other things. "You not only want to throw away *our* money and precious time, which you might spend with me and the children, but you're ready to take your brother's money as well."

"If I could explain it to you, Clara, I would. But I haven't figured it out to my own satisfaction yet, so it would be difficult to put it into words for you right now."

"Make a portrait of it, then, why don't you?" she said. "You're supposed to be good at that." With that she then walked past him into the hall. He could hear her footsteps on the stairs. Through the ceiling came the rowdy noises of children, wild before bedtime.

He found the whiskey bottle in the cupboard and took a swallow, and then another, and walked out onto the back porch and watched the rain a while. His life thus far passed before him as if projected on some kind of curtain in the wind, shifting its shape, changing and unfolding, twisting, turning back. He saw his Pap; he heard his voice: "You must make her understand—if you don't go, you'll die." Or was he just imagining what he wanted him to say?

And without any warning—no blurring of vision, no ringing in his ears—she appeared before him, the clamdigging Indian princess, as present as any visitation of the Virgin Mary he had ever heard reported. "Help me," she said in a plainspoken way, her words slurred slightly because of problems with her teeth. "Help my people, before we fade away into oblivion like everything else."

"But me? Why me?" Edward asked the woman. "I'm just a portrait maker of moderate talent."

She replied, "That is all we need."

Edward shivered in his shirtsleeves, and so filled with this determination, born it seemed out of his own illusions, he turned away from the rain and stepped back inside. He took one more drink. By the time he climbed the stairs, the noisy children had settled into the softer musical sounds and sighs of their approaching sleep. From the hallway he could hear Clara's voice as she spoke to them. "Stop your sniffling."

"I don't want him to go." It was Hal.

"I don't want him to go either. But he has to go."

"Why, Mama?" This was Beth.

"He has work to do."

"Why can't he work here, Mama?" Hal again.

"He has to go where he finds it," she said. "He has to meet the Indians."

"There's Indians here, Mama," Hal said. "I saw some on the street."

"He has to meet special Indians," she said.

"Why, Mama?" This was Beth again.

"Because he must."

"Why are they special?" Hal again.

"Because of who they are. Just as you are special because of who you are. Because you believe in Jesus and respect your father." Her voice wavered a little. "The way I do. We love him."

"I love him here," Beth said. She meant here at home.

"So do I," Hal said. "Don't you, Mama?"

"Of course, I do, Hal." Finding it difficult to speak—he could hear that in her voice—she took a breath. "But your father is a special man."

"Like the Indians?" Hal said.

"Yes, but different. Your father is a great portrait artist with his camera. His work may take him away from us for a while. But he will come back just as soon as he can." Edward was quite moved by the respect and the affection for him that he heard in her voice, moved by how she spoke about him to the children. "I *will* come back soon," he said to himself in the fog of his own youthful illusions. *"This work will not take long."*

Library of Congress, Prints & Photographs Division, Edward S. Curtis Collection, LC-USZ62-112223

five

jimmy fly-wing's story—1

The least movement affects all nature; the entire sea changes because of a rock. Thus, grace, the least action affects everything by its consequences; therefore everything is important.

In each action we must look beyond the action at our past, present, and future state, and at others whom it affects, and see the relation of all those things. And then we shall be very cautious....

PASCAL, PENSÉES, SECTION VII, 505

WHERE DO I BEGIN? In the Beginning was loneliness. And loneliness is no small thing, especially the loneliness of the Spirit. And Sky was lonely. And somewhere around the time that Sky decided he in all his vast expanse was becoming so lonely that he almost wanted to go inside himself and hide and never come out, he settled down onto the earth, which he had always seen lying below him, a territory consisting of smoke and pebbles, with here and there a small lake in whose surface he could see, if he lowered himself enough to catch the vision, his own lonely face.

"Wasn't that a time!" we might say, except that it wasn't a time at all. It was everything, all together, with nothing in the beginning and no sense that it could end—in other words, the best time, when everything was so important that nobody thought about what *was.*

Except there was no anybody and there was no nobody, just Sky, and that smoky pebbly world below him.

And his loneliness.

Yéhe eye ye, á u haíiye, á u haíiye, haíi, haíi, ye á u haíiye!
Yéhe eye ye, á u haíiye, á u haíiye, haíi, haíi, ye á u haíiye!

Sky felt satisfied and didn't need anything to eat. (He didn't know that he had to eat, and we don't know that he did eat, except it's the kind of thing we as People tend to think about, the first needs: food, shelter, clothing....) He didn't know where he had come from. Maybe he never came from anywhere because he had always been there, where he was. But if that was true—and I probably would agree that it was, just for the sake of comity—we can hardly even talk about how he thought and felt, because he was just so different from all of us who came after.

So different from us and yet he felt lonely, and so we have this kinship with him, because never before on our Earth has anyone felt the loneliness of my People, not since Sky. Sky made us so that he would stop being lonely, so that he would have People to converse with. People—on long winter nights, with the wind howling, and the fire flittering this way and that in the wind, and the food settling in your belly, and the smoke from a pipe circling overhead—seek good conversation. Of course, there are those who want nothing more than to satisfy their bodily needs. Warrior clans often gain that reputation. But since they are only People like the rest of us, you wonder how those stories got started. And it could only be because of conversation, particularly the conversation of women, who on nights such as these will talk about things they have known and things they have done, just as the men will, and as always in this world of perpetual congresses and intercourse, the women will correct the stories of the men.

I was a middle child, with two ahead of me, tall and strong boys, and two behind me, two, as it happened, mewling and puling girls. My brothers took care of themselves, and I looked forward to the day when I would live that way. The babies below me stayed on the tit and made for worries during the winters when it became difficult for them to eat and breathe. But whatever ailments the little ones contracted, our grandmothers always seemed to be able to combat them, with cures passed down to them from their mothers and the mothers of their mothers, and their mothers before them—a long line of mothers going all the way back to the time Sky came down to Earth.

Oh, Sky! So lonely, so filled with the hunger for company in the vast expanse of the heavens that was his domain. He changed his mind and gave in to his hunger. (Gods do that.) With his long arms he could reach out into the night sky and pluck several stars at once and nibble on them, until it was time to wake the sun and start the next day. That taste of star was quite delicious, a zesty spice that came of warring elements, exploding atoms, and burning minerals. Alas, stars were not enough. The hunger they appeased returned too soon, and though there were sufficient stars in the heavens to last Sky for all eternity plus even more millions of years, which to him were like the passing—if we can use our word to describe what would happen between one day and the next back in that time before ours—between one gesture and the next in a vigorous conversation between two spirited men.

Fortunately, a lot of things were always going on in the warm seasons, even as we traveled across the distances between one edge of our land and the other. I ran with the boys my age, playing many games that prepared me for the life of a warrior: fight-the-stick game, cross-the-circle game, wrestling, throwing contests, racing ponies, Skipping stones on wide rivers in springtime. Now and then my older brothers would include me in their games and chores, but I was still too weak to get knocked about as hard as they knocked me. They protected me, but they also pushed me into the middle of things to see how I would fare. Soon I had gashes on my legs and arms, and knots on my head, and I was happier than I had ever been since I left off drinking from my mother's tit.

We were a horse clan, and my father had duties that took him away and around the dry country where we lived, often for weeks at a time. In his absence my older brothers took charge of me, and because of this, I wasn't free to cry when I got hurt or to complain about throbbing limbs where I had fractured a bone.

Bones healed. My heart grew with each new day of play and each night's dreaming. It was like living in two countries at once—life under the sun and life at night in dreams. In the waking world I had my family, clan, and tribe, and all of us went about the living of a life that we knew was the life our People had lived ever since Sky had come down to Earth.

Before that the world had been a smooth place, a division of water and land, with few clouds, and now and then a thunderstorm, with lightning zigzagging down to connect the sky and water and flat places where nothing lived. If Earth was lonely, she did not know it. She flowed, she quaked, and she shuddered, in an endless round of shapings and reshapings. Steam pushed out of the stony parts of her. High waves furled and crashed upon themselves on her. But though she was not lonely, she was certainly ready to meet Sky—there was no one else to meet, and her destiny took her around and around, like the water in a vortex out at sea. Nothing but Sky hovered above her.

But as I said, Earth was not unhappy. In fact, she sang to herself, making up songs about the ocean and songs about the flat land that stretched all the way to the other side of the world, where the other side of the same ocean met it. That music was so sweet, if we had been there we could have taken life by breathing it. She did not need to eat but only sang. She did not need to shit but only sang. She did not need to sleep but only sang. And the songs purged the air of all hateful gases and stored up in the rocks and land all the power and nourishment our People would need if we were to live and grow.

So I suppose it was our destiny to live on Earth, but it didn't seem that way before Sky finally worked up his courage and made her acquaintance. Nothing seemed determined; nothing seemed destined. Sky was big and handsome, with his spectrum of colors as the sun crossed over him, and his expansiveness that stretched out to where the light of the sun no longer reached and the air turned empty and sprinkled with stars. Earth was beautiful, in her mix of land and ocean, in the moodiness of her storms and serenity, in the intensity of her lava flows and the stalwartness of her mountains. You would say it had to happen this way, but what is our say under the immensity of all the space and stars? There might have been another thing to happen. What if Sky had suddenly felt a call to attend to another world? Or what if when he leaned down and made himself known to Earth and said a few important words to her, she had balked and buckled and taken herself away and hidden herself amid the pounding waves and sprouting forests?

Who knows what Sky said to her? We can only imagine, you in your body of sea and land. Might he have said, "How in my loneliness I long to keep your company. Or, as your mountains impinge on my body and your flocks of birds fly across my face in the seasons of their migrations, would it not be fitting for us to come together and make a wholeness not yet realized?"

Ah, youth of ages! Oh, Sky and Earth! Then all this became a dance under the stars and Sky was dark, with a piercing of billions of points of light—these stars! his eyes! his hair and teeth and the very nails of his feet!—when Earth inclined toward the other time of her turning.

All this made her suddenly shy, and then she laughed, and he laughed on top of her laugh, and the ground shook, and she bowed her head toward him, and he sang to her a song about his ache of loneliness, and she listened carefully, not saying anything, and he sang her another song, about what a grand life they could make together, and she smiled, laughing again, and he took a deep breath and turned sideways, revealing the length and breadth of his penis before stretching even more and putting his penis in the Earth-hole. Earth sighing. Earth moaning. (Just like the sighs and moans of girls we had heard, while eavesdropping outside the tents of newly married folk.) Mountains jounced in their rocky roots. A cloud passed across the face of the sun. Sky gave a large shout and squirted out the stuff from which we were made.

Days, weeks, moons passed. And Earth became full of a new presence, until one morning, just when the dark of the passing night was about to yield to the rising of the morning sun, her belly convulsed with the tremors of our readiness. Clouds furled up just above the rising sun. Birds and animals suddenly appeared. A flock of snow geese heading south from near the land of eternal ice crossed the sun and honked their greetings. Thunder rolled across the tops of the tall grass. And in a miracle of sound and contradiction, horses unborn as yet into the world of Earth whinnied and pawed the ground.

And so a new way of being came into the world, which was us, the People, first just a few of us, who like Sky and Earth came together and made others, and these made others, and soon there were hundreds of us emerging from the mounds in the Earth where the first seeds had been sowed. We climbed up into a world of Sky as blue as the ocean, and it was cool if not cold most of the year, and some of us set out on a long journey over land, a journey that was a long time in the traveling, in which hundreds of families over ten thousand years walked and walked in the direction of the rising sun, through cold lands covered in snow, and then south toward the mountain passes. Another ten thousand years passed, and we kept moving, and another ten thousand, if a number says anything at all about passing time, and by then we had made our home in the high plains, not far from where I was born, the son of the son of the son of the son of the son of the son, and so on, whose father was among the first to set his feet down on the narrow neck of land that stretched across the waters.

This took so long it seemed to us like nothing and everything, like the distance between the hand I held up toward the stars and the stars themselves. It seemed impossible to a young child that time existed at all, time was a question he never asked, a thought he never held, and yet all of us had come from that first moment, when our fathers and mothers as children emerged from the ground where the seed of the Sky and the loamy soil of Earth came together. No place and no moment seemed more distant, and yet, as one of my grandmothers showed me, if I closed my eyes I could go there in less than the blink of an eye. In me there was time and time within that time. In me there were worlds and worlds within those worlds.

And nothing more so than in the world that appeared when I slept. I was a strong boy, but games often wore me out. When

the sun went down, I went with it. I listened to the stories at
night, enjoying them as much as anyone, for where else would
I learn about where we had come from and where we were
going? But the harder I played during the day the heavier my
head and limbs felt at night, and I couldn't understand how my
brothers and cousins could stay awake in the pool of talk and
chant and smoke that swirled about the inside of our sleep-tent,
when mothers and grandmothers and uncles and cousins and
fathers gathered for the evening in celebration of the day that
had passed.

I suppose I was just much more of a dreamer than they were.
When I closed my eyes, the darkness opened up for me, and I
could see as deeply, perhaps more so, than I could see under the
sun. I ran from my brothers and, unlike during the day, they
couldn't keep up with me. I ran like a pony, racing but with an
easy breath, all the way to the end of the surrounding prairie,
where the land fell away and the air hovered above a drop of a
hundred feet or more, at the bottom of which I saw the sun-
polished bones of buffalo.

Up I leaped, and wings sprouted from my shoulders. In the
company of a pair of hawks, I scoured the country below,
looking for mice and lizards to eat for breakfast, because it was
morning in the night world, the reverse of the darkness of the
end of the day in the waking world. I soared, I swooped, and
suddenly the birds who had guided me had fled, and I was alone
in my stooping dive, talons ready, snatching up a plump mouse
and taking it back to my nest in a niche of rocks near the edge
of a small village.

"Please don't eat me," pleaded the mouse.

It had bright pinpoint eyes and quivered as it spoke, revealing
all the more the juicy flesh of its back and rump. Mercy for a
mouse? Who ever heard of such a thing? With one flick of my

talons, I ripped it apart and nibbled on its remains, enjoying the salty taste of its lukewarm blood.

A flowering cloud, a dark curtain of sudden rain, caught my attention just then, and I fluttered up and then down into a nearby cave, where I waited out the heavy downpour of the storm. Beneath the cave, rivers flowed. A horse swam by, its rider trailing along behind in the swirling white crests of the current.

"Father!" I called out, recognizing his face. Before I could fly to him he sank out of sight beneath the waters. And so I was on my own.

The world turned the colors of the rainbow, and I scrambled like a fox to get out of the way of a vengeful corps of scorpions, whose venomous tails dangled over the rim of the cave.

"Don't go just yet," one of the poisonous insects called out to me. "We were wondering if we might talk over with you a particular problem that has been troubling us."

"And what might that be?" I inquired of the scorpion.

"It has to do with the difference between dreaming and waking," the creature said. "You have heard the elders talking their way through and around such matters in the lodge at night, have you not?"

"I have," I said.

"And have you formed any opinions of your own?"

"I am too young for that," I said. "I am still only a listener."

"But as you listen, you must still shape and form what you hear."

"That is true, but I merely take it in and don't ponder it."

"So you have a view of the matter, but you won't express it."

"If I express it, I will change the way I think about it, and I still have not yet fully figured out what I do think about it."

One of the other scorpions spoke up. "But if I could look into your mind what would I see?"

"Haze and clouds," I said. "Unshaped earth and transparent sky, beyond which the stars glittered and stretched away."

"I think you know more than you tell," said another of the insects. "You merely don't wish to engage us."

"It's true that I don't," I said. "But that's because I have so little to engage you with."

"Waking," the leader of the insects said, "as opposed to dreaming."

"Or," said one of the other scorpions, "to put it another way—dreaming, as opposed to waking."

"They are like the difference between—"

"Ah-ha!" the leader said. "He's going to talk with us."

"We'll have a brilliant debate!" the other scorpion said.

Meanwhile the rest of them had turned and skittered back to where we stood in discussion.

"Between?" the first one said.

"Between air and water?" I said.

"Between air and water? Air and water!"

"Water and air?"

"As you like."

"Each medium is different from the other. Air, because of its transparent nature, would seem to be usually invisible. Whereas water has a weight to it, which we can measure with the eye and feel when we cup it in our hands."

"And how does this apply to the question of the moment?"

"Night is the absence of light, but it has no less a substance to it than day, with a full sun burning through it."

"Go on."

"How we think during the day and how we think, or stop thinking, during the night changes the texture, and perhaps the very nature, of the two halves of the complete daily cycle. I walk on land, I swim, or at least float, in water. But I am still myself.

And yet there is something different about the way we view the world under the sun and the world under the moon. There is a presence in the night that we can hardly account for, but which is true nevertheless about what belongs to the time without sun. A day is like a year, and the hours are like moons, and at a certain point in the turning day, the dark settles over us, as the cold does during the winter part of the year."

The scorpion reared up and shook its tail.

"Light is the season of the daily round?"

"You can say that."

"I did; I did."

"And just as in certain seasons, we experience different varieties of weather—heat in summer, cold in winter, and in spring—"

"Go on; go on!"

"Blossoming of the desert in spring torrents, and in autumn the dying—"

"Ah, yes, and it is poignant."

"—of certain plants, or at least their hibernation, we can think of the changing states of waking and sleeping as seasons of the body and of the mind."

"And yes, and yes," the first scorpion said. "And all that follows from that. Well, well." And he gathered his troop and off they went over the rocks.

I danced up into the air with a few slaps of my wings. They had disappeared, but coming over the rocks, singing, shouting, was a band of men with long, wild strands of hair, dragging behind them another who was clearly a prisoner. I hovered above them, allowing the currents to keep me steady.

When they stopped and threw the prisoner to the ground, I felt myself rising against my own desires, higher and higher and higher. Up into the pale blue of the morning I soared, as if pulled on a rope by some invisible hand, and soon I reached the border between air and the space beyond, and miraculously I could still breathe.

Below me the blue Earth turned, and above me, in the darkness, many shapes became clear. Oh, and was my bird heart ever beating hard! Cougars and horses, buffalo, buffalo, buffalo, a million of them roaring across the sky, and beyond them the fields of light where stars flowed like water, and waves of stars even farther beyond lapped upon this closer ocean. And I turned around and around, like one of my own feathers floating on a gust of warm air, and when I looked down I saw the Earth spinning rapidly, but in a backward direction—land, ocean, clouds all whirling back—and yet I thought nothing of what was happening, because just then I turned again toward the deepening spaces beyond me, where the star animals roamed, and saw the great hand of a keeper come pushing toward me. "Hand of Sky?" A voice called to me in my secret name, one that I cannot even say here, and it sounded like my father, and yet like the voice of a stranger, but a stranger without menace, my grandfather's voice, perhaps, or the voice of an old chief.

He said my name again—let's say he called me Jimmy. And I spoke as a hawk but he understood.

"I am glad you have arrived."

"I am glad, too."

"I was away, attending to things on another side of the stars."

"Very far away?"

"So far I cannot explain and you would not understand."

"But you will stay with me now, won't you?"

"Oh, ho, you have a lot more to see before we meet again."

And he directed my gaze to the stars, which began to tumble in waterfalls of light, moving with such force that I could hear them rush along in their various courses. It seemed at one point to be raining stars and then snowing stars and then singing stars—though words fail me here when I try to describe what that particular sensation, hearing the stars, was like. How long this went on I can't say, but it was quite a while, and I remained fixed in place, a soft breeze from who knows where holding up my wings.

After some time passed, I felt a shift in my position, whether it was an hour in the night (of my dream) or a thousand moons that had turned in the sky, who could say? But slowly I began to turn, and none too soon, because below me the Earth was spinning in the direction opposite from before, and I felt a nearly imperceptible tug at the tip of my wings, and then I was floating slowly downward, downward, toward the spinning mass of blue and brown and green and white.

And as I floated closer to the rapidly turning planet, it became clear to me what was happening. I saw the enlarging of the already large masses of land, the turmoil of the oceans in transformation, volcanoes spouting fiery plumes of gold. And as I settled toward the clouds that covered one large part of the land, I heard loud trumpeting and the yip and yaw of men on the hunt.

A huge beast came lumbering over a rise, pursued by hunters, who were naked except for tiny strips of leather that bound their sex in such a way as not to hamper their movements as they ran. The beast bellowed, a loud harsh roar that rose up to my hawk-self and made me fear for its life. But then I could feel the hunger of the hunters and the hunger of their children. Nothing would stop them, nothing should. And when they hurled their spears at the monstrous animal, my heart leaped into the air along with the weapons, and I gave a hawk-sigh and felt the pleasure of seeing the animal go down on one knee, a spear through its eye, and then down on the other. And under the attack of more spears in its neck and chest, it crumbled onto its side and gave a single gasp—a raw expulsion of hot breath—before death shut its lungs forever.

I felt a surge under my wings, almost as if the last wind of the dying beast shot up under them, and I lifted and turned, and saw a spear flying up at me, and I rolled out of its path. Taking myself up higher, out of the range of the weapons, I floated above the men while they set about to cut and dress the meat of their kill. Their art was a keen one, and I could see that little of the animal would be wasted, and that even the giant sacs that had trailed and bounced along under its sex would turn into bags to haul the meat of their former owner.

Suddenly I felt a huge craving for a taste of the flesh of this freshly killed beast, and who was to say I shouldn't try to satisfy it? After only a moment's hesitation, I descended slowly, trailing just behind the men as they finished up their work, and when I touched the ground I hopped in my bird-like way up behind them. Oh, my hawk-belly danced and hopped around, too, as my hunger increased by the moment. The trail of blood from the dead animal's carcass hooked me in the nose, and I bent to taste a bit of its flesh, which had dropped to the trail from the bloody fingers of one of the hunters.

Boom! Someone hit me from behind, and before I could even flap my wings, he had grabbed me by beak and talons, and stuffed me into one of the sacks just on top of all that fresh meat. I struggled, but there wasn't much room, and there wasn't much use, and so I got to pecking at the flesh while bouncing about with my captors as they raced along the trail toward home. By the time we stopped, I was drunk on the blood and flesh, and without much will to put up a fight. Someone reached into the sack, held me up to the light—laughter all around—and tossed me aside.

I hit the ground hard—my first time on Earth since I began my dreamy climb toward the stars earlier that night—and lay there a while, unable to move. A sharp poke in my side got my attention, and I looked up to see a young boy, naked except for a few wisps of woven threads around his wrist, staring at me in surprise. He called out, and another boy came running.

Soon a circle of boys, all ages, all sizes, surrounded me, and they jabbered and jabbered in the speech of animals. No one from our People ever spoke in such a way. That first boy reached down and pulled at my wing. Another joined in. I began to struggle, but I was weak—still drunk, I thought, from the blood and the meat in the sack—and they easily held me up. It was terribly painful, with me feeling as though each of them would tear a wing from my body.

But it was feathers they wanted, and they plucked at me, and plucked and plucked, the pain momentary, but constant and sharp, until they were done, and they threw me onto the ground and ran off with my feathers.

Misery washed over me like cold rain, until a young woman, naked except for that same wispy wristband, came and lifted me and carried me over to where other women stood around a pot. I was shivering, and at first welcomed the warm water into which they dropped me. Looking down at me, the women smiled and nodded, their breasts, mostly small and boyish, staring at me like eyes. My thoughts were whirling, the heat increased, and I began to beat my naked wings at the water.

"Oh, please!" I cried out. But either they didn't understand my speech, or, worse yet, they didn't hear me.

"Oh, please!"

And the water grew hotter. My body began to feel crushed and expansive at the same time. Pinpoints of pain spread out across my naked flesh.

I was burning, boiling, dying!

"Oh, please!"

I shook. I shivered. I quaked. I writhed in the fiery water.

Library of Congress, Prints & Photographs Division, Edward S. Curtis Collection, LC-USZ62-51436

six

descent

DEPARTURE

From the notes of William E. Myers:

In a hotter than hot July we descend into the Grand Canyon, traveling with a Mexican guide called Negro. (This man's face, a near-chocolate brown, seems to have given him his name, though his arms and hands were as pale as our own.)

Our mules are laden high with supplies, and the beasts we ride are weighed down with our bodies. The sun is rising up over the eastern walls of this great and glorious declivity, a monument to time so vast that none of us can any more imagine it whole than the mayfly can picture the turning pages of a calendar. Cliff upon cliff leads away in ranks to the north and west, and yet it appears as though no dimension exists but the one in which we're standing. All else around us remains only an arm's length away. This makes me think of the childhood notion that one had only to reach out with a hand to snare a star.

Could that thread-thin river, traveling between the great walled ravines, have carved out this great canyon of multifold cliffs and cuts in the very body of the earth? The immensity of the space before us turns my imagination upside down. The idea that there could be enough time and force for the river to have made its solitary way, ledge upon ledge upon ledge, through all this rock and space—I might as well have conjured up all the space between us and the moon as stone and waited for the air to carve its way through.

At the rim you stand three thousand feet above the bottom of the chasm. Looking down into this bewildering gorge, you see many fanciful forms, fashioned through the eons from rock: castles, citadels, pyramids, pinnacles, and sphinx-like sculptures, tinted and mystified with the incomparable atmospheric coloring of the desert, and ever wrapped in death-like stillness. As you stand there and gaze out over the emptiness of stone, there is nothing to suggest that half a mile below and twenty miles away, at the bottom of this awful gash, there is a garden and a human village.

The coughing of a mule interrupts my thoughts, a comment on my philosophical musing. The animal breaks wind and snorts, and I look away from the distances that surround us and focus on the necessities of our travel.

"Ready, you?" Negro looks around at us, touches a hand to his forehead as if in anticipation of the sweat that will pour down all of our brows, and then signals us to move forward. Edward gives his beast a kick and I kick mine. After a moment's hesitation, we lurch forward along the trail.

Tall pines line the path down the hillside, wind whirring through the outstretched limbs. A hawk hovers about a hundred feet below us. We work our way forward in an odd downward-turning motion, as the day opens from the east with the lifting of the fiery orb over the lip of the canyon walls. We joggle our way along and down, and down again, switchback upon switch-back, beginning and then seeming to begin again. Downward toward the age when the river began.

Descent is a subject that those of us trained as classicists know quite well. The word in Greek is *katabasis*, which basically means getting to the bottom, and that's what we intended to do. All the great heroes made descents before climbing back upward. Achilles went down into the bottom of his anger. Odysseus climbed down into the lower pits of Hades. Christ certainly made the same downward climb before ascending out of hell after he harrowed it. Now here I was, seeing myself as a traveler in the same downward path, which we had to take in order to eventually make our way upward with our project fully underway.

First hour or so seems relatively easy, once we adjust ourselves to the somewhat annoying rhythms of the animals. Odd to ride so high off the ground and yet feel so close to it—that is, on one side. In a single turn, all empty space opens up at our elbows and as the mule plods along, one hoof…after another…after another…I feel as though I am half-flying, half-crawling.

I breathe in the dust, cough, cough again, and my mule snorts, coughs along with me, coughs and spits like a camel. Thoughts come and go. On the wind comes a memory out of only the week before, of my fiancée and of Edward's wife Clara and his children waving goodbye to us at the train station. And yet, against the setting of this rock and sky, in this place of singing air and dusty trails, not just this memory but the thought of it itself seems a thousand years old, though it had been only yesterday. Other memories, different voices, other times.

Second hour, and now we're well below the top of the cliffs, so that the cool winds seem much colder without the sun to warm us. It's as if, by descending, we've slipped back to the time before sunrise. The sky directly above us is a much darker blue than it was when we began our descent. There's dust in our nostrils and every breath carries with it the dry odor of the trail, the musk of the mules, the tangy stink of their urine, the high piney scent of the small trees that cling to whatever tiny space they find along the winding way down. Our bodies shift and sway to the rhythms of the plodding beasts, as our eyes adjust to the transformed light.

Yet even as we descend, the heat increases, and after a while we reach a slightly concave indentation on the cliff-side. Negro halts the mules, and we sit there on our beasts—not enough room to climb down and rest on the ledge—and quietly sip from our jugs while our mounts noisily make water, spattering dust in the wake of their hard flows.

"Look," says Edward. He gestures with his head. An eagle is swaying in the wind about a half mile out over the canyon, nearly at a level with where we stand. And above us, a hawk is balancing on the wind like a kite. And below us—

"Look!" I say.

—another raptor is gliding along as if the air were made of ice and the bird were a sled, tilting its wing against the slippery surface of the sky.

"Two ways to go," Edward says, "for us. Straight down. Quite fast that way. Or this endless circling down and around."

"I choose the endless circling," I say. "Straight down takes you much less time, but you're dead at the end of the trip."

"You're right, William," he says. "I also vote for endless circling and climbing down and around."

"Negro?"

"Sí, señor?"

"How do you vote?"

"Eh—vote?"

"On this issue. Do we just jump over the edge or keep on walking these mules?" He looks at me with those dark brown liquid eyes, and I don't know what he is seeing, but I don't think it's me, the me who I really am.

"Mules, señor," he says, but not a hint that he catches the fact that we're joking. If we had decided to fall straight down, voted on it, would he have gone with us, a perfectly devoted guide?

"How many people come down this trail each week?" I ask. He looks at me as though I haven't yet completed making my question.

"Cómo?"

"How many? How many come this way?"

"How many?"

"Travelers," I say. He shrugs and holds up two fingers. "Two people a week?"

"Week?" he says. "No, no," he adds with a shake of his head. "Mes," he says. "Month. Two gringos a month." He pats his saddle blanket. "Sell tings," he says. "Vender, es es-sell."

I nod. "Two a month. Well, for this trail, I guess that's a lot. Makes this a sort of turnpike, even. Precarious turnpike." I lean over my beast of burden and look out over the river, but a rush of vertigo makes me draw back quickly. Mustn't do that again. It's a long way down, but a man would fall rather quickly. Better the long way around and down. Around and down. And down and around and down. That's life, at least. The way of life.

Down we go again, step and step and step and step, and though I've just taken a drink of water, the sweat rolls down my forehead and neck and beneath my arms and down my back. We began in July, we began high on the rim where the winds blow cool even in this hot season. But now as we descend, we move closer, step by step by step, to the heat of our actual season. And the sweat runs even as we move at a mule's pace.

And as we turn up toward the rim again for a mile or so, plodding along, Negro hums a simple little tune under his breath, and because we move so slowly, when the wind dies all of a sudden, as it does now and then, it seems as though we can hear him

sucking in the very air that he needs to expel the melody across
the top of his tongue.

Lie-dee-die-dee-die,
Pal-oh-ma-a-a....
Paloma! Pigeon of love! Lie-dee-die-dee-die, pal-oh-m-a-a!

But no doves here, though we had seen the eagles, and hawks
now circle, as if drawn by the magnetism of some stray rabbit or
rock mouse, dying and ready to become a noon meal.

Noon! The sun is swinging high in the sky and clearing the
lip of the southern rim of the canyon. And our path turns
downward again, downward toward the frothing river, which
now and then, as the sweat distorts my salty vision, comes
muddily into view. A small shelf of rock just ahead, with room
enough for us to dismount. Aching leg muscles, tired rump—
difficult to stretch out even though we had the space to do it in.

Negro unpacks our meal, spicy cooked beans wrapped in
tortillas, neat slices of cactus fruit. I devour these, ask for more.
He must see this happen at least twice a month, because he's
ready with seconds. I chew and chew, and wash the meal down
with good, fresh, if tepid, water. Odd how after a half-day's ride
along this twisting, winding trail it seems almost normal to look
out to one side and see nothing but the north rim of the canyon
across the far distance. Nearby a ground squirrel chirps rapidly,
rapidly, chatters and chatters and chatters, demanding that I feed
it scraps from my meal. There aren't any. Edward offers some,
and the jittery, little bushy-tailed critter snaps it up and rushes up
the rock face to eat a vertical lunch.

"Vámanos," says Negro, and we groan and stretch, and soon
we're on our way down again. Dimmer down there, more than
midway toward the bottom, and the cliffs rise around us, making

sharp dark lines against the sky, so blue that it seems almost liquid, like the sea in good sunlight. Above the plodding and scraping of the mules some Latin verses float in my mind. *Humano capiti cervicem pictor equinam / jungere si velit, et varias inducere plumas....* Yes, I remember that, from old Horace, and my eye and memory blur together, I see the lake, an ocean, my fiancée's face; in the tinkle of bells, I hear her laugh.

I snap upright in the saddle, completely awake, and look around. Here's our Negro, slumped over on his mule, leading us down the winding trail in a stupor all his own, and I look up to see Edward turning in the saddle and giving me a wink.

"Slow work, William, eh?"

I nod, brush a buzzing insect away from my face. Flies follow the mules, and the mules follow the trail. I adjust my discomfited self in the saddle and close my eyes again, listening carefully to the whining, whirring of the wind. No voice comes along with it. I was imagining it; I was mistaken. Sun-genies. Sun-devils. Dust-devils. Whirligig dervishes in the fantasy of our down-turning wanderings. I whip my neck around, only to see Edward staring at me from his plodding mount.

"Yes? What is it?" he asks.

I shake my head. "Flies," I say. "Damned flies. And the heat."

"Well," he says in a voice loud enough to continue our conversation, "up on the rim it felt like early June. Down here I'm beginning to be convinced it's really summer in the desert."

"Yes," I say. "Indeed."

But I've already closed my eyes, hoping to see I know not what, and I release myself from the talk, wondering if I'll hear what I thought I heard—a voice, a familiar voice on the wind, a voice reciting Horace, my girl's face. Up a winding turn and then level, and then slightly down again, and then up, and I look into the gorge and see actual details in the passage of the frothing river, which before had appeared no more than a still white trail between the lowest rocks. There's hope for an end to this descent, visual proof of it.

"Scree-cree!" the voice of a circling hawk. *Scree-cree!* Something triumphant in the sound.

Whoa! now, whoa! These mules now want to kill us with speed after more than half a day of nearly strangling us with lassitude. Whoa! Yet all this plodding will be worth it, I hope. And yes! Now I can see the tops of trees at the bottom of the canyon and imagine, when the wind winds down from time to time into a lower pitch, that we can almost hear the rushing of the river.

"Nearly there?" I say over the pommel of my saddle to our guide.

"Soon," he says, without looking back at me.

"Not soon enough for me," says Edward. "William, how thirsty are you? I could drink that entire river dry."

"Quite thirsty," I say, gazing out over the rushing water as we plod along on our trail, which now runs only a few hundred yards above the river. The water gushes caramel and white, as though it might be some liquid confection served up at a party back home, instead of the ancient waterway that gouged out this canyon, which now towers above us on all sides, the walls keeping out the direct sun, bathing us in the dry white air and seeming to gather the proper heat of the season now that we had descended into it.

"Look!" Edward points down along the trail where it enters a small stand of willows near a turn in the blue-tinted river.

"Good," I say. "I think we're here."

"After quite a long ride down, I have to say."

"This must be the place," I say.

"Esto," says our guide. "Aquí están."

My mule stops dead in his tracks in order to make a long and noisy piss, and the stink of it, cutting through the already baking air of the canyon floor, lingers in my nostrils, marking for me our arrival in this special location in its particular stinging way. After our long journey, our winding descent, I feel as though I have awakened in the middle of a dream of heat and light.

"And now?" I say to Edward. He seems quite overjoyed.

"Our first time in the field!" he says.

"And now what, maestro?" I say.

"And now we go to work."

ARRIVAL

The home of the Havasupai tribe lay at the bottom of Catarack Canyon, a branch of the Grand Canyon of the Colorado River. Without question it was the strangest dwelling place of any tribe in America. In all the long miles of the river's windings, there was but one small spot where the river gorge widened. Here was an amphitheater. Its bottom had filled with earth, the weatherings of untold ages, and at the place where the narrow rift began to widen, water sprang from the ground, and it was of the most peculiar transparent blue.

The floor of the amphitheater was half a mile wide, scarcely two miles long, and contained an area of less than five hundred acres. The never-ending stream made life possible in the depths of this gorge, flowing through the length of this little green spot and then in a cataract leaping from the floor of the canyon to be caught in a pool below. Above us in the high-plateau region, the land of the piñon, cedar, and pine, the wind usually made for a cool high-desert summer afternoon. Down here it seemed almost subtropical, with luxuriant vegetation and fruits of several kinds—figs, peaches, and apricots, growing on trees planted in rough rows.

Next came rows of corn, and then patches of beans, squash, melons, pumpkins, and sunflowers, the large black eyes of these last looming before us as we made our way beside the length of the stream that bordered all these plantings. A dog barked, the only sound that broke the silence except for the plodding of our mules. And then we heard the stream, and the light wind blowing through the brush-shelters, which had corn husks for roofs and were held up by four posts in the ground. Figures stirred within them as they heard us approach.

A man suddenly stepped into the path, his long dark hair tied into a knot at the back of his head. He was dressed in a large deerskin serape with breechcloth leggings. A leather belt loosely held the serape to his middle, while loose baggy sleeves lay open at the elbows. On his feet were high-topped deerskin moccasins. He greeted us with an upheld palm.

"I am Wipai," he said. "Chief."

It might have been the heat, but Edward, as he told me later, was momentarily overcome by a distinct but unidentifiable emotion. The man seemed to shimmer in front of his very eyes, as though he were, like the old clamdigger woman before him, appearing on a photographic plate with the assistance of certain chemicals.

"Chief," he heard himself say. The Indian nodded to Edward and greeted the guide, whom he had obviously met before. To me, he held up his other hand.

"Washington?"

"No, no," Edward told him, recovering himself. "Seattle. From the north and west. On the great waters of Puget Sound."

"Does our blue stream flow there?"

Edward looked at me and I at him. We both climbed down from our mules and offered our hands to Wipai.

"We wish to speak with you a while," Edward said.

Wipai held up both palms to the deep blue of the sky above the canyon.

"We will speak," he said. "But first you rest. It is a long trail down from the rim to our valley." In imitation of our new host I turned both palms to the sky.

Negro helped us unload. Wipai made it clear that we were his guests and that he was giving us one of the tribe's little brush-huts to sleep in and another in which to shelter our equipment. A group of four or five men dressed in similar fashion to the chief stepped out of the corn rows and assisted us with the equipment. From beyond the farm came the noise of children and the scent of cooking.

Wipai told us the names of the men, but we forgot these almost at once when we met some of the women of the tribe. I can recite the names of these women: Chekucheku, which means "Dancing between Two Men"; and Matekalíwa, which means "Flapping Ears"—not very flattering, and as far as I could tell not true, at least as much as I could see of her ears, since she wore her jet-black hair long and straight to her shoulders.

And then *she* came into view, ducking her head and coming out from under one of the bush-shelters, her hair a thick sheen of black jade that moved as a counterweight to the gentle motion of her head, her skin a deep mahogany, her eyes set perfectly in her face, her nose a beautiful, petite ornament. But it was back to those eyes that our own eyes went, as the two of us stared at them, into them, and that night Edward told me he felt as though he looked into them and saw back in time a thousand, yea, two thousand years. Her name was Tasáwiche and she was Chief Wipai's daughter.

"What does that mean?" Edward asked her father.

Wipai inclined his head toward Edward, proud of the girl he raised, pleased that Edward had asked. "Sunlight through the Leaves," he said.

Sunlight through the Leaves.... Sunlight through the Leaves.... I went over and took him by the arm.

"You look faint," I said.

"The descent," he said. "I need water."

"Water it is," I said, and handed him my canteen. I watched him take a drink. "Have you stopped descending?"

He sighed and tried to explain what he was feeling. "Look at her," he said. "She's the essence of what I want my pictures to become. The look, the light, the face, the eyes. A certain glow overall, yet something grounded in the earth."

"So," I said, "you've met your Muse."

Tasáwiche.... Tasáwiche.... Tasáwiche....

"I believe I have," he said.

~~~

WORK

Edward slept badly that first night in the canyon and upon awakening felt slightly feverish. From the descent, he told himself, though if he were truthful, he would have admitted the cause was something else entirely.

On this first foray into the canyon lands of the Havasupai— and then onto the homes of the Yuma and Mohave tribes— never had he felt so ill-prepared. As soon as we began our research, he told me that he thought to himself, "I know nothing about the language, nothing about the mythology, and much that we're hearing about from the old men of the tribe is just plain indecipherable to me." But still we had to begin some- where. And so, sitting with Wipai and his lieutenants for four hours the next afternoon and evening, we made a schedule for our research. Wipai designated one man to tell us of the tribal religion. Another would tell us about agriculture. A third would explain their medicine and such, with some assistance from one of the wives, who is the local expert on such matters.

I was nearly overwhelmed with the task that lay before us, and Edward even more so. To investigate the essence of an entire tribe! However, this was a good place to begin—with only several hundred Havasupai still in existence. Never more than a few thousand lived here, scattered along this section of the river, Wipai informed us. In the old days, before the white man and the Spaniard, they made up the entire world. They had little contact, only here and there, with a few other high-desert tribal groups. And each of these tribes had the same view of things. They were the world, the entire People in it.

Night again in the canyon. Music of the wind in the delicately entangled aspens. When the wind dies down, you can hear the chorus of the stream. We've spent the day talking to Wipai and his adjutants, recording their stories in our notebooks, beginning to make out some patterns. I never labored so hard only to see so much work beyond the next task.

Yet, I suffered little fatigue. We set up to make portraits. Edward asked the chief if he could photograph his beautiful, silent daughter, and at first Wipai seemed reluctant. He spoke to his wife—her mother, we presumed—and she gave him a solemn nod.

Tasáwiche wore a gingham dress. Edward asked the chief to ask his daughter if she might change into a traditional costume. "I want to see a thousand years," Edward said, setting forth for the first time the principle that ruled in all of our subsequent work together. "Not just this year."

Wipai spoke to Tasáwiche, and without looking at him, she went into the house and emerged a little while later dressed in a

blanket robe, the color of the sky. For the next hour Edward
worked with her. Light at the bottom of the canyon presented
an interesting problem, and he was interpreting the light as he
made the portrait. The Havasupai girl's face remained, like her
mother's, solemn throughout our session.

"My name is Curtis," Edward told her. She listened but said
nothing. His hand trembled as he loaded the plate. "Curtis," he
said again and was met once more by silence. "Isn't she exqui-
site?" he said to me.

"She certainly is," I said.

"So different from us." Edward had a flickering thought
about Clara and his own daughters back in Seattle. He was
embarrassed by his building desire for this young girl.
Mustering his strength, he went on with the work. The girl—
Tasáwiche—remained silent all the while.

His notes for this trip conclude:

*Long meal with Wipai and his family. His beautiful, silent
daughter Tasáwiche. Tomorrow we climb back up to the rim and
travel to the Yuma and the Mohave People.*

On that last night after our meal, I retired to our little lean-to,
and by lamplight—the only lamp in the canyon, and it was our
lamp, of course—went over the mechanics of the new-fangled
recording machine, which I myself had never used. Edward,
never one for the way things were put together, only for the way
he found that he could use them for his own ends, left me there
to fiddle over the wheels and screws of it while he lighted a cigar
and went for a stroll along the running blue stream.

As I mentioned, we possessed the only lamp in the village.
Wipai and his tribe, those who were left, naturally went to bed
quite early, almost immediately, it seemed, after the sky above
the canyon rim turned from inky blue to blue-black and the
stars winked on. The Havasupai had no trouble moving about

in the dark if they wanted to. Whether beneath the many-pointed glow of the summer stars or the thick blanket of a winter sky, they could walk about the canyon after dark, as though it were the large parlor of a city house, without worrying about bumping into trees or stumbling over rocks or roots.

Given that habitual sense of place and the fact that Edward's cigar must have left a trail of smoke in the dark air as broad as the stream itself, what happened next was no accident. "Myers?" he called out when he heard the step on the path behind him. Not a word in response.

He looked back down along the dark trail, and saw no one, and then stared down in the direction of the gushing stream. Water flows at night with such an exaggerated sound. To his ears that rushing stream might have been a leak sprung in the wide dam of time.

He took a few short steps right up to the edge of the stream and dropped to one knee before it. His mind rushed along as swiftly as the water. He plunged a hand into the flow, dangling it in the rushing current, cold, cold, hoping for a hand to clasp his own, a fish to swim into his grasp, something, something! What was it that he wanted? What? What? Down on both knees he went, leaning closer to the water, thirsting for just a taste of the blue—well, at this moment, black—stream. As he was kneeling there, he heard the sound again.

"Hello?" In response, only the churning of the stream. "Hello?" He stared into the dark, and the dark seemed to shift a bit even within its sameness. "Hello?" Now a wisp of sound drifted out of the darkness, as though the noise were emanating from the spirit of the night itself. "It's not you, is it, Myers?"

He was befuddled, confused, slightly ever so slightly wondering if there was some lurking danger out there, despite the welcoming atmosphere of the canyon by day. "If not you, then who?" he called. An owl called back. "Nothing more," he said to himself aloud. The owl called again.

Decades before, when he had been a child in Minnesota, an owl had called outside his window, and it turned out to be, as he told me years later, the signal of one member of a passing band of Indians. He listened to the sound again. "Come out," he said. A rustling in the dark, something like a cross between the clicking of a squirrel and the chirping of a small bird. "Hello?" he said. Again the sound.

And then, as if they were standing together on a stage and the time had come to cue the lights, a pale half-moon slid up over the southeast rim of the canyon, and he saw the palpable darkness of her against the greater dark, the dark outline of her against the pale—I could almost say feeble—lunar light.

He said her name. She corrected his pronunciation. "Tasáwiche."

"Tasáwiche," he said.

"Tasáwiche," she said again, to confirm his new rendering of it.

"Hello," he said again. "So you're not as silent as you seem."

"Buenas noches," she said.

"Buenas noches," he said. "But do you speak English?"

A tiny sound came out of her throat, a sigh, subdued so much that he could scarcely hear it, so many paces apart did they stand at that moment.

"Do you?" he said.

The moon slid further up over the canyon, and in the new light he noticed the whiteness of her teeth as she opened her mouth to speak and caught the quick sparkle of the same light in her otherwise tar-dark eyes.

"No mucho," she said.

"Not much?"

"No much English." Eeenglishhhh…the sibilants shushed off her tongue and lips and faded into the splashing of the stream.

"And not much sleep either," Edward said, glancing up at the moon. She stood her ground in silence, facing him. As his eyes adjusted to the new light he could make out the lithe her body, over which she had thrown a blanket, a type that the older women in the village invested many months of their time to create.

"No much," she said.

"Difficult to sleep so early," he said. She gave a shrug. "That's why I came out for a walk."

"Sí," she said.

"Yes?"

"Es-sí," she said.

"Tell me the word in your language for walk," he said. She tilted her head toward him. "You don't understand?" She turned and looked into the dark. A bird called in the night, coarsely, with no consideration of the tranquility it disturbed.

"Shakwakwa," she said in a quiet voice.

"Walk?" he said. Again the bird called out in the dark.

"Shakwakwa," she said.

"The bird?" He made as if his hands might flutter toward her. She nodded. "Bird…pajaro," she said. "Shakwakwa."

"It sounds a little like walk to me," he said. "I thought you were saying your word for walk."

Again she shrugged, and this time he paid closer attention to that small delightful gesture, and the feeling it engendered pulled him toward her. "Walk," she said as he drew close.

"Walk," he said, inhaling her scent, the odor of dry corn silk and tart berries, with a hint of something brusque but compelling, like tobacco, and beneath that a tincture of some odiferous night-blooming plant. He touched her arm and

stepped forward along the trail, and she followed him about a
pace behind. "Come along," he said, as if he knew where he
was going.

"Walk," she said, stopping when he stopped and turned to
urge her forward, starting again only when he picked up his step
and continued along the edge of the flowing current. In this
fashion they proceeded toward the far western corner of the
canyon, followed by the rising half-moon and accompanied by
the music of the stream. Edward would have kept on going, if
their passage had not been interrupted by the interposition of a
large fallen rock.

"We'll go around it," he said, motioning for Tasáwiche to
follow. But it was she who then motioned for him to follow her.
The smell of her—berries turned to wine, the perfume of that
night flower mingling with the acidic bite of the tobacco.
"Tasáwiche," he said.

"Curt's," she said.

"We must...go back...."

She laughed lightly, high in her throat. And sang a few words
in her language. As if in reply, some night bird high in the
canyon immediately trilled out.

"We should...." The bird called again.

"Curt's," she said, and the moon rose up behind the high
rock rim.

"Tell me," he said, but she gave no reply, merely stood and
peered out into the dark. And sang out again.

"Who?" he said. "What?" The birdsong singer responded.
"Hello?" he said.

Tasáwiche touched his arm and laughed that same childlike
giggle, a laugh that dispersed Edward's cares like clouds in the
wind. Though his cares returned immediately upon seeing the
man step out of the shadows.

"Hel—"

"Curtis," I said.

"Myers? Was that you singing?"

"It was," I said, coming close enough for me to see the way his mouth turned up in a smile.

"I didn't know you had the talent," he said.

I looked over at his companion and my smile grew bolder. "I didn't know that you had, either."

"We were…." He stopped himself, gave it up.

"I heard you," I said. "The girl's song, that is. Very pretty. Now that I've got the noise of it, I think that I'll try and figure out the words. But not tonight."

"It is late," he said. "We were…." But he stopped himself again. "Yes, late. Very late. I was just out here wandering about, chasing after the moon, you might say, when I heard the singing."

"It is beautiful," I said, turning toward Tasáwiche. But she was gone. "What the hell?" I said.

"My thoughts exactly," Edward said. "When I heard the singing." We started back toward the village, keeping the rushing stream to our left.

"I can keep secrets," I said.

"Very good," Edward said. "But there's nothing to keep. Nothing."

"Of course," I said.

He took a deep breath and kept on walking, hoping, he later told me, that one day there might be something. We reached the edge of the Havasupai camp and stopped, staring into the dark above the little hut where we would sleep that night in close proximity.

"Time for bed," Edward said.

"Tomorrow, I'll record her song," I said.

"That would be splendid," he said.

"So bird-like," I said.

"Very like a bird," he said.

He followed me into the shelter, ducking his head and planting himself immediately on the pallet where he pulled a blanket over himself, clothes and all, removing only his shoes before feeling the night fall on him like a second blanket. He tried to recall the sound of her song, but his memory of it was imperfect. In his mind, in his state close to sleep, as he imagined it—the song flew, like the night-bird, from place to place on the mesa, and settled now and then back in time, at a point where the melody had not yet descended into language, and Tasáwiche could sing her messages to her father and to others, trilling them like a bird, and could wing her way across the space that gaped between two people. Something shifted in Edward's heart, confirming for him, in a higher way than ever before, that his soul had found its calling.

Library of Congress, Prints & Photographs Division, Edward S. Curtis Collection, LC-US62-101259

seven

jimmy fly-wing's story—2

WHEN I CAME OUT of my fever, feeling all of a sudden as cool as I had felt hot, I noticed a flock of flies buzzing above my head, and I spoke with them.

"What is it like?" I asked.

"What is what like?" came the reply.

"What is it like to buzz about and live only for a day or more under the sun and under the moon."

"Don't you know?"

"I don't," I said.

"Only because you haven't yet thought about it," the flies buzzed back at me.

I lay there, watching them make their circles, and their zigzag runs beneath the tent hole, and it occurred to me—though "occurred" is probably not the correct word, since I was still only a young boy, and young boys don't have things "occur" to them in the same way that people who use that word have things "occur" to them—that I shouldn't be able to speak to them and they to me, but nevertheless we were doing it.

"It's a short life," the flies said. "Full of activity but rarely action. You must try to live another way, with action always standing out over activity."

"I flew like a hawk and now I feel hawk-like," I told them. "Will I now feel like I'm buzzing about, if you help me?"

"Why should we help you?"

"I am your cousin," I said.

"You're one of the People, not an insect."

"But we are all related."

"How do you know that?"

"I know it," I said.

"You could be right; you could be wrong."

A gust of smoke rose up from the fire, stirred by the wind swirling down the tent-hole, and the flies scattered and then just as quickly regrouped.

"Little flies, little flies," I said. "I am your brother."

"You, yes, Jimmy, fly like a fly," they said.

"I will," I said.

"But do you know the difference between us and you?"

"No, what is that?"

"You thought of this and we didn't. We were just buzzing around your head and never had the notion that we could speak with you."

"And now?"

"We're pleased."

"I'm pleased."

"And me," said another fly. "And me, too," said another. "And me, and me."

Here was my great opportunity, the first in my waking life (because all of my previous conversations with Sky and my life as a hawk had, of course, taken place in my dream-vision, that other state of being) to talk with creatures other than my own kind.

"Really?" said one of the flies, as he circled downward and landed on my nose. I crossed my eyes as I spoke to him.

"Yes, yes, I want to know all about your days as you live them."

"The cold in the morning, the heat bringing us back to life?"

"Yes."

"The thrill of meat?"

"Yes, yes."

"The delirium of decay?"

"If you say so."

"You'll never know of it, unless I tell you."

"The circling, endless circling, and lightning down, and feeling the wind stir us to action again."

"Not just movement but action?"

"We're alive and need to live, and so what seems like mere movement to you is action to us. It all feeds our hopes, the hopes to feed, and breed, and hatch."

"And how do I then discern the difference in my own life between action and what seems aimless—say, the way we boys kick around a small piece of leather hide to pass the time under the sun of an afternoon?"

"Everything is aimless," said the flies, "and nothing is aimless. An animal was born and lived and died to make that piece of leather. Its ancestors bred for hundreds of thousands of moons—"

"You're going backward," I said.

"And didn't you in your dream?"

"How do you know about my dream?"

"We all know nothing and we all know everything."

"You buzzing, zigzagging flies know about my dream? I haven't told anyone, not my father, not my mother, not the shaman-doctor. And you know?"

"You've told no one, and one day you will tell everyone."

"You are a paradoxical fly."

"You are a paradoxical boy, that you can use such ideas as this."

A dog barked somewhere in the distance.

"Does that dog have ideas, too?"

"We all do, in our own ways."

"What is that dog's idea?"

"To avoid its destiny."

"And what is that?"

"Being boiled and eaten, to please you and fatten you up."

Again the dog barked.

"Perhaps your father has returned," the flies buzzed at me.

"I miss him," I said.

"Yes, we know."

"Do you know everything?"

"We know you are hungry and that your mother's aunt is coming to bring you a bowl of dog soup."

"Now?"

"She is almost here."

"But tell me one more thing before she arrives."

"And what is that?"

"All of you and I are connected. And I am part of a family, and a clan, and a tribe and the People...."

"Yes."

"And all of us are connected to everything else?"

One fly zigzagged close to my nose and buzzed about the tent high above, before zeeing down to land on my chest. "Leaves and stones and flowers and stars and worms and prairie dogs and comets and creeks and salamanders and cacti and the sun, your mother's braids and your father's chaps, the hair in your nose and the swoop of a hawk or an eagle. Don't you know that yet? Sky, and the width of your hand, volcanoes and your little toe."

"What are volcanoes?"

"We thought you knew everything."

"Not yet, not yet. Does anyone know everything?" But before he could answer I heard the shuffle of my great-aunt's feet outside the tent.

"Little one," she said, kneeling before me, as the flies buzzed around us. She had always been kind to me when I was a child, but now I felt grateful that she had decided to dedicate herself to my return to health. Her dark eyes showed depths within depths, like a stream that eddied beneath the roots of a large tree. Her touch was as firm as a man's as she helped me to my feet and took me to the waters, and bathed me and dried me.

"Oh, yes, yes," said my mother, observing me when I returned. "Good," she said to her aunt. "This is good."

Moons rose and moons set, and I grew stronger and stronger. Soon I was playing with my friends again, and they seemed to give me a larger role in the play we performed.

"They say you had a powerful vision," one of them whispered to me as we climbed to the top of a nearby ridge. "They say you died and came back to the world."

"I didn't die," I said. "I lived another life as a hawk, but I myself never died."

"You are supposed to die," the boy said. "And then if all is well you return."

I gave a violent shudder. I didn't know what he was talking about. We went about our play, pretending that we made up a raiding party and rode out to attack a passing war party from another people. My friend was wounded, but I escaped unharmed, carrying back evidence in a pair of birch limbs of two successful coups.

Much time passed. Moons rose; moons set. We had rain and then we had snow and ice. We traveled; we stayed in place. My father, still away on a horse-gathering expedition, stayed away most of the winter. My great-uncle, husband to the woman who had nursed me back to health from my vision-fever, took over our care, making sure that we had plenty of firewood for our tent and giving my mother generous amounts of meat for our evening meal. My great-aunt accompanied him on his visits to us, and she and my mother talked quietly together while the rest of us played with shadows on the far wall of the tent.

After the coldest weather passed, mother told us to gather up our things and she moved us into the tent of our great-uncle and great-aunt. One of my brothers whined like a bear cub, and one of my sisters cried, but it did not trouble me at all. In fact, I felt the warmest sensation, a soft glow at the pit of my belly, because my great-aunt had taken such good care of me when I had my fever. Seeing her welcoming us into her own home gave me a feeling unlike anything else I had ever known, except when I was very young and saw my mother hurrying toward me across the compound after I had been lost.

I was also amazed—remember, I was still only a boy—that we had enough room in our new lodging. Mother slept in the corner with my great-aunt and her husband, and we children piled up together on the other side of the fire circle. As the weather grew warmer, we all spent more and more time outside.

On one of those warmer nights, during the moon of early planting, we sat quietly around a low fire, my great-uncle telling of earlier times in our life as a People. In the distance dogs barked, and now and then a horse snorted like a man afflicted with a stuffed nose. From across the compound voices rose toward the moon like smoke, some in song, some in declarations that I could scarcely hear.

"—across the river…"

"…along alone…"

"I am the warrior who will!"

"…yes, yes, tomorrow!"

"Ah, tomorrow, but what about yesterday? Yesterday was a fine day. What kind of a day will tomorrow be?"

My great-aunt was singing a song about the flow of light from the moon to our eyes. The evening air settled gently over us, creating a kind of stillness despite the other sounds.

"It was a long time ago, a time before time," my great-uncle was saying, "when the moon had no face, and the rain in spring came up from the ground rather than down from the clouds...." As he was telling his story I leaned back against the legs of the person sitting behind me, who brushed a hand across the back of my neck. It was his wife, my great-aunt, and it felt warm and good when she touched me with such affection. I turned and smiled at her, and she smiled at me; and we sank back into the tale of old times.

"The largest animals walked the earth," he told us. "These great beasts, with long whiskers and broad backs, with spears standing out from their long, winding noses, so that one of them might just as easily skewer you as breathe. And the men decided, before the weather turned cold, that it was time to end the feast and prepare themselves for the hunt...."

Around me everyone nodded, eyes nearly closed, and I could easily picture this beast, because it was the same giant animal that I had dreamed of, and I wondered if all of us had at one time or another dreamed of it, just as I had dreamed of flight and the air and the earth turning beneath us. The way I felt just then, as I listened to my great-uncle speak, gave me the hope that just as in story and dream, I could shift and change from one place and one state and one being to another. And what a hope that was! I had already dreamed of life as a hawk and of soaring to the stars and back again, of flying from the present to the past and back again as well. Who knew where else I might travel, and what shape my being might take!

His words soared as he described the preparations for the hunt, and I pressed back against the chest of my great-aunt, and she soothed me by rubbing my neck and shoulders, and I gave myself over to the story in that dreamy way, so much a part of it, and so steeped in it, that I could see myself moving among the hunters, and I could smell the horses, and hear them whinny, and feel in my own hands the heft of the bows, and hear the cries as the men set out on their journey.

A sharp whistle! A call and shout!

Was this in my dream of the story or in the world around me now? My great-uncle stopped, and others stood, and the young men in the family leaped up and left the tent, the rest of us following.

"Back!" my great-uncle urged us, pushing me back inside.

Horses thundered through the camp.

Shouts! Screams!

Stillness has a million words; chaos has few. The raiding party stole seven horses from us, left one warrior for dead, several of us were wounded, and a number of hearts were broken, because one of the horses they rode in on, which fell and broke its leg and so remained behind, belonged to my father.

I bit my lip and walked out away from the camp until I could no longer hear the dogs bark and the women wail and sat down on the ground and shouted and screamed at the sky and pulled at my hair until I was exhausted. And then I started again. And I grew more and more exhausted, weaker and weaker, just at a time when I needed all my strength. I lay stretched out on the ground, face toward the earth, calling to my father, calling to him in as loud a voice as I could find. Insects crawled over me. I thought of the scorpion in my dream but I did not care if one of those poisonous insects found me and stung me. Nothing mattered, with my father gone. At the sound of a deep cough I turned over and stared up at the sky. The sun passed over me, and the clouds of a prairie evening darkened the sky above, but the sound was coming from below me, echoing up and out to create the illusion of the voice of someone above the ground.

He called me by my secret name.

"Father!" I sat up and looked around. Again he spoke to me, from below, in that voice that seemed to call from above.

"I will tell you my story," he said, "if you will only listen."

My heart was beating rapidly, and I felt near tears again, not a state in which a young warrior (which is, of course, how I saw myself) wants to be found. But it was my own father, and so I stiffened my voice and told him that, yes, I would like to hear his story. And so he began:

"It was late afternoon, and we—my two brothers and our cousins—were crossing the river not very many miles away from our camp. The sun had flattened out against the horizon, and the birds sang their last songs of the day, swooping just over our heads to feast on the swarming insects that followed us and our string of horses. I was singing quietly to myself a song of happiness and praise over the sound of the animals splashing their way across to the other side.

The god, the god, who gave us horse....

"And the light was fading. The sky, the roof of the prairie, took on the color of the lessening day, the blues turning to green, the pale white clouds becoming paler still and then, as if brushed with the feathers of the gayest birds, shifting to yellow and red.

"I had been away a long time and was growing tired of my loneliness, thinking of your mother, and you and your sisters and brothers back here in your camp and how it would be when I returned.

"Such was not a good thought for a warrior to hold. It took me away from the moment in which I was traveling, as a dream takes you away from the immediate life of your body, and so I missed the sound of the enemy taking in his breath just before he let loose the arrow that flew at me with such force as to knock me from my horse and send me tumbling onto my back into the river. Before I knew it, another warrior leaped upon me. As my brothers shouted and fought, I looked up to see a man wearing two eagle feathers and a strand of river pearls bought from a far eastern tribe—by then I was paying the kind of attention a warrior needs to practice if he is to survive—drive a long knife down into my chest.

"I tried to hold onto this world. I grabbed dirt, I grabbed the blade, I grabbed stones, I grabbed water. In the next moment I coughed up my soul with my blood, and both ran into the river and washed away.

"Now, son, I am wandering in the limbo of the prairie, a man without a life and without a home, hoping that you can hear me tell my story and that it will teach you never to let down your guard...."

But I did, because while listening to him speak I lost all sense of time, of where I was. Evening had come upon me, and clouds covered and then uncovered a rising moon as red as any I had ever seen. "Father," I called, getting to my feet, "is it your blood that paints this moon so dark a red?" Silence greeted me. "Father?" I called again.

But he had gone, and I was left to shiver in the growing breeze, beneath that moon the color of his blood. My legs faded away, my hands disappeared from my wrists, and one last time, before I fell through the ground, I heard my father's voice, saying directly in my ear, that it was time for me to become a man.

eight

eastern adventures

OH, TO BE EDWARD in those days at the turn of the century! Light shone down on him from the heavens and Indian maidens sang to him in the darkest nights! Even while he was still traveling about the tops of mesas and photographing his first Navajos, events were transpiring thousands and thousands of miles away that would change his fortune even more for the better.

⁓

A sandy-haired fellow with a full ruddy face chewed the last of his breakfast sausage and lowered his newspaper to peer through his half-spectacles at the children seated with him at the table. Beautiful creatures! And in this world of chaos—assassinations, war in Africa, the destruction of the West, the end of the buffalo, rivers filled with beasts of prey, all the world buzzing around them and rushing them along—shouldn't he have a record, a simple record, of this particularly beautiful moment in his life and theirs in the Eden of Oyster Bay, New York, so that one day they might look back and recall how marvelous life had once been, before he became president?

⌒

The luck Edward had! Oh, in those days he had such luck! Each link in the great chain of circumstances that led him from his—as he saw it—singularly obscure life to doing the work for a fading people slipped inexorably into place.

His luck even held with Clara. She had missed him terribly while he was away, but she had also enjoyed having complete command of the household and the children. With the help of Edward's mother, all went smoothly, no fevers, no tantrums, not even a skinned knee or bumped elbow. The children were as happy as she was to see him return, and she had prepared them, as best as she could, for the imminent trip that even Edward was unaware of when he stepped off the train.

"You needn't unpack your bags," she said. His heart dropped down to the pit of his chest. Was she leaving him? Was she throwing him out?

And then she explained. His booster and supporter, Merriam, had sent a telegram followed by a letter, which Clara had taken upon herself to read. The Easterner had recommended Edward as a portrait maker to none other than Theodore Roosevelt, T. R. himself. Another telegram followed, from the president, commissioning Edward to create a picture of his children and setting up a rendezvous at his home in Oyster Bay.

"It's thrilling," Clara said. "I'm so proud of you."

"And you don't mind that I'm heading back to the train station tomorrow?"

Clara gave him an approving look. "Edward, I couldn't be more thrilled for you."

"Except that I am even more thrilled and proud than she is," his mother said.

"Thank you," he said to Clara, taking her in his arms.

"Oh, stop that," she said. "It's something you must do. For all of us."

And the children? At first they were not so thrilled. But Edward had brought them trinkets from the Grand Canyon and the mesas he had visited after that. Beth especially loved the dolls. Hal played with the toy warriors. "Zum," he chanted. "Zum! Zum!" He described arrows flying and sparks shooting down from the sky. And who knew what toys Edward might bring back from the East?

The East! Edward had never been farther East than Wisconsin.

Traveling back along the train line that had once taken him West, he mused happily that Clara had been so understanding, and then his thoughts drifted to his encounter with the pagan beauty Tasáwiche at the bottom of the Grand Canyon. He grew worried about how he was going to find the money to pay for more fieldwork now that he had spent most of his older brother's contribution, hoping perhaps that Roosevelt might pay him enough to keep him going for a short while. He thought wistfully about the old family days, about his Pap in his high stance at the pulpit and Mama in her kitchen, and all of them around the table for her good meals. He slept, too, and as they rolled through the Middle West his dreams seemed to be connected to the old home place, and more than once he woke up thinking he had heard the voice of an owl, or some such creature, outside his bedroom window.

But once the train passed east of the middle part of the country, and he found himself in new territory, which was the old territory of the nation, his thoughts went forward, especially east of Chicago. He took notes:

Traveling all day through the thick of the country, where even the air seems heavier than at home. Must be more moisture this side of

*the Mississippi. No mountains to speak of. Many of my fellow trav-
elers seem to cramp themselves into their seats, a more compressed lot
than us Westerners. But then there are more of them living out here,
so they have less elbow room.*

"Is that your theory, sir?" Teddy Roosevelt said to Edward
while they were taking sherry in the study of Roosevelt's Oyster
Bay, Long Island, home.

"The mental crowding?" Edward took a sip of the sherry and
swallowed, thinking about this. "Yes, Mister President," he said,
finally, "it does appear that way."

"New York City, then, you see as some sort of a rabbit warren
filled with the mentally anguished of our species?"

"It did seem a bit more frenzied compared to the way we
move out West," Edward said.

His host raised a cigar to the height of his temple and paused
thoughtfully before sticking it between his teeth and biting
down. "You weren't impressed with it then?"

Edward said he hadn't been. "I'm a sea-level fellow, but once
you've climbed Rainier, these tall buildings appear more like
molehills than mountains."

Roosevelt allowed himself a smile and sipped more sherry.
"Yes, I believe it would help my friends in Washington to
stand on a mountaintop and look east rather than sit in an
office in the capitol and look west. I've been thinking something like that myself ever since I first climbed the
Matterhorn. And confirmed it for myself when I went West,
and then took my oath of office."

"And when was that first trip you took to the plains, Mister
President?"

The president told Edward of his first tour West, to the Great Plains, and of an expedition he had planned for the coming year. He owned property out there and it was making part of him become a Westerner. "Perhaps you might meet us on the plains when next we travel there and serve as our photographer?"

"I'm honored that you ask, sir," Edward said, "but I have another project that I'm committed to."

"Tell me about it," Roosevelt said. "Come. We'll walk and talk. Expatiate."

And that was how, after doing the portraiture of Roosevelt's children, Edward found himself walking along the shore of Long Island Sound with their father, talking of his plans. And a new part of that plan came suddenly to mind. The wind blew off the water, carrying the familiar salt-scent of home, but when he looked out across the Sound he saw little to remind him of Seattle. No island proudly standing against the horizon. Even the trees they walked among seemed sadly diminished even by the Middle West standards of his childhood. No, he had plans commensurate with Western trees, rocks and mountains and glaciers!

"And Grinnell, you say, suggested it?"

"He planted the idea in my mind, yes, Mister President."

"But *all* the tribes, every one of them ?" Roosevelt said. "Why, there must be hundreds. It will take you—"

"Years, I know, sir," Edward said.

"Yes, years. And thousands of dollars. Tens of thousands. How will you ever finance such a project? Curtis, when Merriam recommended you to me as the best portrait maker in America, I didn't know that I was going to play host to a holy fool. No offense intended, but this project of yours is truly mad."

"I know, sir," Edward said. "But I can't get it out of my mind. And I've already begun the fieldwork." And he talked of the canyon journey, and the time on the mesas that followed.

"Well," said Roosevelt, turning to face the wind, "surely there are others who might join forces with you, other photographers, that is. You might make, say, a small army of you and divide up the territory in that way, so that you alone don't have the burden of the entire Indian population. Curtis, that is truly a vision worthy of a Caesar, of a military man who wants to conquer half the known world." He looked over at Edward, a small smile quivering at the corners of his thin mouth. "Admirable, yes, sir, an admirable mission."

"I don't want to lead an army, sir," Edward said. "I want to make my own pictures. And not just that, but to record their habits, their beliefs, their songs, their prayers."

"Astonishing," Roosevelt said. "Think of what the task would be like if you were doing it for the Christian world. Who would be up to the job?"

"It would be difficult, even impossible, I have to admit," Edward said.

"So what makes you think you can do it for the pagans?"

"Maybe I can't," Edward said. "But there's more necessity in this project than there would be in the other."

"Do you mean because the savages are dying out?"

Edward nodded, feeling his heart sink at the use of the word. "They're *dying* and *dying out*," he said. "Their populations are growing smaller each year as civilization encroaches on their territories and those that survive lose more and more touch with the traditional way of life."

"Which is our traditional way, isn't it?"

Roosevelt halted, and Edward stopped with him, both gazing out over the dark blue water of the Sound. A few sailboats dotted the water, and some high cumulus clouds sailed heavenward as they—or he, at least—wondered if it might storm later in the afternoon.

"That's how we do it," Roosevelt said, removing his spectacles and wiping them clean with a large white handkerchief. "We settle in their lands and then remove them and study them, classify them, characterize them, before they become like us."

"Our national pastime?" Edward said.

"Ah," Roosevelt said. "But when a civilization—if that's what these tribes all collected together can be called—if a civilization loses its vigor, what's to be done except make a record of them before they pass on?"

"They are living people, sir, Mr. President," Edward said.

"Well of course they are, Mr. Curtis. I know that. I've lived, if not among them, then certainly in close proximity to them on my property out West. Now don't misunderstand me. I'm not making a definitive statement about the red-skinned race. But most of those I knew were scarcely more than mud people. Virtually evolved out of the rock and earth itself."

"If, like me, you have some Irish blood in your veins, sir," Edward said, "you'll know that the same has often been said about us."

"I quite understand—but, to be fair, it is true about those for whom it is true. There are, of course, many exceptions."

"To be frank, sir, I find, as far as I've gone in my fieldwork with the red man, that each tribe is an exceptional group, and that within it many of the individuals are exceptional. If I didn't think so, I couldn't devote my time to making their portraits."

"So you are saying"—and here Roosevelt, having finished the job on his spectacles, returned them to his nose and stared out over the water—"that you equate them in their own way with the making of the portraits of my children?"

"Exactly."

"Bully," he said. "It might be true. Perhaps I've seen only the bad small part around the edges. It happens. Each man looks and sees what he takes to be the main part of things. I know that I do so, and find myself mostly correct. But I could be wrong about these people."

"Will you help me then, sir?"

"Help you? Do you mean financially? Do you think—?"

"No, no, I ask only for some letters of introduction to those who might be in a position to help."

"Such as—?"

"Morgan, perhaps. I've been reading about him. I've met Harriman. I might try him also."

"They're terrible enemies of each other. You must know then," Roosevelt said, "if you have one, the other won't even consider it."

"Do you have a suggestion then as to which is better?"

"Better? Well, they're both quite different, and similar only in that they're monstrously rich. I'll take this under advisement. Meanwhile, let's return to the house."

"It's a beautiful house if you don't mind my saying so, sir."

"Yes, we miss it terribly, even with all of the history that comes with the other house I now occupy. That's why we come here to hide out as often as we can." Roosevelt touched his elbow as they walked. "But if you're going to be talking with the monstrously wealthy," he said, "don't be telling them that you like their houses. The entire thing is mighty unlikely, Curtis. It would take rivers of money, wouldn't it?"

"About seventy-five thousand dollars," Edward said.

"So you've already worked out a plan? That's promising. But that is still quite a lot of money even for the monstrously wealthy."

"I know that. But it's my plan. And my...life," Edward said.

"Bully," said Roosevelt. "A visionary. I like that in a fellow."

"I take pictures," Edward said. "That's what I do."

"Yes, and if the pictures you've taken of my children turn out to be something I like, well, then, the world's your oyster, sir. Or"—and here he made a huge guffaw—"at least your Oyster Bay!"

Library of Congress, Prints & Photographs Division, Edward S. Curtis Collection,
LC-USZ62-52192

nine

jimmy fly-wing's story—3

I DON'T KNOW WHAT it would have been like to have been born into another tribe in some other place in the world—at least I didn't know when I was still young—because the tribe I knew was the entire world to me. Before all this that I am recounting here happened to me, I hadn't even seen a white man, let alone become aware of the wide horizons that included Italians and Japanese and New Yorkers and Chicagoans and Mexicans and Jews and Fillipinos and even Mohawks and Irish. (And jazz, motorcars, cocktails, museums, umbrellas, restaurants, shoe stores, bow ties, and birthday cakes, what were these to me?)

As our ways would have it, after I came back to my senses, I was blessed by our shaman and cared for by my mother and my great-aunt, though I never saw them, since I came out of my new solitary lodging outside the boundaries of the village only late at night to find the food they had left me earlier in the day.

It was my time to prepare, and I kept to a regimen of strength-building and practicing my focus. After a few bites of food, I walked out onto the prairie, dug myself a small hole with a special stick, and cleanly evacuated my bowels. And then I walked down to the creek and there, under cloud or moonlight,

I would bathe, staying in the cold water so long that it began to seem warm to me, and then rubbing myself dry with a handful of leaves.

"Good," the shaman's voice stayed with me, "you have now cleansed your body and it is time to cleanse your mind."

I walked back to the village, imagining the shaman sitting on my shoulder. (In fact, one night I dreamed that he had been reduced, or had reduced himself, no doubt, to the size of a cricket and rode me like a giant horse, commenting on my behavior as we went along.)

"Here is all human activity," he said, as I made my way back to my tent, "from the first to the last."

An infant crying.

Dogs barking at the approach of a man.

Inside a nearby tent, the cry of a girl poised on the edge of a waterfall of ecstasy (though what did I know of that yet, except that the shaman revealed it to me?).

From another, the thick cough of an old man—or was it woman?—caught in the grip of illness.

Men raising their voices in discussion.

Women laughing together.

The odor of cooking meat, the rhythm of a drum, the chatter of teeth, the scent of crushed sage, a fart as loud as a distant thundercloud, the rush of a small flock of birds, music of the rising wind, the crunch of stone underfoot.

"When you can put all this together," the shaman told me, "you will then be released into the world again. But before this, you must prepare your body."

My mother and great-aunt became a part of this training first, because of the food they prepared for me, simpler than simple roots and grains, with once a week a piece of charred meat. These meals appeared much the same as the meals I had eaten all through my boyhood, but they tasted different, flavored in a subtle way that played off the simplicity of the ingredients. It was almost as if, each time I tasted them, I was tasting and smelling for the first time.

And eating the stories.

Biting into a chunk of meat, I saw the animal and all that the animal itself saw, the sea of brown bodies milling in front of it, the crowded prairie at either side of it, I heard the thundering of storm clouds that stirred the herd, and felt the same fears and terrors, and the power of the millions of them, the stench of their dung, the bellows and roars of their warnings and challenges and desires—and when they began to run, pounding out their own storm on the land, running, racing toward the horizon, I ran with them in my mind.

And it was the same for the roots and tubers that I feasted on, sometimes following them all the way back to the first appearances of their kinds, out of volcanic earth, tens of millions of years before, when the world turned with that velocity that I had noticed in my earlier dream, their first fragile shoots breaking through the soil, their first feeling of the wind.

I felt the same way—like a new beast, like a plant, like a creature who had never before been born but just now broke through the surface of the earth and tasted the wind, and bent with it as it changed directions.

A number of moons wheeled through the sky.

One night, while making my usual nocturnal way through the village, a stray dog came racing up to me and nipped at my heels. I kicked at him, but he kept charging me. Leaning down, I gave him a swipe with the back of my hand and sent him rolling over in the dust. A young girl poked her head out of a nearby tent. "Stop that," she said.

"It's only a dog," I said in reply, staring at her eyes, oddly blue like the best skies.

"You warriors are so cruel," she said.

"That is how we survive," I said. "But I am not yet a warrior."

"I know that is true," the girl said.

"Who are you?" I asked her. She might have been one of dozens of young girl-children whom I had seen about the village while growing up, but I didn't recognize her.

"Go hunt dogs," she said and ducked back inside the tent. From within I could hear the grunts and sharp words that made up the beginning of a quarrel.

Fool that I was, I was thinking I might ask to speak with her again and was approaching her tent when someone came up behind me—as I spun about—and gave me a shove. I fell against the tent but not before grabbing one of its ropes so that I instinctively pulled myself to my feet.

Someone pushed me from another direction, and I went down again, this time with a thud as I landed on my shoulder and heard something crack within. Did I cry out? Fortunately, no.

"We are ready for you," one of my assailants said. "Are you ready for us?" Within a few minutes we were heading out of the village on horseback, five of us, my shoulder still aching, my mind full of puzzles, but my spirit bound with the spirit of the hunt.

I hadn't known that girl; I didn't know this horse. The young men who collected me belonged to a secret society of warriors, and their horses came from the best stock of beasts rustled from the corrals of our enemies, a thought that made me deeply sad, because that was the business my father performed for the tribe. Perhaps the very horse I sat on had been one of those that he had brought back to the village. As we trotted along in a westerly direction, catching faint hints that dawn was rising at our backs, I lost myself in thoughts of him—the games he played with me, the sweet roughness of his talk, his hand on the back of my head, the smell of his leathery skin after returning from his labors—even as I put behind me, in the company of my mysterious companions, the place that I called home.

It wasn't necessarily because of his death that I had been tapped for initiation, but that terrible event accelerated the pace of my life. My mother, now without a husband, needed at least one man in her household, even though she had been adopted by her great-aunt and her husband. I was to be that man. The thought of it made me proud. Pride made me incautious.

One of my traveling companions shouted something to me, turning his horse toward the south, and the others pulled up. I kept trotting forward, only to come to the edge of a wide precipice, down which my horse and I nearly pitched. A distant river flowed through the deep valley below. Behind me, the others laughed in disgust and made nasty remarks.

I dropped the reins and held up both hands, as though surrendering to a greater opponent. They laughed even harder, and their mouth-noises made it clear to me that my gesture had been the wrong one. The leader of our small band rode up to me and, without warning, roughly punched me in the head, nearly knocking me from my mount. I came back and swung at him. But he blocked my punch, and grabbed my arm and twisted it behind my back in such a painful way that I nearly cried out.

"Come," he said, "we have a long ride ahead." He released my arm, our horses pushed away from each other, and we took to the trail again as dawn splashed its golden news across the rocks and hills that lay miles and miles ahead on the other side of the valley, riding steadily until the sun rose midway in the sky. These young men were tireless in their roving, and it was clear to me that I was going to have to measure up to their standards if I wanted to survive. Fortunately, my horse was strong and so I kept up with them, even though my own will might have lagged behind that of the animal's.

We stopped at a small stream and watered the horses and ourselves. My companions talked among themselves, ignoring me. I stretched out on the rocky ground, trying to enjoy the heat of the sun. My shoulder had stopped aching but my haunches stung from riding. Above me a hawk made wide circles in a cloudless sky, and remembering my dreams of such flight, I tried to picture how I might have appeared to the eye of that circling bird, a long-limbed young man with aches and pains, fatherless now, and without much heart for this journey, stretched out on the ground like some wet thing left out to dry.

"You!" One of the men stood over me.

"Here!" I sat up and then leaped to my feet as he handed me a palmful of crushed leaves.

"Eat!" He stared at me with eyes as dark as the middle of a night without stars.

I nodded, stuffed the leaves in my mouth and rushed over to the stream to wash them down with a handful of the icy water, and then another. Behind me the men laughed and mounted up. They had ridden about a quarter of the way down a narrow canyon trail before I had mounted my own horse and followed along.

We rode for a long time, while the sky darkened with clouds and the air turned cold. My mind went to sleep and then awoke again, and my horse slowed down, picking his way among the rocks of an old streambed with the care of a mother walking with a child on each arm.

This trail we follow....

A song-poem came into my thoughts, something that had never happened to me before, and wove its way around my awareness of the canyon.

Riding up toward the sky....

A clap of thunder brought me back. Within moments the world grew dark, and rain fell so hard and fast that I lost sight of the riders ahead of me, though I did hear the cry of one of them calling out, perhaps to me, perhaps to his companions. The rushing noise of the rain and the thunder that clanged overhead drowned the words. As if following a command I had not heard, I urged my horse up the side of the canyon and took shelter in a small cave.

More thunder boomed above me. And then, with a huge crash, it sounded as though it fell to Earth. The very ground beneath my feet shuddered and shook. I peered out from the cave to see a moving hill of water sliding down the canyon. My horse gave a loud whinny, and I heard the shouting above the roar of the water as man after man and horse after horse rushed past, caught in the terrible grip of the sudden flood.

One of the men, the tall one who had given me the leaves to eat, cast a sad eye up at the cave as he floated by and held up a hand. I reached toward him, but within seconds they had all gone, and the water rushed past where I stood, horrified at the calamity I had witnessed. My heart was shaking; my throat closed up so that I could not let out a grunt, let alone a wail.

As quickly as it had risen, the water subsided. Carefully leading my horse back along the now-sodden trail, I went looking for the other riders. I found them within minutes, heaped up upon one another, men and horses, as though some giant had taken them and flung them against the canyon wall.

I left the horses, but I slung each man over behind me on my
own mount, carrying them up, one at a time, out of the canyon.
It took me the rest of the day and into the dark of another night
to build a burial platform out of wood. As I worked I sang songs
in a tongue strange to me, making odd clicking noises and high-
pitched words. When I had finished, I built a fire and ate strips
of dried buffalo, which I had found in some of the pouches
carried by my dead companions, and finished my meal with
more of the leaves that I had eaten before the flood. I chewed
and thought, chewed and thought, and the stars pulsed above
me, brighter than I had ever seen them.

"What were they?" I wondered. The eyes of the dead, the eyes
of spirits, of gods? Now they formed shapes, and I could see a
hunter with his bow in hand, taut and ready to send an arrow
arcing across the distance between him and an antelope
standing unawares, and a giant holding above his head a large
stone that he might toss down upon us, and two maidens, hand
in hand, standing off to the side of the universe, observing in
their shy, demurring way, and a herd of buffalo grazing upon a
prairie studded with other stars. Many others appeared to me as
the night wore on, keeping me company as I passed the time
with open eyes and a heart full of wonder. So many spirits lived
above and around us, and now they floated above me, so close
it seemed that I might reach out and touch one of them, something I restrained myself from doing for fear of disturbing them
in some way that might prove harmful to me or to them.

Absently chewing on more of the leaves, I discovered that
with some concentration I could allow myself to float above
the ground. This disturbed my horse, who whinnied at me in
distress as he watched me rise above him into the night sky.
It gave me a pleasant tingling sensation, something resembling the feeling I got when I was small and saw my mother

after a long day apart from her, along with the satisfying sense that came with filling my belly after it had been empty a long time.

"Goodbye, horse," I said to him in my mind as I drifted away, thinking that I was headed once again, as in my dream of long ago, for the stars. But I rose only high enough to see what I needed to see, and as soon as I made my sighting, I settled back down upon the earth and mounted up again—"Hello, horse!"—riding hard in a southerly direction.

A full day's ride later, drawn by a force I can call only greater than myself, I was passing through a strange landscape, dark mountains to the south, a day-moon full above me in the bone-white sky, and the odor of old fires and roasted meat in the air. The wind died down, and those scents settled over me as I came up a low rise and saw what I now understood was what I came for: a pile of bones, dull-white under the sun, strewn across rocks and cactus shrub.

"Father!" A voice cried within me.

Animals had gnawed on his skull and ribs. A man isn't supposed to weep, but I was not yet a man, and so I allowed the tears to flow from my eyes, wetting my cheeks, and running onto my lips so that I could taste the salt-flavor of my grief.

I chewed more leaves and sang songs while I buried my father's remains (save for one long thick rib, which I had the good sense to hold back), wishing all the while that I had floated up into the sky and never returned. When I had finished my task, I stripped off my own clothes, keeping only my waistband, and set them afire, scattering the ashes of my soiled garments in the four directions. Naked I sat a while, filing down the point of my father's rib with a stone, and still naked, I led my horse along, feeling a pulling and a grasping at me from the very air of this awful place.

Soon I mounted up and gave the horse its direction. The beast knew better than I did where we were going. Yet, I don't know how long it took us to make this ride, though I noticed that clouds passed overhead and moons rose and set without me counting. But it seemed to be some time before I saw smoke on the horizon. A small village lay nestled on the side of a creek-bed near a stand of cottonwoods. I dismounted and approached, unclothed and unafraid. Although the sun shone down, I walked into the village as though I were on one of my nocturnal strolls, and all of the people I noticed seemed fixed in their places. Women, children, old men, all stood as still as though they had been frozen in a chill beyond measure.

The few warriors I saw were frozen also, and one of them had a glow just above his head, which I understood almost at once. (Why this had happened, I could not say, but I was prepared to take full advantage of the event.)

Stepping up to this brave, I drew the sharpened rib from waistband and pulled it across his throat. He dropped immediately to the ground, and I went off in search of the others. I found two more seated silently around a fire in a tent near the center of the village and sent them off to the next world in the same fashion. I don't know how I knew it, but two more remained, and I sat before the central fire, with all of these people still frozen around me, and waited. The sun stood still in the sky. No one came and no one went. Even the dogs remained in place, unmoving, tongues drooping from their mouths, but not a drop of their saliva touched the ground.

It came to me then that I had to look for the others outside the camp. I found one almost immediately, seated atop his horse, stopped in place just outside the village on the north side. I leaped up and speared him in the neck with my father's rib. He slid off the horse and fell hard. I had to place my bare foot on his chest and push in order to pull the rib from his neck.

The other took me a while to find, but at last I discovered him in a stand of cottonwoods, his clothes tossed aside, caught in the act of penetrating a naked, young woman from behind. With that same sharpened rib I skewered him, and he collapsed on top of the frozen woman. He was the last of my father's murderers, and with a proud gesture, I tore the rib from his back and secured it in my belt.

I felt a sudden surge of hunger in my belly, and I returned to the center of the village and took meat from a cooking pot. I ate, then found my horse and mounted up again. We set out in a westerly direction at a walking pace. Coming upon a vast herd of buffalo, I had to take a slight southerly detour. I kept my eyes on the ground for signs of more animals.

When I raised my head the sun had moved and clouds had gathered, and I looked around for a spot where I might take shelter. Just as hailstones as big around as my fists began to fall straight down out of a dark and whirling sky, I ducked under the outcropping of a small hill. My horse whinnied as the brutal hail spanked onto its rump, and I pulled the beast closer to me, nearly smothering myself as a result.

"Closer," I said to the horse. Closer it inched. "Closer," I said, as the hail kept falling. The horse pressed against me, and I pressed myself against the side of the hill. Thunder roared overhead, a zigzag strike of lightning lashing out across the plain. The horse shrieked in fright, bucked, and threw all of its weight sideways. In a burst of dirt and dust, the hillside collapsed under us, and I went tumbling through into a cavern that had been hidden behind the thin wall of earth. I fell through the dark and damp at a steep angle and a speed that would be trouble when I reached the bottom, the falling horse just above my head.

Miraculously, I grabbed at something in the dark and found a handhold, while my horse went tumbling over my head and on into the cavern. Whatever it was I was holding pulled loose, and I continued my fall, head over heels over head, until I landed with a loud thump on the soft body of my horse.

I lay there a while atop the dying—or dead—animal, trying to catch my breath and accustom my eyes to the dark. Bright lights and whirling shapes danced before me, as though the night sky had come alive here below ground. I heard music and the drumming of a shaman at work on a cure for the dead. Invigorated by the rhythm, I got to my feet and left the horse behind me in the dark, following the sound of the drumming. A running current splashed nearby. Soon I was up to my ankles in water, then up to my knees. But I kept on moving, until the water, which was rising up to my chest, slowed me down. By now I could see in the dark and noticed several large insects buzzing over my head.

"How do I get out of here?" I called to them.

"Ask her," one of them said.

"Her?" At the side of the stream, a woman wrapped in blankets kneeled down to scoop up shells from the water. "Where am I?" I asked her, pausing in my push against the rushing stream.

She looked up and said something in a language I did not understand. Her face was the color of clay.

"How do I get out of here?" Again she spoke, but I still didn't understand.

All at once, in a voice clear as a morning sky, her words came to me. "I know about water, because I live beside the great salt sea, and I gather these animals each morning when the tide rolls back."

"You don't belong to our People, do you?" I said.

"My people sail on the ocean," she said.

"What is an ocean?" I asked her.

"One day you will know," she said.

"Why not now?" I said.

"Everything in its good time," she said.

"But I want to know," I said. "I want to know everything."

"Come here and help me, then," she said.

I waded to her side of the stream and she offered me a hand, pulling me onto the shore. I could smell salt and the earthy odors of her body. It was sandy there, as a desert is near a watering hole, and she had a sack into which she put the shells she gathered from the gritty stream. She showed me where to reach, and I worked a while, looking up now and then, and receiving her approval.

Hooded in her blanket, the woman seemed older than she really was, and her eyes took on a certain glow that softened the dark around us.

"One day you will meet him," she said, "and we hope that you will be his guide. He will need all the help we can give him."

"Who?" I asked.

"Him. You will meet him."

All this was too much mystery for me, but even if I had asked more questions, it would not have done any good, because at that moment I heard a loud whistle, and when I looked up the woman had gone.

The insects again buzzed around my head.

"All these comings and goings," I said, "they are confusing."

"Keep moving," said the insects.

And so I stepped back into the stream and moved along.

A few yards ahead the stream turned and flowed around a large rock. On the other side stood a shaman wearing a head-dress made of small birds, and he waved a beautifully carved stick of stars and lightning as I passed.

"Welcome," he said.

And I wondered what it was to which I was welcome.

He must have had the power to read my thoughts because he made a long speech about the land around us, its perfect skies, its transparent streams, the lushness of its grasses, and the richness of its soil, which gave birth to vast herds of buffalo. Until then it seemed as though I were traveling in the dark. It was only as he spoke that I looked around and saw what he was describing.

How could I be traveling under the earth when dawn came up so beautifully? I wondered. How might there be wind and the smell of the grasses and small trees? Birds flew above me, and in the distance I could see mountains with snow on their peaks, and it was as though I had discovered a world below the world in which I lived, a world which had always been here and always would be.

It was beautiful here, but empty of people. Where were mine?

An answer came to me soon after I stepped out of the stream and started walking toward the mountains. A band of warriors, one for each finger of my hand, came riding out of the west— if that was what I could call that direction in this world beneath a world—directly toward me.

I took a deep breath and ran toward them. Much to my surprise these were the same men who had murdered my father and against whom I thought I had just taken my revenge. The lead horseman raised a spear, giving me little time to think about what was happening. I took deep breaths as I ran, zigzagging across the plain as he let loose his weapon. Catching the spear in mid-flight, I slung it back at him as he passed, an angry grin on his face, and took him in the shoulder, knocking him from his horse. With a rage I hadn't felt before, I raced over to him and pushed the weapon deeper into his wound and watched the light fade from his astonished eyes.

Behind me I heard the other riders approach, and I whirled around to confront them, taking the mane of the first horse and pulling it down with a strength, like my anger, I hadn't known I possessed, and watched the man slide to the ground. Before he could gain a stance, I shoved the horse at him—my strength! oh, my strength!—and it knocked him into eternity. I picked up his weapon as the other two warriors came fast upon me, and with an ease that also surprised me, I skewered one in the chest and spun him around on the end of the spear to knock the other man from his horse.

A scream of triumph echoed across the land.

My scream!

The last man staggered to his feet only to have me take his head in my hands and snap his neck. I sent him falling into the land of the dead, a path to which opened at his feet as I released him from my hold.

But where were we, if not the land of the dead?

Some other world, some other time, some other life, some other boy but me? I looked up from my wondering and saw more riders coming across the plain. Squinting into the light, I could hardly believe whom I saw approaching, but it was true nonetheless. The warriors, lost to drowning, rode hard and fast toward me, as though they had never left this world for another.

"Come, boy!" The lead rider, the same man who had taunted me when we first rode out together, gestured for me to follow. With an ease I had always admired in my father and other warriors, I ran to one of the now-stray horses, leaped onto his back, and rode off along behind the living dead-men.

We rode and rode, sometimes slowing at moonrise and even, for the horses' sake, now and then pausing at the edge of streams, but mostly pushing straight ahead with such power and relentlessness that when I allowed myself a thought or two—

which did not come frequently because I had to bear down on my horse to keep it from running away with me, so much strength he possessed, and so much vigor—I wondered if I had not died myself and come back to life in a grander and stronger way. My companions never spoke to me, gesturing only when it was necessary to keep me on the trail, but it was clear, by the looks they gave me and the ease with which we rode, that they had taken me in as one of their own.

Still, I knew that I was not one of them, unless I had died when I fell into the cavern. And I did not think that was true, because when I considered the feel of my horse's back beneath my rump and the strain in my arms as I held onto his neck while racing along in the company of those warriors, I was convinced that I was still quite alive, despite what I knew about my companions. My heart beat strong and steady. My long hair blew behind me in the wind. My stomach growled like a young bear after a long winter.

Could the other riders read my thoughts? The leader trotted up alongside me and tossed a piece of jerky in the air. I caught it, chewed on it, and enjoyed the tang and spice of the leathery dried meat.

And when only a short while later a fierce rainstorm washed down on us, I leaned back on my mount, opened my mouth to the flow, and drank. However, the rain troubled my companions, only recently dead in that canyon flood. As soon as it began to fall they turned and raced to higher ground. It was all my horse could do to keep up with them, so fast they rode and over such difficult terrain.

There was a range of small mountains that seemed to rise sharply out of the ground in front of us like rows and rows of giant teeth—dark clouds floated above them, threatening more rain. My guides raced toward these rocks, and then took a trail around to the north of them, a route that revealed to us a long straight pair of iron lines running east to west as far as I could see along the flat terrain.

The white road, they called it, when I caught up with them. These ghost-warriors pretended to know everything, but I could see in their eyes a certain puzzlement about what this meant. One of them dismounted and kneeled to touch the iron line. He bowed his ear toward it, silent, poised to listen. Another dismounted, walked a few feet west, and pissed on the metal, to the accompaniment of great laughter from the rest of us. Hah!

In a moment they remounted and went racing off around the base of those tooth-like mountains. By the time I had caught up with them, they had moved well into a stand of dark trees, and when I pulled up on them, I found them leaning forward on their mounts, all of them pointing to a place deep within the next rank of trees.

I dismounted and walked straight ahead, motioning the warriors on toward the edge of the trees. The rain stopped as abruptly as it had first fallen, and as I walked into the woods, I caught a glimpse just to the west of me of a broad rainbow shimmering in the sky. Would I live to see it again? That was my question as I strode forward, pulling my weapon, my father's sharpened rib, and holding it in front of me. Because I knew where I was going. All of a sudden I knew.

After a few steps I could smell the beast, the greasy-lipped animal coated in thick fur, breathing with a raspy susurration that sounded like a terrible windstorm gathering its strength just over the horizon. Rotting meat, foul water, and the excesses of its stomach and its rear made a weather of its own within the confines of the woods. When the animal looked over at me, it seemed to be asking if I was enjoying the confines of its ferocity.

My legs felt weak, my belly flipped and twisted, and for a few moments I couldn't raise my hands or arms. The beast roared quizzically.

"Oh," it seemed to ask, "who are you that have come to face me in this wood?" Its eyes burned so hot with this question that I wondered if our peoples' shaman wasn't standing there on long legs, peering out at me from beneath the skin of an animal. But when the animal rose on its hind legs and stood nearly twice as tall as any man from our village, I knew it was the beast itself.

My chest went cold and empty. Piss ran down my leg. I bowed toward the bear, about to speak, but the words stuck in my throat. The bear squinted, moving its nose, sniffing the breeze, and no doubt catching the taste of the astringent liquid staining my thighs and calves.

Mustering all my strength and courage, I choked up my words, saying, in as steady a voice as I could conjure, that I had come to relieve him of the burden of his life. The bear cocked its head at me as if he understood, and taking three or four long strides toward me, as delicately as a child on stilts, it raised a paw and knocked me to the ground. I tumbled over and as I regained my balance, I said, "Brother Bear—"

The beast swiped at me again, tearing open the flesh at my neck. I got to my knees—somehow I was still holding my weapon, the rib of my father—and crawled toward the bear, as though I were approaching a king. The animal gave a roar and lurched to one side, slamming me with one of its hind paws so that I fell over on my back. The bear looked down at me and raised a paw again, fanning me with a great wind as I rolled to one side. A chunk of earth and shrub went sailing away into the woods, showering me with dirt and bits of plant. I kept on shimmying away, holding the rib overhead as though I were protecting something precious while wading in neck-deep water.

The bear roared, nearly deafening me, and sidled over in my direction. "Stand up or you die," it said to me in a perfect imitation of my father's voice.

Without another thought I leaped to my feet and took a narrow stance as the animal stepped toward me. It opened its mouth and roared again, bathing me in the filthy steam of its breath. Down into its red-lined mouth, I stared and stared, as if I could see something there besides my imminent death.

Within seconds, if that is how you're counting, I raised the rib and shoved it into his gullet with an upward tilt, so that the rib sheared up into his roaring brain. Blood gushed from his mouth, soaking me with his death. I barely escaped my own as the animal fell toward me, and I twirled away, like the fleetest of dancers, just before he hit the ground with a shuddering thump.

Library of Congress, Prints & Photographs Division, Edward S. Curtis Collection, LC-USZ61-2088

ten

chief

ANOTHER GREAT STEPPING-STONE fell into place when some months after Edward's return from the East, there was a loud knock at the door to his Seattle studio. I opened it, and in strode the Nez Percé delegation, with the stalwart Chief Joseph in the position of honor, and several of his young nephews, or perhaps grand nephews, preceding him. Chief Joseph was a man of medium height with thick black hair done in braids, which fell to either side of his ears in the customary manner; he wore an oversized, dark, striped, double-breasted suit-coat and the expression of someone about to undergo surgery or an execution.

When he noticed Edward was staring, he gestured toward him and then beckoned for one of his attendees to help him remove his outer garment so that Edward could see he wore a deerskin vest and blouse, and a beautiful belt of red seed-beads with patterns of elk heads and stars. More than a dozen seed necklaces covered his chest, and those ears past which the braids dangled bore large, round silver earrings with three moon-like crescents stamped into each circle.

He nodded to Edward and offered his hand. Edward nodded back, taking in the traditional splendor of the chief's attire. He shook that thick, tanned paw of his, wondering why this chief, whom he had never seen before in his life, seemed so familiar. And as he bade him to sit on the sofa and make himself comfortable, it came to him why this feeling struck him.

It wasn't that he knew Chief Joseph, but fresh from his visit with Teddy Roosevelt a month or so before, Edward understood that whether big Eastern politician or Western chief, these were men with the power of command in their persons. Anyone who stood in the same room with them had to admit that at once. In the case of Chief Joseph, he was the commander of his people, who had outwitted and then for a good while outfought the best units of the U.S. Cavalry in Montana. If it hadn't been for a lieutenant's miscalculation about the location of the U.S.-Canadian border, he'd have been presiding over a free band of his people up north of the Hi-Line instead of taking some time off the reservation to get his portrait made.

I hovered over him, saying a few words in my newly acquired Nez Percé language, and Chief Joseph gave up, for a moment, the stolid mask of sadness that he wore and said something in return. I helped him to settle in his pose. This gave Edward a chance to study his head and face, and what he saw didn't entirely please him. Whatever great mental ability Chief Joseph possessed had not translated itself into physical attractiveness, or even the often-compelling posture of strangeness that many of his kinsmen carried. Edward supposed if he had met General Grant or, better example, General Lee, he might have presented himself in the same fashion, just a weary fellow approaching old age with a deep resignation known only to those who had looked into the eyes of ferocious and unrelenting battles.

"I'm very pleased that you could come and sit for me today, sir," Edward said to him.

Chief Joseph nodded, then looked up, as if he heard a translation of the words and wanted to see the source. "Unless I meet some unlucky shadow-catcher soon after, this will be my last portrait," he said, his voice surprisingly high-pitched but steady. The sure-footedness of his English pronunciation surprised us. The Indians we had worked with so far had not had such a command of it as this. I asked him in his own tongue if he was thirsty, and he looked up at his assistant with an inquisitive stare and said a word.

"What is it?" Edward said. I could see on his face, though he tried to guard it, a look of frustration that I was the one who spoke the native languages, which he could never learn.

"Uncle would like to have some tea," one of the other men said.

"I'll fetch it." I said.

Edward went to the sofa and politely urged the chief to turn slightly to the left. "Are you comfortable here, sir?"

Chief Joseph regarded him in that instant as someone from another world. His dark, tanned, leathery face, crease-lines running out like spokes from the corners of his eyes and mouth, seemed rather alien to Edward as well, and if he hadn't had his eyes open and blinking now and then, and if his chest wasn't rising with the power of his breath, he might have seemed already preserved, embalmed.

"He doesn't care," that same nephew spoke up. "He does what he must do."

"If he can be patient then...." Edward walked back to the camera and took a look at him through the lens.

"What is that?" the chief turned a little on the sofa.

"Please, sir, be patient," Edward said, as I returned with the tea. The chief said something in his language that I didn't catch.

"Uncle says he knows how to do that," one of his nephews said.

"Yes," Edward said. "Indeed." Edward made some initial renderings of the chief and then nodded for me to hand him the cup of tea. The man sipped and posed for about another thirty minutes. Nothing seemed out of the ordinary, if having one of the great Western Indian chiefs sitting for a portrait in your studio is ordinary.

It was midway through the session that a sudden fatigue seemed to overcome the chief, and Edward called a halt as the old warrior closed his eyes and seemed to slump into a deep slumber. Edward glanced over at me as if to ask whether or not I thought something was wrong. I allowed that I didn't know.

Suddenly one of the nephews jumped as if touched by a hot coal, and the chief sat up in his chair, raised his arms, lowered them, opened his eyes, shut them again, and began to speak. "Curtis," he said, his head turned straight forward, "I had a dream-vision for you."

"You did, sir?" Edward leaned forward over his camera.

The chief opened his eyes and gazed steadily upon Edward. "Last night when I slept, I saw you with this machine. And now again when my eyes are closed, I see it. I see you."

"Machine? The camera?"

"Yes, the camera. I saw you making portraits, portraits of the People."

"Which people is that, sir?" Edward said, trying to keep his attention on his work.

"I saw you making portraits of all the People. Of every nation. I saw you working for many years to do this, and I saw you at the end, when you had made pictures of all of us."

"Everyone? Every Indian?"

"I saw you making portraits of us all, of every Red nation on the land, in all the four directions."

I had been listening quietly, and then I spoke up in the Nez Percé language, which I had been studying, and I was answered in kind by the chief.

"What is it?" Edward said, standing up to full height and giving up all pretense of working on this portrait for the moment. "What did he say?"

"The same message," I said. "His vision has you making portraits of everyone in every tribe."

"I hope I have enough lifetimes for all the tribes," Edward said.

Chief Joseph spoke to me in his tongue. One of his nephews added something.

"What did he say?" Edward looked the chief in the eye while he addressed me.

I cleared my throat. "He said he took off his coat because he wanted you to see his true garments. He said that you must always show the red man in his true garments, no matter what new things you find them wearing on top of them."

"Yes, of course," Edward said. "You're absolutely correct, sir. I will do that. I will. That is something I have already tried to practice." The nephew translated this into the chief's language, and the chief nodded his approval. The chief spoke again.

"He said," I translated, "better for you to use your eye and show what you see rather than use your tongue and speak. He said you must dedicate your life to this, because one lifetime can be many lifetimes or no life at all."

And then he crooked his finger at me, and I went up to him and he leaned toward me and said in a whisper in my ear, *Tell him that I dreamed him. He is my son. And he has a sister and a daughter, and they have spoken to him and they will speak again.* He then sat back and stared directly forward, waiting for Edward to complete the portrait, as though he had never spoken a word.

Edward was in a terrible state of agitation when he returned home that evening but tried to keep it all to himself. He did well through dinner, but after bedtime sleep eluded him, and his tossing and turning awakened Clara.

"Edward, what is troubling you?"

He tried to avoid it, but Edward finally told her about the chief's vision.

"A silly pagan superstition," she said.

"It may not be," he said.

"And if it isn't?" Oh, the tone she used that night, it was enough to make him want to race out immediately for the desert or some canyon far from any city lights! He knew she was only speaking in defense of herself and the children. He knew that. And yet every defense of them he took to be an attack on his new project.

"Do you know what this means to me?" he said.

"I suppose I don't." She shifted in the dark, away from him.

"It means everything," he said. "Before this I've just been fumbling around in the dark. What the chief told me confirms everything. This is my mission, my life."

"I understand, Edward. There's only one difficulty in making portraits of all the tribes."

"Is it the money?" he said. "I see numerous problems myself, beginning with the money to support the work."

"That's not the greatest difficulty, Edward. You're a charming man. And you work hard. You'll find the money."

"I hope you're right. What then do you see as the difficulty?" Edward stared into the dark.

"The greatest difficulty is it will take not just your lifetime but mine as well."

CLARA, ALONE

The way Edward talks about what the old chief told him! Even as we need him most at home, his mind seems to wander to other places, places he can't even imagine, where live all the Indians the old chief told him he would photograph. Our business is growing, yet we don't have such large amounts of money that would allow him to make any such plans. It would take a king to pay for the grandiose project that he sometimes talks to me about, late at night, when he cannot sleep, and I lie there, also awake, listening to the beat of my pulse in my ear drum, thinking, I want him to be happy, but I want us to be happy, too. But as far as the business has come we don't have anywhere near the money for this. Is there a way that both things might be possible? I think of what my father would say, how we are just simple Christian people trying to make our way under the benevolence of God. I work very hard in the studio each day. I don't understand why Edward wants to find a fortune so that he can throw it away on pagans!

Ah, if only things were perfect, and we were nothing but Indians. He could have us all then.

eleven

jimmy fly-wing's story—4

ALTHOUGH ON MY JOURNEY I had—I knew it in my bones—
often crossed the line between waking and sleeping, and had
gone back and forth between this world and others—of death,
of the afterlife, worlds where nature did not abide by the same
rules as our everyday existence—I did have evidence that the
bear was real.

Without knowing how long I had been gone, I returned to
the village on horseback, wearing the animal's head and
shoulders as a kind of hood and cape. Children squealed at
the sight of me. Women cried out. The few men who sat
around the central fire looked up at me and gave approving
grunts and cheers.

My mother, her long hair much whiter than when I had left
the village, greeted me with lavish embraces. "The blood," she
said, rubbing her palm on my chest where the bear's blood
had dried. "I cannot forget your father. You are wearing the
bear's spirit. It reminds me, too, that I live now like a dead
animal."

"No, mother," I said, "you have family to care for you."

"It is not the same."

Soon after my return we took a stroll through the village, and were greeted by encouraging cries as we went. "They are happy for you," my mother said.

I nodded, feeling my chest swell with a sense of accomplishment. "My time came and I did what I needed to do."

"Not every boy comes back," she said. "Of those who do, not every one is so admired."

"I did what I did for my father," I said.

"You served him well," my mother said. "He has now gone to his resting place in the other country."

I thought of him, of his rib. "Did he visit you and tell you that?"

"Yes."

We left the center of the village and kept on walking. A few of the youngest boys trailed along behind us, and I turned to wave them away. We came to the small stream that marked the western edge of the village. A few stray dogs had gathered there to drink from the swiftly flowing water and carouse. They scattered at our approach, running back behind us to engage the small boys who followed in a trail of yips and barks. My mother gathered a few leaves, made a prayer, and sent the leaves sailing on the water.

That night around the fire we ate roasted rabbit, boiled roots, and pudding flavored with wild fruit. My great-uncle passed around a pipe and sweet-tasting smoke curled in our nostrils and filled the tent with perfume. My mother had asked the village flute player to perform for us, and so we sat back on our blankets and listened to the simple but attractive melodies that floated from his reed. The sounds carried me along into the world from which I had just returned, with its big skies and open spaces, its hovering birds and the holy bear that I had slain, and it took me down into that other land, the country of old times, when our people first had congress with Sky, and where in my earliest memories I had flown as a bird. I closed my eyes to see all this, and now and then, when I opened them, I saw my relatives seeing the same things, with eyes closed and open.

Sky and Earth mating, fish enjoying the flow of streams, birds taking to the air as fish do to water, the air and my lungs, things of this world and my eyes to see them, skin of mine and how it felt to touch all manner of things outside myself—I drifted on the pleasures of the music and the smoke.

Quietly, my great-uncle began to chant along with the music, as did his wife, my great-aunt, and then my mother added her soft voice to the music. For myself, I wanted to sing also but wasn't sure of the melody. And so I watched and listened, as my mother got up and tossed wonderfully odorous wood-chips on the fire.

And she began to move, swaying to the sounds of the music and the sparking of the fire. My great-aunt got up and joined her. And then my great-uncle. And then me, up onto my feet, chanting, swaying, dancing in place, not going anywhere out of the tent or out of my body, but feeling the same sensations nevertheless. The pipe went around again, and I took in more smoke.

"Oh, child," my mother said, "you have grown, grown, grown...."

I stayed quiet, sad that she felt as though she had lost me now that I had reached a certain age. The flute player lashed the tent with his sounds. I closed my eyes, still swaying, chanting.

"Oh, young man, young man," my great-aunt said at my ear. I opened my eyes and she took my hand and led me to the great pile of skins that lay on the other side of the fire.

I looked around to see that everyone else had departed, I knew not where. Mother? Great-uncle? The air was silent. The flute player had gone. I sank onto the skins, listening to my music, that of the wind above the tall grass, the hawk's wings brushing the Sky, the whir and turn of the star-shapes in the broad prairie of Sky. Outside the tent the world lay still. From the feel of the air, the night had dropped over us, heavy with its darkness.

"Nephew," my great-aunt said, dropping the distance of kinship between us.

"My aunt," I said, doing the same.

She took me by the hand and lowered herself to the bed of skins, leading me down with her. Within moments she had pulled away my clothes and was doing the same with hers. Seeing her naked, I felt a flush of fear exactly the same as what I felt on the hunt. Her breasts were small, the nipples like pips on a prairie flower. Her belly was smooth and tight, because she had never brought a child into the world. Her legs glowed white and stork-like in the wavering light of the fire.

Between my legs my staff lumbered hard and long. She lay back but at the same time motioned for where I was to move and guided me in between her thighs, so that in a moment another shock ripped through my body, and she herself—my dear great-aunt—rolled with the tremor like a canoe in sudden rough water. Never on the hunt had I felt such a feeling. Never, even when I took my revenge against the killers of my dear father.

Taking myself back into myself, so that I became me again and she became who she was when we began, I found my strength redoubled near to bursting. But she encouraged me to forebear, and I did by following her instruction, so that as she told me to think outside of myself and turn my thoughts away from the instant of this moment and our sweet time—for what I had thought had been sweet in my life before this was sour tart and full of salt compared to this—I went far away, up and out to those same constellations of lights that I had flown half the distance to when I first took to serious dreaming. My mind went spiraling upward and away, out past the hunter and the deer and the spider and the crab and the beehive and the hill of horses—and who knew just how far away all these figures stood, I could not have said, if anyone knew, anyone at all—back up and out to the same place where I had once seen Sky—

And now the figure turned, whirled, spun, teetered, the entire universe tilted first to one side, then the other—

A child appeared to me, a child that grew quickly into a young girl, and then a woman beautiful with fat and heft. My great-aunt! Covering the world above us, blocking out the stars. I strove to rise as high as she was floating. And when I did soar nearly to that height, I saw another woman standing behind her, someone darker and younger, whom I did not know. And this woman called out to me in a voice like a bird's!

Without knowing that I knew it, I called her name. "*Tasáwiche!*"

"Find him," she said.

"I already did."

"No, you have not."

"I used his rib to avenge his death."

"Not your father."

"Who then?"

"The shadow catcher," she said. "He will need you."

"I do not know this person."

"You will. You will find him. And help him."

"I will."

"Good. Tell me again."

"I will. But when I do?"

"You will know what to do," she said.

And in the fluttering of a wing, of an eyelid, of a leaf in the wind, she was gone. I lay on the skins, naked, with my great-aunt, filled with a purpose I had never known. Never, not even when I went out to avenge my father's death, not ever before.

Library of Congress, Prints & Photographs Division, Edward S. Curtis Collection, LC-USZ62-106478

twelve

a death

AUTUMN, 1904—OH, AT that time Edward, too, believed he was quite content, though at the moment he had a head cold, and he was berating himself because he had no more money yet in hand for the project of his dreams. On this particular day, which turned out to be a significant one for him, on another of his outings by ferry to the island where he and his father first homesteaded, he was walking the beach like a seabird whose clipped wings made it impossible to take more than a few feeble leaps above the sand, looking east and north toward white-sloped Mount Baker and the Colville Reservation.

And then an ocean-deep movement overtook him, chilling his skin and making him quake all over. A wave passed through his body, a ripple of recognition, as though he were a pond and some god had just dropped a pebble into the center of him, perfect circles echoing out from the core. This movement— taking little more than an instant—produced in him a deep sense of humility and frustration.

But along with this came a certain corresponding warmth, and he turned his face into the wind, assured by whatever invisible force it was that bore down on him that he still had many years of life to hold onto and that rewards would come to him if he pushed ahead with his business. Yes, yes, he was a businessman, and a father and a husband, that was what he was!

Seabirds, floating in on the winds along the Sound, called to each other over his head. And from far off in the trees beyond the shoreline came the cries and shouts of his children, whom he and Clara had once again brought over on the ferry for the day.

"Papa! Papa!" the young girls called out to him. And he freed himself from that otherworldly mood and went stalking off in their direction.

Hal came running toward him, a bearer of news both good and bad. "Mr. Myers is here, Pap!" he shouted.

"Really?" Edward made his happiness visible on his face, enjoying the way his son addressed him, the same old way that he had spoken to his own dear father. (He could say without embarrassment that he'd encouraged Hal in this.)

And the girls. "Pap! Papoose, Daddy!" they called to him, racing along behind their older, faster brother.

"Beth, Florence!" He welcomed them with open arms and whirled each of the girls a full circle around before depositing her on the sand.

"How is your treehouse going?" he asked.

"Fine, sir," young Hal said in reply. "But Myers, Pap."

"He'll catch up with us. I want to know what progress you made while I took my little walk."

"The platform needs to be nailed in," he said.

"I want to hammer," Beth put in.

"You're too weak," Hal said.

"I am not," she said.

"Children," Edward said.

"Me, too," Florence said.

"You, too, what?" Edward said.

"I want to hammer," she said. "Hal said we can't hammer. Can we, Papoose, can we hammer?"

"Yes, we all will work on the treehouse," Edward told them, "just as soon as I see what Mr. Myers wants."

He saw me coming through the trees, dressed in an old coat and khaki trousers, the same outfit I wore in the field. "Ho!" Edward called to me. I waved but kept my slow pace, because I was carrying news I didn't wish to deliver. "Welcome," Edward said.

"Lovely spot," I said. He could tell by the way I looked at him that we needed to talk.

"Children," he said, "let Pap and Mr. Myers have a little walk now."

"Back to the treehouse!" Hal gave out a shout and ran in the lead toward the tree line, with the girls scampering after.

"What is it?" he said to me. He was staring up at one of the swooping gulls, almost as if the bird were the subject of a portrait and his eyes a lens.

"Chief Joseph is dying," I said. "He is not that old in years, but his heart is old. All those defeats make a man age."

Edward's own heart sank at this news, almost as if his old Pap had just died—again. "How did you hear?"

"It was on the telegraph," I said. "A friend of mine at the newspaper picked it up."

"We must go up to the Colville Reservation for a last visit," he said.

"I'll go for us," I said. "You've got the children."

"I'll bring them home and then we'll go," he said.

I looked at him. "Are you sure? When I went to your house looking for you, I saw Mrs. Curtis."

"What did she say?"

"It was nothing she said. Just the way she looked when I told her why I wanted to see you."

"You told her?"

"She asked," I said.

"Of course."

"Pap! Papee!" The voices of the children drifted up over the trees, drifted toward where we stood at the waterline.

"Let's go to them," he said, and we began walking toward the trees.

"A great chief is going," he said.

"Yes," I said.

We walked in silence through the trees to the doorway of the old house where his family first took up residence after their long train trip West. Clara greeted us as we entered with a soft look and a sympathetic voice. "I'm sorry, Edward. William told me the news."

"Yes, it is a terrible thing," Edward said. "A part of our history, soon to be gone."

"At least you have his portrait," Clara said. The children came trooping in the door, whooping and squealing. "Children," Clara said. They ran out the back door, squealing and whooping.

"I must go. We'll go, William and me."

"He's probably dead by now," she said. "You've made his portrait. What's the use, Edward?"

"I must go to pay homage," he said.

"You speak of him as though he were part of our family. As though he were your own father or brother."

"He's very important to me," Edward said. "He gave me that prophecy."

"A pagan prophecy, Edward. And a very expensive one." She rolled her eyes dismissively, all her sympathy suddenly withered away, turned, and went inside. Edward wanted to follow her, to explain, and, as only a guilty man can, to ask for forgiveness. Except he hadn't, in his own eyes, done anything wrong. And, as he saw it, he had a journey to make.

"Whoo! Whit! Whit! Yeeeeeee!" The children came storming in through the front door again, grabbing at Edward's coat tails as they went whipping past.

"Children!" Clara called out from the next room.

———

We left on the next ferry for the city, and from there we hired a wagon that would take us north to the Colville Reservation. The sky clouded over early in the evening. We camped that night under a wet sky, and not much had changed by morning, except that we had talked a little while sharing a bottle of Seattle-made whiskey.

"I'm embarrassed, William," Edward said when he first brought up the subject as we sat staring into the fire. "Clara is a devoted wife and mother. And what I admire in her, her tenacity on behalf of the children and the family, is what makes for such hellish moments as you witnessed—" He passed me the bottle.

"Well, sir," I said, "I wouldn't use so strong a word."

"It does seem hellish to me, the way I put her in such a terrible state. She wants me to stay, for her sake and the children's, and she wants me to go, for my sake."

"But here you are, sir. You have acted on your desires."

"Yes, I'm the wayfarer, whose homelife doesn't add up to much if you want to count it."

"Edward, if I may make an observation?"

He shook off a tremor from the cold, took the bottle back from me, and leaned closer to our fire. "Make your observation, sir."

"Your wife and your children are devoted to you."

"You've said that."

"I want to emphasize it."

"Duly noted."

"In many ways, your household—"

"Oh, Myers, I'm not sure I want to speak about my household. My household! When Pap and I took the train West I never imagined I would end up having a household." He drank and passed the bottle back to me.

"But that is life," I said, taking another swallow of the bitter whiskey.

"Profound, sir. And now will you quote to me one of those old poets whose study you took up when at the university?"

"I profoundly will not," I said.

"I never attended the university," he said.

"No, sir, but you have made much of life so far."

"Yes, the university of the household."

"And the Grand Canyon."

"Ah, Tasáwiche," he said with a sigh and took the bottle back.

"We'll drink to her."

"To Tasáwiche," he said, taking a swallow and then passing the bottle back to me.

"And to the chief," I said.

"Yes, yes, of course," he said.

"And to the underwriting that will come to us."

"That's your job," he said.

"No, no, sir, you are the one who can bring in the money."

"I meant the writing part of underwriting. What you write will become our foundation, under it all."

"I'll drink to that."

"Good, good," he said, taking the bottle back from me. "And I will make one more toast, a proposal in the form of a toast."

"And what is that, sir?"

"That in whatever fieldwork we perform in the future, and I hope there is a great deal of it, because only in that way will I...." His voice trailed off, as if he were lost in thought.

"Because what, sir?"

He had been staring at the fire, and now he looked up at me. "Be…because…because only in that way will we fulfill the prophecy and charge of the chief."

"In what way, sir? I'm not sure I understand."

"Without this," he said, holding up the nearly empty bottle and then hurling it into the dark. "No more of this in the field." He stared out at the proximate place where he had tossed the bottle. "If there is a field. Do you think, Myers, there will be?"

"I don't make prophecies," I said.

"But you know a lot from your university days."

"I know what other people have said."

"And from all of that, will you say something yourself?"

"I'll say that I can't say, sir."

"You won't say it?"

"I can't."

"I have no university wind at my back," he said. "But I'll make a damned prophecy, I will. I'll say we do go out into the field again; I'll say we're going!"

So there we were, two men soaked through and through, the picture of discomfort and desolation, with aching heads and downward-turning eyes, arriving at the entrance to the reservation the next afternoon.

"Joseph?" The first person we encountered, a wrinkled, old fellow wrapped in a blanket, gave us the bad news. Belying his features, he spoke with the voice of a man we might have encountered on a street corner in any American city. "He left two days ago."

"Is his family here?" I asked. "So that we might pay our respects."

"Oh, they ain't going to want to see you," the old fellow said.

"We know—we met—some of his nephews," Edward said. But the old man had already turned away.

"We might go and look," I said.

After one more inquiry we found the wooden house where one of his nephews lived, one of the fellows, in fact, who had accompanied the chief to Edward's studio. We smoked a pipe and an old woman, one of Joseph's wives, as it turned out, boiled some tea for us. The house smelled of the incense burned for the departed chief's soul.

"He was a great man," Edward said.

"He told me he liked the photograph you made of him," the nephew said.

"I am glad to hear that."

"He told me he would speak to you."

"We did speak during our session," Edward said. "He gave me a prophecy."

The nephew turned his head away. "You heard him."

"I did," Edward said.

"You listened; you heard."

"Yes, I did, sir."

"And will you follow him?"

"Eventually."

"No, no, will you follow to the end of his prophecy?"

"I hope to."

"Then his spirit will rest."

"I hope so," Edward said. "I wouldn't want to disturb him."

Joseph's nephew stood and said something that I couldn't quite catch. The future, truth, his uncle's spirit....

"Might you speak more slowly?" I said. "I am trying to understand."

The fellow looked at me, at Edward. "Listen more quickly," he said.

———⌒———

Edward sank very deep into a dark state on our return journey. "We must work faster," he said, "because before too long none of them will be left."

"What did you say?"

"The elders," he said. "They'll all soon be gone. We must help to save them. If only…." He wrung his hands together. "The money, the money, the money…."

All his hope hung on one slender thread. I asked, "Do you think that Roosevelt will get you an audience with J. P. Morgan?"

"It's been too long," he said. "I have just about given up on it." And saying this, his heart grew even heavier than he could have imagined. "Perhaps it is supposed to happen this way," he said. "It's what Roosevelt predicts, and what he wants to happen. That's the prophecy of one of *our* chiefs. All the red men are either dying off or turning into white men with red skins. He has helped me the way a taxidermist helps the hunter. He wants to have us stuff and mount our subjects. Hang them on the wall. Put them in the museum."

Before I could respond to this, and I wanted to, because I didn't believe it, Edward drifted off again into thoughts of the old chief. And of his long-departed father. There was some connection between the pair of them, I suppose, that he couldn't figure out. Or didn't want to. Or perhaps wasn't meant to.

———⌒———

It rained again before we reached Seattle, and the weather inside Edward's house was colder than it was outside. Clara said nothing specific to him about the trip, which was worse than if she had asked questions and then responded in a biting way. It felt as though something else had died besides one of the great old chiefs. If only it could be reborn. If only he could find a way to make this happen, to undo somehow the awful change that was taking place between them.

"I'm going for a walk," he said.

"In the rain?"

"In the rain."

"Go then. Get soaked. Catch a chill. I'll take care of you. I always have."

"Clara," he said.

"Are you going?" she said. "Go."

He walked for miles, soaking through and through. He didn't know what he was waiting for, but he was waiting for something. "Chief?" he called to him in his mind. The rain came down. "Chief?" He was up there—or somewhere—with his Pap, he knew, he knew. "Chief?"

But the Chief didn't answer, and Edward sank suddenly to the sodden earth, on his knees, while the rain poured down on him, a man with nowhere to go and nothing to do, his life stuck in place like a wagon whose wheels had lodged in a great mud-hole and every effort to free it dug it deeper in.

Library of Congress, Prints & Photographs Division, Edward S. Curtis Collection,
LC-USZ62-83601

thirteen

jimmy fly-wing's story—5

NOW COMES THE VERY plainest part of my story but also, I believe, the most important. Not so long after my coming together with my great-aunt, I took a wife, as it turned out, the young girl from a nearby family who scolded me for my would-be ferocity and teased me and told me to go hunt dogs.

Her name was Herb-Gatherer, and she had soft hands and a warm smile, with eyes as blue as the space between the clouds. My secret name for her was Blue-Star, and I moved her into our family tent, taking a place across from my mother. Our tradition would have it that after a year's hunting I would have enough materials to build her a tent of our own in whatever location our migrating tribe had settled on, however temporarily, as its next home.

Nothing I had ever done prepared me for the bliss of living with only one other person, and the skills in lovemaking taught to me by my great-aunt helped make this new life a happy one. One day Herb-Gatherer came to me with a broad smile on her face and told me that she noticed her belly was rising.

To provide for my new family I hunted long and hard, with the goal of making our own place as quickly as possible. I rode with other young men in quest of buffalo hides and meat. I often rode alone when in quest of antelope. Quite soon my supply of hides and skins grew to where we could trade and exchange, making us ready to move to our tent together.

Such as it had been for thousands of years for our people. The only difference between the early days and now, or so my great-uncle explained to me, was that once in a while white-skinned traders and mountain men would come to our village, offering us knives and guns in exchange for the spoils of our hunting. But there were few of them and many of us, and so we paid them little mind, except to use the guns in our buffalo hunts. One old man spoke out against the use of these new weapons. It was not our way, he said. It disturbs the horses; it disturbs nature. But his voice was drowned in a rush of talk from younger hunters, myself among them, who praised the guns as a more efficient way of taking the meat. "Was there a time before we had horses?" someone asked. "Yes," the old man said. "And so there will be a time before we had guns," the other said. We all laughed. The old man went into his tent and six moons later died of a cough.

Heat came in summer, the streams dried up, leaves fell in autumn, winter snows buried us—what happy months we hibernated away!—and spring brought melting, and the lush-ness of the fields and flowers and trees. Such as it had been, such as it would be. After all my high-flying hawk-visions and dreams that took me into the stars, my life seemed to hug the earth and never leave it. Herb-Gatherer and I made love, but it was nothing more than that, by which I mean, it was complete and wonderful in itself. By springtime our daughter arrived in a chorus of shouts and prayers, and with a spray of beautifully red blood. Everything—earth, sky, trees, sun, streams, the prairie itself—seemed in tune with everything else.

I carried this deep sense of goodness-of-the-world with me as I rode out one afternoon in early spring, under a sky that appeared to take its color from the waters of certain rushing streams, a slight wind coming from the south. My horse surged along, and when we came to the flats of the prairie, it moved me with it as I might have been moved along by a constantly rushing river down a canyon. (Oh, I had seen some of this, I had, yes!)

A pair of hawks circled overhead, nothing but hawks on the prowl for their morning meal, which even now would be racing toward cover somewhere in the tall grass ahead. The sun rose over the rim of the prairie to the east, and within an hour it was pushing at my back with long, hot fingers, urging me onward, onward, to the west.

"Pony," I said to my horse, "we will have a good day's hunt together." My horse responded by keeping up its westward pace.

When the sun had risen above my left shoulder we stopped and drank. With only a short way to go to the hunting ground I had chosen, I still felt the pull of my wife back in the village, and the slightest shift of wind or gust of light would have turned me around and sent me riding back in that direction. How I would have loved at that moment to have seen her before me and taken her in my arms and lain with her upon a bed of skins! Instead I hoisted myself onto the horse's back and urged the animal forward.

When the sun stood almost directly overhead, we reached a small rise—all these hills that rose above the plain gave us a sense of flying surpassed only by the flying in my dream-visions—below which ran another of those rows of iron. A large, dark bundle lay on the prairie. Thinking it might be something worth taking (guns or tools), I urged my horse down the rise. He whinnied in surprise when just as we reached the flats where the bundle lay it suddenly rose from the ground and turned into a man with a black face dressed in long trousers and a shirt. He held up a hand, pale palm forward, to show he meant no harm.

"You have been too long in the sun," I said. He made noises, nothing I understood.

Had anyone, alive or dead, spirit or mortal, from past or future, warned me about what was to happen next, I would not have believed a word of it, not if the clamdigger woman herself, the Princess of the coast of Seattle, had told me in a dream, nor if Tasáwiche, the chief's daughter from the deep canyon, had floated above me in the night while Herb-Gatherer was sleeping and whispered in my ear that my destiny was to change forever from this moment on. Do I even believe it now, even as I am about to describe what happened? I just barely believe it. Just barely.

Why? Because what happened next took place in everyday time but had every marking of a dream. The black man speaking and gesturing to me. Peace, yes, he wanted peace, that much I could understand. Aside from his mouth noises, the air was still. Far off in the highest part of the cloudless sky, a hawk hovered, drifting slightly on the wafts of invisible winds.

"What?" I said, shaking my head.

The black man went on making noises, showing me a smile, keeping his hands in front of him. The hawk drifted in our direction. My horse whinnied. The black man gestured, smiled, stopped making his noises. Everything became still again. And my horse whinnied.

The black man looked down the iron rows, and I turned to see where he was looking. At first I saw nothing, and then, staring hard, I caught the slightest wavering disruption in the air above the horizon far down the end of the rows. And my horse snorted, and stamped a foot. A black speck appeared at the edge of the horizon and both the black man and I followed its progress. Only my horse lost interest and wandered off a few yards behind me, nibbling on dry grass.

The black man pointed.

I nodded.

He smiled.

The train—yes, of course, it was a train—approached, making a long stain on the eastern horizon as the white smoke from the engine—yes, of course, a train had an engine—trailed behind it. As it grew closer, the black man began to speak to me again in his language. The longer he spoke, the louder grew the train, and by the time the brakes screeched and the engine screamed to a halt near where we stood, the black man was sputtering and sweating because he could not make himself understood.

I was not a man easily frightened in battle, but a sudden whoosh of smoke from the engine sent me jumping back. High up in the cab another man—this one a pale-faced man wearing a white beard—leaned out of the window (I learned all these names of things much later, of course) and called down to the black man. He waved up to the white man and then pointed to me. The man in the engine called back down.

From a door that slid open in the car behind the engine, a ladder lifted down and a man in a rough gray uniform descended to the prairie floor. My horse made a questioning noise, signifying how strange this all seemed to his horse-knowledge.

"Come," the black man said, motioning toward the ladder.

Years later, I now understand what he meant. At that moment I took him to be telling me that I could take the ladder. Which I walked over to and touched, and tried to disengage from the train.

"No, no," the black man said with a gesture. He motioned for me to climb the metal steps.

At first I stood my ground.

He insisted.

And on this next moment everything turned. The black man came up behind me and gave me a shove. I whirled about, knife at the ready. But the black man was still standing several feet behind me. I became suddenly quite confused. The engine was steaming; my horse began to whinny.

And then a voice whispered in my ear, and I understood.

"*Go on,*" she said. I couldn't see Tasáwiche, but I recognized her voice.

"*You must,*" said the clamdigger woman at my other ear.

My love, my life, my wife, my daughter, my village, my sky, my prairie—all of this kept me rooted in place.

"*Go!*" Tasáwiche said, giving me a shove, and I stumbled forward, nearly stubbing my foot on the bottom rung of the ladder.

I grabbed the railing and climbed straight up as the train gave a roar. The black man jumped up the ladder behind me, and we went chugging off along the iron rows. I leaned into the wind, watching, watching, watching, until my horse was nothing more than a dark spot on the horizon.

fourteen

the great patron

Goddess-born, let us follow our fates, whether
they seem to lead, or to withdraw.

No matter what shall be, all fortune can be
conquered by endurance. (709–10)

AENEID 5

THE RAINS CAME, THE rains went, and Edward, gloomy enough
already since the death of Chief Joseph, slid down into an even
darker place. He and I were walking the beach, a light mist was
falling, and he was bemoaning the demise of the late chief and
the general dissolution of the tribe.

"The Nez Percé, the Nez Percé, how long will they survive?"

"We'll go back there and find out," I said.

"We must," he said. "Even if it means that I have to mortgage
the house. Even if it means that I have to mortgage the studio."
Picture him walking the beach as we talked this over, his eyes
turned down, his thoughts heavy as rocks. Even his limbs
looked weighed down with disappointment.

Are we merely creatures of the weather? Would not a classical
hero attribute what happened next to the intervention of the

gods? On the wings of ferocious winds, the rain blew east, and by the time we had turned back along the water's edge in the direction of the cabin, the sun—young handsome god Apollo!—appeared to the southeast, lighting up the snow-capped mountain whose presence on clear days dominated the view in that direction.

"I don't know how she's going to take it," he said, meaning Clara and the news that he intended to use the business as collateral in a loan.

"You mustn't be too hard on her," I said. "It's not easy being wife to genius."

"Is that why you have not married yet?" he said, with a laugh I had not heard from him in many a week.

Clara was sitting at the kitchen table when we returned, enveloped in what appeared to be worse gloom than Edward's.

"You have news," she said.

"Oh?" He didn't like the sound of her voice—news? Must be awful news, he figured. She held up the telegram and he took it from her.

"Mr. Morgan will see you...," it read, followed by details. These were among the most thrilling words Edward had ever read. Tall fellow that he was, he curled himself into a taut, compressed bunch of flesh and muscle and sprung up into the air.

"He has done it! Roosevelt has done it!"

It was January, light snow on the pavement and in the gutters of the great city, a wind sharp as a skinner's knife raced off the water. Edward lugged his portfolio in the cold all the way from the hotel to Morgan's midtown mansion-office figuring that it might be healthy for him to take a good bracing walk in this winter air. It took him half an hour. His shoulder hurt; his nose was running. And his heart beat much faster than usual. It was almost like a romantic encounter for him, this rendezvous with one of the richest men in the world. Passed from doorman to butler to secretary, he at last stood in the place he had traveled thousands and thousands of miles to reach.

"I read your letter," said the man behind the huge mahogany desk. "And Roosevelt's." Edward nodded, unable to take his eyes off J.P. Morgan's engorged dark red nose, even as he felt Morgan's eyes bearing down on him like the headlamp of a rushing train. "And I've decided against it," Morgan said.

Edward felt nothing in that instant. Next came a shuddering in his heart.

"Not that I'm against modern methods," Morgan said. "Why, I've given up gas light for electric lights in my home as you can see. But when it comes to this project of yours—"

"Let me—"

"I'll finish," Morgan said. "I have a lot of sympathy for the red man, mind you. I know full well it was people like me who drove him off the plains and crowded him into those miserable little reserves."

"Reservations, sir," Edward said.

"Whatever you call them. But this is a question of art. I have seen Catlin's drawings, and they preserve the old ways rather nicely, don't you think? They're not great art, but they do the trick."

"I—"

"Thank you for coming to see me, Mr. Curtis, and I know you must be disappointed. My secretary may have been a bit overzealous in inviting you to come all this distance when I hadn't yet made up my mind about this proposal. Knowing that you were going to appear gave me some cause to think over the matter. I see it this way. Electricity I will gladly pay for because it is clearly superior to gas light. Photography, however, hasn't proven itself against the painting, and that is what I have decided." He looked past Edward, as if he could see through the thick wooden door to the outer office. Immediately the secretary stepped through the door.

Edward's nose began to drip again, and he wanted furiously to staunch it, but there was no time except to raise up the portfolio and splash it across Morgan's desk.

"Sir," he said, "I've come all the way from Seattle. If you will only take a look at these pictures...."

The secretary appeared at his shoulder and lay a soft hand on his sleeve. "Please, Mr. Curtis...."

Something in her voice reminded him as much of a nurse as a business person—she had seen others like him in this situation, no doubt about that. Edward felt like nothing, like an old shell cast up on the beach. "Very well," he said. "Thank you."

But just as Edward, with trembling hands, was gathering up the portfolio, about to turn aside, Morgan slapped his palm onto the smooth leather cover.

"Show me the damned pictures." He motioned with a stubby finger, and Edward hastily opened the portfolio. He turned to the portrait of Chief Joseph. Morgan stared at the picture and made a noise in his throat.

Edward opened to some women of Taos, carrying their water jugs on their heads as they made their way along a forest path, a photograph he had taken on our way back from the mesa country. Morgan made that sound again. And then Morgan became quiet.

And then Edward showed him a Mohave girl, Mosa, a younger version of his Tasáwiche. Her beautiful face seemed almost to have been that of a doll's carved out of a single piece of mahogany.

"I've changed my mind," the red-nosed rich man said. Now it was the secretary's turn to make a sound in her throat. Clearly, she was surprised, perhaps even astonished. "Take these away and come and see me next week."

He looked down at some papers on his desk, and it was as if Edward had become invisible. Only after closing the portfolio and turning to leave the office did Edward notice that there was a window overlooking the street, facing the other massive building opposite. Descending into the Grand Canyon had been an easier feat than what he had just accomplished, and he seemed to have accomplished nothing just yet. It was snowing. And he was sweating so hard it was as though he had just chopped down three trees and then rowed himself across Puget Sound in high summer.

He couldn't recall most of the other business he performed while waiting around in New York City for his next appointment with Morgan. Perhaps he went to galleries, to the theater. He did remember wanting to visit with Edward Steichen, who had photographed Morgan only a short while before. Edward had seen a copy of that, with its bold figure in the foreground and nothing but darkness behind. The darkness he knew, seeing himself teetering above it when the great man had at first turned him away.

There was a library at the hotel, and there he found a copy of Francis Parkman's *The Oregon Trail* and read for several days. Sitting in Manhattan, he traversed the trail, marveling at the Indians and the landscape and the weather. "This life, this life!" he recalled thinking to himself. "It is a trail I am traversing as I discover the way." Once he stood upon the south peak of Mount Rainier, looking out toward the Pacific, and then he descended a canyon to the navel of the earth and found a beautiful creature living there, and then he climbed mesas, and now he was parked in a small room in a hotel in the largest city in the nation, waiting

to speak again to one of the richest men in the world. And he had
not yet even reached the age of forty! This trail of hopes and fears!
"What lay ahead?" he asked himself. "What years?"

He nodded to himself and took a deep breath, feeling as alive,
and yet as isolated, as he had ever been. What years, yes? But
what *cash?* That was the big question as the time for his next
meeting with Morgan at last came around. Edward had already
spent, by his calculation, nearly twenty thousand dollars of his
own money over the past few years on this project (in addition
to all that his brother Ray had given him), and he needed a great
deal more to complete it.

"How much more?" the great man with the red nose inquired
a few days later, as he stared—glared might be a better way to
put it—from behind his beautiful leather-covered desk in the
library of his midtown mansion.

Immediately after receiving the telegram, Edward had sent
back a letter laying out some initial amounts. "I wrote to you,
sir," he said, glancing over at an assistant who stood to his right.

"Yes, Mr. Morgan, I have those in hand," the fellow said,
bending stiffly and keeping his eyes averted from his master's
face. You might think that it was a sort of religious veneration
that kept him so.

"Curtis," Morgan said, "why don't you step across the hall to
the library for a moment?"

"Very good," Edward said, and left him and his assistant in
the office, with its thick Persian rug and dark wood paneling,
and the ceiling that seemed made for a foreign church rather
than a Yankee's counting room.

Edward had not had much time to admire the library, or to
take in all of the figures in the cupola above the entrance from
the street. But as he passed from the study to the east room of
the library, he allowed his eye to stay a moment on the figures

out of myth and legend and history that decorated the niches above the doors. And in the library he lingered at the lowest rank of shelves, picking out a signed copy of the English poet John Keats, and a medieval Bible with jeweled binding, and then a scroll in some language he could not make out, which by its very configuration seemed to tell an important story of gods or kings.

"May I be of some help to you?" The woman's voice caught him by surprise. He turned to see her standing in the doorway, demure but hardly plain, in a dark green velvet skirt and white blouse that seemed, despite the dim light of the library, almost to set her upper body aglow even as her face took on a certain dusky impermanence. "I'm Mr. Morgan's librarian," she said. "Belle da Costa Greene." She touched a finger to the rim of her spectacles and gave him a tepid smile.

He hurried to introduce himself, as Morgan's assistant appeared in the doorway. "Mr. Curtis," he said.

"Miss Greene," Edward said. He was about to say more when she gave a toss of her head and waggled her finger at him in schoolmarm fashion.

"Go," she said. "He doesn't like to wait."

Morgan was standing at his desk when Edward came back into the study. "We have an agreement then, Curtis," he said. The assistant handed him some papers, and Morgan told him to come back and speak with him the next day. The assistant ushered Edward out to the foyer where he stood in a daze, staring at the figures on the paper.

Taking a deep breath (and feeling in a celebratory mood), he went to the library door and turned the knob. Locked. He knocked. No answer. Immediately he went out onto the street to find a telegraph office and wire the good news to Clara and me. Fifteen thousand dollars a year for five years!

It was snowing again, and the drift of flakes down from the street lamps seemed more theatrical than natural. He took himself out for a good dinner, a wonderfully thick steak and delicious beer, and then strolled the avenues a while, staring at just about every gentleman he passed, saying to himself, what would he say if I told him I had just made the richest man in America a partner in my project?

Snow kept falling past his hotel room window as he made ready for bed. He studied it for a while after he turned down the light, recalling nights on board the ship in the far north when the stars shined so ferociously. Men were dwarves, he thought to himself, so tiny and feeble when put against the backdrop of the broad canvas of the world, let alone the universe. But as he climbed into bed and settled down to sleep, he overcame that sense of his own puniness, recalling to himself his vision and his mission. He thought of the light in the ice cave high up on Mount Rainier. He recalled the erect posture of Chief Joseph, who showed thousands of years of the life of the tribe in the way that he held himself before the eye of the camera. Even as Clara's face and the faces of his children swam into view, he could not help but think beyond them to the task Morgan had now underwritten. It disturbed him to imagine what Clara might say when he told her upon his return just how much fieldwork he would be undertaking now that the money was assured.

Would she understand? Could she ever understand?

He hoped, and dozed, and woke himself up with a dream that seemed so out of keeping with anything else of recent notice that he wrote it down so that he would not forget it, ever.

Adrift on an ice floe. Seabirds swooping and calling overhead. An old woman's face appears out of the snow fog, smiling. I wave to her only to discover that instead of an arm, I have a flipper!

Although no words pass between us I have the distinct sense that I know this woman....

The next morning he returned to the Morgan mansion. The great man had left for Newport to fish for deep-sea monsters or departed for Baalbek to gaze upon the pyramids. Oh, he had gone somewhere, wherever it is the very rich go, leaving behind his assistant to deal with Edward. The two of them worked out a schedule of payments and the plan for the publication of our findings and photographs in a series of volumes that would serve as the first and only comprehensive study of the American Indian Nations ever produced.

It was done, and it was as simple as that.

And yet Edward lingered there in the foyer, in a strange and intangible mood, contemplating this latest feat of his. And this act of good fortune. It seemed perfectly fitting to him that the man who had made the most money out of the settling of America should pay to record everything that would soon be lost as a result of his work. Would that we could have undone it all and returned to that moment in Spain when Cristoforo Colombo reached down into himself and made the argument that turned Isabella and the Spanish Crown in his favor!

George Catlin—Edward's rival, apparently, in the minds of some—asserts in his writings that if the Plains Indians were not the direct descendents of the Lost Tribe of Israel then they were in some of their elemental rituals at least heavily influenced by them. This made great sense to Edward. What if there were more of a connection between us all than the great accident of geography and time? What if there was a pattern in life that somehow emulated the pattern in art and poetry? As he studied the paintings in the cupola of Morgan's house, thoughts came to him about the passage of knowledge from the oldest times to the youngest, and it tickled him all of a sudden, as he scrutinized these works that were hung so high in the hallway of this mansion that he had to strain his neck to see them.

"Hello?" Belle da Costa Greene's voice startled him from his daydream. She stood demurely in the doorway to the library. "You must have a lot on your mind," she said. "Mr. Curtis."

"You remember my name?"

"I'm a librarian, Mr. Curtis. Names are almost everything to me."

That made Edward smile, and he took the occasion to study her, dressed as she was now in a blue velvet skirt, with another startling white blouse, and her dark brown hair piled high on her head, the wisps of it tucked under the collar. She peered at him through the same pair of spectacles, her eyes showing some amusement, and yet behind this mood a certain—what?—disdain?

"And I understand," she said, "that we're going to have to make room on the shelves here for some books of yours in the near future. I just learned yesterday that you are going to produce several volumes on the North American Indian for Mr. Morgan."

"That's correct," he said.

"So you're a writer and photographer? A wonderful and unusual combination."

"I'm a photographer, first," Edward said. "The writing follows along after the pictures."

"To my taste, it works just the other way," said Miss Greene.

"You're a librarian, and so it would follow," he said.

"Words before pictures, do you mean?" A light sparkled in her eyes as she spoke, and when she stepped back inside the library, Edward immediately followed.

"Do tell me about your book, Mr. Curtis," she said. "I'm quite interested. Mr. Morgan obviously believes in books as works of art."

"I'll tell you all about it," he said, "if you'll have tea with me."

She squinted at him, as though she were reading small print, and then relaxed her face.

"Can you come back at four o'clock?"

"Tea time?" he said.

"Where are you from, Mr. Curtis?"

"Seattle," he said.

"Home of the great tea drinkers, I presume?"

Edward gave a shrug. "I never drink it."

"But you're willing to start now?"

"I am," he said. "I am."

She laughed, and with a half-wave of her hand, dismissed him.

The mansion was not far from Edward's hotel, but instead of returning there, he paced the avenues, weaving back and forth between them at intervals, until he had nearly reached the park. Only a few snow flurries in the air today, and a weak sun struggling to take a peek at the city from behind thick gray clouds. This was certainly not his favorite part of the country, but he had to reckon with it. In exchange for a few weeks of the year, not all of it in such unpleasant weather as this, he would secure enough cash for the next five years of his working life.

After loafing along all afternoon, gazing in shop windows, staring at passers-by, he scarcely had time to return to his hotel and change his shirt before heading back to the Morgan house for his rendezvous with Miss Greene.

"I'm sorry," was the first thing she said when the doorman gave him entry into the cupola. Her eyes seemed empty of the sparkle he'd first noticed in them, and she worked her hands nervously together.

"Is there something wrong, Miss Greene?"

"I...we just received a shipment of books from Paris and I have to work late."

"Oh," Edward said, feeling a little sting of cold in his chest. "I'm sorry, too, then. What new books are they?"

"A number of illustrated Bibles that we've been waiting for for months now. I do have to get to them directly."

"Bibles," Edward said. "But you've only been waiting months. The good news the book proclaims, it's been around for years."

She smiled a touch, but then regained her serious composure. "Are you interested in books as old as the Bible, Mr. Curtis?"

He watched her hands, the long pale fingers twining about each other, snake-like almost. "I've known the Bible, Miss Greene, ever since I was a child. My Pap—my father—was a minister back in Minnesota."

"A minister, really? So you might be interested in this shipment?"

"Definitely, most seriously and undoubtedly," he said.

Her smile grew at the corners of her mouth and her eyes gained a little of their former brightness. "Where are you staying, Mr. Curtis?"

He named the hotel.

"And they do serve tea there, I'm sure."

"I'm sure," he said.

She relaxed her mouth. He noticed now for the first time a small dark speck of a birthmark just at the left side of her chin. He wondered why he hadn't seen it before.

"And if I said that I would meet you there in two hours?"

"I would be utterly pleased," he said.

"Well, then," she said. "I'll meet you there."

Torture by city time! That is what he had been enduring ever since he had arrived. Two hours in New York City, he learned, can pass like a half-minute, or go on and on and on like most of a lifetime. For part of the first hour he stood on the street and watched the traffic pass by, and for another he went up to his room and changed his shirt again. In the lobby he composed a wire, sending a copy to Clara and a copy to me:

MORGAN WILL SPONSOR. DETAILS FOLLOW.

Still there seemed to be an enormous amount of time to pass when he was sitting rather nervously in the parlor of his hotel awaiting her arrival.

He was counting the seconds, thinking now and then of work to do, when Miss Greene appeared, the sparkle gone from her eyes again and looking rather fatigued. "Hello, Mr. Curtis," she said. "I—"

Standing to greet her, he said, "Please call me Edward."

"I can't stay long," she said. "I must get back to the library."

"Those Bibles call out to you."

"Yes, they do," she said. "They do. And a dozen other new volumes that I must catalog."

"Mr. Morgan loves his books, I must say."

"Fortunately for you."

"For all of us, I must say."

"For your family, do you mean?"

"Not just my family," he said. "For the People."

"The people?"

"The Indian Nations," he said.

She raised her eyebrows, and then gave him a look as such that he might have just told her that Jesus Christ Himself had come back to Earth and wanted to check out one of her new Bibles from the Morgan library. "Tell me about them," she said, settling onto the sofa next to him. A faint scent of floral perfume caught his attention.

"Tell you about them?"

"The People," she said. "I want to hear about them."

"Let's have our tea first," he said.

"I don't have that much time, Mr. Curtis."

"I'll begin telling you about them and we'll see if the tea arrives."

"Begin," she said.

"I don't know where to begin."

"When did you first begin thinking about them?" she asked.

"It doesn't begin with thought," he told her.

Between the time he had arranged for the tea to be served to them and its arrival, he must have covered the first several decades of his life. Though he intrigued her with his story, he still hadn't gotten to what she wanted to know. "I know some of their names," she said, adjusting a proud little smile on her lips. And taking a breath—her breasts rising with this glorious intake of air—she said to him, *"...and for the past I pronounce what the air holds of the red aborigines. / The red aborigines, / Leaving natural breaths, sounds of rain—"*

"Miss Greene," he said, not knowing at first what she was saying.

But she merely fluttered her large eyelashes and continued. *"—and winds, calls as of birds and animals in the woods, syllabled to us for names—"*

"Miss Greene?"

"—Okonee, Koosa, Ottawa, Monongahela, Sauk, Natchez, Chattahoochee, Kaqueta, Oronoco, / Wabash, Miami, Saginaw, Chippewa, Oshkosh, Walla-Walla, / Leaving such to the States they melt, they depart, charging the water and the land with names...."

"Miss Greene," he said, almost as a release from the tension she had, with her chanting, instilled in him.

"Did I say the names properly?"

"As far as I know."

"But you're the expert," she said. "Mr. Morgan is investing a lot of money in your expertise," she said. "I hope that we can trust you."

"Is this some sort of test?"

"Not at all, Mr. Curtis."

"Edward," he said. "Please, call me Edward."

"Edward," she said. "Edward Curtis."

"You say *that* name pretty well."

"But what of the others? I did say them passably well?"

"I told you, yes, but where did that come from? Is it something you wrote? I didn't know that you were interested in these matters."

"Something I wrote?" She laughed easily in her throat. "Not me. But Walt Whitman. Walt Whitman, our untamed poet. Did you like it?" She took another deep, fascinating breath: "*Starting from fish-shape Paumanok where I was born, / Well-begotten, and rais'd by a perfect mother, / After roaming many lands, lover of populous pavements, / Dweller in Manahatta my city or on southern savannas....*"

Somehow the tea had materialized before them, and he watched enthralled as the memorious—or should he say memorable? or memorizable?—dusky-complexioned Miss Belle da Costa Greene—was she Portuguese?—raised her cup to her delicate lips and sipped. And touched the tip of her small pink tongue to those self-same lips. Glancing at him over the rim of her cup, he could see that she was paying close attention to whether or not he was paying close enough attention.

"And so from here," she said, "will you be going out on one of your field trips again?"

"First home," he said. "We'll organize ourselves for the coming year. And then start out."

"Now that Mr. Morgan is underwriting you," Miss Greene said, "you'll feel a lot more confident, won't you?"

"It is a good feeling," he said. "A very good feeling. My assistant will be quite pleased to hear about it. I wired him, actually."

"And Mrs. Curtis? I assume there is a Mrs. Curtis."

"I wired her," he said.

"Will she be pleased? It must require you to be away from home quite a long time each year—and will more in the years to come."

"She is devoted to our family," he said. "She holds the fort while I make my expeditions into the field...." Now it was his turn to sip some tea and allow himself the luxury of rolling the warm, sweet liquid around in his mouth while he attempted to figure out how to say what he wanted to say. "There's so much yet to do."

"'Sauk, Natchez, Chattahoochee, Kaqueta, Oronoco...,'" she began again in her little recitation.

"Yes, all of those and more," he said. "It will take me away from home for a long while."

"Months and months?"

"Years," he said. And when he explained how methodically he and I intended to undertake our research, she said that she understood. "Though I am not a scientist. I am a photographer."

"And a writer."

"I'm trying to be a writer," he said. "I make my notes. My assistant makes his. I keep a journal."

"Very good," Miss Greene said, as though she were his teacher and he was eight or nine years old again. Something flared up in her eyes—or was it just the gaslight flaring and her eyes reflecting it?—and she set her cup down on the saucer on the little table that separated them. "Time to go, I'm afraid."

Edward stood up and helped her with her coat, inhaling a deep draught of her special scent, some Parisian perfume, no doubt, brought back from fabled Europe by her Croesus-like employer, a man with enough money to underwrite a history of all the dying tribes that he and his compatriots had worked faithfully to displace, if not destroy.

"You must tell your wife about this wonderful tea that we had. And promise to bring her here one day."

"I'm sure she'll be terribly jealous when she hears of it," Edward said. "There's nothing so European as this in Seattle."

With a wave of her now-gloved hand, she feigned the writing of some script in the air. "You must write to me," she said, "and keep me informed about the progress of your project." The doorman moved to hail her a carriage.

"You want me to do that?" Edward said.

"Of course, I do," she said, and with a smile and a touch of her gloved fingertips, left him standing before the hotel as confused and convinced as any wanderer across the plains upon whom some conjuring Indian medicine man had cast a spell.

That spell lasted a long time, not only all through Edward's tedious train trip back to Seattle, but also striking him now and then while he was out in the field. Thus, he wrote the first in a series of letters to a woman who was not his wife.

Dear Miss Greene:

I am writing to you from our camp in the high desert where once only the Comanche roamed. My assistant—partner, really—Myers and I have spent a week now making our portraits of some smaller tribes that inhabit this part of the Western plateau. Tonight we find ourselves exhausted, spent from the work of wading through impromptu translators and organizing what is really, in bits and pieces, a sort of variety show for the Broadway stage.

Not that I have seen one of those, but I do hope to one day. Just as you might long to witness a cavalcade of Plains tribesmen returning home from a deer hunt, as I did the other afternoon, or have explained to you the toilet of a young Comanche girl, whose mother graciously agreed to allow us to witness the daily ceremony in which the girl awoke and performed her ablutions necessary for a particular holy day.

Should you ever decide that you might like to witness some of these events yourself, or at least attend a portrait session, you would be a most welcome guest.

But my surmise is that you turn your eyes more toward the Old World of Europe than you might to our new West. I trust you won't take this in the wrong way, but it seems to me that most Easterners look more to Europe than in our direction. What an odd country this makes us! Divided between North and South—some time I might tell you, if you are interested in the subject, about my father's life and his service in the Union Army—and between West and East, it's a miracle of politics that we do all ultimately work together to make one nation.

I have thought of you now and then, in Mr. Morgan's library, cataloguing all of the knowledge in those books that arrive—is it almost daily or weekly that they come?—making up a wall of learning about the subjects of the Old World. I wonder if now and then you might have a thought or two about what is going on in the Western part of the country, in our truly New World, all of this life we live on the other side of the Mississippi and the Rockies, where the land once belonged to the now defensive and worn-down People of the Tribes? For certainly I cast my thoughts in your direction, thinking of how on my next trip East we might again take tea together.

This is of course an invitation offered in the spirit of colleague-ship and amity, as we both work now for the same employer. I hope you won't construe it in any way but that. As a married man with several children and a most dutiful wife who tends to our home with great success and care while I am away on my frequent field trips I am quite a fortunate fellow. And even more fortunate now that our mutual benefactor Mr. Morgan has endowed my photography project.

But in an odd way, New York City, with all of its millions of inhabitants seems to me a much lonelier place than the wide plains of the West, where often I camp out in the company of one assistant and, aside from several dozen Indians, have no other human beings around me for hundreds of miles. So it would be a pleasure and an honor to spend an hour in your company on my next trip to 'Manahatta.'

fifteen

jimmy fly-wing's story—6

WHY HAD I DONE it? I asked myself that same question for many years thereafter.

I left my horse, my land, my wife, my child, my village, my people, all for a ride on a train.

Why had I done it? Because they pushed me, is one way to answer it. Because in visions the clamdigger woman and the beautiful Tasáwiche pushed me toward my future.

And I had done it—and here is where the mind of the aboriginal and the modern American man come together, in agreement on the possibilities of existence—because I could.

My people followed a trail of ten thousand miles and ten thousand years that took them from Siberia to North America. My half-adopted people sailed across the ocean and then set out on foot and on horseback to trek Westward ever Westward where they met my native kin. And they fought war upon war with each other upon this beautiful land. Why? Because they could.

And who would help to make both sides see things clearly, to see where we all came from and where we are going?

I climbed up into the cab of the engine—years later, telling this I have the words to describe all of the strange things I saw back then but couldn't name at the time—and the black man followed. And I roared off, trailing smoke, saying to myself, I am only going to ride this monster to see what it is like, and soon I will return to my family, to my wife, to my child, to my people, to my land. I never thought of that train ride as going off to meet (what I would later think of as) my destiny.

The engine hauled us across the border—yes, I learned to read maps! and everything else, as I'll explain soon—and rolled toward Minneapolis, where we stopped over a night before entraining again, for Chicago, and the museum where the black man studied.

What he studied, I soon learned, was me.

The black man's name was John Willoughby, and he was a student in the new science of anthropology, having worked under Boas (who had emigrated to the United States from Germany some years before) during the great man's brief stay in Chicago.

Student. Science. Anthropology. Boas. United States. Germany. All words whose meaning I eventually acquired. Fortunately—and unfortunately—I learned quickly.

By the time the train approached Minneapolis I was speaking a kind of pidgin English with Willoughby. By the time we reached Chicago—Big Village of Tall Tents, I was thinking of it to myself upon first sighting it—I was beginning to speak his language in a serious way.

"You learned fast," Willoughby said, a few years later looking back on our travels together.

"It's a matter of survival," I said. "If you don't learn quickly you have less of a chance to stay around." I tugged at my shirt collar, still somewhat unused to dressing like a city Indian.

"I understand that intelligence is distributed across the population of every group—there are smart Italians and dumb ones, smart Germans and dumb ones, smart Jews, all of that. But it's taken me a while to accept that the first Indian I came across in my studies would be as smart as you, Jimmy."

"Call it destiny, John. As far as the rest of it, I don't know how smart I am. But I knew men who were a lot smarter than me. Smart enough not to be curious about a black man standing at the train tracks, like a bit of meat set out to draw a bear."

"Oh," John said, "you had then and you still have great curiosity. Most men would have ridden over to see what was there."

"Which was you."

"Me, in person. My biology instructor at Harvard told me that all the knowledge in the world doesn't mean a damned thing, if you don't put your passions into it. So there I was, with all my knowledge, and damned passionate about it, waiting for you to ride down that rise. So I could continue my studies."

"You couldn't have predicted that I was going to be there."

"I knew someone like you would come along sooner or later. It was a big game crossing, according to the railroad. I had my bedroll and some supplies. I was prepared to camp there until someone like you arrived."

"You caught me like a fly in a web." (I hesitated to tell him, even after all the work we had done together, about the two female spirits who sent me right into his arms.)

"Yes, Fly-Wing struggled in my web."

"Very funny. I hadn't thought of it that way."

"One of the few things you haven't thought of."

"Oh," I said, reaching for a glass of water. (We were sitting in his office at the Field Museum, with heavy snow falling outside the window.) "I haven't thought about a lot of things, some of which I deliberately avoid, because they're so painful."

"I know—"

"You don't really," I said.

"But I do," he said. "I left my own tribe to study and work."

"You didn't leave your tribe to study and work on the plains,"
I said, "giving over your automobile for a horse."

"And my fieldwork? Don't I do just that?"

"Knowing you can turn around and go back to your city."

"And you can—"

"I know. But I haven't wanted to go home," I said. "I understand why, and at the same time I don't understand. It's been all too interesting here. I don't like myself for saying that, and sometimes I hate myself for living this way. One day I will go back, when I'm ready."

"I suffer that same illusion from time to time," Willoughby said.

"Do you?"

"Yes, I picture myself putting on a pair of dirty coveralls and climbing out of a horse car in Harlem and walking out into the old neighborhood. 'Hey, Johnny, boy,' old pals will call out to me. And I'll sit down on a stoop and drink homebrew from an old pickle jar, and things will begin to whirl around me if I make the slightest move, so I stay put, but they'll also get brighter and brighter the more I drink, and pretty soon someone will be playing an old breakdown on a harmonica, a blues that pulls your soul down and up the length of your body before extracting it with forceps from your heart, and girls will be up and dancing, and I'll have a hunger for one of them greater than any other appetite in my entire life, and I'll jump to my feet, crash that by-now empty jar onto the pavement, and charge into that dance until that black girl and I are mashing together up against the side of the alley, in the dark, but illuminating ourselves from within from our mutual raging desires...." He paused, and sipped tea from a cup. "But I couldn't do that."

"You couldn't?"

"No, not anymore than you could go back and participate in the Sun Dance with every bit of your heart and soul."

"We didn't—don't—practice the Sun Dance in our tribe," I said.

"Of course," he said. "Protestants are different from Baptists are different from Catholics. Rituals vary."

"We were—are—more like red-skinned Episcopalians," I said. "Nothing too deep. The Great Spirit hovered—damn!— *hovers* over all."

"So you don't see yourself as ever going back? You don't dream about it?"

"Is this an official interview? Am I informing you about Indian life now?"

Willoughby laughed. "We are just talking."

"Good. But I really don't have much more to say about the subject except what I am putting in my dissertation. You've read my draft. You know where I came from and what I look back upon."

"Yes, from pure aboriginal to city Indian in less than the time it takes to, pardon my metaphor, fatten a calf for market. Quite extraordinary, Jimmy. Quite extraordinary." He sighed deeply. "But then you are quite extraordinary."

"Sir, you should meet the rest of my tribe."

Willoughby clicked his teeth. "There are differences among us all. There is the difference between us and Boas and Willis. They have nothing mutual to look back upon. Europe. Indiana. Where's the depth for them that matches your old Indian soul or my old African one?" He caught himself and snorted out a laugh. "Soul! Listen to me! Whoever can measure that? Soul? I feel it sometimes, but I can't measure it."

Perhaps, I mused, I had traded my Indian soul, a Plains spirit, for a city soul. I hadn't looked back since the day I hopped onto that train. (At least, not during the day. At night it was a different story, which I'll get to in a moment.) Does that sound terribly cold and callous?

I knew that my family and clan would take care of my wife and child. We did well in that regard, because in a warrior culture we were losing men all the time and had an immediate and helpful reaction to such losses. Look at the way my family reacted when my father was lost. Yes, in a time of war, which was all the time in the time we lived in and had been for thousands of years, we did well. Our problem was how to live in a time of peace. And in a time of defeat, after which there would be no further wars.

But that matter lay outside the immediate boundaries of my scholarly work. The fact was, I worked for a number of years at the business of my education, packing in the first twelve years of school into about two or three, and then beginning the graduate work that Willoughby—and Willis, and Putnam, after him—said I was born for. I was quite successful at it, to be sure, but it also took quite a toll on me. To become a modern wonder—and go from an oral culture to a literary culture in a short space of time—took quite a toll. To write about myself in an objective manner could not have been more difficult than if I had become my own physician.

To be quite honest, I sometimes felt as though I were taking myself apart bone by bone and scrutinizing myself with an objectivity usually reserved for a pathologist. And yet I was as alive as anyone I knew! I immersed myself in knowledge, world upon world of knowledge flooded into my mind. And on top of that I was present at the birth of a discipline the world had never known before! And how many scholars could say that they were present at the birth of something new?

And yet even as anthropology was growing, one of the major subjects of American anthropologists, the native people, of whom I was obviously one, North American aboriginals, Indians, redskins, were dying. As it happened, I had grown up in a relatively isolated part of the Dakotas, and our people were not aware of much that was going on in the West, where Sitting Bull had commanded a vast army of us and defeated the hubristic Custer, a turning point in aboriginal–European American history.

Ironically, in the wake of that great victory, American Indians went into a great decline, beset by large numbers of Federal soldiers across the West and herded into reservations. If Sitting Bull had been defeated, the result would have been the same. History, which I discovered as a subject when I began my schooling in Chicago, had smiled on the Europeans and turned her back on us.

I knew from the Bible study I began along with my university courses that thousands of tribes had faded away and died over the course of thousands of years. Sumerians and Canaanites, and others too numerous to name, but when it came to considering the fact that my own tribe might be fading away and dying, I felt certain emotions that did not fit into the rigorous program of study I had set for myself. My Herb-Gatherer, my daughter! Mother and great-aunt and uncle! The fact that I had abandoned them only made my feelings for their loss deepen. (But how else was I to fulfill my sacred charge? I asked myself that question as often as every night, with a shot glass in front of me. But more of this—and there will be more, much more—later.)

"Do you feel something similar?" I asked Willoughby one night at the bar called the Hawk, which we frequented after our seminars. "Do you feel as though not only your people are disappearing but you too are fading away?"

"I fade," he said. "Because of my color, I do fade. Each day at twilight when the lights go down I fade into the shadows."

"You know the feeling then."

"But each sunrise brings me back again. And since most of the night I sleep, it's not such a bad way to live."

"For a part of the day, then, you become invisible?"

"Yes, I am, in that way, invisible."

"You are a fine scholar, John. Against the crowd of mediocrity you stand out."

"Except when I am invisible. At night. And on a street I stand out in my invisibility. Men stare. Women look away. Though sometimes it is just the opposite."

I raised my glass, and he raised his. "To visible invisibility!"

He repeated my toast and we both drank. "And yet...."

"Yes?" I said.

"I am a man full of hope. I could not be any other way. I grew up in the gutter. I went hungry. I wore rags. And yet here I am." He held up his glass as a sign of victory.

"Here you are," I said, touching my glass again to his.

"To me," John said.

"To you," I said, and we drank again.

"And now to you," he said.

"To me," I said.

"The disappearing...and reappearing Indian."

"Is that who I am?"

"If not, then who are you?"

"A good question," I said. "Who can answer that for himself, let alone for me?"

"You have to answer it for yourself, or else someone else will answer it for you, Jimmy."

"Is that why...?"

"Why what, sir?" He stared at me, and I stared back, matching eyeball for eyeball his strong inquisitive gaze.

"Why you plucked me from the prairie and put me to school?"

"Jimmy, I did no plucking. You moved yourself. You became your own pivot point and moved yourself onto that near-moving train, and then things began to move."

"True," I said, "I have to admit that. I was my own mover. Although"—and here I squinted into the haziness of the crowded bar, wondering if the spirits of the clamdigger woman and Tasáwiche might be hovering near, even in this foggy mob—"I had some help."

"Of course, of course," Willoughby said, thinking I was referring to him. And I let him think so.

I saw those spirit women again, later that night.

I had returned home, feeling quite woozy with drink, scarcely able to put one foot in front of the other. I was pleased with the conversation the two of us had had and felt a kinship with Willoughby, which I had suspected was always present but until this particular evening I couldn't really identify. We were brothers at the level of our skin, and beneath the skin as well.

"Although, he had an advantage over me," I said into the shadows of the park as I took my unsteady way home. He might fade at night, but he returned during the day. I felt as though I were in a constant fade, and that even as my hair and teeth and bones went invisible, I could only replace them with the knowledge that they once existed. I know this sounds difficult, if not opaque. But here is what came to me—that Willoughby's kin would grow stronger, breeding hard and fast, while my people, herded into reservations and sinking into a spiritual decline, might never regain our old advantage, of knowing who we were in relation to the land and lightning-filled sky and stars. We were, to use a phrase that was fashionable in my day, a vanishing breed.

And I? I, I, I…I stumbled up my steps and trembled with key in hand, as I unlocked the door to my apartment and pushed my way into the flimsy dark. Suddenly the world came crashing down on me in every way foreign and forbidding—the city street, street lamps, the steps to the door, the door itself, locked until I opened it with a key! Who was I to be living in such circumstances, in such a place as this, as if on another plane, in the world of spirits, as someone being punished for deeds beyond the ken of human beings? And yet even though I was standing in this here and now, I felt as though I were vanishing before my own eyes. All that I had studied until then had convinced me that everything I had once taken as truth was illusion, everything that I believed in now made a lie of everything in the world into which I had been born.

Once inside the door I could barely stand. What was I doing here? I summoned up all my will—and it took even more strength than I had to muster when I killed the bear—and told myself that my sense of fading away was exactly the point, and that I was here to prepare myself to help make a record of our fate before we vanished completely, or became so distant and strange to our old selves that none of us in the future would know ourselves in the old way—a fate worse than fading.

That's why I had done it, left all the old ways behind and embraced the new. In order to study the old and make it known.

"And to help him," came a voice in the dark.

"Oh, yes, and that too," I said to the clamdigger woman. "And who is he?"

"You will meet him," said Tasáwiche, whom I knew well enough now to recognize her voice in the dark.

"And until then?"

"Do what you're doing."

And so I did.

Library of Congress, Prints & Photographs Division, Edward S. Curtis Collection,
LC-USZ62-118599

sixteen

clara, clara, clara

AND ON SOME OF *those nights, when Edward, home from the field and exhausted, goes early to bed, I lie awake and think awful thoughts. What if he fell off a wagon and suffered a terrible hurt to his legs? What if this kept him from traveling? He could hobble to the studio each day and make portraits. We could arrange for that. But now he is planning another journey and thinks all the time about boarding a train, and traveling to the plains, and mounting a horse, and spending two days riding into the wilderness. Oh, no, he would not be able to do that. Oh, for a home-bound husband!*

Over he turns, like a large fish turning in the waters of the Sound, and I wonder about his breathing, which seems even and calm, and if I might take a coverlet or a blanket and put it over his mouth, and he would breathe no more!

Might he have similar thoughts about me?

These sinful thoughts of mine! I am a bad person in my own eyes, thinking these vile thoughts, until I see the children in the morning, around the table, eating breakfast, and I must laugh and sometimes sing a little tune and smile and keep the flag flying, because I can

*see it in his eyes, that their father has departed even before he has
left the house....*

*And when he left again, not that I wasn't expecting it, I felt such a
letting down, such a feeling of falling off, that it was almost as
though parts of me had sloughed off the rest of my body, my face, my
breasts, my knees, my feet. The children found me that morning,
curled up in a ball beneath the bedcovers, trembling, as though with
fever.*

*Hal—so helpful. "Mama, I'm going to fetch the doctor." I
pleaded with him to stay at home.*

*And Beth? Her father's daughter, she seemed to have little
sympathy for her mother's plight. Yet she insisted, "You must sit up,
Mama. You must drink water."*

*While Florence curled up with me and wept. That helped me to
calm myself because I had to remain calm for her. "There, there,
child. There, there."*

"Is Papa coming back?"

*"Of course he is," I told her. And I knew that he would. It wasn't
as if he had abandoned us for good. But the finiteness of his leaving
did not help to lessen the loneliness—felt more intensely by the children than me, I believed—or the despair (an emotion children
cannot experience, or so I believed). Oh, alone, in this crowded
house! I decided to get up and get dressed. The last thing I wanted
was to have everyone gathered around me, caring for me when I
didn't need that kind of care.*

*Still, there were moments when sadness and longing seemed
inevitable.*

"Mama," Florence whimpered, "where is he?"

*"There, there," I told her. "He's climbing a mesa. He's making
portraits of the Indians who live on the top of it."*

"What's a mesa, Mama?"

"A mountain, but with a flat top, with a top like a table. 'Mesa' in the Spanish language means 'table.' Did you know that?"

"No, Mama," Florence said.

"I know it," Hal said, but he was imagining that he knew Spanish. He had become good at his numbers, and he could read. But where in our city he could have learned Spanish, I could not have said. "Chabama la moka dalada...." He spoke made-up words, proving me right.

I stood a while in my nightclothes, staring out at the blue sky beyond the bedroom window. A rainless day, and there might be a few whitecaps on the Sound, as often there were in windy weather. I felt buffeted by a wind at my back. Something called to me from the water, perhaps the water itself. It said to me, you can be free as you like out here on the Sound, you can sail, you can swim, you can float with the tides. But I was nothing if not practical. The children needed me, an old, old story. And so after a short time of folding pity around myself like a blanket, I put on a dressing gown and prepared to cook breakfast. If I was going to have to conduct myself as though I were a some-time widow, I was also going to have to play the part of mother and wife.

"Come, children," I said. "Time for school for you and you."

"And me, too?" said perky, little Florence.

"No, you doll of a child, you get to stay home with me."

"But I want to go to school."

"Next year," I said.

"Chicklada pamada," Florence said, trying to sound like Hal and thinking it would help.

"Oh, Spanish girl. Sorry, sorry, not until next year. But think of it."

"What, Mama?"

"While your brother and sister go to school, you can come with me to the studio and watch your father's helpers make portraits."

"No, I don't want to" she said.

"Yes," I said. "Mama has to help with the business."

"No, I want to see water."

"You sweet girl," I said, taking her hand, "you want to take a boat ride to the old house, don't you?"

"Yes, Mama."

"You love the water, don't you?"

"Yes, Mama."

"Perhaps you were born part water," I said.

"Yes, Mama."

"Then," I said, taking her up in my arms, "can I drink you?"

"Oh, no, no," she said in a rapid series of giggles. "No, no, no, no, no...."

The fact of that child giggling, so happy, kept me alive through the rest of a long day. Only at night, alone in our bed, did I think about the days and weeks and months they were living without their father. And me again without a husband.

Library of Congress, Prints & Photographs Division, Edward S. Curtis Collection, LC-USZ62-66669

seventeen

in the field

THE CAMP OF LONE PINE, Chief of the Salish, or Flatheads, stood on the banks of the Red Willow River, a beautiful stream flowing through the forests of the Bitterroot Mountains, in what we now call western Montana. Its cold, translucent waters come from the springs and snows far up among the mountain crags.

Beautiful lodges or tepees made from the dressed skins of buffalo and elk were scattered everywhere among the pines. The village was like the camps of hundreds of other Indian chiefs, or local head men, which stood beside the forest stream, by the quiet brook of the open plain, by the lake in the mountains, or on the grassy bank of the prairie lake. These people never adopted a campsite by chance, but chose them for a definite purpose. In some cases, the object was fishing; in others, to hunt the buffalo, or elk and deer; or to dig roots and gather berries and other wild fruits.

The hour is that of a new day, just before the sun lifts itself from the forested peaks to the east. Here and there low voices of mothers speak to children; a woman calls to another to be awake, and not to hold too long upon the sleep. Now the smoke curls upward from the lodge-tops and from fires built in the open just outside. To the nostrils comes the fragrant odor of burning pine. Soon the savory smell of roasting meat will announce that the women are preparing the morning meal.

There is a hushed feel of excitement and anticipation. Only yesterday a rumor reached the chief of two strange wanderers who on this day would arrive at the camp. The wanderers? Edward and yours truly, his faithful assistant.

Only two days before, at the westernmost reaches of the high plains, we had ridden with Grinnell to the top of a high bluff and witnessed the gathering of the Blackfeet, Piegan, and Blood tribes, who had come together for the annual Sun Dance. Hundreds and hundreds of tepees stretched to the horizon, and the sound of thousands of horses rose erratically on the wind.

"My God," Edward said. "An ocean of Indians!" And sitting atop his horse, he let the reins fall slack and held out his arms as wide as he could, as if to hold the great gathering of people within his own embrace. "If there were someone, a chief, a god, anyone, to whom I could swear an oath," he said in a voice suffused with passion, "I would swear it. I will give my life to all of this!"

eighteen

jimmy fly-wing's story—7

*Standing on the bare ground,—my head bathed
by the blithe air, and uplifted into infinite space,—
all mean egotism vanishes. I become a transparent
eye-ball; I am nothing; I see all; the currents of the
Universal Being circulate through me; I am part or
particle of God. The name of the nearest friend
sounds then foreign and accidental: to be brothers, to
be acquaintances,—master or servant, is then a trifle
and a disturbance. I am the lover of uncontained and
immortal beauty. In the wilderness, I find something
more dear and connate than in streets or villages. In
the tranquil landscape, and especially in the distant
line of the horizon, man beholds somewhat as beautiful as his own nature.*

—EMERSON, NATURE

MY STUDIES CONSUMED ME. That powerful engine that had first
carried me away out of the prairie world I had known was nothing
compared to the force of my desires when it came to what I needed
to read and what I found myself writing, about myself, and my

people, and what it meant that we all found ourselves becoming ghosts even before we found ourselves fully alive.

I came to suffer an odd condition. Newspapers proclaimed in headlines various events, large and small, and though I slept easily after long days and nights of study, I never had a dream, not one, about myself, only about the passing parade of the world around me.

February 23, 1905
TWENTY YEARS HUSBAND HE IS LOVER STILL
Theodore Sutro of New York Sends Missives to Wife on Each
Anniversary
IS ARDENT IN DEVOTIONS
His "Dearest One" Has Assertions Perpetual Love Printed as
Gifts

TEN COUNCILMEN REJECT GAS LEASE

DUNNE IS MAYOR
VICTOR BY 24–454

GENERAL STRIKE NOW THREATENS

WHEN INTERCESSION COMES, IT IS BELIEVED
ROOSEVELT WILL CONFER DIRECTLY
WITH THE CZAR

ROOSEVELT RAPS DISHONEST RICH

The world, oh, the odd world into which I had been born again! I became my own engine, devouring book after book, day after day, reading works that introduced me to the beginning of the history of the world and its various peoples—and what a shock that would have been to my old self, that all these other people abounded all around the world, who saw themselves as The People!—and building a geography in my mind of places so far beyond the territory I had first known that I might as well have been living on another planet. Perhaps I had been.

The nomadic life of my first family seemed, when I was a child, to be as much a part of nature as the earth and sky—oh, Sky! My earliest guide and hope, in dreams and in waking life!—but when here, now, I was sitting in a library in Chicago, surrounded by stacks filled with books, each one opening a new world, and much more convincing to me as I stared at them than any dream-vision I had when I was younger. As a child I had known only one "book" and that was the world in which I lived. Now each of these volumes made a world, and I stepped from one to another to another, as I might have stepped on rocks to take me across a raging stream in springtime.

I moved along at a rapid pace, like a starved man who has suddenly discovered food. I devoured books, taking in one volume after another after another, until I began, after a year or so, to feel that I had some direction. Like a tracker on the wide prairie who has found a new sign in the dust or picked up a new scent on the air, I became even more relentless in my reading, even as I widened my studies to include physical science and the new field of psychology, as well as the history and literature I had first taken to so well.

Oh, Scythians and Egyptians, Indians and Bactrians, Libyans and Cyrenaeans! I sailed with Herodotus and met him and his odd customs, and I speculated with Plato about lost undersea civilizations and roamed ancient Gaul with Julius Caesar and wandered across Asia with Marco Polo. Oh, the many voyages I took in my mind!

And acquired mathematics, for which it seemed, along with many languages, I had a certain propensity, which made physics a lark, and chemistry, and biology, where I found the work of Darwin as interesting as any of the great novels by Cervantes, Manzoni, Stendhal, and the proliferating fiction of Balzac, which consumed the few hours I allotted for leisure each day. And Homer and Chaucer and Shakespeare, yes, and Boccaccio, the only writer I discovered who wrote about what transpired in the dark between the sexes with any real joy and appreciation!

This last of course was the only part of my new life that I found wanting. The affection bestowed on me first by my great-aunt and later by Herb-Gatherer gave me a great reserve of calm, but the longer I stayed in the library and in my apartment, the more of it I expended. So that if Plato is correct, my desire built up in me, filling up the cavities in my body until it finally reached my brain, and one night, while deep in the reading of Gogol's *Dead Souls*, I suddenly slammed the book closed, putting all thoughts of Russia and serfdom aside, and jumped up from my desk. Within minutes I was walking through the cold moonlit Chicago night toward the lights of the neighborhood tavern where faculty and students gathered.

I was ready, oh, I was ready, but, oh, what was I ready for?

The air was exhilarating, the stink of sour beer and cigar smoke in the bar nearly overwhelming. The familiar faces of a number of fellow class members and thesis students lightened my heart. Here I could find sympathy, if not for my feeling of loneliness and isolation, at least for the burden of work that I had taken on, so similar to that of the others (though more so).

"Hey, chief," said the bartender, a red-nosed young man with hair too silver for his age. "What'll it be?"

"I'm not a chief," I said, as I always did when he called me that, "only a warrior."

"Whatever you are, I've still got the same question, fellow. What'll it be?"

"A deep philosophical question, pertaining to existence."

"Sure, Mike. And pertaining to whiskey, too."

I ordered a drink and drank it quickly. And then another. A few fellow graduate students came up and tried to engage me in conversation, but I pushed them away.

The Irish liquor made a swirling mess of my thoughts and by the time Willoughby came in through the door I was in distress. All of my enthusiasm for the night had withered away. My heart felt like a stone chilled by the icy regions at the bottom of a winter ocean and yet, amid the smoke and above the din of voices raised in conversation—with many of my fellow students arguing one point or another about the methods and conclusions of our discipline, about the differences between science and history, and between ontology and evolution—I heard voices more persistent than any of the rest, urging me, now that I had nearly completed my studies, to see beyond them and keep focused on my quest.

And what would that be again?

To help the shadow catcher, said the sweet voice in my head..

Of course, of course.

"Are you feeling unwell?" my black mentor asked me.

"No," I said, "not at all."

"You look a little under the weather."

"Not at all," I said again, and to demonstrate my good health and good cheer, I downed another whiskey.

"What an extraordinary fellow you are," Willoughby said.

"No, no," I said. "I see plenty of men in here drinking as much as I am."

"That's not what I meant."

"You're referring to my studies?"

"I am."

"I amaze myself in that regard."

"You should. No one I've ever heard of since J. S. Mill has studied so much in so little time."

"Mill? What tribe was he? How did I miss him?"

Willoughby leaned so close to me that I could see the very pores on his dark cheeks.

"Church of England, I believe."

"Not a pagan like yours truly?"

"He worshipped the past." His eyes glazed over like pond-ice in winter. "Or was that Ruskin?"

"Are you confused? I haven't known you to be confused."

"I haven't achieved perfection yet. If a black man ever can."

"Or an Indian?"

"You are in a good place, sir," Willoughby said, lowering his voice so that, because of all the raucous conversation in the room, I could scarcely make out what he said next. "I hear good things are coming."

"And what might they be?"

"I understand that your advisor has spoken to the head of the press."

"Spoken about what?"

"Your story."

"My story?"

"Your dissertation."

"Willoughby, with all due respect, there is a great distinction between a story and a dissertation, and you are quite well aware of that."

"Your advisor, yes, he is—and he, we, have great hopes."

"As do I. But since I haven't revised it yet, I'd prefer to put my hopes aside and concentrate on the work that comes first." I emptied my glass and looked around for the bartender.

"Jimmy, do you always drink this much?"

"This is a case of the pot calling the kettle black, isn't it?"

"I already am black," Willoughby said, and we had a laugh at that.

I took him by the arm. "Listen to me. I am shaving a bit of time from my work. Drinking helps me to avoid thinking about what I need to do when I return to my desk. Otherwise, I would be thinking about it all the time."

"Fair enough," Willoughby said. "I know you don't need my permission, but please continue."

"I intend to," I said. "Whether or not you give me permission."

"Touché," he said. I watched him as I might have watched a man teetering on the edge of a precipice, and then pulled him back.

"I appreciate everything you have done for me, John," I said.

"I don't think I've ever done a better thing," he said. "Not even for myself."

"Five years, now," I said. "And it's still a great adventure."

Willoughby nodded his head. "It's a monk's life is what it is."

Visions of monasteries and dark-robed, holy men—images of rock-hewn fortresses of the Christian god—pictures I had seen in books that I had riffled through in my recent studies in everything not myself.

"Monks," I said, feeling now ever so slightly intoxicated.

"It is not easy," Willoughby said, reaching across the space between us and laying his hand on mine. I straightened up and stared at him, as I withdrew my hand. He stared back at me, and then looked away. "I must go. I have an early…." His voice trailed away.

"Goodnight, John," I said, and watched as he slowly disengaged himself. I noticed that the bartender was staring at me.

"Another whiskey," I said, in as sharp a voice as I could muster, as Willoughby slouched out the door.

"Chief?" A plump young woman with a gray streak that ran vertically across her otherwise dark head of hair sidled up to me at the bar. "You're a chief, aren't you?" she said, an appraising look in her eye. I could feel my heart thudding in my chest, as if I had just been surprised by an animal on the plains. Or as if I were an animal, surprised by a hunter.

I cocked my head, feeling both annoyed and proud that she had singled me out. "I'm a warrior," I said.

"Oh, you are, are you?"

"Yes, and who are you?"

"A clerical," she said, with a little wink. "Not a cleric, because the good Church doesn't recognize women as...."

"As?" I said.

"As? As independent," she said. She told me she considered herself an independent woman and had come for a drink with a friend, another secretarial worker from the museum, who had since gone home. The students in the place bored her. Working at the school, as she did, she knew too much about them. But she didn't know much about me.

All this she told me while I drank another whiskey, and another, and she drank along with me. "I'd like to know more," she said. And then she slid off the stool onto the floor.

You—Western-minded readers—know that I have killed men in battle. But in my mind, having left my wife and child and family and clan and tribe behind was the worst act I had yet performed. Watching that woman lying at my feet, turning slowly in the sawdust, the pale flesh above the border of her dark stockings revealed for all to see, I could not bear to commit another horrendous deed.

I climbed off my stool, reached down, and hauled her to her feet. "I am going to take you home," I said. And with the effort it might have taken to carry several large buffalo robes, I helped her stumble to the front door and out onto the street. "Where do you live?" I asked.

She rolled her eyes up into her eye-sockets. Saliva dribbled down her chin.

Two men stepped out of the bar.

"Do you know this woman?" I asked.

They waved me away and walked off along the street.

"Where do you live?" I asked again.

She mumbled, dribbled, staggered along.

I could do nothing else but bring her to my house. Once I had helped her up the steps, she seemed to gain a bit more control of herself, standing against the wall on her own while I unlocked the door to my apartment. But that was deceptive. Once inside, she staggered forward a few steps and fell onto the sofa. I kneeled before her, hoping she had not broken any bones or injured her face. Sure enough, a thin trickle of blood ran from one of her nostrils down onto her upper lip.

"Miss?" I said. "Miss?" She lay there absolutely still, and I began to worry, because having read, among other things, the necessities of American jurisprudence, I knew that I might be thought responsible if she died here in my apartment.

"Chief...." The words bubbled up through her unsealed lips.

"Ah," I took in a breath. "Miss. Where do you live?" She answered me by vomiting all over herself.

I, who had dressed deer with great ease, found it difficult to strip the clothing from a woman who was all deadweight. But using a kitchen knife and my natural manual dexterity, I removed her stained dress, cutting and peeling down to her undergarments, which I would have left alone if she had not, with a second round of vomiting, soiled herself again down the front.

Propping her up against some pillows, I left her for a moment to wet some towels and returned to find her still upright but sleeping peacefully, her pale skin a canvas on which moonlight illuminated the delicate pink of her nipples and the shadow of fine dark ash between her legs. After I had cleaned her up, I put my ear to her mouth and listened to her breathing, and then put my ear to her chest and listened for a moment there. A faint odor of bile still clung to her skin. Again, I cleaned her face and neck, and left her to fetch a spread from the bedroom. I gently lay her down onto the length of the sofa and covered her with the spread.

It was a long while that I sat there listening. The moon disappeared. Shadow upon shadow engraved themselves on the finer dark of the apartment. What animals did I see in the air? What spirits? I blinked. The woman still slept.

"Now," the voice came to me.

I counted what money I had and packed a small bag. Dawn was rising, as I made my way to Union Station, where I bought a ticket on the first train West.

Library of Congress, Prints & Photographs Division, Edward S. Curtis Collection, LC-USZ62-110962

nineteen

the zigzag years—1

AND FROM THE FIELD to home again, where he began to despise himself for not being able to give himself completely to the children when he was finally able to spend time with them. As to Clara, the situation sometimes veered toward the intolerable for both of them.

"Again?" Clara said to him in bed one night in the winter of their thirteenth year of marriage.

"The tribes," Edward said. "There's not enough time."

"They've been here a thousand years or more before you arrived," she said. "I expect they'll be around another thousand after you die."

"But unrecorded," he said. "Unphotographed. Who will know what they were like? Who will know?"

"Who will care?" Clara said. Her voice was suddenly harsh—as if she had drunk a bitter potion.

The next morning, while Edward was working at the studio, Clara left him a note and took the children on the ferry and visited with Edward's mother and younger brother who had moved back across the Sound. It shocked him to come home that evening and find the house empty. He took a boat to catch up with them, appearing somewhat breathless and upset when he arrived at his mother's house.

The children came running, as always, with Beth in the lead and Hal bringing up the rear, hand in hand with Edward's mother.

"Papa," Beth said. "We missed you."

"I was only working at the studio, darling," he said.

"Away is away, Edward," his mother said. "Except for Asahel, I am all alone myself, as you know. And it has not been easy."

"I know, mother," he said.

"I was very happy when Clara brought the children over."

"Yes, I'm sure," he said, as Clara appeared in the doorway. "I missed you."

"You know something now of the way it feels to us," Clara said.

When they were alone, he said, "That was an awful thing to do, absconding with the children like that. I didn't know where you had gone."

"And do you think your absences have no effect on them?"

"Edward," his mother said, "you must pay them more attention."

"Is this a civil war?" he said. "And have you chosen sides?"

"It is not a war, Edward," his mother said, "but it is a struggle."

Clara smiled triumphantly, and he looked down at the floor. To be caught like this, between his familial duties and his aspirations—it was more than intolerable. Where once at the beginning the project overtook his finances only, it had now overtaken his everyday life. In what he later thought of as his zigzag years, as he made more and more field trips—to the Hopi, the Crow, the Hidatsa, the Arikara, the Sioux, among many others—an odd condition began to affect his memory. The more pictures he made, the less he remembered other parts of his life, and when he looked back, even after just a month or so, the only thing he could recall were the portraits and the odd bit of information, usually pertaining to the project.

Out in the field with the Mandan tribe, he missed Clara's birthday. Out in the field with the Kalispel, he missed their wedding anniversary. Not to mention all the children's birthdays that he missed. None of them was pleased.

"I beat a birthday drum with the Sioux," he told Hal returning home the next year about a month too late for his seventh. "With a man named Jimmy Fly-Wing."

"That's a funny name," Hal said.

"It may sound strange to us," his father said. "But he is a very smart fellow, and he showed up out of nowhere and has become very helpful in our research. He speaks a large number of Indian languages, and he knows everything about their religions and their dreams. He's even been to college, a rarity among his people."

Hal looked glum. "Pop, am I smart fellow?"

"Of course, you are, Hal." Edward took his son around and gave him a bear hug. "I'm sorry I missed your birthday."

"Did you miss me?"

"Truly, I did," Edward said.

"That's all right, Daddy," Beth said, giving her older brother a look that said never mind.

"It's not," Hal said. "We want you here."

"Your mother has been coaching you to say this, hasn't she?"

Hal lowered his head, his body weighed down with gloom. "No."

Beth gave him a big, wide smile. "Yes, she has."

Hal glanced up at her. "Liar," he said.

"No, I'm not," Beth said.

Their quarrelling only made him feel worse, and the cure for that was to head out again.

Once again, having left Clara and the children in Seattle, he descended for the second time into the canyon of the Colorado to do further work with the Havasupai, the Blue Water People,

and, of course, to see Tasáwiche, his beautiful aesthetic obsession. Clara faded in his mind, and Tasáwiche rose in his
thoughts like a full moon above the canyon. The closer he got
to her, the more he studied her portrait in his mind's eye.

When we arrived at the bottom of the canyon, the shock of
catching sight of his Havasupai girl standing outside her father's
house turned his head upside down. It was as if his art had come
to life, and it was all he could do to remind himself that all the
while we had been away, she had gone on living.

"Hello!" he called out to her.

She stepped inside and then came out again, as though
waking herself from a dream. "Curts," she said as he came
walking up to her. "You went away."

"And now I'm back."

"Time passed," she said. Or was it, "time past?"

Down in this vast declivity, time flowed forward like the river,
rushing in the center of the stream, pooling at certain places in
the bank. We worked all day in the heat of the canyon valley. We
grew hungry. We ate tortillas made from the corn whose silk
rippled in the warm wind of the canyon floor. All the while he
kept his eye on the girl, and she made her presence known to
him, flitting here, appearing there, as a spirit might, trying to
communicate from another world.

The ups and downs of his life in these years were something
Edward could scarcely bear to think about. But down here in
the canyon of the Blue Water People, he suffered the deepest—
and purest—emotions about any woman he had ever known, a
woman for whom without even touching her, he had betrayed
his wife. Time, wind, and water might wear away his own frame,
and all earthly creatures might bend against the strain, but she
would stay with him always unchanged and unfettered, the
emblem, the engine, of his mind's longest desires.

Tasáwiche.

That night he dreamed that he awoke on a ledge, in the dark, the stars flowing above him in the narrow slot of the canyon opening like a river below and in the sky above—his body came alive and he pressed close to her in his dream and she became a bird—*shakwakwa*—and he became a fox and then a hawk. The momentum of their affection knew no bounds, and yet it boxed them in everywhere and every which way. He heard an owl cry out in the night, the music of his childhood home, and for a brief while, it calmed his mind.

Ay, dream! Ay, Tasáwiche. Ay, *shakwakwa*…and the fox ran along with the bird.

twenty

meeting jimmy fly-wing

IN ALL THAT I have written so far about Edward, his life, and our work together in the field I have tried my best to stay as close to the truth as I can. This doesn't mean that I have not gotten some of the facts wrong, too. Where I have depended on Edward's recollections of events, within his family and without, to which I have not been witness, there has always been the possibility—as in the recollection of any human being—of his getting the facts wrong. There is also the chance of me further compounding error by mistranscribing some of his descriptions and recollections—though I would hope that if this has happened it has not happened in any major way. (Any errors in dates and order of public events are mine, and I take responsibility for them.)

The errors—that is just the cost of employing memory, the foundation of storytelling, which, by its very nature, changes and shapes the facts into something larger than just one thing happening after another. Telling one thing after another is chronicling; shaping and forming belongs to history and poetry. Memory is about the shape of things we see as we look back. Aristotle says in his *Poetics* that history is a record of what happened, and poetry is a record of what ought to have happened, and in writing this story so far, I have to say that the distance between the two seems to grow more and more narrow by the word. All of which is merely to preface my account—my recollection!—of Edward meeting Jimmy Fly-Wing for the first time.

A man of dark skin and long, dark hair twisted into two braids, wearing the trousers of a city dweller and a cowboy shirt, riding a big mahogany horse into our campsite near Flathead Lake—that was my first sight of Jimmy.

It was summer, and we had been enjoying a stretch of good weather, warm sun, light winds, with cool nights only making the dawns more enjoyable because of the warmth they promised. That particular morning Edward had arisen before me and had gone off to the lake to inquire about a young man, Blackfeet, I believe he was, who was supposed to have several beautiful grizzly-bear robes. So I was alone, out there on the edge of an encampment, when Jimmy came trotting up to our tent.

"Good morning," he said, reining in his horse, whose loud breathing gave evidence of a long ride.

"Good morning," I said.

"Beautiful morning," he said.

"Quite beautiful," I said. I immediately took notice of his accent, or lack of it. This man had the appearance of a Plains Indian but spoke like one of my instructors at Northwestern. The only thing missing was his tie, jacket, and shoes. Jimmy wore beautiful tooled leather boots, each emblazoned with the zigzag sign of snake and lightning.

"Are you Mr. Edward Curtis?" he asked, staring down at me with a pair of piercing brown eyes.

I laughed and turned aside. "I'm not that gifted," I said. "But come on down off that horse. You're making me nervous, sir. Edward should be back after a while."

Jimmy immediately dismounted and stood before me, about my own medium height, in a ready stance, balanced on the balls of his feet, as though he could begin almost anything—from a footrace in which he would leave me behind in the dust, a spelling bee, hand-to-hand combat, or a brisk discussion on the ontological argument for God. (It wasn't that this man seemed to be a person unsure of who he was and what he wanted to do. On the contrary, he seemed, more so than anyone else I had ever met, "to contain multitudes," as wrote our poet Whitman.)

"You don't mind if I wait?" Jimmy glanced up at the sky and then to the north in the direction of the lake, as though he might almost have been able to detect Edward's presence over some distance.

"Not at all," I said, introducing myself. "I'm William Myers."

"You're the amanuensis," Jimmy said. "Ah!"

"I don't use that word in these parts," I said, amused, in fact, at his use of it, "but yes, that's who I am." "Erudite fellow," I said to myself. "Scholar on horseback"—which turned out to be quite true.

"I've got to water my horse," he said in his next breath.

"Of course," I said, watching him lead his animal over toward the stream that ran along the northern line of our camp. "Quite a man," I said, again to myself, "at ease with the likes of me and with his animals."

"We've been riding almost all night," he said when he returned from the creek. "Came in on the train to Missoula, and then rode the rest of the way in under two days."

"And you came from where, sir?"

"Been all over," he said. "East to Chicago, north to Saskatchewan, west to the Pacific, south, well, almost all the way to the Mexican border."

"Sounds a lot like everywhere to me," I said. "And you said Chicago? That's my home territory. Grew up, went to school there."

"That's how I got there," Jimmy said, "school."

He talked a bit about his studies, leaving me quite impressed. I have to say that I immediately concluded that in many ways he would be a much better assistant to Edward in our work than I was, but I got over that quickly—mainly because he was so likeable a fellow. In fact, I don't know that I ever met anyone quite like him, outside of hearing about many-skilled heroes in some old Greek poems. Was he too good to be true? Yes? But when I looked at him, heard the timbre of his voice, looked into his eyes—he had a deep, deep look, but not one that gave you the shivers, as was sometimes the case when you met shaman-istic Indians along the way. His look was more one that reas-sured you, gave you the news that however much this fellow might be tied to the very old traditions of a past almost all disap-peared except for a few people like him, he was also someone with his feet planted firmly in the here and now—and taking all this together my body gave a little shudder of recognition, as I admitted to myself that this man could be very helpful in our investigations.

"You must be tired out," I said. "Would you care for some breakfast while we're waiting for Edward to return?"

He did care for some. And while I cooked—oh, I've picked up some skills in our years in the field, and who knows what's to come?—he asked about our project, about which, he said, he had heard quite a bit from meeting people in various tribes around the West.

"What have you heard?" I asked.

"I heard a few grumbles from some professorial folks about how Curtis is asking the people to put on the old robes and headdresses to pose for his photographs, but from people who live out here, I've heard nothing but good. Even when Curtis buys a carving here or a necklace there, he does it to put some money in the hands of people who need it.

"I've heard that. And how he sees us not the way we will become but the way we have been. We don't want to lose that, because that would be losing our way. God damn, we're already well down that road."

"God damn?" I thought to myself. "God damn? Who is this fellow, anyway?"

Edward had no doubts, not from the first moments of their first encounter. He came riding up some hours later, a lush bearskin tied onto the back of the horse, and made his beast trot faster, the closer he came to where Jimmy and I stood, still talking in front of our tent.

As if in some old story, as if in some myth—and why it happened, Edward told me later, he could not, could never, explain; it was just a feeling he had, just a hunch—Edward jumped down from his horse, as excited as I'd ever seen him, and thrust out a hand toward Jimmy. "Well, well," Edward said, "I thought you'd never get here!"

Jimmy gave him a big smile as they shook hands, as though he were hearing music the rest of us couldn't hear and was about to pass it along.

twenty-one

some close calls

I DON'T KNOW IF it was Jimmy's presence among us on many of our new field trips, or if Edward had decided in his heart that he did not want the family to feel neglected—he never told me —but he began to make plans that would bring him and the children together in a regular way. When the Seattle schools let them out for summer, Clara would pack for them and all of them would ride, most of the way by train, and then by wagon, to Edward's latest worksite. In the summer of 1906, this meant that they traveled to Holbrook, Arizona, where we were working with the Apache nearby. Great mesas to the north, the mountains to the south, the dusty plain before them—the children would remember this all of their lives.

"I knew how much I missed them when I was away," Edward said to Clara, soon after they arrived in the hamlet of tents on the outskirts of the large Apache village, "but I hadn't anticipated how much of a joy it would be to see them at play like this...."

Hal raced around the encampment with the son of one of the chiefs. The girls rushed up and down in the dust, touching a pole at one end of the Apache village and running to the other end, and then back again. Dusty, dusty, dusty play, and delightful!

During this visit, we were working with the medicine chief, a leathery-skinned old man named Gosh-o-ne, who had only one good eye. The medicine men of the Apache are most influential personages. They are usually men of more than ordinary ability, claiming, through their many deities and their knowledge of the occult and the ominous, to have supernatural power. In sickness, any individual may make supplications to the deities, but the prayers of the medicine men are accepted as being the most efficacious.

Gosh-o-ne was quite wary of us, but since a younger rival of his was trying to present his vision to the tribe, Gosh-o-ne seemed to think it was a good idea to work with us rather than let his rival take up our interest. Our first few days were grueling exercises in diplomacy. Gosh-o-ne did not want to give away anything. Every Apache medicine man has a medicine skin inscribed with the symbolism of the tribal mythology. With his prayer wands, he beseeches the symbolic figures, praying to the mythical characters that are regarded as attached to the particular ailment under treatment.

Gosh-o-ne was gracious; he had the children of his acolytes show the Curtis children many of the sights around the camp. He fed us; he smoked a pipe with us. He showed us his buckskin. But he would not take the next step and talk about it. Even after a week, we had gotten nowhere. We understood that he was holding back from us, that he didn't want to tell us the truth.

Edward's family occupied one tent, and I lived in a smaller one where we worked, all of us just outside the perimeter of the Indian village. Jimmy usually rode out into the far field, scouting for new informants, disappearing at sundown and reappearing in the mornings, his whereabouts at night a mystery to us that we never thought too much about. After Clara put the children to bed, she often drifted over to our work tent.

"They're in dreamland, Edward," she said.

"Both waking and sleeping," he said. "They appear to be having a wonderful time."

"They wore themselves out. I worry about them playing so hard every day for the next few weeks."

"Children thrive on it," he said. "Don't fret."

"I'm not fretting. I do just worry sometimes."

"Worry? About what?"

She looked over at me.

"How long will this go on?" Clara asked.

"A few weeks. I've told you that, Clara," Edward said.

"I meant the entire project, as you call it."

"Until our work in the field is complete," he said.

"That could be months," she said.

He nodded. "Perhaps two or three more years," he said.

Clara took in a deep, deep breath. "The field," she said. "The field. I don't like it in the field, Edward. You see how I worry about the children and I'm too uncomfortable." I didn't want to hear the remainder of this conversation, but unless I left the tent and walked to the edge of the village, there would be nothing else to do but listen.

Fortunately, two of the medicine chief's helpers approached the tent, and Clara was the one to excuse herself, going back to where the children slept, so that, as she told Edward, she might get some rest herself.

Gosh-o-ne appeared, with his buckskin, for some reason finally giving in to our request. With the painted deerskin spread before him, he crooned songs and prayers, in the hope of hearing the voices of celestial messengers, and told us stories (which I approximated in English) of creation and destruction, of the origins of things and prophecies for the end of this world, until the fires settled to flickering embers in the tent. Edward and I spent a while transcribing our notes into longer stories. It was tedious, working by lamplight, but it was better than using a flickering fire or candles, though I wonder if we had known that this would be our lot for so many nights for so many decades, if we would have pushed forward with as much attention and vigor as we did.

Two weeks of nights filled with work went by, and when we grew tired, we sometimes stepped outside the tent and stared up at the stars—or rather, Edward did, more than I. He would stretch his arms toward the sky and wiggle his fingers, as though he might, if he stood on tiptoe in his heavy boots and added just another tiny bit more of a stretch, touch fingertips to the hot, flickering pinpoints above and pull himself up there among them.

His family lay sleeping, but he could not have been more awake. His thoughts whirled about the sky, splashing from one galaxy to the next, and lighting, as it happened, on the slender crescent of the earliest rising moon in the southeast. Suddenly, in a quite uncharacteristic state of mind, he found himself muttering a quiet prayer, just as his father might have done when finding himself in a period of what might pass as peril.

"Oh, Lord," he breathed out, "please give me the strength to continue this work until it is done and the wisdom to allow me to do it right."

From in the distance came the whinny of a horse, Jimmy's perhaps, skirting the edge of the camp. "Is that you, Lord, speaking to me in the voice of that animal?"

Silence, silence, silence, silence, silence. A breeze blew up out of nowhere, quite cool for the place and the season.

Silence....

The children were sleeping. He cast his mind over them like a protective blanket—and over Clara, too. In his mind, he touched a gentle hand to her sleeping head. She was in so many ways one of the most skillful people he knew—the way she raised the children (except that she was a bit too cautious) and the way she ran the business while he was away. (Oh, what disasters might be in the making with both of them away right now!) There was just some *something* that had gotten between them, some irritant that kept them from meshing and running smoothly together, some speck in the lens of things. And he would say that it had never been there before he had begun working on his project, except that, he would be the first to admit, he had paid so little attention to her wants and ways of seeing things before he began what he took to be this great work of his that he couldn't say for certain that the trouble hadn't been there waiting from the start.

There was a rumble of thunder from somewhere in the darkness, far away toward the western mountains. The gods are trying to tell me something, he decided. But what might that be? Could the answer to his question come in the form of the young Indian assistant to Gosh-o-ne, who appeared suddenly in front of him?

"What?" Edward gave a shiver. "You startled me," he said.

The young man didn't understand English, and so Edward had to rouse me from the tent to speak with him and translate. Within minutes we were meeting with Gosh-o-ne in his medicine tent, where the air reeked of herbs, dried blood, and other odors we could not identify. We sat on robes before a low fire in front of the chief, who had bowed his head and remained silent while his two young assistant medicine chiefs chanted in low guttural voices, and now and then picked up drums and beat them lightly with their hands. We waited and waited.

Finally, Gosh-o-ne spoke. "I have hesitated," he said (all this I translated for Edward), "until the spirit came to me and said that I could go on."

"Good," Edward said, "very good."

The chief spoke on, as though Edward had not said a word. "The knowledge that I am going to impart to you is dangerous. To give this knowledge to the wrong person can bring a judgment of death. Do you want me to go on?"

"Yes, yes, please," Edward said, nodding.

I added my assent.

"I will tell you why I am telling you things that I—we—have never told a white man before. There has been no reason for him to know."

"We thank you," I started to say, but Edward, though he did not know what I was saying, shushed me down.

"Please go on," he said to the medicine chief.

The chief began again, "This is the knowledge that holds up the world. This is the knowledge that makes the water flow and the grass and trees and flowers blossom. This is the knowledge that makes sunlight and makes the moon glow in the darkness. This is the knowledge that explains the air and the stars, the bear, the honeybee, and the snow. We the People have known this since the beginning, because our spirits have stayed with us. Here is what I did to find out what I should do, because you asked for this knowledge. I bathed in the cold stream every hour the first day and fasted for three days. I drank a magic soup made in a magic bowl. I ate the dried heart of a bear. I sent my sperm flying in the air after a butterfly. I slept without dreaming and I dreamed without sleeping. Ten days later I am ready to tell you that you have good friends in the spirit world. They asked me to help you."

"That is good to know," Edward said.

"Yes," I said. "Yes."

The chief spoke, "They told me it was a good thing to tell you. I said that I would not. They told me I must. I said it was too dangerous. They talked to me, two female spirits, holding hands, floating over my head. And an old chief. He spoke; they spoke. It was night, it was dawn, it was daylight, it was twilight. The music of a drum sounded in the air. They sang to me. I listened. 'Where are the buffalo?' they asked me. I could not tell them. 'Where are the children to come after?' I could not tell them. 'What is that dark haze floating across the face of the sun? The world may unravel like an old rug. And will you not help to keep this from happening?' 'I will try,' I told them. 'But I am afraid that if I tell the white man, he will destroy our knowledge the way he destroyed the buffalo.' They told me this is an old story, a fight against the end, against the danger of disappearing as air. They told me you are helping to keep the old ways known in the white man's mind. Hey, what a terrible turbulent demon-swirling place that must be! Hey, he has come to steal our lands. Hey, he has come to take our food. Hey, he has come to spoil our water and make his poisons flavor our minds."

The assistants drummed steadily and louder, as the chief raised his voice. Edward glanced at them but mainly kept his eyes on the chief.

"What man wants his people to disappear? What man wants his children's children never to be born?..." The drumming stopped.

Edward and I sat there silently in the silence. In his mind— he told me all of this later—he went through that litany over and over, because he did not want to think about the other part, about the spirits whom the medicine chief said had come to him, two spirits? He wanted to ask what they looked like, but he dared not. Shivering before the dying fire, he reminded himself of who they were. He *knew* it; he *knew* it. The daughter of Seattle, withered, old clamdigger princess, she was one of them, and the beautiful Tasáwiche, she was the other. And the old man? It was Chief Joseph—he *knew* it, he *knew* it—returned from the spirit world for a short while to tell this medicine chief how important it was to speak about this with Edward and me.

Edward knew this, and yet he refused to admit the truth of it. He was truly a man of two minds, and each aspect of his thinking was growing greater and greater in itself, and greater and greater in opposition to the other part.

Who would have admitted that he knew three people appeared to this medicine chief to plead his case for his fieldwork? But two of them were dead. If the third was Tasáwiche, did that mean that she had died? Oh, he hoped not! Could her spirit be so strong that she could send her soul to appear in the medicine man's vision even while still alive? It was a difficult question. It was not rational. Any rational person would have walked away. But I am a rational person—I am sure I am—and I did not walk. And he did not. No, his rational mind did not walk away from his Dionysian mind. He kept both ways of thinking together, and I was beginning to see this was the reason why I admired him enough to make the sacrifices I was making. My schoolteacher fiancée had recently written me a letter breaking things off. I had stored many of my belongings in an apartment in Seattle, but I had no permanent home. I certainly had no family, except for thousands of Indians, most of whom did not know me.

I was ruminating painfully about this, while Edward, in the ecstatic mood of his working state, felt his brain nearly ablaze with the possibility that those spirits had crossed over from wherever it was they now inhabited and pleaded his case with the medicine man. He wanted to tell Clara and the children, but it would frighten them. And so he would hold his tongue, until he told me later.

The drums began again. And then one dropped away. The assistant who had been playing on that drum left the tent and returned bearing a bowl of what we took to be the "magic soup" to which the medicine chief had referred. He offered it to Edward, and without hesitation Edward tipped the bowl toward his lips. A slight flicker in his eyes, muted by the firelight, I took to be a warning. And when I tasted the "soup" I understood why. It had, as Edward said later when we were going over our notes, the flavor of bird stool and mud, horse piss, rotten cactus fruit, stale tobacco, old berries, old flowers, hot pepper, and salt.

And it took only a few minutes before we began to feel its effect. Edward got clumsily to his feet, staggered over to the wall of the tent, and vomited profusely. This startled me, and I stood up. Unhappily, I never reached the wall, spewing out my stomach onto my shoes and the blankets. Just at that moment, Edward cried out, not in disgust but in amazement, pointing up over our heads. The smoke hole in the center of the tent glowed with the intensity of a volcano about to explode.

"Mother!" Edward cried out.

The tent flew up and away as if in a great wind, and we were left standing under a vast canopy of stars, shivering, because our clothes had turned to shreds, but as happy in our hearts as we ever might have imagined. Thousands of tiny spiders dangled on delicate threads, each of these silver in the starlight, each of these in time with the others, so that they might have been performing a dance that connected the heavens to the earth. Edward stared up beyond them, hoping to catch a glimpse of the spirits who had interceded on our behalf, the old clamdigging princess and the bird-like Tasáwiche, and, of course, the old chief, whose death had affected him almost as much as his own father's.

The fathers were dying, he reminded himself, and he was left to pay tribute to their lives. But it wasn't just these individuals. No, as the medicine chief spoke of, it was the antique way that was dying, fading into oblivion with these old men, women, and even the children who would grow, if they lived, to become leathery-faced elders, with faded dark eyes that hinted at fathomless time and space, surrounded by the new monuments and signs of the civilization that was overtaking all of them.

This was not right! Edward raised his fist at the stars. Not right at all! "I vow," he called out, "I vow, do you hear? that I will do whatever is within my power to fight this!" Edward then charged off into the grass, and I followed.

A bright light burst in front of us, some odd balloon of prairie gas, he figured, but then we heard drumming and singing, and the songs that rose in the voices of the men came to us in a language I had never before heard. A great shaft of light, a roadway, descended from the stars. Edward stood with his back to me, his hands outstretched as three figures approached, in faintest outlines only against the velvet dark upon dark.

"This!" Edward cried out. "This is what they are losing! This is what we all are losing!"

Neither of us had any memory of what happened between that last moment and dawn, when the early light found us, naked and aware, wandering upstream in a nearby creek. In hurried, embarrassed fashion, we found our clothes scattered under various bushes near the stream, and we dressed and wandered back toward the tents.

Clara was awake, waiting for Edward, something he feared might happen and for which he felt quite ill-prepared, his head still spinning as it was. "Where were you?"

He took a deep breath, inhaling from himself an odd odor that smelled to him of the soup he had drunk and something he could only recall as the smoke and dust of the roadway from the heavens. For a moment, confusion overtook him, and he sank down onto the pallet where Clara lay, fearing she would be repulsed by his odor, yet needing her near him as intensely as he had ever felt such a need.

"I went to a ceremony," he said.

Clara showed him her disgust. "Edward," she said, "I don't think it's good for the children to be so close to these pagans."

He heard small animal noises. The children were stirring. Edward and Clara lowered their voices to whispers.

"I wish I were free," she said.

He sighed and pushed himself back against the wall of the tent. "If I could do something about it, I would."

"You can do something."

"Clara, I can't stop doing this." He waved his hand about the tent.

She let out a sharp short breath. "No, I believe you can't."

"But they are having a good summer so far, aren't they?"

He watched as first Beth and then Florence sat up and looked around, while Hal still slept soundly. Clara watched them, too.

"Yes, they are," she said. "I know they are." She reached for his hand. "I will try," she said, "to do as you do and do both things."

"The business and the project?"

"Our life and the project," she said. "Our life...."

"Good morning, Daddy," Beth said.

"Good morning, Daddy," Florence said.

"Oh, what a day, what a new day!" Edward jumped to his feet and rushed to pull open the tent flap and stick his head outside. "A new day! Not a cloud in the sky!"

And there were no clouds all morning, either. The children went on a stone hunt with one of the older Apache girls—each was

given the task of finding a stone in the shape of an animal—
while Clara sat with the women and watched them repair
clothing. Edward and I went about our work with the informants we had cultivated, adding to our picture of the Apache view
of life and the world—and death.

At around noon—with the sun high in the southern sky—
we learned through Jimmy of an old medicine chief who lived
by himself out in the desert to the south, and with the help of
a young Apache man, we hitched up the wagons and set out for
his abode. There was no road; there was scarcely a trail, and so
we shifted our course down into a dry creek-bed out of sight of
the mountains.

Our trouble began when we cracked a wheel crossing a near-
blockade of small rocks. Fortunately, we had unloaded the
wagon when we first arrived at the camp, so that two of us, the
Apache fellow and I, could put our shoulders to the wagon and
keep it raised while Edward removed the wheel. We were all
soaked through and through by the time we completed our
repairs and felt fortunate that the sky had clouded up, shading
us from the raw, hot sun of early afternoon.

Edward had begun to develop great patience in this work—
making the photographs and the anthropological record, not
repairing wagon wheels!—but he felt a surge of annoyance when
the wheel would not turn on the axle, and we stayed a while
longer to complete the repair. "Patience is an absolute must," he
said. "But even while we're standing still in our patience, for
whatever reason, the Indian world is fast disintegrating."

"Aaaargh!" We put our shoulders to the wagon, grunted and
grunted, and finally got the wagon moving.

"These dying worlds," Edward said when we were riding
along again. "They are alive, or at least give us that illusion, even
as we were fast flying to pieces. It is a matter of time and

patience. We have the latter. The question is, do we have the other. And cash. Oh, yes, that. Which without it, we are utterly doomed to failure. Cash…cash, cash, cash, cash…."

He leaned toward me and whispered something for the first time, which I took to be quite shocking, "I talked to Jimmy about this. I have decided to collect some artifacts and sell them, to put money into the project."

I wasn't sure how to respond, and before I could say anything at all, the sky ahead of us suddenly turned ominously dark, with zigzags of lightning slashing here and there, and the temperature must have dropped all of a sudden about twenty or thirty degrees. The Apache fellow shouted for us to leave the creek-bed at once. He jumped from the wagon to grab the lead horse's halter and tried to turn it toward the low embankment to our right. A distant roar caught our attention. From up the creek-bed, a five-foot-high wall of frothing brown and white water rushed toward us.

I shouted to Edward, and he looked up, with eyes full of fear, something I had never before seen in his gaze. The children! Clara! The thoughts rushed upon him in that instant. What will they do? Even as the wall of water roared along.

"No!" he shouted. "Turn!"

Because we were already turning, the wave hit us nearly broadside on, spinning the wagon a quarter of the way around, which, fortunately, meant we didn't capsize. The horses shrieked as if being torn to pieces. Equipment and supplies went flying, or rather, sailing. I went soaring over the sliding body of the horse, and Edward shot past me.

"William!" he called, catching his balance as the rushing water flowed beyond us. He pushed himself to his feet, blinking, blinking.

"Where are you?"

The Apache had me by the hand, pulling me to my feet.

"Here!" He said in his language.

Edward looked around as though temporarily blinded. And then he saw us, and he let out a cheer as loud as his initial scream. The rush of the high water disappeared around a bend in the old creek-bed, and almost at once the sun returned full bore as we set to digging ourselves out of the long, muddy swathe that the flood had left behind.

And as it happened, all this was for naught; we had gone on a wild goose chase. When we finally arrived, a bit shaken by our near-demise in the creek-bed, at the hut of the old medicine chief, his ancient wife was there to tell us she was a widow; the old man had died a few days before of an illness of the lungs. We expressed our regrets, sat with her as the sun climbed higher in the sky, and eventually returned along that same creek-bed, which was as dry once again as it had been when we had first started out. We kept our eyes on the sky for any gathering clouds.

"Another elder gone," Edward said, sounding utterly disconsolate, even as we talked through a few notes about the mourning ritual the old woman was undergoing. His mood did not improve by the time we returned to the village, even though Clara's state of mind seemed to have changed almost completely.

"Edward, Edward," she said as he climbed down from the wagon. "I was so worried about you."

"Daddy, Daddy!" The children rushed to him, as always, tugging at his coat.

He held out his arms and took them into them. And then told them to run off and play. They retreated, but not all that far. Clara then pressed herself to him, despite the audience of the children, a few Apache, including our informant, and yours truly.

"You saw the rain clouds?" he asked her.

"One of the people here told me what could happen. I...I...nearly fainted."

"Someone told you?" He still held her close, a rare thing to see.

Clara spoke quietly, not wanting to frighten the children. "They saw the clouds; they knew."

"They do know these things," he said.

"I don't know what they know," Clara said. "But I know what I know."

"And what is that, dear Clara?" Edward said.

She pressed herself to him even closer, despite the gaze of all who were looking on.

"While you were away today," she said in a whisper.

"Yes?"

"One of the women told me something."

"And what did she tell you?"

"In the next village over, there is a sick child."

Edward released her and looked over at the children. "I'm sorry to hear that."

"What if it were...?"

"Our children are fine," he said.

"But they're playing with these Indian children...." Her voice trailed off.

"Nothing is going to happen to them," Edward said. He could hear in his own voice an annoyance that he hadn't wanted before to acknowledge. "They will be fine."

He—we—went back to work, and the children returned to their games, with Clara watching over them a little more closely now that she had heard the news about the sick child. Gosh-o-ne seemed more helpful than ever, showing us various designs, one in particular that was a woven cap, which he explained cured the illnesses of anyone who wore it.

"I would love to try it on," Edward said to me that night. "Not that I have any ills. But if I did, I would wear it."

"You believe in their medicine, don't you? While I always thought we were only studying it."

"I believe, and I don't believe," he said. "Photography has taught me a few things. To the Indian what I do may at first seem like magic, but you and I know it is simply chemistry. What if the miracles they perform for their people turn out to be chemistry, too. The heretofore unrevealed secrets of the natural world. What if there is another world in our own world, one that we need a particular pair of spectacles in order to see? I believe this, and I disbelieve this at the same time." He tapped his pen on the page of his notebook. "Once when I was a boy I was lying in bed and heard an owl call, and I knew it was an Indian spirit. Ever since, I have believed and disbelieved all at once."

Suddenly, in a cloud of dust—as if out of an old dime-novel—a rider came galloping toward the camp. The Apache dogs barked. The children looked up from their play. Clara, from her post nearby, where she chatted with some Apache women while keeping an eye on the girls and Hal, glanced up and then returned to her vigil. And we watched as the dark-skinned, shirtless rider came racing toward us, slowing only at the last moment and, in one smooth and synchronous action, leaping from the horse as he brought it to a halt.

"Jimmy!" Edward applauded, but Jimmy was too distressed to notice.

"That child who had taken sick in the next village over? The medicine chief there, desperate to show some knowledge of the problem, told the child's family that your presence had brought a curse down on the encampment."

"How did you learn this?" Edward asked him.

"I was there," Jimmy said. "I just rode from there. And now you—we—have to leave at once." You could see the urgency in his posture.

"Edward, this sounds serious," I said.

"We have only just gotten to the heart of our work here," Edward said. "If we leave now—"

"If you don't, you won't be safe," Jimmy said. "You're not safe now."

"I'll speak to Gosh-o-ne, the medicine chief," Edward said. "He will help us."

Jimmy looked down at his feet. "He will be the first to denounce you," he said.

I was still uncertain, but at this point, Edward looked past our new acquaintance and called to Clara and the children. "We will come back," he said to me as they came running. "It's just temporary; we will come back and finish our business here."

"You will," said Jimmy. "I think I can promise you that."

Within the hour we had gathered up our belongings, packed the tents into the back of the wagon, and were rolling out of the canyon. Clouds sailed overhead. Jimmy rode along with us for a good while and then turned his horse toward the south and rode off on his own.

"He asked where we were going next," Edward said. "He told me he'd catch up with us somewhere along the line."

"Somewhere," I said, studying the figure of the man on horseback as he grew smaller and smaller on the horizon. And then I blinked, and Jimmy was gone.

Edward turned to me and said, "That's how I'd like to go one day. Ride and ride and ride, until I'm only a dot on the horizon."

From that year on, Edward saw a lot more of the children than ever before while in the field. Aside from that terrible problem with the medicine chief, one visit in particular stood out for him: the first trip that Hal, an adolescent now, made, without the girls, as it happened, since Clara could not come because of the business, and she wanted the girls with her at home.

Edward met Hal at the train station in Missoula, and they drove east and then north in a Ford automobile he had just purchased. They were enjoying an unseasonably warm autumn day in Nez Percé country, among the few straggling villages on the U.S. side of the Alberta border. Hal started off having just the grandest time—sighting elk and what they both decided was a large bear, just a moving blur about a hundred yards up the road—as they drove along, and it kept on getting better and better.

Late in the afternoon they stopped at the side of the road and made camp. For supper they roasted some birds that Edward had brought along for the occasion, dressed with berries and greens for a salad. To drink they had well-water from town, which had stayed fairly cool during the drive. As the light seeped away, like water running out of a basin with a small drain, father and son settled down to watch the stars come out. First one or two, then another pair or three here and there, and then thousands, and then a filigree of more than millions draped the entire broad range of the sky.

"Do you like it out here, son?" Edward asked him.

"I do, Dad," he said. "It'd be scary if you weren't here, though."

"Why, I'd feel the same if you weren't here."

"The same as you do now?"

"Scared, scary," Edward said. "Interesting, isn't it? One of us alone feels naked and weak, and just a pair of us makes us feel like a million."

"I wouldn't be here except for you, Pop," Hal said.

"No, no, I guess you wouldn't. Well, I'm just out for stars."

"Really, Pop?"

"Oh, stars, and quite a lot of other things."

"So many up there," Hal said.

All of this talk under that glittering net of stars, which before they slept Edward pointed out might possibly be the glowing, winking souls of millions upon millions of Indians who had once lived on the very ground they were sleeping on that night.

"How many?" Hal asked.

"Millions upon millions."

"Hah! You can't make that many pictures of them," Hal said.

"No, son," Edward said, "I can't."

That night they slept well, unworried about bears, because Edward had drawn a border around their camp with an herbal mixture, which a medicine chief had given him, that gave off an odor that is noxious to the animals. In the morning they drove on and reached the Nez Percé camp by late afternoon.

On a high plateau, looking west toward the mountains, they spent the evening around a fire with some of the tribal elders, who spoke among themselves in a language Hal didn't understand, and Edward, without me to translate, could not make out a lot of it. From what he could discern, it was talk of family mostly, about what brothers and cousins were doing, most of whom had scattered throughout Canada a long time ago, some of whom had moved west to Seattle; and about weather and horses and hunting, which was still the main occupation and preoccupation of this small band of people.

Hal was tired, and drifted in and out of sleep, sitting up and alert only when one of the men, working hard to make the story clear to the visitors, told a tale about an old relative who had climbed the mountains and taken a big leap up into the starry sky, holding onto a ledge of light by his fingers.

"What do you think, Hal?" Edward asked. "Do you think
that happened? Or is it just a way of talking about things."

"A funny way," Hal said, before falling into a deep sleep.

They were up early the next morning. It was still dark and
absolutely still, like water before gravity took effect or air before
the earth began to rotate. Fishing was the order of the day. One
of the boys in the camp had volunteered to lead Edward and
Hal to a creek that he said was bustling with trout. He called the
place Little Mist Creek.

"Fish," he said in the tribal language.

Neither Edward nor (of course) Hal understood. But Edward
had the idea when the young Indian shook his long spear in a
downward motion, as though to skewer a swimming trout.

"Fish," Edward said.

"Fish," Hal said, after his father.

The young Nez Percé warrior nodded, and they kept on walking.

A half hour or so up the trail into the cleft of the mountain,
they found the creek. The air up there, they discovered, was thick
with swatches of fog hovering above the swift-flowing water, and
the water itself gave off the surprising odor of licorice.

Hal was nearly delirious. "Pop! I want to eat the water!"

"Not drink but eat it?" Edward said.

"It smells so good."

"The fish must like it," Edward said as the Nez Percé boy took
up a still pose at the creek-side. Hal stole his way quietly alongside. Minutes went by. Edward marveled at his son's own stillness, admired him for it.

And as quickly as the shutter on his camera might snap, he
blinked and caught the Indian boy spearing a big scarlet-
throated trout. They all laughed at the swiftness of it and the
skill of the thrust. After a few more catches, the Nez Percé boy
handed Hal the spear.

Hal watched, waited, watched, waited. Bogs of mist floated above the river. Birds called, sang. Suddenly the boy struck the water with the spear—but came up with nothing. The Nez Percé boy said some words. Hal nodded, as though he understood, and retreated into himself again, waiting, watching.

Again, he struck.

Nothing.

Again.

Nothing.

Hal looked back at Edward just then and gave his father the grandest smile, as if in his failure, he had found great happiness.

Later, around the fire, the trout tasted delicious, flavored somehow, miraculously, with the taste of the licorice from the waters of the creek. More stories. The elders passed around a pipe.

Before sleep, Hal said to his father, "I have a question, Pop."

"And it is?" Edward said.

"In the story about the man who leaps up into the sky?"

"Yes, son?"

"He couldn't really hold onto a ledge of stars, could he?"

"In the story, he could."

"But really?"

"No, I don't think so, son," Edward said.

But in his mind he said to himself, "Perhaps he could. Perhaps he just might be able to do it."

twenty-two

jimmy fly-wing's story—8

THAT FIRST TRAIN TRIP from Chicago to Missoula carried me
with great finality into the most important part of my life,
though I felt quite numb, having left the city so precipitously.
I slept as much as I could, dreaming initially of buffalo that
raced on either side of the car. The farther west we traveled, the
less I saw of the great animals and the more I became aware of
a dark hawk soaring through my sleep.

"You knew it was time," the bird called to me.

"Yes, yes," I replied.

But it was not the hawk that gave me the signs. In the
distance, near the horizon of the great country of my dreams,
I could see lightning flickering, beautiful zigzags of terrifying
light by night, elusive slashes of brightness under the sun in
the day.

That was how I came to understand, to know when I should
attend to the photographer, whose name came to me only in the
final hours of my journey, when I stopped at a small encampment at the edge of a Montana hamlet and sat with the old men
and listened, and learned whom I must seek when that lightning
raced sideways and down across the sky of my dreams.

How beautiful to see at last the deeds we need to do, without the prompting of a touch or a word!

On that rough ride up to Flathead I heard myself singing with joy. I felt like a serious man again, on horseback, the wind in my face, sleeping under hillsides, listening to the animals, to the birds, to the insects, to the grasses. Things were nearly visible! I was going to see; I was going to meet this man whose charge the spirits had given me!

I was never so happy as when I first arrived in his camp, though I had to laugh at myself when, in my enthusiasm, I mistook his assistant for the man himself. This fellow, plain, medium height, with a dark mustache, was good enough to cook me breakfast, and we talked and talked, and I knew that we could work together in a way that I never could have understood before.

Still, though our talk came easily I was growing quite nervous—that modern condition, which I had only acquired after my stint at school in Chicago—and I fretted to myself about whether or not things would go right almost as if I were worrying about an examination in my major subject.

But when the man finally arrived, I was completely at ease. My cheeks and jaw hurt from smiling. It was as if some electrical field leaped to life between us, the kind that sometimes happens between friends and should, but doesn't always, between lovers. We immediately, after shaking hands, sat down on the ground and talked about the day, the work he had just done, and he told me, at length, about his project, as if he seemed to understand that I was present because of him, not because of anything I had done, and that, for the sake of my family and my clan and all the People, I was placing my life at the service of his work.

That was the good part of my act of sacrifice.

There was another side.

And I lived it when Curtis and Myers returned, as they did now and then, to Seattle, or went on business because of the project to the East or other cities. During those times, I wandered here, I wandered there, living in small towns, sometimes drifting into the few cities of the West where I could satisfy my recently acquired reading habits in the cool, high rooms in new public libraries, and finding always that when I needed to be at Curtis's side, he was never more than a day's ride away.

To support myself, I sometimes took whatever odd jobs were available, enjoying the physical labor. I also spent time on the campus of several universities, where it became known among the student body that the smart Indian was the fellow who could write you a paper, or a doctoral thesis, for a good price and without fear of discovery. (I wrote about Homer; I wrote about Aristotle and Plato, about Virgil; I wrote about Chaucer and Shakespeare, and about Vico and Dante, and even Malthus and Adam Smith.)

Whenever I saw a brown face on the street of a town, I turned the other way, and during this time I fueled myself with whiskey and ate few meals, not because I didn't have the cash but because I didn't have the hunger. I often went out the door whenever I saw one of my own come in, having quite a visceral response to the scattering of the members of the tribes.

Sometimes, though, I wasn't quick enough.

In a bar in Tucson, a mean little Apache fellow hit me in the chest for no good reason as I was walking past, and if the bartender hadn't leaped over the bar with a pistol in hand, the mayhem might have been more than I could have borne. In Denver, two Gros Ventre men, cousins as it turned out, caught me on the street just as I was making my escape, and if a policeman hadn't been strolling past the establishment, I might have ended up in the hospital.

Divine intervention is what the Christians would call it, I decided. As I saw it, I needed little or no explanation. I had a charge, a duty, and a mission, and I was carrying it out, whenever he was needed.

But it was such a lonely vigil I made, sometimes just plain torture when I was in a city or a large town. The only place that made me forget my loneliness, or perhaps put it in perspective, was the no-place, the wide-open spaces of the country that I traveled, where mountains and tree-filled valleys ran with good streams, or where cacti and scrubs populated the horizon in every direction of broad desert lengths. Out here, in the everywhere and nowhere of the Western part of the continent, I found both my home and my exile all in one. The odors on the wind, the small cries of animals in the night, the people and creatures who populated my dreams, swelled my heart with a deep and exultant sense of being in the right place.

Towns, cities, meant money for my basic needs.

The mountains and desert meant life itself.

Though each had its dangerous temptations, as in those saloons of the towns where I gave in now and then to the pulverizing elixirs poured out by various barkeeps and sometimes had those desperate encounters with other dangerous men. And out here on the broad span of earth, where now and then I would camp, and sleep, and dream those dreams of lightning splashing its patterns across the sky. In those dreams I knew I had to mount up and ride in pursuit of it to wherever it was Curtis, at that moment, needed my assistance, to villages where I became my old self again, in gesture and in the tone of my voice, in the way I moved my eyes, and in the way the very juices in my stomach and mouth seemed to turn into fluids of an older variety, and in making links in my mind, certain parts of my brain leaped to others, forming connections I recalled with pleasure, and which, augmented by the training of my city life, gave me—I more than sensed this, I used them—powers beyond the normal abilities of most men, of whatever tribe or caste or culture or country.

For all of my learning, both in the world and in the libraries, I could not explain it. Either I had always been this way, or something had changed in me and I lived a life I doubted many men could speak of without sounding as though they had gone mad. How else could I explain to anyone who had not lived as I had lived what happened when, after months and months of wrestling with the trouble in my mind, I retraced the first part of the long journey that had taken me to this point, boarded a train to the nearest town, and bought a horse and ridden to the territory of my old life—or the early part of my present life?

It was both delightful and delusionary! Entrancing and maddening! No animal or dream figure had prepared me for it, perhaps because none of the spirits who were guiding me could have expected that I would try, having felt the exhilaration of my new charge, to return.

The closer I got to the old places, the more the air swelled with the finer familiar odors of my early days. Desert flowers and low trees called out to me, as if I were an insect guided by air currents and titrated scents and patterns imprinted on a rudimentary nervous system millions upon millions of years before. What a life! That I was an insect and I was a man, a rider and a beast of burden, or so it seemed that I partook of the latter condition, because as I rode and rode, I found myself listening to the worried thoughts of the horse—thirsty, getting tired, soon be hungry, too—as well as remaining mindful of my own fearful notion that if I appeared in my village—if I was fortunate enough to find that the People had remained in the particular location for this time of year—that I would be ridiculed and then cast out.

Thirst, getting tired, soon be hungry—

I reined in the beast and gave it a few minutes' rest, taking the time to stare up at the cloudless sky, an azure beyond the blue of any ocean I had ever seen pictured. I imagined nothing beyond it, in the conventional sense, and yet I sensed all of the cosmic passages behind the flat near-turquoise scrim, all of the rush and swirl of the atomic level, the name for which I had yet to learn.

And then it was time to mount up again and ride a while longer. When the sun had swooned westward in what had once been the morning sky, we approached a stand of trees that I recognized as one of the known places of my early world, and I slowed again, stopped, dismounted, and tethered the horse to a drowsy cottonwood. An underground spring bubbled up in the center of the small woods, and I knelt and drank. The water, with an infinitesimal tang of salt, gave me all I needed to carry on. My horse whinnied a query, and I untied the beast and stood back, while the animal set its feet in the soft turf and slurped and slurped itself back to full strength.

I did not ride the rest of the way. I tethered the horse again and set out on foot. Soon I was running low to the ground, covering much more distance than a man, intoxicated by the foxy odor of my own musk. My now quite-small animal heart nearly leaped out of my chest when I crested a rise and saw the smoke rising from the tepees on the plain below. I stopped all of a sudden and rolled over in joy amid the dust and stones, and yipped and yipped my pleasure.

Home! Oh, Sky, it was home!

I pissed on the nearest rock and went scampering toward the encampment. Before I traversed a hundred yards, I felt my wings sprout and I worked them atop a rising breeze, enjoying the return of my old power as I rose—oh, the sweetness of it, like nothing I had ever known before and everything I should have remembered—above a young scout dozing at the beginning of the marked path, soon soaring on a wind spout to where I could glide back and forth directly over the center of the village.

The people below, the smoke rising, the clouds above, the mountains on the horizon all around, nothing, oh, nothing ever equaled this, at least not while still within the pull of gravity! Circling and circling, I watched mice scamper and smaller birds peck about at the air that kept me buoyant, and within my bird-heart beat another heart, that of my long-time love for where I had lived and who I once was.

The wind, the wind!

Sounds rose to my ears, still recognizable, and I watched the children emerge from the tepees and race to the center of the encampment, and I saw an older boy take them each by the hand, and I closed my eyes against the vision, nearly plummeting as a result, until I came to myself again and watched as I circled and circled, and when *she* came out of the tent to speak to the children, I felt as though a warrior had skewered me in the chest with an arrow.

Oh, my life, my love!

Oh, this world, this passion, this mission, this task!

Convinced that if I did not immediately depart, I would die in midair and drop like a stone into the center of the village, I wheeled with the wind at my back and pumped my way higher and higher, and then turned and headed toward the western mountains where, without pity but also without hunger, I stooped in a dive at the first mammal I spied, tearing it apart and leaving its bloody pieces scattered for many feet around.

Library of Congress, Prints & Photographs Division, Edward S. Curtis Collection, LC-USZ62-48228

twenty-three

the zigzag years—2

THE VIEW FROM WALPI clears the mind, Walpi, which sits atop one of the three sacred mesas of the Hopi. Vast expanses of light, like the optical memory of the vast sea that once covered the plains below the mesas, and horizon upon horizon suggesting ranges of mountains where none exist, a trick of the heat, or perhaps a memory inherited from the mind of the ancient tribe to which we all belong, our ancestors who once escaped the Great Flood.

There atop the Western desert, Edward made a rendezvous with me because, after several years of trying, we had been granted permission by the Hopi, in the person of a man named George Runner, to photograph—and film—the Snake Dance ceremony. So it must have been for stalwart explorers, finally gaining admission to a port outside of which they may have anchored for years and years.

We made our notes:

The Snake Dance is a biennial, sixteen-day rite conducted by the Snake and Antelope fraternities as a dramatized prayer for rain. The Antelope Chief (Tsóp-monwi), who must be of the Rattlesnake clan, impersonates Isanavaiya, chief of the Rattlesnake People who

*lived, according to clan legend, under a mountain that was covered
with rattlesnakes. Each morning, before the Snake Priests hunt
snakes, their chief goes to the Antelope kiva, the sacred underground
gathering place of each clan, and asks for pahos, the sacred sticks,
that the Antelope priests have made, which show the four directions.*

*The Antelope chief says, "Now you will go and gather snakes for
me. If it should rain, you may drink."*

George Runner, his face painted with sacred stripes and dots,
looked over at Edward where he stood, his camera at his side,
while I held onto the motion picture camera and tripod, trembling (in my mind) in anticipation of my first close encounter
with snakes and my first attempt at movie making.

"And you may keep on taking photographs until it pours."
And Runner gave him a wink, the sign of a man with one foot
in one life or dimension and the other in another. Edward had
met him shortly after his climb up to Walpi, this humble
collection of adobe houses carved into the side and top of the
cliff. All around you, the land stretches out below, the bed of
a vast evaporated ocean. Was this Earth or Mars that he gazed
upon? The feeling Edward had could not have been much
different than if he had landed on another planet.

Look at this man, this living paradox. When we first met
Runner he wore denims and a cotton-print shirt, a neckerchief
made of red cotton, with belts of leather and turquoise and
bracelets of silver. But after Edward spoke with him about what
he was looking for—telling him what he had begun to tell all of
his Indian subjects, if they had questions, about the old Nez
Percé chief's injunction to him—he was now ready for a
portrait, covered with muddy paint, white streaks running
down his sides, his hair daubed with corn-dust and mud, and
his bare chest coated with the same mixture.

Edward knew that by ignoring the everyday life of these people and focusing only on their old ceremonies—and showing them dressed only in the old way—he might be leaving himself open to charges of fakery and a forced romantic view. But the old chief had spoken. As Edward saw it, this was the way to memorialize all that had gone before: show them as they had once been, had always been, if not might still remain.

Moody light that morning. He posed George Runner standing tall, space all around him. He wanted to reproduce the emotion in his heart, that here was a man who was the son of a man who was the son of a man who was the son of man, etc., who had stood this way a thousand years ago, ready to make the rain come again. If most people in our world could never be that man, Edward hoped, they might catch a glimpse of such a way of being by looking at his photographs, before all these red men died out, or their descendants dressed forever in the clothes of the present day and bore children who would forget all the old ways.

"Look here now," he said, and Runner stared directly at him.

And what did he see? What kind of a man was Edward becoming? If you turned the lens around, what would you see? A tall man, on whom years of leaning over the camera had bestowed a slight stoop. A serious man, with a slight twinkle in his eye when he spoke to his subjects. A sweet baritone voice that must have come to him from his father, who had intoned messages to his flock from the dais back in the middle part of the country, a voice that his loving wife and children back in Seattle longed to hear in person but still could sense the echo of in his absence.

And how did he seem to himself? As a man who had meandered about for years without real intent, who had one day discovered his mission in life. And now strove to fulfill it.

Atop this mesa we waited for eight days, during which the ceremony seemed to be held up, and we turned patience into a virtue rather than a penance. The delay gave us time to make more pictures and gather a great deal of information and lore from the elders of this high place.

Even after the announcement of the Yunya Assembly on the eighth day, things moved slowly, and it is not until the tenth day that the actual hunt for snakes commences. The Snake Priests enter the kiva immediately after breakfast and strip to loin cloths and smear their bodies with red paint, which they call "snake pollen," and pray that the snakes will not harm them.

George Runner sent his minions out on the hunt, and in his incarnation as Snake Priest, he let out not a hint that he knew us or that we were huddled there in the *kiva*, Edward and me, watching attentively. The odors in there grew thick—the paint, the body smells, breath, and other stinks—and we were glad to leave the *kiva* and follow the clan members as they dispersed around the valley below the Walpi cliffs, planting their *pahos* at various dry springs and going after their prizes.

When they find the first snake, cries go up and they all run together to surround it, throwing cornmeal on it, and begging and pleading with it.

"Don't be angry! Quiet down!"

"Don't harm us!"

"Don't be angry! May the Sun, our Father, help us!"

Then the one who found the rattlesnake tames the reptile by reaching down and brushing it with his two-eagle-feather whip (his wuvápi), until the snake straightens out and tries to escape, and then—my heart leaped this first time I saw it happen—he quickly seizes it by the neck.

Edward caught this in a photograph, bending with the man as he bent, but slowing, just enough to capture the blur of his motion, the sweep of his own catch. Just then an adolescent boy from the village who had been trailing along behind in the dust came running up to us. The snake-catcher turned and motioned for him to watch as he set the snake back down on the ground.

"You!" He motioned to the boy, meaning that the little fellow should attempt to catch it.

This boy, perhaps sixteen years old, immediately burst into tears, which made the men gathered around us laugh out loud.

"Oh, no," Edward wanted to say, "he's not that much older than my own boy, who I'd never set to chasing down a rattler. Have mercy on him, please. Please!"

The men waited until the snake had begun to make its wriggling escape across the dry ground when they charged it again, tugging the boy along by the hand and directing him to kneel and hold his sack open as a snare while they used their sticks to drive the deadly reptile into the bag.

"Well," Edward said to himself, and he wondered if his Hal would be able to perform such a little trick when he got a little older.

The boy was smiling now, holding up the sack, showing off his accomplishment.

Dozens more moments like this, dozens more snakes found their way into the sacks. But to catch that first snake so quickly was a good omen. Over the course of the morning Edward watched carefully and saw the method in all of this.

The rattlesnake is moved about with the stick until the opportunity arises to press its head into the sand. The pressure causes the mouth to gape and the blade of a wooden hoe or other flat stick is slipped in between the jaws. The thumbnail of the catcher is placed against the fang near the base while the point of the fang rests on the blade or stick. Then its body is handled and rubbed while the head is still pressed down, and after a while the snake becomes passive and is easily pressed down, and it is then easily picked up and dropped into the bag.

Toward noon the Snake Priests assembled at Puhu-va ("new spring"), on the north side of the valley lying west of Walpi, to partake of a light meal, and after a brief rest some of them went about the business of shaking the snakes from the sacks so they might cool off on the sand.

The boy who sacked the first snake of the day dumped his catch out and when it merely lay there without moving, he bent close to it, taunting it with his stick. As though tied to an invisible spring, the snake whipped around and leaped at him, lodging its fangs in his right wrist.

The older men gathered around him and pulled the reptile free, and then several of them led the boy away, back to the village. Edward and I followed the main troupe of snake hunters throughout the afternoon, but later that day we returned to the *kiva* to find the boy sitting in the corner, his head bowed, his arm swelling up as though someone had inserted a second limb beneath the flesh of the first. Edward alternated between watching him and watching the men set loose their catch of the day, allowing the huge mass of vipers to roil around in the sand before the fireplace and rear wall, until after sundown when they gathered them up and placed them in ventilated earthen jars for the night.

Edward and I became quite concerned for the young boy with the snake bite, but when we approached George Runner—shirtless and still smeared with the ceremonial paint but wearing his denims and shoes—he assured us that the boy would do better to wait out the progress of the poison right where he sat.

"Shouldn't we take him to town?" Edward said.

Runner did not agree. "Bouncing around like that, it will stir up his blood and kill him."

Edward pondered that and looked at me in the firelight. I nodded.

"I will stay here all night with the snakes—and with him," Runner said. "Don't worry."

But we did. Edward did. He lay awake for hours in the small house they had set aside for our use and while I snored away— ah, the deep sweet innocent sleep of a man without a family— Edward went over and over in his mind all that could go wrong, with that young boy's life and all that had happened with his own. Sleep finally overtook him. And mercifully, it came without dreams.

First light speared his eye and he sat up, breathing hard, feeling as though he had escaped from some earthen jar himself, like those snakes that, as it happened, had crawled out to freedom in the night, only to find themselves tracked down by the Snake Priest, George Runner, and returned to their enclosures.

"And the boy?" Edward said, after Runner gave him an account of his work during the night.

"He's holding on," he said, looking over at the young fellow who sat exactly where we had left him the evening before, head bowed, and his arm swollen even more.

"Can we—?"

"Don't touch him," Runner said. "He's still alive."

"I know that," Edward said. "But I worry if—"

"This is our worry," Runner said. "You asked to observe and ask questions. We allowed that. But here." He dug his heel into the sand and dragged it in front of him. "This line. Do not cross it. Or we will ask you to leave."

Edward demurred. "We won't cross it, of course not," he said, though in some important ways, he already had.

Last days of the feast. More snakes. The hunt grows furious. Now the singing in the kiva begins as the men prepare a large sand mosaic in the center of the space. In the middle of the mosaic and facing east is the mountain-lion, surrounded by four differently colored snakes parallel to the sides. At regular intervals along each side of the sand-painting are placed eight nolokpi, which are syringa shoots about thirty inches long, curved like a shepherd's crook at the upper end where a down feather hangs. The lower ends are embedded in a ball of clay, and at the back of the mosaic the Snake Chief stands his tiponi.

The colors charm Edward, the sand seems to glow from within, the body of the lion, a sepia shade almost, and the shoots and the beautiful blue-red-green sheen of the arrow feathers. He set up to photograph the mosaic, hoping against hope that some hint of it might emerge on his plate. Surrounded by all this color, he had to live with the paradox of making pictures only in black and white or sepia.

The singing started up in earnest, and as the voices rose around us, Edward stole a glance at the ailing boy, still huddled in the corner, his arm still swollen, though no greater than the day before. He took a step or two toward him, but Runner held him back.

"No," he mimed with a shake of his head.

"Alright," Edward nodded.

Around them the music swirled like dust. And the men at their prayer made the *kiva* tremble with deep-throated voices.

> *Taaí, itá-naa, Pá-lölökanu umita muioqatuwun*
> *Pa-lölökanu, itamu u-sinomu. Oviya, natko takamui*
> *ep salai-totini. Taai, ita-naa, chuchu-pökokani nok*
> *ka-hákam humuwa nákyatani. Pai lólmani.*
> *Yókuvani. Amútsvi mónvas-toni. Yántani.*

"Now, our Father, Water Bullsnake, have pity on us. Water Bullsnake, we are your People. For them let there be here abundance. Now, our Father, pacify the rattlesnakes, so that none will be angry. That will be well. It will rain. On their account, good will come. So be it."

"Time for the *chú-yutu*," I said.

"You are a quick study," Edward said. "Translate for me."

"The rattlesnake running, of course," I said.

"Of course."

Chú-yutu ("rattlesnake running") occurs on the last day of the ceremony. Before dawn, a clansman goes along the western side of the mesa and plants a paho in Anwús-pa ("crow spring"), another in Kanél-va, a third in Wípho; and from each spring he collects ooze and water in a gourd. Then he returns to a place about half a mile south of Wípho and five miles from Walpi, where he plants the remaining four pahos.

At the foot of the mesa stands a shrine where, according to the Rattlesnake legend, some old men were turned into stones. Here an old man of the Rattlesnake clan stands with a short stick, on the bent end of which a paho is tied. This represents an old hunchback. Runners who have earlier set out from the mesa approach him, and he urges them on, crying, "Run! Run!" As they pass him, each touches the crooked stick, and when the last runner has gone, he hurries after them. Meanwhile the Antelope clan leaders have appointed four Horn clansmen, who separately go in the four cardinal directions to place in the dry watercourses pahos and round balls of mud, such as are found after heavy rains. They gather the debris washed down by the last freshet and scatter it over the ground as they run toward the course of the racers, to join them and enter the village with them.

On the way to the starting place some of the runners visit the gardens about Wípho and there gather bunches of cornstalks, bean-vines, and pepper-plants, and as they come running into the village, women pursue them with shouts and laughter, and take the green stalks from them.

The sight of this called Edward back to a reading I had suggested to him about the innocence of the harvest festivals of the old Greeks, the earliest of them, the ancients of the ancients. Edward trailed along behind the runners, his mind racing faster than the young boys, turning their chants into our sensible language, imagining that all of us had been cast back to a time before time—if we had ever left it.

Earlier in the morning the men who are to handle the snakes in the dance go into the valley to make certain hidden deposits of herbs, and they return about the same time as the runners. When this occurs, the Snake Chief goes for his medicine-roots, which are not the same species as those he uses for "man-medicine." Nobody but the Snake Chief and the man whom he trains for his successor knows their identity. Sitting apart from the others, and working in the concealment of a blanket drooping from his shoulders, the Snake Chief pounds up the roots. While it is still morning, he takes the pulverized substance to the principal house of the Rattlesnake clan, there to place it in vessels of boiling water, which the Snake women have provided and which they watch as the water boils during the rest of the day. (And which, with the permission of the women, after the Chief departed from the house we watched a while, seeing the roots and stems spinning about and about in the steaming swirl of the large clay cauldrons, a vortex of herbs and water that drew in my eye and held me there, rapt in the passion of the steaming fluid.)

The washing of the reptiles—that came the next day in the early afternoon.

"Look up there," Edward said, gesturing toward the western sky beyond the cliff town, where large, dark clouds had begun gathering, as if in anticipation of the ceremony, which was picking up in intensity now.

"They'd better hurry," I said, "or it's going to rain before they finish the magic."

"Or it just might be magic so strong," Edward said, "that the rain is coming on early."

"Whichever you choose to believe," I said.

"I believe both," Edward said. "Which do you believe?"

I said. "I'm just taking notes."

Meanwhile the song in that mystical language was rising above the circle of priests in the middle of the dry, dusty square.

> *Haíiye haíiye haíiye, haiyí!*
> *Haíiye haíiye haíiye, haiyí!*
> *Hóshke hóshke pinawi másaiwa toní!*

Though chanted in low tones, the men rendered the song with great spirit in double tempo, beginning with the next verses.

> *Yéhe eye ye, á u haíiye, á u haíiye, haíi, haíi, ye á u haíiye!*
> *Yéhe eye ye, á u haíiye, á u haíiye, haíi, haíi, ye á u haíiye!*

"And you don't know what any of this means yet?" Edward said over the noise of the song.

I held out my empty hands. "I'll inquire."

And then Edward gave himself over to the song, bobbing his head, moving his limbs, almost as if he were about to fling himself into a dance. It was unlike anything else he had ever felt in his body before this—how strange, how strange! The singing went on for hours. He wandered about the little plaza, soaking in the words—or the measured noise, we should call it— thinking to himself, "So this is what it must be like to be a ghost," because his free movement throughout the village seemed to come about because no one acknowledged his presence. Eventually, he set up his camera and prepared to photograph the dancers where they would gather in a line just outside the Snake *kiva*—forewarned by one of the Antelope priests as to precisely where they would begin the next phase of the ceremony. Though the priest spoke to him as if he were invisible, aiming his words somewhere past his ear.

Edward was leaning over his instrument, working on the focus, when someone brushed past him, and he looked up to see a trio of young Hopi girls, their hair arched up in the traditional wings at either side of their heads, their large brown eyes liquid and full, like the eyes of deer, almost, and he felt again a sudden pang of recognition of an image he had yet to make.

Yehe eye ye! Síyapatu síyapatu yóyo!

The song rose full and rhythmically thunderous over the top of the mesa.

Ná u haíiye, ná u haíiye, á u haíiye, haiye!

"I've got some of it!" I ran up to him, nearly out of breath.

"Tell me," he said. And he led me around the corner of one of the adobe apartments, where we leaned in the shadows, and I told him what I had garnered from some of my old informants in one of the other clans.

"The corn god and the rain god are related," I said.

"I'm not surprised," Edward said. "The corn needs the rain to grow."

"Yes, yes, but the snake, do you see how the snake comes in?"

"Crawling," he said. "Slithering along...."

"Amusing," I said. "Very amusing. But seriously, listen...."

"I'm listening," he said, and he was listening, to the rousing double time of the song, to the stomp of feet on the earth, to the faint rumbling of storm clouds gathering to the west.

"I think I've figured out the link between the two," I said.

"And it is?"

"The corn god and the rain god, their names are Máisawa, Másewi, or Másou...."

"Máisawa," he said. "Másewi," he said. "Másou," he said, feeling a rippling chill of a shiver pass through his body like a wave.

"You see," I said, "these names, almost nearly alike. So they might be brother gods, you could say. But when I spoke to them...."

"Spoke to the gods?" he said.

I leaned over and touched a hand to his shoulder. "No, no, no. But are you alright, Edward? You look a bit pale." He seemed almost delirious, and I was feeling quite excited myself.

"Pale? No, I don't feel pale. You mean as in pale-face? I am a pale-face. But there's also something darker in me...."

"What?"

"These gods," he said. "Their names."

"Yes, but as I was about to say, when I spoke to the old clan leaders, they told me things. And I've made some connections in my own mind."

"And I in mine," he said, blinking, blinking at the light approaching from the west beneath and between the great unfolding clouds of thunder that rolled almost like grand ocean waves off the coast beyond the Olympics. "Máisawa," he said to the clouds, "Másewi, Másou...." And the singing gathered around us, drifting like the smoke from the ceremonial fires, and the smoke rose around us, and the wind tore at it, like a child pulling out tufts of grass, and the smoke blew away, joining the greater smoke of the storm clouds, and the fire and the air around us and above and the light behind the clouds all seemed to bunch together into one single coruscated wave of dark and light together, a rhythm of coming rain.

"They're one god," I said. "Three different names for one god. In the Keres language, which nobody here seems to understand except for the name of the god...the corn god and rain god, all in one."

"Or like our Holy Trinity," he said, coming abruptly down to earth, the earth of fellow Christians, after his instantaneous ascension into another world of clouds and light and wind and smoke from fires. "Though not *mine* anymore. I've long left my father's God behind, I must confess. What do you believe these days, William?"

"Believe? It's not a question," I said. "I don't believe in any religion. But I want to understand them...."

We stood aside as the priests emerged onto the plaza, holding handfuls of writhing snakes in each hand, gathering around the large tubs of liquid that the women had hauled to the center of the plaza.

"See their *shape* as they move, the *shape* they make in motion?" I pointed to another group of snakes slithering away from the center of the plaza with another clansman almost literally on their tails.

"The zigzag?" he asked.

"Exactly," I said. "The zigzag. The pattern of lightning in a thunderstorm."

"So!" he said.

"Yes," I said, "they show the shape of the lightning that connects heaven and earth in the rainstorms. They're the living embodiment of the lightning, and so they form the center of the dance for rain."

"You figured it out," he said. "How did you see this?"

"I ruminated," I said. "I meditated upon the shape and the form of it."

"While I hid my face in the camera. Good work," Edward said.

"The zigzag of the lightning," I said. "I saw the connection also in the smoke from the fires. The smoke rises up from the fire here on the ground, on our earth, and links the builder of the fire to the clouds where the smoke gathers and makes shapes and forms in the sky."

The priests passed the snakes in groups to the Cloud clansmen, who grasped them carefully, and dipped them into the sudsy mix, moving them about in the water and still holding fast to them by their necks. They then lay them at the base of a small altar, where young boys—novitiates in the clan—used feathers to whip them into further motion so that they dried themselves.

"It's him," Edward said, pointing out to me that one of these young fellows was the very boy who had sat in the *kiva* near death from a snake bite. Now he moved about the plaza, his health apparently fully restored.

"He's been through it," I said.

"A sort of miracle, I suppose," Edward said. He glanced up into the sky, seeing that the clouds appeared even more ominous than before, portending another miracle.

"See that," I said, calling his attention back to the washing ceremony.

"What's that?"

"The priest just held one of the snakes up to his lips. Almost to test to see if it's ready, clean and dry, I mean, for the next part of the ritual."

A chant rose from the closely gathered group of Snake Priests, grew louder and louder, and then subsided.

"Do you know what they're singing now?" he asked me.

"I believe so," I said, "if the old fellow who informed me wasn't pulling my leg."

"What is it then?" Edward said.

"Well, they're becoming the servants of the snakes," I said. "They're showing their gratitude to the creatures, and they're cleaning them as a duty. And, here's the logic, Edward, they're washing the snakes in the same way that they want the rain clouds to wash them. So you see the snake connects them to the rain in a number of ways."

The singing rose to a high pitch and then came to an abrupt halt. A wave of approval traveled across the crowd of onlookers, who formed a large half-circle in the plaza and stood on the rooftops, beyond which the dark clouds hovered. The priests released the snakes and their apprentices, boys not much older than the one who had been bitten and survived, chased after them, as the scaly creatures wriggled and writhed their way out of the circle, some of them gaining so much ground that they passed right by our feet as we stood there admiring the ritual.

"Yiee!" I let out a cry.

"Close call," Edward said, watching a big rattler that had come disturbingly close to us slither away at top speed toward the edge of the cliff as a junior priest came running after it and scooped it up around his arm and returned it to the circle.

A rumble in the distance, loud enough to call our attention away from the singing, chanting priests. Clouds gathered darkly nearly above us. Others in the village looked up to this promising configuration in the heavens.

One of the Antelope priests drew a circle of cornmeal on the ground and, when finished, cast more meal to the four directions, and the Snake Chief, in like manner, made a superimposed circle. Then they carelessly cast the reptiles into the circle, and the men rushed wildly forward to seize handfuls of snakes at random and dashed away out of the plaza and down the trails into the valley, arranging the snakes in more orderly fashion in their hands and on their arms as they made their way downward.

"Where are they headed?" Edward asked.

"I inquired before the ceremony," I said, "about how it would end. They're going back to where they placed their *pahos* the night before. It's a sort of magnetism, the prayer-sticks calling the men and the snakes back to those old locations."

"And the singing and the exaltation of the snakes, that calls the rain?"

"You can see as well as I can that the rain is on its way."

But it still took a while. And in the interim, the elderly men and the boys who took no part in the ceremony formed a line and marched four times around the plaza and then to their *kivas*. The Antelope clan members did likewise. Eventually the runners who descended into the valley to distribute the snakes returned and gathered at the western edge of the mesa to bathe in the snake medicine, which had been boiling all day, and drank small portions of it as well.

"What next?" Edward said.

"To the pits," I said, and we watched as the purgative took effect, sending the men running again, to purge themselves both from their bowels and from their stomachs of any evil influences they might have picked up from the snakes when they handled them and took them in their mouths. The Snake clan women came forward then, bringing food and carrying away the clothing that the men had worn during the dance, washing it in the remainder of the snake medicine to purify it, and then wringing it out and returning it to them. Each woman carried home from the *kiva* a cup of medicine of which each member of her household took a sip—we peered into several of the stone apartments and saw this happen, the passing around of the communal liquid—and then returned the remainder to a single jar left standing in the plaza.

It wasn't until he heard himself say it that Edward knew he wanted to drink from that jar. "I do, I do."

"Are you serious?" I took a step back and gave him a questioning look.

"I want to know what it's like," he said.

"We've drunk before, with the Apaches."

"I want to know what *this* batch is like," he said. "Myself."

"We should ask," I said. "They might get angry if you just did it without asking."

"Where's Runner? Do you know where he is?"

I held up my empty palms.

"I'll just go ahead then," he said, walking toward the large earthen container.

"Wait," I said. "I'll see if I can find him."

Edward stopped and stared at the jar. "No," he said, with a shake of his head.

"Edward, I wouldn't—"

But he had already done things that he shouldn't have done, and this seemed like something he must do, and so he reached down and picked up the heavy container, raising it immediately to his lips. No thunder just then, as if in warning from the gods. Though out of the corner of my eye, I caught the flicker of lightning just off to the northwest.

The women had used wooden ladles to offer portions of the liquid to the men. Edward had no spoon or ladle, and so he used all of the strength in his arms to tip the jar and let some of the stuff run into his mouth.

Nothing could have prepared him for the taste of it—dead animal and live reptile, scales and dung and must and raw flesh, metal and stone, pulpy and putrid and hot, biting, stinging—

nothing he had ever dreamed of had prepared him for this wild flavor or the burning in his mouth and throat and chest. (The Apache brew he and I had drunk together that helped us to hallucinate tasted like the waters of Eden compared to this, he told me later.) Just as he set the jar back on the dusty ground, it struck him in his stomach and bowels.

He turned, dashed past me, making for he knew not where, some lonely corner of the mesa village where he might relieve himself in peace. The pain, his twisting innards, it was so intense that when the first lightning flashed just above us, he couldn't tell if it was flaring out from his eyes or sparking toward them. He was already pulling at his trousers when the rain began to fall, a heavy slashing downpour whipped about by churning winds, and down a few ledges on the eastern side of the cliff, he found a little spot beneath an overhang where he squatted and felt as though his entire insides, bowels and stomach and heart and lungs and liver and all else, his woes, his worries—his old life itself!—were trying to release themselves from the imprisonment of his skin.

"Edward?" he heard me after a while, calling out to him in the rain. And he saw me go by, a few feet above his head, on the higher ledge, following behind a lithe shadowy figure, who pointed here, there, in quest of him, though he remained hidden to us behind the heavy curtain of rain.

"Curtis?" I called a name that didn't belong to him but rather to the huge mass of muck and guts that had just burst out of him onto the stones below. He rose painfully from a squat and turned and looked up and over his shoulder as the two of us walked blindly past, separated from him by the dark sheaf of rain, and he recognized, with the stinging complicity of a fellow chief, that the figure I was cleaving to, holding to his arm in the downpour, was the same young Hopi boy who had suffered and recovered from the bite of the holy rattler.

Seeing that boy made him suddenly so lonely for Hal that he turned his eyes aside. A cold wind blew through his lungs and his groin burned with the terrible fire of a life thrown away on strangers. The beautiful strangeness of what he had seen, now from the inside, lent his mind a certain fiery amazement.

"Oh, my life! The snakes, the lightning!" He pushed himself back onto his feet and there I was standing just in front of him.

"And," I said, a grand smile on my lips, "in addition to all this, I got it all on film."

Library of Congress, Prints & Photographs Division, Edward S. Curtis Collection, LC-USZ62-60394

twenty-four

sun dance

IT WAS 1907 WHEN Hal accompanied Edward on a trip up through the Rocky Mountains and over to eastern Montana and the Arikara camp, where we were gathering preliminary material on these tribes that were new to us. The boy rode with Edward over to Wounded Knee, where they'd made a big feast for Red Hawk, two other chiefs, and several hundred of their tribesmen. And then they rode west together, along the Dakota-Nebraska border, on a journey that took them more than a week, to where the big Montana battle between Custer and the many nations had taken place a little more than thirty years before.

After a day of riding about the Custer battlefield, up and down the ridges and into the small creek-beds where the government soldiers took it badly, and out onto the meadow where the last of them fell under the rain of arrows and bullets, father and son spent a night under the stars and Edward told Hal stories— about Chief Joseph and how he had showed him the way to pose his people for photographs. And how he had used the light and the faces and the old way of dressing to make the best pictures he could make.

"They don't wear those clothes now, Pop?" Hal seemed interested.

"Some do, some don't, son," Edward said. "I ask them all to wear the traditional costumes, so I can make a record of how they all used to appear."

"Makes sense to me, Pop," Hal said.

"I hope the scientists will be as forgiving," Edward said, as much to himself as to the boy.

"I'd love to wear a war bonnet," Hal said.

"Who wouldn't?" Edward said. "But it's only the warriors of a certain rank who can wear one."

A rustling in the underbrush startled them. "And the snakes Mama said you danced with?"

Edward told him about the Snake Dance and the young boy who had been bitten. "I was missing you," Edward told him. "Looking after this young wounded boy and thinking about you."

"When you're away, I miss you, too, Pop. But I'm happy now." He was even happier to climb on a horse and survey the rolling prairie, which had been sculpted a very long time ago—before what we call time even began—by the ice of retreating glaciers.

They were only half a day out on their ride back east to Pine Ridge in the Badlands of South Dakota, when ice began to fall from the sky—hail stones, or hail balls, they should be called, because they were large enough to give them a good pelting. After riding fast and hard for about twenty minutes, they found refuge under a stand of small cottonwoods.

"Oh, Pop!" Hal shouted out, both exhilarated and full of worry. And then lightning struck all around them, a sizzling spatter of celestial electricity that had the trees bending and their horses dancing on the verge of hysteria.

"Let's get out of here!" Edward reached over and took Hal's horse by the mane, and the two of them trotted out of the trees just as a large slash of lightning whistled past them and set the leaves smoking.

They galloped away, the rain soaking them to the skin, nothing a man wants for himself, let alone for his son. The winds roiled up, the winds whined down, and after about ten minutes or so of moving fast, they slowed their pace and spent the next several hours walking along behind the fast-moving storm clouds, feeling more like swimmers in the ocean than riders on the land.

That night, when they were camped out in a wet patch of woods, huddled around a damp, smoky fire, Hal began to tremble and shake in his sleep. "The hawk," he said aloud in the dark, "the hawk head...."

"What, son?"

"Handle-bar," he said. "Pick a whistle. Vermilion."

"Vermilion?" Edward didn't even know that Hal knew a word like that, let alone could say it in his sleep, and it was then that he realized just how feverish the boy had become. "Calm yourself, son," he said. "I'm going to fetch something to cool you down." He wet his neckerchief with water from his canteen and touched it to the boy's forehead, suffering a feeling akin to a knife-wound each time Hal twitched under the grip of the fever.

Morning came and they had to mount up and continue their journey, though Hal was not feeling much better than he had been in the middle of the night. He rode along, slumped on his saddle to one side or the other, only now and then sitting up to look around, as though he had suddenly awakened from a dream.

And all that day they rode east, back toward Pine Ridge, the wind blowing in their faces and Hal's forehead hot as a rock stowed in a campfire, and once when they stopped beside a creek and Edward washed Hal's face with a cloth, cool with the waters, he cried out for his mother.

And then there were a calm few hours as they rode further.

He called out that night as they tried to sleep. "Pop! Oh, Pop!"

"More hawks, son? You see more hawks?"

"No, sir," he said when he came fully awake. "Only the calvary."

"You mean the cavalry?"

"Yes, sir."

Suddenly he was quite lucid. That battlefield they had toured had been haunting him, he explained to his father, and they talked a little about what had happened back there—the final rising of the Indian Nations against the encroaching federal cavalry, and what a good punch in the nose it was to the army, the last blow of any consequence struck by the Indians.

"Why did we do it?" Hal asked.

"Lose that battle? Because there were many more of them than us, and we were full of pride."

"No, why did we attack them?"

"Attack them? They attacked us."

"The first time. At school, Pop, somebody always throws the first punch."

"A good question." Yes, a good question, from a feverish young boy lying next to this dying fire in the midst of the wilderness. "Land, I suppose," Edward said.

"But we have plenty of land, Pop. We have a whole city back at home."

Edward couldn't help but laugh. "Some people just aren't satisfied," he said. "And also there's more and more of them."

"More Indians?"

"Fewer and fewer Indians. More and more of us. We kept coming over on ships, and we kept moving West, always Westward. Some people stayed in the cities, but it's harder to live there, so people came out to look for land to work, and they kept moving West, and they met up—or they used to meet up, anyway—with the Indians."

"Well, the Indians were here first."

Edward nodded, marveling at his boy's way of making a fair game. "Yes, they were."

"When we play at school, whoever gets to a place first can stay on that place."

"I know it seems simple, son. I truly wish it were."

He explained that it was a man's game, not for boys, the greed and lust for all of the land within the compass of one's vision. So, we'd do a lot better going back to being boys, then, is what Edward saw. Boys weren't greedy, just strong-headed. Boys didn't care about gold. It was a different story for the adults. Gold made all the trouble. When the first gold came tumbling out of the rock in the Black Hills into the hands of some itinerant miners, the end had begun for the Indian Nations. Gold was land, concentrated, value you could hold in the palm of your hand. No need to work it. Just mine it and sell it. Problem was, you had to mine it on land that belonged by sacred treaty to the Indian Nations. So, when the miners came in large numbers, the troops arrived to protect them, and the Indians fought back, and we were left with massacres and victories that lead only to defeat.

Hal, his eyes already lighted up with fever, brightened even more. "All for gold, Pop?"

"I don't pretend to understand much of it, son," Edward said. "I suppose I'd agree with that old saying that money is the root of all evil, because that sure seems to be driving all this we've seen. When I was growing up my father tried to teach me that Christians do better with controlling their greed than others, but that doesn't seem to be the case. Getting all puffed up about

Jesus just seems to make some people worse than those without Jesus. These people I've given all my time to, these Indians, you never see them killing for anything but maybe a horse or an insult." He sighed and took a deep breath, reaching over and feeling Hal's forehead. The boy was hurting, and he, like any good father, was hurting, too, because of it.

"But for money? Never. They have no use for money. Or didn't used to. And they never heard of Jesus until a couple of hundred years ago. Though they seem to have had a notion of a messiah coming to save them back about twenty some years or so when this Ghost Dance business got started. Makes me wonder about George Catlin. He's a writer and painter who talked a lot about Indians, and when he talked about the Jews being the ancestors or at least the cousins of the Indians, it didn't make a lot of sense. Who knows? He could be right after all. But finally it's more pagan than anything, the Indian religion. The more I learn about it—and I'm learning huge amounts about it every trip I take—the more it seems like the way we all probably were, all people were, when the world first got started."

"That's why you take pictures and write it all down, right, Pop?"

"Right, son."

"Mama says what you do is important."

"She says that, does she?"

"All the time, to all of us. When we get, well, not me, but the girls, get weepy about you being away, she says, 'Children, your father is out in the wilderness doing important work for all people.' That's what she says."

"She's right, son. It is important. Though that doesn't make me important. I'm just a messenger. I make my pictures, son, and write down what I learn about the customs, so that there's some record of what they lost, and what we lost."

His face brightened even more. "And I'm here in the wilderness with you." He didn't say another word, lapsing suddenly back into the depths of his fever, and looking like nothing but an orphan boy whom people called "poor," as in the story of the origins of the Sun Dance that Edward was putting together in his notes.

He helped Hal get ready for the last part of their ride, worrying terribly about the way the boy sat slumped over in his saddle. He looked too much like a young dead man and too little like the boy he'd been when they first started out.

"A hundred miles more, son," he called to him.

"Yes, Pap," he said, his voice as weak as Edward had ever heard it.

And then, fifty miles. He kept on talking, but Hal stopped responding.

And thirty. His throat went dry.

And twenty. And he didn't open his eyes. By then, Edward was trotting alongside him, working to keep him from sliding off his mount.

The last ten miles Edward sat Hal in front of him on his horse. He could feel his son's feverish heat right through his rough clothes.

"Just a little longer, son," he said, hoping to soothe him.

When they arrived back at Pine Ridge, Hal was burning hotter than ever. An Arikara medicine man waited for them in front of their lean-to. His hair was greased and small seashells dangled from slender braids. "Curtis, you called me."

Edward appeared puzzled. He hadn't said anything, but who knows if some scout had seen them on their way and made out by their postures that something was wrong? Or perhaps he read the terror of his worries on the air?

Immediately the medicine man went to work on Hal (lost to the tremors of incessant shivering as his fever increased), setting small mounds of herbs afire and beating out special rhythms on the back of a turtle shell. Now and then Hal would open his eyes but didn't seem to see them.

"Leave us now," the medicine man said to Edward.

And so he walked out and around the camp, climbing a slight rise and fixing his eyes on the western horizon, chiding himself because of how stupid he was, how selfish, how ignorant, how stubborn, how mean and narrow-eyed! "Please, God of the Ghost Dance," he prayed silently, "even you, Jesus, Pap's old God, please get together and help my boy, please!"

The day went dark and half a moon rose, and he wondered at the shadow part of the otherwise glowing sphere. The thought of suffering Hal came back to mind. I have been a bad father, he accused himself, and a bad husband, throwing away my life for people who—

An owl called out. He hurried down the hill to the lean-to to find the medicine man still lost in his curative singing. When he saw Edward, he paused, looked him in the eye and said, "I don't know. Send for the boy's mother."

I was away for several days, gathering data from outlying encampments and in my absence Jimmy had arrived to assist Edward with his research. Edward asked Jimmy to take a telegram message and ride over to the nearest rail stop.

"Boy's not doing so well, eh?"

Edward lowered his head, as though he could feel the weight of Hal's fever pressing on him. "No, Jimmy. If you could hurry...."

"Hurry is my middle name," he said. "I'm already on my way."

Edward watched him walk away toward the corral and sat down in the dust outside the lean-to, listening to the medicine man's songs, telling himself that Sun Dance story we had just learned from one of our recent Plains informants.

Poor was unaware that his new friend was Morning Star. They played together, and as the day advanced and they became hungry, Morning Star disappeared into the undergrowth and soon returned with food. So for many days they amused themselves, their favorite pastime being the construction of a miniature sweat-lodge of a hundred willows and a round lodge of poles, and then singing certain songs that the stranger knew.

His body felt as though it was weighed down by a mountain, but he got up and went into the lean-to, kneeling next to Hal, and telling the story into his sleeping ear, while the boy tossed and turned in his fever. If he heard him, he didn't acknowledge it. Eyes shut, fingers wriggling, chest heaving—he frightened Edward more than he could say.

Days and nights went by, and Edward told Hal one tale after another, or told himself, trying to keep his own soul together, bound in words and accompanied by the thumping of the medicine man's small drum.

Another night passed, and Hal was breathing harder than anyone Edward had ever heard breathe, even his father on his deathbed. "Please," he said to the medicine man.

The medicine man ignored him, pounding out a small rhythm on his drum, turning back to his work over Hal's trembling body.

Sun passed his hands through the smoke, rubbing them then over the young man's left arm and side and face, and then over the right, to purify him and to remove the odor of earthly people. And then the youth's body was like yellow light. Next he began to brush lightly with a feather over the boy's face, obliterating the scar and causing

*him, with the final touch of long yellow hair, to look exactly like
Morning Star. Finally he led the two youths into his lodge and
placed them side by side in the position of honor at the rear.*

"Old Woman," said he, "which is our son?"

She pointed to the young man, "That is our son."

*"You do not know your own child," answered he. "This is not our
son. We will call him Mistaken for Morning Star."*

*The two became close companions. One day Morning Star
pointed out some large birds with long beaks, warning his foster
brother that he must never go near those creatures, for they had
killed his brothers with their beaks. Suddenly the birds began to
pursue them. Morning Star fled, but a warrior named Scarface
picked up a club and one by one struck the birds dead. When
Morning Star related to his father what had happened, Sun made
a song of victory for his warrior son, and in gratitude for the saving
of Morning Star's life gave him the forked stick for lifting embers in
making incense and a braid of sweet-grass, emblems of the sweat-
lodge medicine.*

The medicine man brought in a colleague to consult, and the
two of them began to chant over Hal's sleeping body. All the
next night Edward tossed and turned on a blanket next to Hal,
waking at the slightest change in his breathing.

Dogs barked. Far away in the night there was a howling, and
another and another, in coyote chorus. "I'm sorry," he said in
prayer to every god and no god at all. "I've thrown my life away
on Indians, and this is what I've got for it, my feverish child. Is
there nothing I can do that will save him?" He went back over
his life, trying to find wrongs he could ask forgiveness for, and
hoped that that would do it. His little brother, how Asa both-
ered him—forgive him for that. For thinking lustful thoughts
about Morgan's librarian while married—forgive him for that.
And for his flights of fancy with Tasáwiche—forgive him for

that. And for not really caring for his father's religion—forgive him for that. (But to whom was he praying? To Jesus? The Great Spirit?) Help, help is all he asked for.

"Tell you what, Lord," he said in the moment of his greatest desperation. "Heal my boy, and I will give up this project. Make him well and whole, and I will return to Seattle and stay in the studio for the rest of my life." Such exhilaration overtook him once he said this that he began to laugh and shake all over when the idea caught hold of him. "Yes," he vowed, "I will give it all up and return home." But there was no change in Hal.

Some days later, Clara, led by Jimmy, came riding over from the railhead. Edward had no idea so much time had gone by, except that his clothes were filthy, and he was sleepless and soaked in sweat and fringed with an old beard—but Jimmy had sent the wire and waited for a reply, and then waited several days for Clara's train to arrive.

"You got my wire?" Edward asked.

"Apparently," she said, allowing him to help her dismount, as Jimmy wandered off into the middle of the encampment.

"How was your trip?" Edward asked.

"I don't like horses," she said, looking around at the camp as though she had just awakened into a nightmare. Her usually carefully brushed hair was all askew, her eyes were red from lack of sleep, and her dress was rumpled.

"Where is he?" she asked.

"He's here," Edward said, leading her around the edge of the encampment.

"Is he still alive?" She spoke with an urgency that he had never seen before in her.

"He is alive, and almost still," Edward said.

"Edward, don't you talk fancy with me. What does the doctor say?" They passed a pair of young girls, who giggled at them and stared.

"There is no doctor."

She pretended that she did not hear him. "The doctor. What does he say? You did bring a doctor in from town, didn't you?"

"Clara," he said, "there is no town, only the railhead. Town is hundreds of miles from here."

"Who is caring for Hal?" She clutched at his sleeve. "Who?"

"Come with me," he said.

"There is no doctor here," she said, pulling at him. "So you have some medicine man, some savage—"

"Clara, please." He reached for her hand but she pulled it away. Behind them, more giggling. A gaggle of children followed along in their wake. The children fled at Clara's shriek upon seeing Hal.

"You've killed him; you've killed our son!"

The medicine man, like an embarrassed guest at a party, shuffled off to the side, out of the way of her wrath.

"He needs a doctor," she said, kneeling at Hal's side.

"Mama?" the boy said, as though he were seeing her in a dream.

"He has medicine," Edward said, speaking to her back. "He has his own entire medicine man!"

That was when she turned and looked up at him as though he were some offensive stranger, not the father to the boy lying in front of her. "Leave us alone," she said. "Leave. You are good at leaving. Go!"

Shaking his head, Edward ambled away, using the time to walk along the creek that bordered the south side of the encampment and eventually stopping to strip off his filthy clothes and wade out into the chilly water. "Jesus," he said, squatting in the creek up to his neck. He was so worried and tired and confused, he didn't know if he was exclaiming or praying.

And then he ducked his head under the water and held his breath, thinking his vow again. "Make my boy well and I'll do whatever I have to do"—thinking, next, "What I have to do is finish my project." Oh, he was a confused man, and worried, ever so worried. If the boy dies....If he dies....Edward's mind went around in awful circles, digging him deeper and deeper into woe.

But he had to take a breath. When he raised his head above the water, he noticed a bunch of children, boys and girls, had followed him and danced, laughing, in circles, pointing at him, almost as if they knew how confused he was.

He pulled on his clothes and returned to the encampment, where Clara sat with Hal's head in her lap, stroking his hair. If she knew Edward was there, she didn't acknowledge it. He left the tent, and she stayed with the boy all the day and night, bathing him, changing his clothes, and only after she fell into a deep sleep in the wake of the descending moon did Edward dare to approach them again. His son's forehead was still hot, and the boy breathed with a slightly raspy sound.

"An old Elk was jealous of his wife," Edward whispered to him, *"and constantly abused her, so that at length she took her two children and fled. Through the hills, down the river, and into the forest, he pursued them, and there, as he neared them, he sang:*

Atsíwashkuyi ni-saám.
The forest my medicine.

The two young Elks heard and recognized the voice, and counseled their mother not to fear, for his medicine was strong. The three stopped, and as the Elk trotted toward them, his wife began to sing:

Omak-nína, nókooskisi taíkimuki;
natósiyi.
Coming man, my children take pity on me;
they are medicine men.

He tried to sing these words to his sleeping son, but he couldn't get his voice to warble and quaver, the way I could. So he really only talked the songs as he went along, in a voice that betrayed his worry and fears.

The moon had set when Clara opened her eyes.

"How is he?"

"About the same," Edward said.

"The medicine man brought me tea. I gave it to Hal. I want more tea for him."

"I'll fetch it for you," Edward said.

"Thank you," she said, as though he were a benevolent stranger.

"Clara," he said, when he returned with boiled herbs steaming in an animal skin sack.

"Leave me alone," she said. "Leave *us* alone. You have work to do, don't you? Why don't you go and do it?"

Edward had notes he was making about the Sun Dance, which by the tribe is called Akuchishhwnahu, for "house whistle," in reference to the constant blowing of eagle-bone whistles in the ceremonial lodge where the dance goes on. It was a good thing in which to bury his thoughts, and he tried to focus on it.

The Sun Dance of the Arikara in its two principal features—
the personal supplication for spiritual strength for the individual
and the tribe, and the forceful promulgation of precepts of virtue
in women—was strikingly like the ceremony among other tribes of
the plains, but in its details it differed considerably....

But it was difficult for him to go further, for all that he saw when he looked at his pages was Hal's face, his shivering limbs.

About noon of the fourth day of Clara's visit, while the people in the camp went about their waking duties and play, she lay down in the tent and fell again into a deep sleep. How strange it was for Edward to see her lying there in that encampment, as if in another dimension, or at least another country or another time, so unlike the way she lived with their children in the city near the salt ocean where civilization reigned. And seeing her there, he had to ask questions about his own presence among these peoples, for what now had been years and, if he was going to be true to his intentions, what would be many years to come. Was any of it worth the price of the life of a little boy, his son? This was Clara's question, hovering in the air even as she slept. And just then he had no answer, not a yes, not a no.

He took his place at Hal's side, whispering to him about the Sun Dance.

The priest went out of the booth and stood opposite the pole. How such dancers as remained steeled themselves for their final effort of endurance. How, joining hands as the priest waved his buffalo-tail fan about his head as a signal, they ran around the pole, each until he fainted from sheer exhaustion. A helper placed cedar leaves on burning coals, and the priest waved his fan over the unconscious men until they revived. As each one regained consciousness he dragged himself to the burning cedar, exposed his body to the smoke, then crawled back to his place. When the last one had been revived they described their visions. Each dancer during the ceremony had promised the supernatural powers some part of his body; he now informed the old man which part he had offered, and it was cut off in further sacrifice to these mysterious powers.

Edward shut his eyes, overcome by exhaustion. He felt as though his arms might be pulled from his shoulders, his shoulders from his torso. The only thing that seemed to offer relief was sleep, and even in sleep he felt this affliction, struck just then by another, let us call it, visitation, a dream, of all things, about a talking seal who was also a priest, who waved a buffalo-tail fan over his face.

"You do this," the priest said.

"Only if my son," he said.

"Only if your sun?"

"Only if."

"And the god will make it so."

"Then so be it."

"And it be so."

"Not at the cost of my tail," said a passing buffalo bull.

"We all must make sacrifices," said the priest.

"I have," Edward said. "I have made many. Perhaps too many."

The priest waggled the fan at him. "Never enough on behalf of the People," he said.

"Don't I give enough?" Edward asked.

The priest looked up at the sky. A hawk circled above the camp. "Never enough," the bird called down to him.

"Never?" Edward felt upset.

"Never," said the hawk.

Suddenly Edward woke up just as Hal, opening his eyes—still tinged with the red of fever—himself sat up and said, "Which part, Pop?"

Edward's heart sat up! And he took a deep breath. "The part in the story? I don't know, son," he said. "Which would you choose?"

"One of my ears," he said.

"Good choice," Edward said. "You can always use a finger, and if you give up a toe, why you couldn't balance yourself properly when you walked. But an ear, that's just the outer part of your hearing facilities, correct?"

"I think so, Pop."

"So you made a very good choice. An ear for the Sun Dance."

"But Pop?"

"Yes, son." He sat beside him and put a hand to his forehead, feeling still the heat that had overtaken him, even on this relatively cool summer day.

"Where do they put it?"

"Put what, son?"

"The ear."

Edward pursed his lips and thought a moment. "Why, you know, I haven't found out about that yet. I'm just going to have to ask someone, if they'll tell me, since it's one of the mysterious parts, as I was telling you."

"You see any one of the Indians cut his ear off, Pop?"

"No, son, I didn't. But I'll take a closer look."

"You'll tell me if you do?"

"Of course."

"And if you see where they put it?"

"I'll tell you that, too."

Hal closed his eyes again. His father watched him until his breath resumed the quiet evenness of sleep, and Edward realized only then that he had been holding his breath. His heart felt swollen and lagging, not at all the excited heart that pounded against his rib cage when he was making his (apparently empty) vow to end his project. A great sorrow prickled his chest and rippled along his arms.

It was a cold wind that blew over them, cutting down aslant from the icy northwest corner of the continent all the way to where they found themselves here on the great plains, and Edward, shivering in its presence, left his son and wife and stumbled around the camp. He was still floundering about in his confusion, going back and forth, back and forth, when he fell into a sort of zombie-like meandering, stopping only now and then to watch a hawk fly overhead.

CLARA

On the other side of the encampment, where she had been consulting with the medicine man, Clara was suffering her own sort of confusion. A hawk flying overhead caught her eye and steadied her for a moment. Then she looked across the plain at the horizon point, where the brown earth faded into the pearl-white sky and lost her composure in the point where all things blurred into one.

A sigh floated from her lips, and then up from her chest rolled a deep, deep moan, the noise of someone who had grown sick in the weather of a long winter and seemed nearly unable to recover. Edward, to whom she had pledged herself from an early age, was causing her such unhappiness, she could barely suffer it anymore. Now and then, in times when she left her heart unguarded, such as when she had just put the children to bed and was preparing to spend yet another evening in the house without Edward, or when she found herself in an odd moment staring out over the Sound and wondering where he might be just at that exact time, she wanted to float away from the earth, leave everything behind, and join herself to all the dreams she had dreamed as a girl, dreams of happiness and serenity, of home.

The children always called her back, as Hal was doing now, poor, feverish, whimpering boy. Someday, when she had no one to care for, when the children were grown, she might consider walking from the house and never looking back, going to the train station, perhaps, and taking the first passenger train heading north or east, or even—her worst fear—climbing into a boat and paddling or rowing out into the Sound and seeing where the currents might take her, exploring the islands, places she could sometimes catch a glimpse of hovering on the horizon on a clear summer day but where she had never been before. Someday she might do this.

Voices on the other side of the encampment brought Edward back to himself. Tucking the blanket tightly around the sleeping Hal, he looked up to see Clara and Jimmy walking toward him across the grass.

"He's a little better, isn't he?" Clara said. "Jimmy said he would be."

"Yes," Edward said, testing Hal's forehead and feeling it still quite warm. But it wasn't burning to the touch, the way it had been for so many days.

"When's the next train from the railstop?" he said to Jimmy.

"This evening, eight o'clock," he said. "Westbound."

Edward looked over at Clara. "Don't you think he ought to rest a bit more before traveling?"

The fire rose up in her eyes, and just as suddenly subsided. "You're right. He can use one more day of rest."

"Thank you," Edward said.

"Thank me for what? He's our child. I came all this distance—"

"I know," he said.

"Please have some understanding...."

He held out his arms, reached for her, and she tilted forward and nearly fell on top of him.

"I've been so worried about him...."

"He's going to be fine," Edward said.

Immediately, she pulled back from him. "How do you know? How would you know?"

"Clara, I will try to make this up to you; I will try to make this up to him."

Without a word she turned and walked away. All the rest of that day, she kept her distance from him, even when she was close by tending to Hal. That night, around the fire, she refused to speak when he addressed her.

"Tell him," she said to Jimmy, "that Hal and I are leaving tomorrow."

Jimmy was a smart man, a learned man, but when he looked over at Edward just then, you could see in his eyes that he was quite unsure about what to do. Edward turned away, feeling his teeth jammed into his mouth. Clara ignored him, briskly going about the business of gathering Hal's belongings together to get him ready for their journey home.

When I returned to the camp, notebook in hand, I found Edward sitting rather disconsolately in our tent. I said, "I have some good new stories. Want to hear them?"

"Of course," he said. And he listened while I read my notes. His thoughts kept turning to Clara and Hal on that train heading west, where were they now? Over in Idaho? And then Spokane? And then roaring down the last few hundred miles toward Seattle through our great green forests toward the clam-white horizon that hinted of the sea?

"You're distracted," I said. He explained why. "If I ever have a family, Edward, I will stop my work here," I said.

"Even you think that way? Then who will do it?" he said. "Who will do it? Who will do the work?"

We spent a long night of work around the fire, with lamps lighting the way for Edward's pen, while I went back to talking to the elders. We put together the old stories as they told them to us, and this time Jimmy came into the tent to hand Edward a telegram that had been sent to the railhead and delivered here by a young man from the tribe. Clara and Hal had arrived in Seattle—and the boy's fever had broken!

"You know, Mr. Curtis, that boy of yours will be doing just fine," Jimmy said.

Edward stared at him, because there was something else in his eyes that he could say but wasn't saying.

"Yes?" Jimmy said nothing, just kept on looking at him.

"Say what's on your mind, Jimmy."

"I wouldn't worry about your boy. It's Mrs. Curtis who's probably not going to survive all this."

"Did she say something to you?"

"She didn't have to say anything."

"At least my boy's fever's gone," Edward said. But he had to admit to himself that his own fever lingered. He had worked with dozens of tribes by now and had another hundred to go! And even after his trouble with Clara and Hal's illness—or because of it?—he was more enthusiastic than ever about flinging his life and work away on the Indians, whatever the expense! To make pictures of a world almost lost, and disappearing faster every day! Yes, he wanted that. But suddenly he charged up to me and pulled me away from the men I was listening to.

"What is wrong with me?" he said, holding onto my shirtsleeve. "My boy nearly died, saved only by a medicine man and his mother's loving care—and I still will not go home?" He didn't wait for an answer, as if I could have given him one, and turned away and walked out into the dark, listening to the animals, seeing the stars like an ocean of light stretched all the way to wherever they end. If they do end.

twenty-five

passing through chicago

LYING IN HIS BED as a young boy, listening to an owl call outside his window, could he ever have dreamed this? T. R.'s endorsement meant the world to him! And to celebrate the publication of this first volume, J. P. Morgan himself was going to throw him a party!

So here he was, traveling across the country again, and even as the train carried him along, he remained lost in writing the second volume, now and then forcing himself to sing under his voice a little song we had rehearsed quite a lot before he left on this trip. He stopped only in Chicago to purchase a suit of evening clothes for the New York occasion.

As though he had just dismounted from a pony that had carried him from the railhead, there was Jimmy, in boots and poncho—living in Chicago again for a while—waiting for him to step off the train.

"What a treat, Jimmy!" Edward said, embracing the lean man from the prairie.

Jimmy pounded him on the shoulder and then stepped back, smiling broadly. "When you wired and said you were traveling through, I was pleased." Jimmy kept Edward company while he made his clothing purchases, and then they went to a steakhouse for dinner and then to a saloon where they drank to the imminent publication of the first volume—a number of times.

"Jimmy," he said, raising yet another drink to his lips, "may I ask you a question?"

"Of course, you can, Mr. Curtis."

"Mr. Curtis? Who is that? I am Ed-sir."

"Ed-sir?"

"My father called me that."

"My father called me...," and then he said a word in his native language that Edward didn't understand.

"What's that? I thought you were Jimmy Fly-Wing?"

"That's my public name. I've got a private name, too, the one only the family called me."

"Of course, of course. I'm supposed to know these things."

"It takes time, Mr. Curtis."

"Ed-sir."

"Ed-sir. When you haven't been born into a tribe, it takes time to learn these things."

"Oh, I was born into a tribe alright. The tribe of troubled white-faces."

Jimmy laughed. "White-faces have made a lot of trouble for us, for all the tribes."

"Jimmy, then what do you make of professed Christians killing off so many of your cousins and then hiring me to make a volume capturing the life that was lost?"

"Interesting question, as my teachers used to say. All I can say is, the spirit moves through this book of yours in a strange way, but it moves." He raised yet another glass, and they drank.

He told Edward stories about his father and grandfather, who spent their lives on the plains. "But they're both long gone." Normally quite stoical, his voice wavered a little.

Edward made a long sigh and stared off into space. "I wish I could have made their portraits. In fact, I'd like to make a portrait of you."

"I have only these clothes," he said, meaning his cowboy shirt and poncho, his denim trousers, his boots. "I know you like to dress us in the old way."

"Yes, yes," Edward said. "To preserve the way things used to look. We could put a hawk feather or two in your hair. Strip away about a hundred or two hundred years."

Jimmy said, "Sometimes I wish I lived back then. Before all of you came here."

"That's the spirit I like to try for in my pictures," Edward said.

"Try for it? You try to catch it. Soul-Catcher, that's why we call you that."

"I don't want to keep any souls," Edward said. "If I catch any, I throw them back."

Jimmy gave him a deep look—making Edward nervous—and then he laughed. "I'm just poking fun at you, Curtis." He took another drink. And Edward took another drink. A waiter came over and took their order. Next thing they knew, they had eaten.

"This America we're living in," Jimmy said, "it's a hard life for us real ones."

"Real?"

"Americans. Not like you Europeans."

"I never lived in Europe," Edward said.

"My grandfather's grandfather's grandfather was born right here. And many grandfathers before them." At which, he pounded the table with his open hand, making the considerable number of glasses and plates sitting there give a jump. "It's a terrible thing happening, this America these days," he said.

"What's that, Jimmy?"

"When the best thing a red man can say to himself is, well, at least I'm not a nigger. First you kill most of us off and then squeeze us into reservations, and then you want to make pictures of us, so nobody will forget what we looked like. That's what the old Conquistadors did to the Aztecs and the Mayans. Have you read Bartolomé de las Casas?"

"No, I'm afraid I haven't."

"You should," Jimmy said. "You should. He was the Spanish priest who came over to Mexico with Cortés and described the old Mayan books made from tree bark, even as his fellow priests were burning them. He wanted to preserve the memory of them…." Jimmy gave the table another whack. "Not the books themselves, only the memory!"

"That's not the only reason I'm making these pictures," Edward said.

"Oh, no? What's another reason?"

"I'm making art," Edward said.

"Out of me?"

"You can make art out of anything. Even you, Jimmy."

"Art is me standing next to my horse?" He stood up rather unsteadily, as though he were about to look for his horse.

"It's the way the angle puts you half in shadow, half in sun. It's the relation of the foreground and background. It's—"

"Edward, have you studied aesthetics?"

"No, I have not. All of my experience is practical." It was his turn to stand. "Our hometown photographer gave me a camera obscura when I was only a boy. And later he gave me a book about photography. The rest I learned on my own."

"So, no Kant?" Jimmy said.

"Kant?"

"Alright. What about Emerson? Have you read Emerson?"

Edward recalled his onboard conversations long ago with Dean Inverarity and Grinnell about the American philosopher. "He's on my list to read," Edward said.

"And you would be well to do that. What about some of our recent homegrown native philosophers?"

"Native?"

"Not as in red man. We don't need philosophy. All of our philosophical questions were answered before we raised them. We had no theories of life. We had—have—life. No, I meant as in Charles Peirce. Granted he hasn't written much about aesthetics but...." Jimmy suddenly stopped speaking and his chin sank toward his chest. When he looked up again, he said, "You have a camera with you now?"

"I have a small camera and a tripod back in the hotel," Edward said.

Jimmy steadied himself with a hand on the back of his chair. "Let's make a picture and see if it's art."

The two of them staggered out of the restaurant, with Jimmy in the lead, and nearly fell while climbing into a taxi. Jimmy was singing to himself some prairie song, grunting and humming it, as they rolled along. Edward tried to grunt and hum with him. They must have been quite a sight staggering through the hotel entrance and across the lobby for one more quick drink at the bar.

"I don't know if I should do this," Jimmy said.

"And why not?" Edward said.

"I don't need a drink."

"Who does? It's a fiesta, sir. A celebration."

"Just one," Jimmy said.

"I'll count," Edward said. In a few minutes they had finished a round. "Jimmy," Edward asked him, "do you have a family?"

"Sure, I do. I've got family going back all the way to the creation of the world out of the big sipapu...."

"And that's funny, because I have a family going all the way back to the time my wife came down with her folks from Canada."

"She's from up there, eh?"

"Yep," Edward said. "And you know what?" He leaned closer to him, melding his spirit-drenched breath with his friend's, amazing himself that he had Clara on his mind even now. "She's got Canadian weather in her veins."

"Oh? Oh, no, Ed-sir, those Canadian woman got to have warm blood to stay warm though the winters."

"I think we know different Canadians."

"Could be, Ed-sir, could be."

"And Jimmy?"

"Yes, sir, Ed-sir?"

"Do you have a w—"

Jimmy sent his empty glass skimming along the bar until it crashed into an array of other glasses. In the next instant, he jumped up from the barstool and said, "Let's go, right now!"

"One more round," Edward said, still seated.

Jimmy was staring at the other side of the bar. "It's time now."

"You didn't answer my question. You didn't even let me ask it."

"No, I didn't."

"Alright." Edward recalled himself to his mission and stood up. And so off they went, stumbling, singing, to the elevators.

Up in Edward's room, Jimmy, at Edward's drunken urging, put on the newly purchased evening clothes and strutted in front of the mirror. "Mother of Thunder," the Indian said. "Holy Prairie Dog! God of the Horses! I just wish I could see a thousand of you Europeans stuffed into those silly suits and a glass of whiskey in your hand! How do you wear this stuff? And I thought our old bear hide and feathers was uncomfortable!" He did a little dance in front of the mirror and sang another old Sioux hymn to himself as Edward set up the camera.

"You should come to New York City for this celebration, Jimmy," he said.

"No, no, you do fine on your own in New York City. It's on the prairie that you need me."

"As you like. You'll be missing quite a party. Alright, ready now?" When Jimmy didn't respond, he looked up from camera. "Ready?"

"This going to be real art?" Jimmy said, running his hands down the front of the tuxedo jacket.

"It's photography," Edward said. "Different from art. But something like it."

"It worries me. I have to tell you that I've been worried all the while I've watched you work. I'm standing here, me, Jimmy Fly-Wing, and you make a flash of light and next thing I know I'm not Jimmy Fly-Wing anymore, I'm a work of photography?"

"You're still you, Jimmy. The picture is extra. It's not part of you. But without you, it couldn't have been made. And when the real you dies, the picture may live on."

"And that's how art works?"

"I don't know about the rest of art. That's how pictures work."

"I'll have to think about that. Meanwhile, would you like me to smile?" he asked.

"You never do," Edward said. "Don't start now."

And thus began what might have been one of the most interesting photographs of Edward's career—Jimmy posing with a cigarette, smoke drifting past his water-blue eyes, his pumice-black hair.

If only Edward had remembered to use a photographic plate! But by the time he was sober enough to notice what he had forgotten, Jimmy had sunk down onto the floor and gone to sleep, and it took all of Edward's strength to peel off the evening clothes he needed for his dinner in New York, put them away in his wardrobe, and throw a blanket over Jimmy before a cloud settled over him and he collapsed on the bed.

The next day, Jimmy rode in a taxi to the station with him, humming, grunting, chanting, laughing all the way.

"I had a dream-vision," he said.

"Did you?"

"It'll make you happy. A wise old chief came to me and told me something."

"What did he tell you?"

"He said I should be happy you're doing what you're doing. Without you, none of us would see the way we used to look."

"Well, I'm grateful to him for saying that. You thank him for me."

"If I ever see him again."

"People come back," Edward said. "I've learned that. I've dreamed of some Indians."

"Women, I'll propose," Jimmy said.

"Yes, they were women. But spirits."

Jimmy gave him an odd look. "Now you're talking like an Indian. Maybe something of us has rubbed off on you. Maybe that skin of yours is just white paint." He got a laugh out of Edward with that. "One other thing," Jimmy said.

"Yes?"

"That chief told me one other thing."

"What's that?"

"He said up in heaven?"

"Yes?"

"He said he was thinking about this country down here."

"And?"

"And he said he was thinking about America, and how we Indians were the first to live here, that we came up out of the ground. Nobody else was here when we arrived. So we could stand still and just live out our ways. But since then...."

"What did he say?"

"He said since then, everybody else has arrived, and we've become strangers in our own country. He said it would be better if we went back into the ground."

"I don't think so."

"But you are worried."

"That's true."

"You are afraid that we will disappear, like the buffalo."

"I don't think you'll die out," Edward said. "Merely melt into the American stew."

"We are not part of a stew," Jimmy said. "We are the...."

"What?"

Jimmy threw up his hands. "Oh, metaphor breaks down at times like this, just when I need one."

"Metaphor?"

"Nothing, nothing," Jimmy said. "Ed-sir?"

"Yes, Jimmy?"

"Have a good trip East. Work well. We are working for you."

"You are?"

"We are."

"And who is we?"

"All of us. The Nation, here and gone, living and dead, mortal and spirit."

"Quite a speech to make to a man in front of a railroad station," Edward said. Did he think Jimmy was a little mad? Could he understand what the Indian was saying?

Jimmy and Edward remained silent for a moment. And there in front of the station they embraced in fraternal fashion. "I will see you when next you need me," Jimmy said.

Edward took this as a joke. "Well, thank you, Jimmy," he said.

So the Indian went West and Edward left the city and headed East, without either of them saying much more.

NIGHT THOUGHTS: A BRIEF MEDITATION IN THE DARK NIGHT OF A TRAIN COMPARTMENT HEADING EAST

Out of nowhere came this impulse, and he acceded to it—

You gods, Pap, your old Jesus, and all the tribal spirits I've encountered, all of you, and to you the Great Spirit, I wish to give thanks for having helped me travel this far along the way toward my end, on the project, with these people. For whatever damage I have done to Hal and the girls, and to Clara, I ask forgiveness, but I know not how to do this any other way. I have tried to make it up to her, yes, I have tried and I have tried.

You know, because you can see into my heart, that I am not a bad man, rather, a man with a mission, and if it is not for the greater good what I do, then I don't know how to do anything at all.

So please, as you have this far, because you have taken me this far, bless me in the rest of the way that I must go.

And he lay there in the dark of the eastward-moving train, many, many pictures passing through his mind *beginning with the old Indian woman digging for clams at the waterside, the first portrait he ever made of one of her kind, and the portraits, children and friends, and Chief Joseph, and all of the unknown braves and chieftains, and the women, old and young, snakes and buffalo he saw, roiling in the dust, tramping out great trails, vast herds moving along the waterlines, clouds rising, zigzag lightning tearing across the sky the way a diamond cuts glass, threatening to slice open the membrane of heaven, rainstorms moving in like vast curtains of vertical oceans, dust-devils and wolves, the crying of the horses when they smelled danger, and pine needles hurtling on a wind so strong that they stuck into trees like arrows, and mules so stubborn that they would not fall over the edge into the deep canyon even if you beat them half to death.*

twenty-six

volumes

Announcement

THE
NORTH AMERICAN
INDIAN

BEING A SERIES OF VOLUMES PICTURING
AND DESCRIBING

THE INDIANS OF THE UNITED STATES
AND ALASKA

WRITTEN, ILLUSTRATED, AND
PUBLISHED BY
EDWARD S. CURTIS

EDITED BY
FREDERICK WEBB HODGE

FORWARD BY
THEODORE ROOSEVELT

FIELD RESEARCH CONDUCTED UNDER THE
PATRONAGE OF
J. PIERPONT MORGAN

IN TWENTY VOLUMES
THIS, THE FIRST VOLUME, PUBLISHED IN THE YEAR
NINETEEN HUNDRED AND SEVEN

He is an artist who works out of doors and not in the closet. He is a close observer whose qualities of mind and body fit him to make his observations out in the field, surrounded by the wildlife he commemorates.

—THEODORE ROOSEVELT

Manhattan's loud and particular music drowned out the memory of Jimmy's song and the night-thoughts in his traveling mind, as Edward opened the door to his taxi and proceeded, bellboys assisting, into the Waldorf-Astoria.

"A note for you, Mr. Curtis," the desk clerk said, handing him a heavy envelope with a gilt edge.

Edward opened it at once, and though the lobby was filled with people bustling to and fro, he felt as though he stood there alone, with a cold wind blowing past him.

Dear Mr. Curtis, the note read, in her fine and even hand, *Mr. Morgan would like the pleasure of your company in a celebratory moment before the banquet. His suite. Six o'clock sharp.* And then her name: *Belle da Costa Greene.*

"Mr. Curtis?" He spun around, as though he'd been surprised alone on the prairie by some wild scout or beast. "Johnson of the *Herald*," the young fellow in a dark coat and mustache said.

"Sorry," Edward said. "Didn't mean to seem so wary."

"What's that, sir?" he said.

Edward raised a hand. "Nothing. What can I do for you?"

"I'm wondering if perhaps you might give me a few minutes of your time."

Edward pulled out his watch and saw that he had some hours to spare. He arranged to meet the newsman in the lobby after settling into his room. He should probably have rested, or gone over the remarks that he would make at the dinner, but instead, he opened the drapes and stood at the window a while, looking out over the buildings on Park Avenue, staring west toward the river and the West beyond. Oh, the twists and turns of the hungering soul! Now that he had arrived in New York City—truly arrived, with a great banquet to be held later that day to honor his work— he wanted to turn smack around and head West.

These emotions still weighed on him a few minutes later as he returned to the lobby and met the inquiring reporter.

"So, tell me now, Mr. Curtis," he put to Edward, "how long have you had this interest in the red man?"

"Red?" he said, fending off an impulse to tell this writer to go to hell with all his annoying questions. "He's actually brown, tan, sort of mahogany, or sometimes like walnut, or the bark of the iron tree, a rather pale gray upon occasion, but then I've seen Indians just as pale as you or I, sir, and with hair quite blonde...."

"Well, when did you first become interested in them?" Johnson leaned toward him, either ignoring or not catching his tone of voice, attentive in his reporter's pose, his pen poised above his notebook.

"It's a long story," Edward said, "and I couldn't begin to tell it to you now. Maybe some other day."

"Not even a hint?"

Edward took a deep breath, and found himself looking far back in time.

"I was a boy; I heard an owl outside my window, and I thought it was an Indian calling to another Indian...."

And when did he first become interested in photography? That brought some powerful memories to the surface, though Edward certainly didn't say much to him.

"Interesting," the reporter said, when Edward mentioned his old stereopticon in passing, the one that he had played with on his first train ride West, all those many long years ago. "And do you do many of these things like tonight's event?"

"More and more," Edward said. "I've given lectures and magic-lantern shows, and I have a short motion-picture of the Hopi Snake Dance that I'm going to show in Seattle. I'm hoping that other theater owners might like to book it around the country."

"Motion picture, eh? And you think that's a coming thing?"

"Like these electric lights," Edward said.

"I hear that J. P. Morgan has his mansion lighted by electricity. Is that so?"

"The better to count his money by," Edward said. And then stopped himself. "If you print that, I'll hire the most blood-thirsty brave that I know to come East and scalp you."

The reporter laughed, and closed his notebook. "I had a question."

"Ask away."

"There are some scientists, students of Boas, who have questioned what you do."

"Questioned?"

"They say—"

"Where do they say what?"

"Give me a minute to ask my question. They say, you take these degraded Indians and dress them up in costumes they haven't worn in years. Just to make a picture."

"First of all, who calls these people 'degraded'? Who says this, and where?"

"It's just talk," the reporter said. "But what do you think of that?"

"I can't speak to a question I haven't seen raised."

"Well, let me ask it this way. Is what you do science, or is it art?"

"A little of both, I suppose. But now I've got to go."

Edward had just enough time upstairs to bathe and shave, and take one more look at the skyline before evening came. Oh, he longed to leap over the tall buildings in his line of sight and head west and west and Westward! To the places where he belonged and to the places out there that he had not yet seen, the prairie havens and mountain encampments, the lodges near swiftly flowing rivers, and the big sky toward which rose the smokes from a dozen or a hundred tepees—and yes, he longed too to be back in the house in Seattle with Clara and the children and take the boat across the Sound to his first house there. If only he could live this life long enough to embrace all that he desired!

The sun slipped away over the lands beyond New Jersey, toward Ohio and points further west, and the sky went from a yolky orange to deep purple to black, and after not too much longer, he went out into the bustle of the New York streets to settle his mind before meeting Miss Greene and his great patron.

He knocked. Morgan himself called for him to enter. He pushed open the heavy door, looking around at the large, lavishly decorated suite, which the great man had taken for the occasion, and the familiar fleshy figure seated before the window.

"It looks good, doesn't it?" Morgan glanced up from the volume in his lap.

"Yes, sir," Edward said, as he reached out a hand for him to shake. His grip was firm—it was the first time that they had shaken hands, since in their previous meeting, Morgan had not risen from his seat behind his desk or offered his hand.

"Miss Greene will be here in a moment," he said. "Here." He held out the volume for him to take. Edward had to tear his eyes away from the rich man's bulbous nose.

"You must be pleased, Curtis," he said.

"Yes, sir," Edward said again, as if he had no other words in his vocabulary. He could not accustom himself to the electric nerves that took him over in Morgan's presence. He focused his eyes on the book, studying the beautiful binding, the gilt lettering, enjoying the weight of it in his hands. And the leathery odor arising from it nearly hypnotized him with its delicious flavor, and he wanted to hold the book up to his nose and breathe in a full draught of it, but politeness—or embarrassment—kept him from calling too much attention to his delight.

Just then Miss Greene entered the room, followed by a waiter carrying a tray of glasses and a bottle of champagne. Edward thought his knees might give out.

"You're here!" She feigned delight, but even the convention gave him a little flick of electricity about his chest and heart.

"I am, Miss Greene, and it's a true pleasure."

"So wonderful that we've had a correspondence."

"I'm pleased that you are pleased," Edward said. She offered her hand. Morgan made a noise deep in his throat, the way a pampered animal might when it was not receiving the attention that it considered its due.

"Time for our celebratory glass," Miss Greene said, studying carefully the machinations of the waiter, as he opened the bottle—with a crisp snap of the cork—and poured out the bubbly liquid for their toast.

"To you, Mr. Curtis," Morgan said as he stood and raised his glass.

"To you, sir, for without you, there would be no book."

"To both of you," said Miss Greene. And they raised their glasses to their lips.

"Wait," Morgan said.

"Yes?"

They both stared at him.

"We should have had one of those damned chiefs here, too," he said. "Why didn't I think of that?"

"I'm sorry, sir," Miss Greene said. "I should have thought of that."

"Could we have arranged it, Curtis?" Morgan stared at Edward with his dark and magnetic eyes.

"We might have, sir, yes."

"And whom would you have invited, if I may ask? One of those big Sioux chiefs who killed Custer?" Morgan allowed a certain amount of mischief into his voice.

Edward turned to Miss Greene who was staring at him. "Yes, I suppose," he said. "Or just some unknown Piegan chief or Cheyenne from the plains."

"The unknown Indian," Morgan said. "To the unknown Indian," he said, touching his glass to his lips.

"May Mr. Curtis make him known," Miss Greene said, and she smiled with delight.

"Thank you, Miss Greene."

"And how is your current research progressing?"

"Splendidly," Edward said. "We have enough material for the next two volumes in hand and plan to gather enough for another two before the year is out."

"Ambitious, very ambitious," Morgan said, even as he set down his glass and consulted his large, gold pocket watch. "But now we must go to the banquet and sell subscriptions to your admirable project." As if on signal, one of his assistants opened the door.

"Shall we?" Miss Greene then beckoned for Edward to follow.

In the hall Morgan went on ahead, and Edward stayed close enough to Miss Greene to sup on the wonderful aromas of her perfume. On the stairs he took her elbow, politely helping her to keep her balance.

"Are you nervous?" she said to him as they entered the ballroom.

"Any sane man would be," Edward said.

"You needn't worry," Miss Greene said. "Above all else they have their manners. If you were to fall down drunk—"

"Which I don't plan to do," he put in. "Though I must say that the champagne has given me great courage."

"Good. Even if you were to fall, they would applaud politely and have someone carry you out. Not a ripple in the air would remain a moment after your departure."

"Easterners are different from the rest of us," Edward said.

"Are we?" she said, leaning along her arm, with her head in the direction of his.

"You are," he said.

She pulled back and laughed with delight. "I'm so glad to hear that."

He took a deep breath, tasted the champagne on his lips. "You know I've thought about you from the first time we met."

"You Westerners are rather blunt, aren't you, Mr. Curtis?"

"I don't mean to be rude, just truthful," he said.

She laughed, and said, "You're very charming. You say that just like a little schoolboy, Mr. Curtis."

"Edward," he said. "Call me Edward."

"And would you then call me Belle?"

"I would."

"Then I have to think it over," she said. She nodded, rather gravely, given her mood of the moment before. "Good luck with your speech," she said, turning and leading the way into the large noisy room.

Who could have predicted this? Pap Curtis's boy having dinner at the Waldorf with dozens of J. P. Morgan's friends—husbands and wives, elderly financiers, antique librarians and rare-book men, society dames, railroad magnates, men who built the tall city in which they dined—all here at these tables to commemorate our labors. All these furs and feathers and face paint—what a tribe the New York rich comprise! If only Clara could see him now!

Instead, he found himself here amid all this hub-bub, seated on the dais only a few places down from Miss Greene—Belle!—with a millionaire on either side of him. To the left was a gruff old railroad man, a cousin to the Morgans, who did nothing but grunt and eat. On his right, blocking his view of Belle—Miss Greene?—sat a lavishly fat woman, wearing such feathers in her hair that she might pass for an old warrior anywhere out on the plains, and rings on her fingers and jewelry ringed about her thick neck that would mark her as the wife of a maharaja or whatever they call the high muck-de-mucks of India. (Indians and India, how the name of the native man spans the globe!)

Farther down the table sat Morgan, and he never once turned in Edward's direction, though now and then he would gesture or cast a word out over the mob of tables that crowded the dining-room floor at the base of the high seats. Edward couldn't complain. Morgan had invited—or commanded, should he

say?—all of these good, rich folk to come and sup and celebrate
the publication of the first volume. And after much wine and
food—grilled birds, squab, pigeon, and roasted turkey, with
tasty vegetables, the likes of which Edward hadn't eaten since
his last cooked meal at home—it came time for the speeches
and presentation.

First Morgan himself, and then Hodge, our editor (for
whom we had developed a system of having me write out most
of Edward's responses to editorial queries, so as not to compli-
cate the process). Roosevelt was off in Idaho hunting bighorn
sheep but sent a message, saying essentially what he had
written for the foreword to the volume. Polite applause for
each. These hundreds of rich folk, how many banquets did
they attend each month?

When it came Edward's turn to stand and make his little
slideshow, he suddenly began to shake, feeling like the latest
snake-oil salesman to come to town. Except that this wasn't
any old town, it was New York, and the crowd he looked out
upon from the dais showed him curled mustaches and thick
lacquered face-paint, half-lidded eyes, fat cheeks, tiaras
entwined with curls, and jewels sleeping in rolls of thick flesh—
old New York, the New York that bought the very island on
which they stood from the local Manhattoes in a simple
exchange of beads and cloth.

It took a few moments and swallowing half a glass of wine
to calm him down. He was allotted about twenty minutes
officially to speak of people and the project, but in truth, he
knew that he had only about four or five minutes, and he
could see that in the eyes ranged below him, so he tried to roll
all of what he knew and felt into as few words as possible—he
knew, only a hope! only a hope!—and make the images speak
for themselves.

He began by extolling these images before them: chiefs on horseback at the watering place, children at play in the dust of the plaza, riders fading into the haze of late afternoon. *Oohh,* some women in the audience made a welcome sound in their throats.

He spoke with his heart, his throat merely serving that better organ, of small huts gathered in the gloom of a deepening canyon evening, of songs reaching to the highest pitch and then falling to the depths while a drum beat out the steady pulse of earth, of dances, toe and heel, heel and toe, turn and spin, spin and toe, dances that marked in time and space the creation of elements, of seasons, of passions, of hunger, of replenishment, birth, exaltation, and dying.

And he knew that out there in the crowd sat a Mrs. Von Putter, her eyes glazing over, her thick legs tingling with lack of circulation of her very old blood, feeling, as she listened to him expatiate on this subject of no consequence to her, that she must relieve herself soon or die. He spoke directly to her. He raised his voice and sang of maidens and braves (he conjured up Tasáwiche), he spun out stories of the Corn Goddess as she descended toward Earth to make a day possible when the real People could truly save a grain for next winter's planting. He talked his way through the little poetry that he knew.

Mrs. Von Putter fluttered her eyelids.

Their gods lived in the grain and the streams, and in the flowering of the seasons, and in the light that poured down from rain clouds, and in the chirping of birds and the yip-yip-yipping of wild dogs out in the night, in the deep snows and the heat of high summer, in the songs on the air above the circles where the dancers moved, and the drummer thumped out the very rhythm of being alive.

Edward surprised even himself with what he did next.

Atsíwashkuyi ni-saám....

He began to sing of the good medicine of the forest.

Mrs. Von Putter sat upright in her chair.

And a few moments later, after speaking of the Sun Dance, which he promised would soon appear in a volume to be published next, he sang again, this time performing the musical memorial of the man who cheered on a fellow named White-buffalo Chief who performed deeds of great merit—and something, as I have mentioned, we had rehearsed before he left on his trip.

Unistái-na, pináttsiksiwut!
Itássapiup!
White-buffalo Chief, do not stop!
We are looking!

His voice rose and fell in that sing-song fashion that the Plains People employ, as though bouncing their sound from earth to heaven to earth to heaven will somehow keep a connection between the two realms and make the world right as long as the sound echoes across the air. And he looked out on a room of faces, their eyes showing their amazement and confusion. And he spoke of how all this magic used to work for the People whose portraits he had included in this first volume, but that it was all fading, fading fast, or else why should he and Myers—he did mention me, God bless him—have to go among them and live and suffer certain hardships?

And Mrs. Von Putter tugged at her rotund husband's coat sleeve....Wake up! WAKE UP!

Why did the project exist? Because it had to, because these native peoples were fast disappearing into the very land that nurtured them, retreating into invisibility, into emptiness, or into the death of folding themselves into our own way of life. And so some folks had to make a record of who they were and what they believed, while they still held to those beliefs, however fast they were fading away. Of how the earth was made, and how the sun played his role in the creation of the sacred plant, and how the waters gave birth to frogs who spoke of gods, and how they learned the words for bringing animals to their houses, and how they mastered the game of growing food in their circles, and why horses loved them, and the nature of the talents of the snakes, and Coyote's genius, and all the thousand and one stories that passed the wisdom along from one generation to the next, even as the words made warmth and pleasure for the listeners on long, cold winter nights while the wind howled above the tent poles and the fire crackled in the circle before them.

Mrs. Von Putter seemed entranced.

It had all begun here, didn't you know? In our own Far West, everything that we had become had gotten its start in this way— with the discovery of such god-like tricks as making fire and planting corn and other seeds, and aligning the people with the strong sun in summer and the weak sun in winter, and tuning the families and the clans and the tribe to the turning phases of the waxing and waning moons, and what we know about the wind and fire and water and earth around us and beneath us and above, and how the light appears and where it goes in evening and night, and how our blood moves and the way that families flow in time and the people make a space, out of earth and sticks and ashes and bone, painting pictures, sewing the proper attire for the proper occasion with the proper materials.

The ancient Dutch matron sighed and nodded to her husband, who patted her on the hand.

Edward closed his eyes, and opened them to see Belle da Costa Greene leaning toward him along the row of seats to his left. The stirring of chairs and voices before him grew like a rising wind. Applause rose up to slap him in the face. Morgan's chair was empty. Edward wasn't sure why, but his stomach turned a little somersault at the sight of it.

Belle came forward to say how much she admired Edward for speaking so passionately and that she was sure that it would help sell subscriptions. In fact, even as they spoke, people were signing small cards at each table place that would declare their patronage for the entire set of volumes.

"Miss Belle da Costa Greene," Edward said, "can we drink another glass of champagne together?" She pursed her bird-like lips and touched a hand to her hair as though some tiny piece of detritus might have fallen on her from the high ceiling above. Edward's heart leaped to his throat, and he felt like a little boy, though he had never felt like this when he had been a little boy.

"Thank you, Mr. Curtis. But only one. I have an early morning appointment."

"I myself have a very early train tomorrow morning, Miss Greene," Edward said.

"Yes, off to Arizona or some such wild place, aren't you?"

"Yes," he said, "to New Mexico."

She gave him a look as though he were one of a quickly vanishing tribe himself. "You'll do well to get to bed early then," she said, offering him her hand. He stared at it a moment, at her, unbelieving. The room still buzzed around them, but he couldn't speak. "I know a place," she said, leading him through a crowd of well-wishers and somewhat familiar strangers.

Opening a side door on the far wall, she led him in to a small sitting room and only then released his hand.

"Solitude," he said. "But no champagne."

She must have signaled as they hurried through the main room, because no sooner had Edward spoken when a knock came at the door and in stepped a waiter carrying a tray with a bottle and two glasses. She thanked the waiter as he placed the tray on a table opposite a small sofa.

"You run a smooth ship, Miss Greene," he said.

"Belle," she said, as the man departed by the same door through which he had entered.

"Belle, of course, Belle," he said.

With a nod of her head she suggested that he sit on a sofa on which she herself settled as light as a feather and said, "This evening went very well. Mr. Morgan was pleased. You should be pleased."

"I'm pleased," he said, "when I remember that this is not just a dream conjured up out of a pipe."

"Mr. Curtis—"

"I turn the tables on you," he said. "Please, call me Edward."

"I will. Edward." She settled back and he glanced at the nearly imperceptible rise and fall of her chest. "And have you ever smoked a pipe?"

"Opium?"

"No, no, no, not—"

"Tobacco then? With many a chief so far."

She seemed to retreat into what he imagined to be a certain mood of wonder, and then took a sip of champagne. "That must be...."

"Exhilarating," Edward said. "The tobacco itself is intoxicating, and when I look around at where I am sitting when I smoke a pipe, in a tent in the wilderness, making our smoke rise up through the hole in the center of the tent, it helps me to

understand a way of life so different from our own that it might
be taking place in another time...."

"The smoke rising...a beautiful thing that must be to see...."
She took another sip of champagne.

"It is one of those moments like no other," he said. "It makes
a bond between one man and another."

"And the rising smoke? 'We raise our crooked little smokes to
the gods....'"

"What's that?"

"Shakespeare. From Cymbeline. The smoke makes a bond
between men and the pagan gods. Between earth and heaven."

He took a breath and said, "Sometimes I'm embarrassed that
my education is so lacking, Miss Greene."

"Belle."

"Belle. I've never studied. Though I have read some."

"But you have a charge," she said. "You have the task of your
project, don't you?"

"I do," he said, swallowing some of the bubbly wine.

"There is nothing more important than a man with a project
or a mission."

"Like your Mr. Morgan."

"Like my Mr. Morgan." She took another sip. "And like you."

"I'm not in his class, Belle."

"No, no, no," she said, sliding toward him. "I am not
comparing you." She touched him on the coat-sleeve and kept
her hand there.

"I suppose I was the one who initiated the comparison."

"Initiated, yes," she said.

He took another sip of champagne and then inhaled deeply,
leaning back and enjoying the combination of wine and the
perfume she exuded like some lovely night-blooming flower.
"Mr. Morgan is very fortunate to have you in his employ."

"Mrs. Curtis is very fortunate," she said, her hand still on his sleeve.

"And why do you say that?"

"Because you smoke a pipe with her."

Edward laughed, but not, he hoped, all that loudly. "Mrs. Curtis and I have never smoked a pipe together," he said. "Would that we had. It might make for more peace between us." Thoughts of Clara! Life on the Great Prairie could not have seemed more foreign to him than his immediate, though fleeting, memories of the house in Seattle and the house on the island.

"Nor have Mr. Morgan and I," Belle da Costa Greene said, calling him back to the moment. She tilted her face up toward his, as if in expectation of something he had not anticipated. "No, no, he and I...," her voice dropped to a whisper, "have never...."

He leaned forward, breathing deeply of that perfume and the alcohol on her breath. "Ever?" he said in a whisper.

"Ever...."

"What?"

"Ever...smoked...." She drew back. "I must go."

He shook his head in disappointment. "Your early appointment."

"Yes."

"And I have my early train."

"Yes, you do."

Edward sat up, saved by the motives of the woman opposite him, not from any good plans of his own. "May I keep on writing to you?"

Regaining an almost regal haughtiness and cruelty, she nodded. "You may. I can pass along news to Mr. Morgan, certainly."

"News?" he said.

"Of the progress of your project." She stood up, and it was as if for her, she had never been sitting next to him, though they had sat so close that the memory of their proximity would stay with him for a good long while. "Good night, Edward," she said.

His name!

"Good night," he said and watched as with a little turn of her wrist and a wistful smile, she went out the door. He followed and watched as she faded into the still chattering crowds.

"Excuse me, Mr. Curtis?" A patron was upon him, with questions about savages and the changing nature of the West. It took him several minutes to extricate himself, and then another gent took his place, with Edward all the while trying to see if Belle had stayed behind or if in fact she had left the hall.

By the time he left the banquet room and made his way to the lobby, she was nowhere in sight. He started when he felt another tug at his sleeve.

"Quite a night," said Johnson, the reporter. He still held his pen and notebook in hand, but appeared to be somewhat fatigued, with a little twitch having appeared—tic, tick, tic, tick—at the corner of his left eye. "Want to see a little of the town?" the reporter asked.

Edward laughed at himself, at his pretensions and his betrayals and his hopes and his vision. Waves of noise from departing diners swelled his head. The room tilted, and then righted itself. No Clara. No Belle. Never, never, never, never had he ever felt so utterly alone, especially in a crowd. Not even in the middle of an encampment of a thousand Indians. His heart contracted into something that felt like a tight little knot, and his limbs trembled as he moved about. This was the night of his greatest triumph! And it made him into a treasonous husband and an agitated animal of a man. His knees ached as he started walking, following behind the beckoning journalist. Leaving the lobby of the hotel, he stepped onto the street as though ascending a gallows. His life, as he knew it, he was sure, he was worrying, he was celebrating, he was fearing, was over.

And that's how, after his dinner at the Waldorf, he came to be sitting in a cave-like saloon called Chumley's in old Greenwich Village, lower than he had ever been, though how much lower he would soon go, he had no idea.

"Nice," Edward said. "Nice. Very old buildings here. Interesting. Seattle was still a patch of woods on some hillsides while this part of your city was thriving. I see." He swallowed more beer and leaned back in his chair. "The city fathers almost named our city New York, you know."

Johnson laughed. "Sorry. But it's hard to imagine any other place called New York but New York."

"That's why they eventually gave up on it, I suppose. But it shows great hope, doesn't it?"

When they left the pub and came back out onto the dark street, it wasn't the same street from which they had entered. "This Village of yours can be just as confusing as a forest," Edward said to Johnson.

"Have no fear," he said, leading Edward onto a narrow lane and down around another corner. Edward stumbled, and Johnson caught him by the arm. They were turning a corner into a small alley, blue lights burning at the far end.

"Is that what I think it is?"

Johnson chuckled like a little boy, deep down in his young throat. "The Blue Mill," he said.

"What do they mill there?" Edward said.

"The souls of men," he said.

"Ground down under...let me think...could it be...?"

"I think you've guessed it," he said. "Come on."

They approached a small door beneath the pair of blue lights, and Johnson rapped hard twice just above the empty place where once had been a knocker. "Yes?" said a woman with a cracked voice on the other side of the mysterious portal.

"Johnson," his young guide announced to her.

"That's your real name?"

He averred that it was, and she laughed. In a moment they were admitted to a dark hallway by a gnarly knuckled, old woman wearing a long white gown. Above them music floated, and a woman was singing a melody without words.

"Come along," the old woman said, as witchy and fairytale-like as any of her kind that he had ever seen. And he understood that old New York was like a place out of legend, and that the brightness and gaiety of the grand hotels burned with the same fire as lighted places such as where he now walked, up stairs and into a small sitting room where several women in near-undress sprawled on sofas and over the sides of chairs.

"Mrs. O'Melviny's," Johnson said, with a little nod and a finger pointed in the direction of the door to another room.

He noticed that the door had opened—what had he been watching that he hadn't seen it?—and out stepped a tall, thick-boned woman wearing a wig of dense white curls, the kind of hairpiece that he associated with the heads of the Founding Fathers in paintings and picture books. Her simple gown, of a color similar to the wig, fell in a single sweep of satin down her long frame, like water over a ledge.

"Mrs. O'Melviny," Johnson said in the tones of someone new to making formal introductions.

"Charmed," Edward said, holding out a hand to her.

Her eyes—ice-blue and recessed far behind the promontories of her cheekbones—sparkled a little, like ice in sunlight, as she touched her fingertips to his. "And what is it you want?"

Edward stared at her, the lights went low, the sounds around them faded, and he leaned close, and she inclined toward him, as though this were not an unfamiliar posture, and he spoke softly in her ear. "A dusky woman," he said, as some reed tore within him, "the duskiest you have."

Library of Congress, Prints & Photographs Division, Edward S. Curtis Collection,
LC-USZ62-130191

twenty-*seven*

the assistant—2

ON A SUMMER EVENING in 1909, in a cabin outside of Billings, just after the birth of his last child, his daughter Katherine—the news of which had put him in a turbulent mood—Edward called for a halt to our labors and without too much fanfare confessed to me the indiscretion that he committed that night in New York City.

"I have always been a man troubled by conscience," he said. "Perhaps too troubled. You know that, William."

"I have listened to you, it's true," I said, "and you have admitted mistakes but never many regrets."

"I have had so much luck," he said. "Such good fortune."

We were sitting on the ground just outside our tent, eating pan-fried trout coated with wheat-berries and washing it down with a jug of fresh water from a nearby stream. We could hear noises of the life of the small village nearby: dogs barking, children crying. Except for the occasional glimmer of a lamp from the village where once only cooking fires glowed, we might have been living, as was often the case with us in our fieldwork, in some time a thousand years ago, or perhaps even several thousand years ago. These were the moments when my old skills at

reading Greek and Latin coincided with my new skills at translation of all these many tribal languages, and gave me a push
back into a time before modern time. Once Edward started
talking, I put this feeling aside and longed for, unusual for me
since I was never much of a drinker, a large goblet of wine in
hand rather than pure water.

"Oh, yes, I have had great good fortune, but of all things," he
said, "I am so ashamed."

"Oh, no, sir," I said. "You're an unusual man but you're not
more than human."

"Yes, that's what I told myself." Edward took a swallow of
water from the jug. "But the guilt and worry won't leave me
alone. Clara and I, for all our squabbling, had a pure life
together. And then I went and sullied it. And tried to make
things better. Now we have another child."

"I'm sorry, Edward. Both sorry and happy to hear about the
new child."

"Balm for her mother is what she'll be. At least I believe that
is the case. Poor thing. Clara has come to hate the field. Though
she has done a fine job managing the studio."

"More than that, Edward. Certainly more than that."

He sighed heavily, and said, "I have always told you everything. And now I have told you more."

"And I have told you everything about me, Edward. About
which there is a great deal less to describe than you."

"You are younger than I am."

"And most of my adventures early in life came from reading,
rather than from living. You can put that on my tombstone. 'He
visited Troy and sailed the Mediterranean with Odysseus.'"

"Nothing to sneeze at," Edward said. "One day, if we live
long enough, the only thing of life we'll have is our reading.
Isn't that why we're writing all this down and making our

portraits? To make a record for the old age of our country. So the country can say on its tombstone, 'Once wild men with great hearts roamed these prairies.'" He paused and took a breath. "But why are we talking about tombstones, when we should be talking about life?"

At which point he gritted his teeth, dug a hand into his saddlebag, and came up with a real bottle. (Yes, we still used saddlebags for our supplies, though by this time in our field-work, we drove automobiles and rode trains rather than horses. Ah, such nostalgic dreamers we both were! Which is undoubtedly why we could work so well together....)

"Aha!" I couldn't restrain my joy. To see him like this, the man for whom I had worked all these years, made me understand that at least part of his heart was a wild heart. Mine, I have to admit, was all science and study. Meanwhile, we put that bottle of whiskey to use, and talked, drank, and talked. And now and then, as the alcohol would have us do, we would stop and listen to the sounds around us.

"I must say," he began explaining to me, "I have never ever returned home with a heart heavier than mine weighed after that trip to Manhattan. The children, as always, welcomed me with yips and outcries; always they made me feel like a warrior brave returning to his tribal encampment. To them I am, *still am*, I emphasize, a hero, though of course someone whom in this past ten years or so they saw more from afar than near...."

"Yes, yes, Edward, we did travel, have traveled, will travel," I said, feeling somewhat conjugational from the whiskey.

"But Clara...." His voice trailed away.

"Yes?"

"You know her."

"I do. We've had the opportunity to talk over the years." And it was true that during our usually brief intervals in Seattle, she did always find some time to talk with me. Ever since my once-intended had written me a letter, breaking off our long-held engagement, I was left with nothing but our work, of which there was a considerable amount, to fill my waking hours.

"She likes you," he said, edging me out of my brief reverie about my own lost girl.

"I'm grateful," I said.

"In fact...." Now he took a long swallow from the bottle.

"Yes?"

"She would rather be married to someone like you than someone like me."

I could feel myself blushing. "What on earth makes you say that, Edward? I have spoken to her, but I have to say that I have in no way shape or form—"

"Calm yourself, William. She meant it as a compliment to you and a complaint about me."

Now it was my turn to nurse from the bottle.

"She is a good, steady woman," I said. "I wonder if I shall ever find someone as good and steady as she is."

"Oh, you will, you will. If you haven't already. Wasn't there someone back in Seattle? Wasn't she steady for you?"

"Edward, yes, there was, but she's dropped me because of my travels."

"Ah, yes, yes. But there will be another girl."

"I'm never home, Edward. Sometimes I don't even know where home is. Where would I meet a girl?"

"Different from me," he said. "I know where home is. I just can't get there very often." He took another pull from the bottle.

As for me, I was well on my way toward traveling to another sphere, listening with one ear to my long-time employer, friend, fellow traveler, mentor. With the other I listened to the sounds of the village, wishing, since I was so lonely in this present world, that I could have lived another life and be sitting even now around a fire with a sand-colored woman in black braid, her teeth as white as birch, her eyes bright from the dancing flame, our child suckling at her breast—and later, before the cold moon rose in the sky, I would go off on the hunt with my uncle and cousins, and it would take us far and wide away from the village, to the fields and mountainsides where bucks leaped and we charged the animals full ahead, bringing them down with our arrows and spears, and not to return until we had stored away in the frozen earth our winter cache of meat. By then my wife's belly would be rising softly with the life of another child.

"It was her eyes," Edward said, breaking into my reverie.

"Yes? What about them?"

"The way she first looked at me, when I was making the family portrait all those many years ago."

"Yes?"

"Compared to the way she looked at me when I returned from my compromised trip to New York."

"Did you tell her?"

"I did not have the courage to confess, no."

"But she looked at you differently?"

"Perhaps I hadn't noticed if she looked at me differently before this. But I certainly noticed how she has changed in the way she looks at me now. Something in her eyes, deep behind her stare, told me I was found wanting. As I was. Yes, I was wanting...." He paused and took another swallow of whiskey. "I was wanting something, and so I was found wanting. I found myself wanting, and she has found me so as well."

"I am sorry about all this, Edward."

"I had never failed her before this. Do you know that?"

"I believe I did. I do."

"Though my heart went out when I first met Tasáwiche, I never moved toward that girl. Though I still hear her singing that song in my heart and in my mind."

"She was, is, a beautiful young woman," I said. "Alas, my Penelope couldn't wait for me. Though I hope she hasn't run off with one of the suitors." He either did not understand my reference, or ignored it, probably the former.

"You will settle down one day."

"I hope to, Edward."

"Whereas for me, the question is not when will I settle, but if I ever will finish this project that keeps me from it."

"From settling?"

"Yes, from the children, who are growing by the day, and from that devoted woman who is always waiting for me at the end of the train line."

"She is devoted," I said.

"She is," he said. "But am I? I have failed her. If she never takes me back I will understand."

"But she has taken you back. She has given you another child."

"Yes, I wooed her. And she softened to me. But mostly I think I wore her down," he said. "I am wearing her thin." He sighed deeply and took another drink. "And the same voice you are keeping to yourself as I say this is the same voice that I hear in my own mind. *Then why not do something to change this? Why not settle down?* Over and over. Over and over. The project moves forward with all due speed, and my life goes around and around, like a carousel, like a whirlpool in a river rapids." He let out a most uncharacteristic moan. "Oh," he said, "don't you ever get caught this way, William. Don't ever." His eyes glowed, burned, even, and he seemed about to weep and laugh at the same time.

"I will try not to," I said, "If I ever do have a family, I will try not to." And my own heart sank a little, like the small orb of the bright moon that had ascended and now was sloping down toward the mountains of this state where we found ourselves caught up—oh, still caught! always caught!—in the necessities of the world of our labors. Would I ever have a home and a family? I might as well try to catch the moon, or catch the lightning.

Library of Congress, Prints & Photographs Division, Edward S. Curtis Collection, LC-USZ62-119797

twenty-eight

clara, crossing

"OH, WILLIAM," SHE SAID to me on a ferry-crossing back to the island to meet Edward, who was visiting there with the younger children on one of our infrequent trips in from the field, "I cannot tell you how much pain I feel right now, just crossing over to rejoin him yet again, all these thoughts and worries mounting up in me, like those clouds over the mountains, the clouds drifting, as though the sky were a river, no, an ocean, and these clouds were shifting islands. How I wish I could have put all of these terrible thoughts into a basket and sent them floating away from me on the sky—or on the Sound as we passed over it. I love the water, I watch the water, I hate the water, it fills me up, fills my mind, makes me feel as though I will remain as overwhelmed as I am now with despair for my marriage....

"The years have gone by and in almost every way things have gotten worse and better....The children are growing, and, to be fair and true to him, I have to say that their father remains loving to them in his fashion, though it is his fashion. And now we have yet another child. All the more of us for him to leave behind. He would insist, as he does always, that it is his only work, and it is obsession and vision that carries him away from us so often—that deprives the children of a true and present father. And yet they still love him, truly, I think. Why should I feel such sadness when I say that? It is a good thing, isn't it?"

She paused, and as she might have done a thousand times or more while writing out a bill for services rendered by the Curtis Studio, she stared up, this time seeing a high-flying bird, a gull, soaring across the Sound in the direction of the mountains.

"All these years I have tried to endure his passions, to tolerate them, to make room for them in the life of our family, and I know that he has struggled, too. And I am the one who has held the business together. I don't say this out of vanity, but it is true. So much at home has depended on me.

"And then to have him come home from yet another trip to New York City and see that news in his eyes!

"And to have him say nothing! Does he think that I can't see into his gaze? Does he think that the same power of the look that he casts through the image-finder in his camera does not, if we look hard enough, show things that live in his mind?

"And to have him say nothing! Though his look said everything!

"I have gone from ignorance to annoyance to discomfort to dismay. I tolerated his passions and his vision, and now I am tormented by them....And I will tell you this, I will confess it, long-time friends that we are, that when he wooed me, I allowed it. And now we have another child, little Katherine, oh, Lord, another child for him to lose!"

I stood silently, listening to the noise of the engines churning in the water, listening to her, watching the gulls skim just above the white-frothed water, scavenging for food.

twenty-nine

jimmy fly-wing's story—9

GOD OF THE COYOTES! Spirits of lightning and thunder! Trying to go home was the worst thing that I could have done. I can't say for sure what I had hoped to find there. But when I returned to Chicago, skulking around, avoiding my old neighborhood, I felt just as bad. I had left everything behind for a second time, and if I woke up one morning with a great weight on my chest and wondered if my notes for my thesis were still tucked away into a filing box in the apartment I had left behind, I did not spur myself on to look for them. Instead, I lay there on a ragged bed in a rented room, as far away from the university as I could live and still stay within the city limits, and dropped into a deep slumber. The next time I awoke I didn't remember where I was and I didn't remember who I was, except that I did not feel well, and I had the great thirst again. I set out to quench it.

I had no family, no wife, no tribe, no clan. Lost to the world I was born into, I had cast myself out of the world I grew into. Couldn't I really feel sorry for myself? Where was I going and why was I going there? The last time I saw Curtis I came out of it so drunk I could not feel my own body, let alone sense the connection between him and me, and between me and the spirits who had commissioned me to watch over him. He was going to New York City. Where I was headed, I didn't know. I just could not live any longer without a tie to one world or the other, and while I knew too much ever to return home, I did not know enough to step completely over the line into the other world I had left behind.

How long after this it was, I couldn't say—a month? a year?—but it was night, there was loud music, and I opened my eyes and I was lying on the floor in a bar near the train station in a place that turned out to be Ogden, Utah, splashed with my own vomit, with two red-eyed policemen standing over me.

"Indian pig! Dog! Scum! Drun-ken bas-tard!"

They beat me so hard they broke my nose and bruised my ribs, so that for days after leaving Ogden I coughed up blood, and I found myself cursing them and not myself for making what they did possible.

Standing at the roadside in a rainstorm south of Provo, I once again considered returning to my own, going back to the family I had left, I thought, permanently behind me, and back to the clan and tribe for whom, I truly believed, I was performing a higher duty by staying away. I had that thirst, too. But a powerful voice still inside of me said, no, you have your purpose, and I walked up into the mountains and found a leaf-fringed cave and lived there a while, eating berries and roots, and wondering if I could survive the winter. I grew as lean as an aspen and turned in the wind in the same wobbly way as its leaves, the better to stay alert. Small fires in the night kept me warm, and I sang to myself and kept my notebooks—the physical versions of which I had long ago lost—in my mind.

After the first heavy snow, which blocked my passage to town, I grew dizzy with hunger, yet I had several visitors.

The first came to me in his white robe, and we discussed ethics and aesthetics, in particular the organic aspect of the play *Oedipus the King*, which I had read in Chicago some years before.

A proper Germanic fellow lectured me on the relation between private and civic morality.

An unkempt German, his breath reeking (and me, dry again, for months now), moved his hands like birds in flight, explaining to me that God was dead and thus all things were possible.

And when Sky appeared, in all his flawless blue-white atmosphere, I knew what I must do.

As though Sky had only to breathe on the land to work his magic, a freak thaw occurred, melting the snow that had kept me from going into town. Thanks to a good Mormon widow, whom I encountered while standing in her backyard patiently waiting for Sky or Aristotle or Kant or Nietzsche or someone to tell me what to do next, I had enough money to take the next train out of Provo. But there was still a period of waiting, I discovered. Two weeks in Denver did me no good. I stayed at a mission house and fell back to drinking during the day. Another month went by—it might as well have been a day or a year or a decade—and I caught a train to Omaha.

Two days, two nights went by, and I truly believed that not only had Sky and the others been hallucinations, but that I was trying somehow to kill myself by conjuring them up. I drank harder than ever before. I fell down in the street and bloodied my nose again. Refused reentry to the rooming house where I had landed, I let the streets take me on as their burden.

It was a Friday afternoon, late, the beginning of another fearful weekend, when I next came to my senses. Snow flittered down across the proscenium of sky, and I watched it from the luxury of an alley littered with old newspapers and rags. An awful odor arose from this ash heap, and I recognized that it was myself. My stomach ached from emptiness, my thirst was monumental. I turned my face into the snow and got to my feet.

"Hey, you!' Someone called out as I peered from the relative safety of my alley. A cop! Coppers! "You! Stop!"

I took off running, and I was miraculously as fleet as when I was a boy. Whistles blew. A car horn honked. And then a siren whined into the night air. I kept on running. Soon the voices of the cops faded behind me, and I found myself slowing down, miserable all of a sudden in breathlessness—I was not the boy I once was after all—and staring up at a theater with a golden-lighted marquee. Light bulbs as large as my fists spelled out a name.

CURTIS

Sky descended lightning-quick into the street and in the guise of a well-to-do gentleman slapped the price of admission into my hand.

Library of Congress, Prints & Photographs Division, Edward S. Curtis Collection, LC-USZ62-104025

thirty

show

Pounding of drums, high sing-song voices (violins and cellos) rise and fall above the drumming.... Mud-heads bend and weave as though their large figures are as supple as grass.... Pounding of drums, the strings singing, sighing, weaving....

(Off to left of the movie screen and to the right—grass huts, beneath which sit the members of the orchestra)

"Now appear the special guests of the ceremony...."

(That voice of his, so rough and raggedy on the soundtrack, he scarcely knows it's his own)

"...the creatures both natural and heavenly whose presence makes all the magic possible...."

The drums, the drums...echoing through the hall.

Snakes writhing on the powdery ground, sliding away into the dust, dancers bending, reaching, pulling them back, tossing them into the air, here one man—man? god-man?—catching the coiling reptiles in his mouth, biting to hold them....

(Off to the left of the screen, off to the right, the musicians twist their bodies to play, and at the same time, strain their necks to watch the images on the screen)

Oh-hey, how the melody bounces up and down above the drums, oh-how-hey, how-hey-how-ho....

(Gilbert's marvelous score, extending the melodies and rhythms Edward played for him from the scratchy Edison cylinders we made far out on the mesas)

Bending, standing, bending, stomping, the snakes writhing underfoot, the snakes whirling like children's toys in the mouths of the dancers....

(And how old is all this? In the books, he cannot speculate, only specify and classify, identify, record, record, with photographs and bars of music, in our strange language, strange so strange compared to all those in which he hears the stories, the histories, the legends, the myths, the tales that dig back so deep into the past that our normal way of regarding time has to be overthrown, and we need to think of time the way the mayfly would need to think of time, if it could think, when it needed to imagine, if it could imagine, just how we big lumbering creatures regard it, not the passing of a single lifetime in a day, but the crowding together of all the lifetimes come before us into a single day, and that day one of hundreds of thousands, hundreds and millions of days)

Pounding of the drums, singing of the cellos....

And now on screen, the scattering of the snakes, the redistribution of the harbingers of rain....

Running, racing, to the four corners, to the four directions, to the four winds....

(Remembering when we returned to the Hopi to make this film, and the priests talked it over, and because of the way he had approached it, he supposed, allowed him to take part in the dance, and the fasting and the sweating and the dancing, all conspired to take his mind and spin it out into the orbit of the moon, and he recalls little of it once it began, except the chanting, the music, and the snakes in his hands and the whispered encouragement of other dancers, his legs grew so weak, now and then they had to bump against him, hold him up, and the last run down from the mesa, he thought that he could never climb back)

"And the stamina of the dancers matched only by the power of these creatures, on whom the rains come to depend...."

(And that's not all that depends on this, the snakes, the gods, the rain, the abundance of the corn, the season of lean winter, spring comes next, because it is also his life that is so intertwined with this now, the music in the concert hall, the images of the dancers on the screen, oh, there, the mesa, a long shot showing the shape of the cliff, the clouds gathering beyond, promising rain, promising rain.... (All the old footage from the first Snake Dance motion picture edited in, intertwined, here on the screen.))

"We can see the gathering storm clouds, the promise of rain hovering above the sacred mesa, even as the dance comes to a literally staggering conclusion as the tired Hopi...."

Dancers stumbling, falling, like old cornstalks before a storm wind, and the camera's eye leads us up above the mesa into the dark heaven of clouds.

(That storm came up out of nowhere, and he said to himself, why, they just always make the dance at this time of year because this is the time of year when the rains come, and I looked at him with a wicked grin and said, Edward, what if they called off the dance one year to see if it was true, that the rains would come anyway, and he said, well, I suppose they just couldn't afford to take the risk, and I said, I have been told, some of the old men have let on to me that there were stories of years far back in the deep past when there would come a year when they *would* call off the dance just to see what would happen, say it had been a fat year the year before and that there was plenty of corn in the storage huts and so the priests might say, let us take a rest from the dance for a year, and they did that, and the time came around for the ceremony and they did not dance, and the rains did not come either, and so they proved to themselves that if they did not dance the snake ceremony, there would come no rain...and so once or twice in a few generations they might try this, to test the power of the dance, the power of their belief...and what if the rains came without the dance? he wondered, and then he told himself that they had not come, so why question, because the causal link had been proven to the satisfaction of the priests and the chiefs, and it brought plenty of corn for the villages, abundant heaps of corn...and what about the old story of Joseph in Egypt and the famine that afflicted the people there, wasn't that a variation on the Hopi corn cycle? an old testament that comes much later than the Hopi dance, and when someone asked about the Biblical parallels in one of the cities where they played the film, and he talked afterward, can't remember where, Cleveland? surely not such ignorance in Washington? but it could have been Washington, and he answered in that way, explaining that the Hopi way goes back, we believe, so much further than the history and lore of the Old Testament, and some stood up to debate him, and some left the hall, but others stayed, listening, questioning, and when he returned home, he told Clara, thinking that it might amuse her, but she became quite angry, and they fought yet again, and he, feeling guilty, tried to make it up to her)

Drums pounding, whining of the high strings,
cellos and drums, eh-hey, ho-hey, hey-hey-oh-hey....

(God knows, in spite of everything, he wanted to hold the marriage together, and after that night, the first time in many, many moons, they fell into each other's arms, weeping, and then kissing, and then came the rest of it, the old Clara, the old Edward, reemerging, but it turned out not to last, in a few weeks he's out in the field again and when he returns, they're back into their old round of regrets and recriminations, and if he could stay home, why then, all would be well, if he could stay home instead of spending only six weeks out of a year in Seattle…on the road with this show now in addition to all the fieldwork…how could he do else but travel? the horizon we head for always seems to be receding the further we push ahead toward it)

You say I don't love you?
You love me but you don't live with me, you live with your
Indians!
I do love you, but I have my work!
And you love your work more than me and the children, don't
you?
I'll show you how much I love my work! I'll show you how
much I love you!
[Picking up camera and raising it above my head—and
smashing it onto the floor!]
Edward!
I'll show you how much I love my work!
[Racing into the studio, snatching up photographic plates and
smashing them to the floor!]

Rain clouds filling the horizon, all eyes, camera eye, human
eyes, eyes of all who watch the screen gather at the horizon.
(Seeing back down the way he has come, and hasn't he always been moving in that direction? with Pap and on the way West,

on the way north, up the mountain and onto the ice, and up
Rainier and looking out across the fog toward the shimmering
Pacific, and, oh, from that way, they came, all the fathers and
mothers of the hundreds of Nations, those Nations we call
tribes, those clans and families, their ancestors, and an
unbroken ten thousand years of small battles between tribes,
and many, many decades of this time without time, a seamless
and unbroken web of family and clan and Nation, with only the
gods above and below to tamp down or push up against the
scattered human beings)

*Pounding of the drums, chanting of the high-voiced violins
and lower throats of the cellos.*

(They know what it is like to make voyages of discovery,
having traveled here—on those big, long water canoes, or on
foot and with dogsleds across the great ice bridge that led from
west to east—and they have made a country on this land and
still hold within them the same sense of wonder that they felt
upon the discovery of this homeland, to live in place and yet to
travel in the spirit, to travel endlessly, while sitting still before a
fire, watching the smoke curl up to meet the nostrils of the gods,
how better to live than that? how better to pray than that? how
better to join the two parts of life, the movement and the stillness, the before and after, the travel and arrival, birth and death,
earth and sky, water and fire, the land and the sea, the visible
and the invisible)

*"…the aftermath of the dancing, the fatigued yet replenished
dancers make their way toward—"*

(But I am only a photographer, he said to himself, and how
am I to know, and how am I to live, the way I have walked, the
path, the things I have seen, this country too large, enough to
contain it all, these disparities, the opposites of us and them,
and how to join these two parts? what I am trying to do with

my images and my recordings, our transcriptions of the stories and the legends, the hawk coyote bear otter eagle weasel rabbit frog stories, the animals alive and speaking…and what of our own legends of the speaking animals in the nativity? some single source for that? who knows? Professor Boas who has written to me about our researches, I could ask him, and do we all share a common religion? what would Pap have said about that? what would he say? Ed-sir, he would say, what makes you ask that question?)

drums again, drums then, drums now, drums

(Drums in all those cities, all those cities that would not exist in a world without the white man's discovery of this continent. Cities where we have played this show, Philadelphia, Milwaukee, Chicago, Los Angeles, Kansas City, the cash it's brought in, not enough, not enough, need the business to pay for the next volume, and the next and the next, Morgan money dwindled and dwindled, not that we spent lavishly, just the rough wagon, the spare supplies, but the money blows away like topsoil in a high windstorm, repairs on the equipment, lost or broken cameras, film, payments to the locals, Washington again, how many times Washington? St. Louis, Omaha, Seattle again, right here in this same hall, again and again, and San Francisco again, am I a Barnum or am I a photographer? Am I a scientist of sorts or am I a showman? Am I an artist or am I a businessman? Salt Lake City, Phoenix, Pittsburgh, Detroit, Nashville, Memphis, St. Louis again, again, San Francisco again, the halls, the orchestras, the tickets, the screens, the sounds of the violins)

drums, drums, drumming, the drums

(Beat of the world, rhythm of the earth's heart, thrumming throb, oh, of the universe, oh, the beat comes the drums beat the drum comes the ear of the beat in my drum and the nights that he learned this sitting out beneath the stars when the rhythm the dancing went on all night the days the nights the dancing went on as in years ago with the Ghost Dance the last gasp of a movement on the plains to bring back the old ones, bring back the dead call them back to arms to war against the government the grim killing government mowing down the people mowing down the old ways plowing under planting over making such noise on the earth that no one could hear the old calls the old sounds any longer...and his own heart sank when he learned of it and fell lower and lower into the canyon of his spirit to the sipapu where the soul appears one day in the body coming out of the crack in space and time that leads to the beyond except that the soul comes from the other direction from there to here and here it is and we are alive, but then he heard the news and his heart his soul sank back down into that first place, nearly leaking through into the non-place the other place where things do not occur do not exist, the not world the not alive not dancing not singing not drumming other plane of the ghosts who are so ghostly that they have not even lived before they died again never to come back, and in that place he languished, so unhappy in the world above— oh, and despite their new child, Clara would not sleep in their bed anymore, saying that he never lived at home so why make a space for him, and there was some truth to that but though he tried to explain and explain that it was all the more reason to sleep in the same bed when he was home he could hear his words falling into the space between them, and he knew in his heart that the better half of him lived in the field—and then that trip up to British Columbia, filming this movie that now flows across the air to dance upon the new screen before them)

Drums, at a fast and steady beat
Chanting high voices in the air behind

(He remembered standing at the pier in Victoria after we had returned from the islands where we made the movie....His cap in hand head cocked to one side and wiggling his nose like a dog tasting the air....He remembered this more clearly than he recalled events in his life that anyone else would call major, his mother dying a few years ago while he was in the field and his brother Ray coming to see this spectacle said to him, "Ed-sir, seems to me you've made quite an improvement over that Snake Dance movie, but now this one new picture of yours it's got a real plot and you make the Indians move around in the world at large outside of the ceremonies at the waterside, and if you're worried that some of those experts might say that you're working beyond your knowledge, then just say to them that you know what you know and that you went out into the field just the way they did and that you had expert informants, which you did, which you did indeed, and which you still do, and opening this movie here in Seattle, why if it goes well you can play it across the country just the way you did the Snake Dance movie, why these movies, they're the coming thing!")

longboat with the bear totem thrusting
forward into the wind, the men digging
their paddles into the deep
approaches
now the large figure in the stern stands
and moves its enormous arms
the bear
bear shaman

huge bear plowing toward shore
boat bearing bear plowing toward

(standing at the pier in Victoria, light rain falling, cold wind blowing off the Strait, and Clara's cousin Will Phillips came running over from the hotel with a telegraph message in hand, and it was the news from Belle da Costa Greene in Egypt, that, oh, gods! Morgan died in his hotel, and all the breath went out of him, and he fell to his knees onto the wet pier, and everything went black, as if he were to die now that Morgan was dead, because it was all over for us, the end of it, the end, and when he opened his eyes, there I was standing over him, and Phillips was standing over him, and he looked up into gray clouds spinning overhead above them)

fast drumming the drums drums

(and he tried to raise money with these shows and it was terribly difficult, so much work for so little return, the news of Morgan took the wind out of him again like nothing since the death of Chief Joseph, and he closed his eyes thinking to himself, "let the tide rush in some great tidal wave and wash me out to sea because the great patron lies dead in Egypt," and he thought of how Morgan's breath must have flowed out of him, the gasping, grasping his hands to his chest, and the way his incredible nose sucked in more air, and the great man fell over like a huge redwood)

and high wailing song wailing song

(it was a cold March day and his heart went colder and it was as if he heard news of the death of one of his children the blow came that hard, and while he knew certain things, such as that he and Clara kept clinging to each other even as they grew apart, that he knew, he also knew that the Indians would go on dying and that their old ways would keep on fading day upon day upon day slowly receding into the deep and dark and unrecapturable past and that unless he kept on with his project that there would be less and less of it each day, all this that he knew in his heart he recalled as he watched the bear shaman cavort in the stern of the longboat, the strangeness of it even now overtaking him that he was considered both man and bear, the man beneath the bear skull a man and yet a god so unlike his old lukewarm Christian beliefs and "sorry for saying this Pap but it's what I believe"—but now—the bear and man, one and the same yet different, a man as a god as an animal as a man as a god is a monstrous and yet sublime encounter with the all in the all, and all these old ways dying, like the song now fading on the lips of the chanting men and the lights come up and the people stand and stare at each other, some of them clasping their sides, others clapping, and all this he would have to enlarge and expand if he was going to raise the money to continue the fieldwork and publish the next volumes because in all this he had never ever given a single thought to the possibility that Morgan would die)

and high wailing song
and drums
and drums and drums and drums

The lights come up and he's sitting in his seat, holding his hands to his head.

Library of Congress, Prints & Photographs Division, Edward S. Curtis Collection LC-USZC4-11256

thirty-one

banana gold

Apache, Apsaroke (Crow), Arapaho,
Arikara,
Assiniboine, Atsina (Gros Ventre),
Brule (Sioux)

SOME WORK HAD BEEN done, but we had so much more to do, which made the next few years the most difficult time of Edward's life. Many things seemed to go into decline. Down, down, down. His mother's death had upset him. Morgan's death in 1913 nearly defeated him. Morgan's son Jack took over his enterprises, and Edward had no promise that the money for the project would continue. The movie we showed around the country—New York, Washington, Seattle—brought in precious little after expenses.

Everything seemed to conspire against us. Among other worries—though this may not seem large, it was important—the supply of paper for the volumes came from Holland, and after war broke out in Europe, we could not obtain any for the duration. So though our fieldwork continued into the past culture of the Indian, Edward was growing more and more desperate about the future of one Western fellow, namely himself, as well as all the dozens of tribes and thousands of Indians we had yet to encounter. The weight of all that had by now made that posture, tall man with a slight stoop, as though he were perpetually bent over a camera, peering into a lens, quite permanent.

He was so desperate that he even overcame his shame and embarrassment, and wrote again to Belle da Costa Greene.

Dear Miss Greene,

It is with considerable hesitation that I speak this way, but it is only fair that you have knowledge of the situation. I so deeply appreciate your assistance, and Mr. Morgan's, over the past few years, that the desire to succeed for the sake of his memory is uppermost in my mind. I assure you that I have made about every sacrifice a human being can make for the sake of the work, and the work was worth it. I just hope that the men for whom Mr. Morgan did the most for and made the most for will not turn their backs and let our undertaking languish, for the lack of a few paltry dollars is maddening, and causes me to have a good deal of contempt for mankind as a whole....

Months went by without an answer. Edward and I headed north for a major field effort with the Kwakiutl and other British Columbian tribes, using our last cash on hand to rent a sailboat and crew, and spend some time moving up and down the coast. Before the first snow, we returned to Seattle, and he became immersed in the gloom of his finances once again.

Dear Miss Greene,

The trouble with the undertaking is not in extravagant use of such money as we have, but rather that we have so little. The fault has been the fearful difficulty of securing orders. According to the original plan, the expense of research and publication was roughly estimated at one million and a half dollars. Mr. Morgan's subscription was seventy-five thousand dollars, leaving to be raised one million, four-hundred and twenty-five thousand dollars. This is no small task when confronted with the fact that the majority of the logical supporters insisted that the one doing the most do it all.

The fact of the case is that, both in the furthering of the work and in the support of my family, the most rigid economy and pinching care have been necessary. When I say this, I do so with the fact before us that we started out to do a real piece of investigation and publish a real book, not a pamphlet at "six bits." As to the effort I have put forth to do the work, few men have been so fortunate as to possess the physical strength I have put into this; and year in and year out I have given to the very maximum of my physical and mental endurance in my effort to make the work a worthy one.

I am enclosing an extract from this year's annual report, in which I briefly review the situation. I wish that you would take the time to read this material. The cash receipts from the latest volume should underwrite our next field efforts—another trip to the northern plains is next in line—and when we complete that business I will be traveling again to New York to show our movie there and in several other Eastern cities. I do hope that we might meet to discuss all this. I am, yours, etc.

I recall watching him compose this letter, because we were sitting there with a map of the West spread out on the table in front of us, with pins bearing flags marking the location of the various tribes, as was our wont, trying to decide how much cash and time we could afford to spend on one variation or another. There had been a time when Clara, who had a fine mind for business and organization, would, despite her misgivings, help us with our plans. But she and Edward hardly spoke about our work anymore. Life together for the two of them had become rather grim.

"I have written to Miss Greene," he announced to me, and in his voice I could detect both the hope and the desperation that such a letter entailed.

Edward visited New York again, but she did not respond to his note, and when he attempted to make an appointment with Morgan's son, Jack, an assistant informed him that young Morgan was not considering any new business ventures. Neither Jack Morgan nor Belle da Costa Greene attended the latest showing of the moving picture.

We departed for the field again and again, adding on a fellow named Schwinke to help with the cameras. Although Edward would not say he had made a success of *In the Land of the Head-Hunters*, he could see that the moving picture was the medium of the future, and it might be his only way to make money to keep the project alive.

Life grew all bunched together—after another trip to Montana; he traveled to New York again.

Dear Ms. Greene,

I do want to call and have a chat with you and within the next two or three days I will get in touch with you by telephone and suggest the time I can come in. I have with me a few proofs of some of the later work and think you will like them. I look forward to seeing you, etc.

He dropped the proofs off at the Morgan office, and then walked the streets of Manhattan in great despair. Never in all his days from boyhood to the present had Edward felt so physically fallen. His legs moved him weakly along the pavement, and his heart whimpered in his chest. It took all of his strength and will to get himself to the train station.

And then things turned up, rather than down. At Hal's next school break, Hal, Edward, and I found ourselves trekking along a dusty trail outside the site of the old town of Cibola where the sun bore down on us like the fabled fiery eye of God. Though the air smelled of mesquite and donkey, the light gave it a distinctive golden hue.

Edward looked at Hal, and he shrugged.

"The Spaniards must have been mighty disappointed," the boy said. "Where's the gold?"

"The Spaniards had a number of surprises," Edward said. "The local tribes weren't terribly pleased to see them."

Hal spoke up. "It was a war, huh, Pop?"

"A bad one, and it went on for years. Kind of like your mother and me."

"Come on, Pop, none of that."

"Sorry, son." The dust made Edward cough, and that was when it happened. He made a spyglass of his hand and peered through it at the ruins. "Well, well," he said. "I've found the gold."

"What, Pop? Where?"

"Take a look," Edward said to him, showing him what to do. The boy held his fist up in front of his eyes.

"What do you see?"

"Bully, Pop, just bully."

"What are you doing there?" I wandered over their way.

"You look," Edward said.

Hal was still holding up his own fist to his eyes. I peered through Edward's rolled up hand. "And what do I see?"

"Everything," Edward said, "the world in a golden tint." And the idea for his new process was born.

"The idea that I thought of on the trip to Cibola?" he explained to the family on his return to Seattle for a brief summer visit. "It's thanks to young Hal here that it came to mind. I've been working on it. It's a way of seeing through gold, but like most things in this business, the secret lies in the printing of it." He patted his son on the shoulder. "Thank you, boy."

Clara had not approved of Edward taking Hal on that trip. But when Edward explained how good his discovery might be for the business, she yielded a little.

"Explain it to the girls," she said. "They're old enough to understand."

"Explain to me," Beth said. "Explain to me."

"Can you keep a family secret?"

"I can, Daddy," Beth said.

"Here it is." He paused a moment, with all of them standing there on the porch, almost if they were posed for a family portrait that he himself might be making. A cool breeze blew in off the water. The sun bore down, gold, hot gold.

"Well," he said, "the way we do it is to reverse the photographic image in the glass, then seal it, and back it with a viscous mixture of powdered gold pigment and banana oil. This gold-tone photographic finishing process, we're going to call Curt-Tone. The banana oil proved to be the major ingredient. My wonderful discovery. The gold-tone process—that will make up for all of the money Morgan would have given us."

"Banana oil?" Beth thought this over with a giggle.

"That's right. Banana oil. Oh, and let me tell you, it stinks to high heaven, that banana oil does, an absolutely ferocious stink that is so stinkful that it has a stink that stinks of its own on top of its usual stink." The girls laughed outright at their father's joke, laughed until he calmed them down. "That's right. The entire studio, sometimes the entire building, reeks of the stuff. Your mother says she wants to help with the process, but she refuses to set foot in the studio because of the smell. Well, she uses that as an excuse, actually. Isn't that true, Clara?"

"The children keep me busy, Edward, as you well know. But yes, the odor in there is awful." Clara pinched her nose closed and everyone laughed, even Edward.

"But," he said, "we're turning banana oil into banana gold."

Clara turned to him and said, "Nevertheless, the stink of it is indelible."

No one knew what to say or do. The children laughed, mostly feebly, while Edward merely sat there, silently for a moment, before clearing his throat and saying, "But Clara, dear Clara, what else then am I to do?"

After a field trip to the plains a few months later, Edward made a little side trip to visit Hal at his preparatory school in the East. Hal had a letter from Clara, and the boy had written back to her. Things were not good between his mother and father.

"Mama wrote to me," Hal said, which thickened the plot.

Edward stared at him, as if trying to see inside his very brain. "And what did she tell you?"

Hal hitched up his shoulders in a shrug.

"Did she say that she agreed to help in the studio with the Curt-Tone work?"

"She wants to keep the business going, despite everything."

"And everything is…what?"

"You know what I'm saying, Dad. *Pop*. I'm old enough to figure out the truth for myself, aren't I?"

"She's quite bitter, yes. I've tried my damnedest, son. So has she. No one's in the wrong," Edward said. "That's the heart of the matter. Two rights banging their heads together, is what it is."

"Something's got to give," Hal said. "I haven't studied geology for nothing. Things give, one thing or another. What's going to give, Pop?"

"I can't stop my work," Edward said. "Since Morgan died, I have to work at it double-hard, doing the research and the writing, *and* help to raise the money to publish the books."

His son ran his fingers through his thick brown hair, smiling at him in a sort of suspicious way. "You're a real artist, aren't you, Pop?"

Edward couldn't help but smile with the pleasure and a touch of embarrassment at this little accolade from his own flesh and blood. "So you understand me a little better than you did a few years ago, when I insisted that you come here to school?"

"It hurt me a little, Pop. But I see now that it did me good."

"All these opportunities back here," Edward said. "I couldn't help but push you toward them."

"And I appreciate it." Something in his eye made Edward question it.

"But?"

"But?"

"But, you wish you could have stayed at home?"

"There hasn't *been* all that much of a home for a while, has there?"

"No, son, not if home is a father and mother presiding over the household."

"So it didn't seem to matter that I should go."

"It mattered to me, your welfare did, your education mattered. But I wasn't there enough, back home, to help you the way I...."

"The way?"

Edward swallowed hard and said what he had intended to say. "The way I should have."

Hal leaned back in his chair and closed his eyes, the way a much older man, a man Edward's age, say, might do, when recollecting some deep sorrow of the days gone by. "Sorry," he said.

"You're sorry? I'm the one who should apologize. I do apologize. I am sorry. You almost died because of me. Your mother never forgave me for that. I never forgave myself for that."

"Oh, come on, Pop. You had this work to do. Who would have done it if you wouldn't? And I turned out alright, didn't I? *Hawk. Vermilion?* That's what I remember saying when I had that fever...."

"I remember, son."

"I remember the medicine man. Wow, did he smell bad! Or was that me?"

"It hurts me to joke about it," Edward said. "It hurts your mother a lot, too, I know. But there's nothing I can do. I couldn't stay home and run a photography studio, no matter how good I was at that. I was made for this project, Hal." And then he said more than he should have. "Maybe I wasn't made for marriage."

"Aw, Pop. I wonder if I will be."

"Sure you'll be," Edward said. "It's not something passed along in the blood. My brothers have made good marriages. They're good, loyal husbands, such as I ever see them."

"You never see them? I didn't know about that, Pop. Kids don't always know these things."

"I had a falling out with Asahel a long, long time ago. So long ago now I can hardly even remember what it was about, if I ever did. I used to see quite a bit of Ray, but now, scarcely ever. I hear he has a lovely new wife."

Edward took a deep breath and settled back in his chair. "That was another life," he said. "All that. Family in Seattle, living there. Your grandfather long gone. Your grandmother gone now. Another life." He sat for a moment, staring out the window at the western darkness, calling back all those years as best as he could. He knew so much less then. The story seemed hazy to him, not like the forward direct line of a train, but more like the meandering, but eventually always forward, motion of a river. "But isn't there something beautiful in that?" he wondered. To see things as they are, instead of as someone changes them to make a better story? He wondered if anyone would ever remember a story out of life that moves along naturally, without the twists and turns that an artist adds to his natural material in order to make it more appealing. A paradox, yes? The truth in exchange for beauty. Like him getting all those people to put aside their modern style of dress and put on the old costumes?

"So, Hal, you plan to manage a mine one day, do you?"

"That's my dream," he said. "But they tell me I've got to finish metallurgy first."

"Then do it. Do what you dream about. Nothing else matters. That way you'll already have found the real gold, son, even while you think you're still looking."

And then down, down, down again, down. Another fieldtrip. And then another train trip East, for a showing of his movie at the Museum of Natural History. Things turned up again. He had written to Belle da Costa Greene. She had written back a cordial note. He had written to President Roosevelt. Edward gathered up all of his desperation and traveled out to Long Island to speak with him.

But on the train ride out of the city, Edward felt himself flirting with absolute despair. Other men made great things happen. Such as T. R., who had served as president and had finished his work, while our project was still as yet incomplete. "Look at him," Edward said to himself when he arrived at the Oyster Bay house. The man had added some girth, but there was a new look in his eye, as though he might be aiming a rifle at an animal, or at a politician, or at some goal in the future.

"I am quite remiss," the former president said, toying with thick fingers at his pince nez, "about not attending the publication banquet."

"Sir, we've moved far along since then."

"But you say that Jack Morgan has not been forthcoming?"

"No, he has not."

"I'll speak with him," T. R. said. "I'll send him a note. He ought to see your motion picture. I should see your motion picture. If there were only time for everything in life, I would have seen it already."

"Perhaps you might come in to see it then?"

"Perhaps, Mr. Curtis, perhaps. As with all in life, a large perhaps. Perhaps...."

Edward took a deep breath and said in a quiet voice, "We are hurting for money, sir. The future of the project is in jeopardy."

T. R. sounded a large "Hmmm...." Nothing so much as kills life as a sound like that. Edward immediately sank into despair.

Down, down. He didn't feel much better when he returned to the city for a long-hoped-for tea at the Waldorf with Miss Greene. For the length of the train ride, past houses and fields, with now and then a glimpse of water, he berated himself for being where he was, for straying thousands of miles from the field. He saw things still as he had always seen them. Each day, each hour, that he wasn't moving the project forward, the Indian Nations were moving backward toward oblivion. Back and forth, back and forth on trains.

His mind in a tumult of ideas and regrets, he arrived for the rendezvous about twenty minutes early, as nervous as a school boy. If he hadn't been here before, he might not have been so agitated, but it seemed like a second chance, and if he missed it, there might never be another. But was the chance with Miss Greene herself only, or did he now mix this desire with the hope that she might give him entry to Jack Morgan? Or was it a mingling of both hopes?

With a rustle of silk, Miss Greene rushed through the door, and as she turned to say something to a man alongside her—before he slipped away toward the lobby—Edward's heart took a dive straight down like a cormorant into the rolling Pacific.

"Mr. Curtis," she said, offering her hand.

Edward feared that he might stink of banana oil.

"Belle," he said, keeping a certain distance as they were led to a table for their tea, "I don't understand why you haven't seen me before this. And you never return my letters."

She smiled, amused, clearly, at his forwardness. "If I only had all those lonely nights on the plains, I would find time to write, Mr. Curtis."

Edward shook off the remark—did she mean to be familiar? Cruel? Flirtatious? "I know you are busy, Belle."

As they sat down she gave him a sly smile but a smile that gave him no clear sign of what she was feeling. "If only you lived here in the city, Mr. Curtis—"

"Edward...."

"Edward…though you are so formal, I find it difficult to call you by your given name."

"If I lived in the city?"

"We might discuss things other than money."

He took a deep breath and plunged ahead. "But right now, that is what is on my mind."

"…I just don't know," she was saying. "Jack Morgan is trying his very best to sort things out still, but there was so much, *is* so much. He could have turned everything over to the lawyers, but that is not his way. So that is where it stands, at a sort of impasse, if I may use that word."

Edward studied her eyes. She seemed as lively as the first time he saw her.

"And how is Mrs. Curtis?"

Without hesitation he told a few lies about how happy he was in his marriage and how much Clara supported him in his project, and then went back to the subject at hand, the project itself, trying to frame a way to speak about all the bills without becoming too abject in the presence of this lovely younger woman. He was finding it difficult to breathe.

"You Westerners," Belle da Costa Greene said. "Why this gentleman I know, who owns millions of trees somewhere out where you live, came to town again, and after inviting me to lunch after lunch and dinner after dinner after dinner and the theater and all the museums and then a ride on the ferry, he asked me what I thought he needed most in life. And I said as a joke, a Reynolds for his sitting room out in the big trees where he lived, and he went to a gallery and bought himself a Reynolds…."

Her eyes danced as she spoke, as she mocked the poor rich man who wanted to please her. "…And the next day we went back to the gallery, and he bought, at my suggestion again, a

Raeburn and a Gainsborough, and at the end of the week, when I asked how he was returning West, he said by train and told me that he had just bought a private railroad car for his trip home. 'Belle,' he said to me (and he says it so that it comes out 'Bay-el, Bay-el....'" She laughed ferociously, as she cruelly imitated the earnest timber baron's voice. "'Bay-el,' he said, 'I would like you to accompany me back to my home, so that I can make an honest marriage with you.' I didn't know what to say. An 'honest marriage,' whatever that is. Can you tell me what that is? Has there ever been one such as that since the beginning of time?" Laughter spilled from her lips.

Edward, who had stood before brave chiefs and powerful warriors, and held his ground, could do nothing more than shake his head in consternation, watching her hands fly and swerve about the angelic facade of her face and brow.

"Now I suppose I know what *you* want, don't I, Mr. Curtis?" Her eyes bore in on him, and he squirmed in his seat, though he dared not look away. "Mr. Curtis, I have never known you to be speechless before this. Please, come out and say what you wish to say."

He reached for his teacup and took another sip in the hope of clearing his throat. "I would like you to come and see a special showing of my motion picture at the museum."

She didn't hesitate in her reply. "Why, Mr. Curtis," she said. "I would be delighted."

"Do you think that Jack Morgan might come with you?"

She demurely gave her head a little shake. "I make no plans for him," she said. "His life is completely beyond my powers. I'm only his librarian." A light sparked up in her eyes, and then quickly faded.

"T. R. told me he would speak to him about it," Edward said, trying to keep the pathos out of his voice.

"Why, then, I'll add my suggestion as well. What is the date for the showing at the museum?"

He gave her the details. They sipped more tea, and then it was time for her to go, and they parted ever so politely and made promises to meet again at the showing. She flowed out of the tea room toward the lobby, and Edward saw the tall man in the brown suit hurry toward her and glide along with her into the crowd before the front doors.

Pounding of drums, high sing-song voices (violins and cellos) rise and fall above the drumming....
Mud-heads bend and weave as though their large figures are as supple as grass....
Pounding of drums, the strings singing, sighing, weaving....
"Now appear the special guests of the ceremony...."

At the showing of *In the Land of the Head-Hunters* at the Museum of Natural History, not a great crowd appeared. And Jack Morgan and Belle da Costa Greene were nowhere to be seen. Hodge, the series editor, did make an entrance, coming directly up to Edward just before the lights went down to make a grand show of pumping his hand. (As I mentioned, I had done most of the correspondence about the editing of the volumes in Edward's name, so Edward himself knew little about some queries Hodge made. Edward said he would write to him.)

But in every other way, Edward was in charge. He put on a grand show the rest of the evening to make his editor feel important, but after hearing that there were few subscriptions for the next few volumes, and so little hope for more, his soul sank into a decline. Hodge offered to stand for some drinks after the showing. Edward demurred, on the grounds of having so much work to do back at the hotel. Hodge seemed disappointed.

"There's a war on," he said. "Not much to be cheerful about. So I thought we might raise a glass or two."

"I can't think about the war," Edward said. "I'm living too far in the past. The only wars I know are the tribal variety, and for all of the cruelty of death by axe or lance or arrow, sir, the numbers of the dead would not make up one tenth of one percent of a single skirmish at the front lines today in Europe, from what I read. I'd rather dwell in the past than shiver in the present."

He and Hodge parted cordially, and he was headed out the door on his way back to the hotel, when he was met by a thin, blonde-haired young fellow named Flaherty, who had seen *Head-Hunters* and wanted to talk about going north—as far as the Arctic—to make a motion picture about the Eskimos there. "Do you have any advice for me?" the Arctic-tending fellow asked.

Edward smiled cautiously, thinking to himself how he could hardly raise the money for his own project and stood upon the earth as if on reeds for legs, but here was a younger man asking for advice. "Yes, yes. See all your rich friends before you leave, and don't fall in love with any Indian maidens."

The man looked at Edward curiously, and then laughed. "A good joke, a good joke. But tell me now...."

Edward tried to tell him, failed, and then went back to the hotel to work on some letters.

The magnitude of the undertaking is such that the fieldwork, the preparation of the text and pictures, and then the fearful struggle to make sales have kept me too busy to give much time or thought to telling my friends about it. Also I have taken for granted that they would know I was doing my very best. Perhaps in this I have made a mistake. No doubt I should have tried to keep closer in touch and explain more fully the problems confronting us. My theory has always been that people do not want a tale of woe from a worker as to how hard it is to do a thing, but rather they want results from a worker who has managed to keep a smile most of the time....

This he sent over to the Morgan Library to Belle da Costa Greene. He wrote to me in Berkeley, where I was spending some months while he was away, working with Kroeber, the ethnologist and tribal linguist, telling me about the encounter with our editor Hodge. He wrote to Schwinke, our camera man:

I wish you would immediately shape up your books and other affairs in Seattle so as to be able to leave on the shortest possible notice. I may ask you to go into the field and do a month's motion picture work and scenic stuff. That is, going out quite by yourself, and instructions will probably come by wire, so lose no time in getting everything in such shape, so that you can pull out for a trip of a month or six weeks.

Though he waited a day, he had no response from Belle da Costa Greene.

A letter did arrive from Clara, in which she complained once again about his absence, though she declared that she had overcome her disgust with the odors arising from the new process and thrown herself into the work at the studio. She included a copy of the sales catalogue:

The new Curt-Tone finish of the Indian studies is most unusual in its depth and life-like brilliancy. Of this remarkable finish, Mr. Curtis says:

"The ordinary photographic print, however good, lacks depth and transparency, or more strictly speaking, translucency. We all know how beautiful are the stones and pebbles in the limpid brook of the forest where the water absorbs the blue of the sky and the green of the foliage, yet when we take the same irides- cent pebbles from the water and dry them they are dull and life- less; so it is with the orthodox photographic print, but in the Curt-Tones all the transparency is retained and they are as full of life and sparkle as an opal...."

Did he want to change or amend any of this? She wanted to know.

No.

Business, business, business. She wrote that Burl Patton was now in charge of sales. Two Japanese printers, Tay Takano and Harry Koniashi, were working at the studio, as well as a photog- rapher named Nels Lennes, who doubled as a retoucher. A sister of Clara's, Sue Gates, had been working there, but she had left, and there were three or four other women doing just about everything else, such as making mounts for the portraits, cutting the heavy papers, and hand-deckling all the edges. And Beth, their little Beth, now a young woman, was helping her manage the business in his absence.

But when will you return? Clara wanted to know.

This gave him hope. Could she consider living as wife and man with him again, as tired and worn as he was?

He responded with a letter giving her in detail all that he was busy with here in the East, all that kept him from coming back to Seattle immediately. When you looked at it from this perspective, he was not just a busy man, he was one of the most successful photographers in America. *Leslie's Magazine* wanted photographs made for a series about touring the scenic spots of

America, fifty-two of them, with a different photograph to run
each week for a year. An editor at the U.S. Forest Service wanted
to turn some of his photographs into lantern-slide illustrations
for use during lectures to the public. He explained that he was
still waiting for a meeting with Jack Morgan. And then he told
her of his encounter with the young fellow, Flaherty, who had
seen his *Head-Hunters.*

"Oh, Clara," he said to her in his mind (but not in the letter),
"what if we could go back to where we were a long time ago,
before children and Indians? To start again—to make a different
way of life? With each of us able to find within ourselves the
right point of spirit, so that we might join our souls in a
marriage both real and proper?"

But the thought didn't last long before his mind got to
wandering, and got to the thought about what he had said to
Flaherty—too harsh?—and wondered whether or not he would
see Belle da Costa Greene again, and wondered just why he
wanted to.

He wrote another note to Schwinke, trying to plan the
summer, wherein they would make their photographs for
Leslie's as well as do more fieldwork. Equipment, equipment
is always on his mind these days when the money is stretched
so thin.

The motor camera and its accompanying equipment.
Both motion-picture tripods. Have old one given any repairs
needed, and if I am right, there is no tilting head to it.
The small dark red tent.
The 6 x 8 camera and accompanying holders, etc.
One small brown tent.

Light blanket equipment for yourself, no blanket or bedding for me.
We will first be making a thousand-foot motion picture of the Grand Canyon. I will work with you a few days in starting it and then leave you to finish. You will next join me at Yosemite and there you will have two or three days with me, and again it will be up to you to finish the picture. After leaving you at Yellowstone, I return to Albuquerque and join a congressional party there, covering certain conservative projects in Arizona, New Mexico, through California, Nevada, Colorado, Oregon, Washington, Montana, and Idaho. We will meet again when our party is in the Yosemite.

He could picture that map of ours, with all of its pins, pointing to our work to come. The thought of it made him a bit tired. He set down his pen, and got up from the desk and went to the window. The city glowed with light as far as he could see, and beyond the dark sky to the west, he imagined even more light, the light of the day that had departed, the light of the day that would be upon them in some hours, the light he had known in all of those Western places, from the sun, from bonfires, from cooking fires, from the pure stars. Out there in the Western dark lay his sleeping children, and Clara, and what was left of his family, and the thousands of Indians, tens of thousands, he had met since he had begun the project. Some had died since he had begun, many others would be born before he had completed it, if ever he would complete it. Clearly at this moment, he stood there with a sad heart, and a despairing sense of mission, that even after having done so much, so few people cared about what he had accomplished, and the future which had once seemed so bright with hope and expectation had dimmed its lights. He hoped that it was only the dark before the next dawn.

At least the work had taught him patience. Another week went by, with a number of false fundraising leads played out. And a number of solitary dinners, during which he could mull over the troubles he carried with him. Such as the wire from Schwinke, telling him that he was quitting and wanted his share of *In the Land of the Head-Hunters* by return mail. Edward wired Clara, asking her to pay Schwinke out of the studio receipts. (No money coming from the moving picture, that's for sure.) She didn't wire back.

A fitful train trip West. Usually the roll of the car on the rails allowed him, when he wasn't working in his notebooks, to daydream and then sleep—not this time. His eyes stayed wide open most of the thousands of miles, and by the time the train pulled into the station, his head felt as though it might split apart. He was a man who never had such physical cares, and now he walked with his stoop and a clanging brain.

He had wired Clara several days before, so that she would know of his arrival, and he surprised himself by admitting that he was greatly looking forward to a few weeks at home. Of course, he envisioned this mainly as time in the studio, so that he might make an honest man of himself in connection with the business, and pitch in and help produce some pictures. (There was just enough money left in the project account for a fieldtrip to California to work among the many scattered and diminished tribes down there—and he wanted to add on another trip to the Grand Canyon.)

As the train came to a shuddering halt, he scouted the platform for a glimpse of her, but after all her lamenting about his many and long absences, on this return home, Clara was nowhere to be seen.

Instead, as he descended from the train, a fellow in a dark suit and black cap came rushing up to him. "Mr. Curtis?"

"That's me," Edward said. "But no interviews right now, please."

"No, sir," the fellow said, handing him a long white envelope.

"What's this?" Edward stood there in a rather befuddled state alongside the train car.

"Self-explanatory," the fellow responded, as he raised his fingers to his cap and walked away.

Self-explanatory was a way to put it. Edward tore open the envelope and read the enclosed legal notice. Clara was suing him for divorce. After all the years of squabbling, raging, weeping, smashing, he felt nothing but regret, regret, regret.

He rushed to the house and Katherine came to the door. "Tell mother—"

"Tell him I will not see him," Clara called from the next room.

The poor, dear girl in front of him seemed about to shrink into the floor.

"Clara," he called to her, "please don't turn this into a—"

She came charging into the room, her skirts all aswirl, as if she were dancing, or in a trance. "Katherine, go to your room."

"Yes, Mama," said their youngest, as she hurried out of their sight.

"You shouldn't—"

"Don't tell me, Edward, what I should or shouldn't do. Now please leave the house. You are never here, so that shouldn't be a problem."

"Clara, Clara," he pleaded with her, "come to your senses. I have always been a dutiful husband and father. I have made a life for all of you—" She made a grand coughing noise in her throat. "I have!" he said. "I have always loved you—"

"It is true," she broke in, "that you have worked hard and made a life for us, true. And I have tried to live that life. I just can't do it anymore, Edward. I just cannot bear the betrayals anymore."

"Betrayals? I have never betrayed you, never."

"Oh, yes, you have!"

The fleeting picture of Belle da Costa Greene's face passed through his mind. But he had not done anything near betrayal, no. "I have not," he said, trying to keep his voice low.

"You have," she said. "You have betrayed me a thousand times, with a thousand Indians. You have given them the life you were to have given me. Now go." His heart broke for himself and for the children as he turned and walked out the door, but even more did it crack for Clara, to see the tears streaming down her face.

"But you didn't turn around and ask for forgiveness?" I asked him when he appeared at the door of the apartment, which I scarcely ever lived in myself. (Although I was beginning to allow myself again to imagine another way to live. In fact, even as Edward knocked at the door, I was trying to compose a letter to my old Seattle Penelope, who had written to me while Edward had been away in New York, saying that she had thought things over and would consider hearing from me again.)

"Clara has been forgiving me for many years," Edward said. His long, tall body seemed to be trying to sink into itself, he was so bowed over with misery. "Apparently, she has run out of forgiveness."

"And you, Edward? What do you do now?"

"Camp on your floor, if you let me, until I find another place to live or go out into the field again."

"Of course you can stay here." I paused and took a moment to think. He seemed as vulnerable as a wounded animal, and just as ready to fight to defend his life. I didn't know if I should tell him anything that might put him more on the defensive.

For a few days Edward slept on a bedroll on the floor in my apartment, and then took up residence at his studio. Clara had left him a note saying that she would stay away until they had sorted out their affairs, and that Beth would manage the day-to-day running of the portraiture business. He couldn't sleep very well. The odor of banana oil permeated his forgettable dreams. A good part of those nights, he sat and stared at his notes, and at shelf after shelf of the photographic plates from the project, which dutiful, capable Beth had catalogued and stored.

"These are worth a lot, aren't they, Daddy?" she said.

"Oh, yes," Edward told her. "They are worth all the years of my life that went into them." He watched her go about the business of the studio, so assured, so competent. He had to admit that Clara had raised her well.

"Don't worry, Daddy," she said when she noticed the sadness welling up in his eyes. "I think she'll change her mind."

"I'm afraid not," Edward said. "I have ruined too much."

Sometimes in the afternoons, Florence stopped by to make tea and talk. Hal, always loyal to him, had sent an encouraging wire from school. Only Katherine kept her distance, completely her mother's girl.

And each evening back at my apartment, we drank a considerable amount of whiskey. He poured out his troubles. There were several awful visits that he paid to the house, when Clara refused to answer the door. He wrote a letter to her attorney, for whom he was paying, of course.

My own life, meanwhile, was going in the other direction. At long last, my long-lost schoolteacher agreed to see me again. And again. When I finally dared to tell Edward, he looked at me in utter surprise.

"Really?"

"Yes, there is someone I have been seeing. My Penelope...."

"Congratulations," he said. "I hope she has more tolerance for your absences than Clara has had with mine."

"Oh, I have tried her patience for quite a while," I said. "I had thought I had torn it loose. Now it seems that it has been more resilient than I had first imagined."

"William," he said, "I tell you this with all my feeling, I would hate to lose your help with our project, but if it comes to choosing between a good wife and a good life, and the project, I will understand if you choose your life."

All my fears evaporated as my old friend and employer, tried in the field and true, put his arms around me and gave me a deep, manly embrace.

"Thank you, Edward," I said, finding the words coming much more easily than I had feared they might. "I think I may sit out the next fieldtrip. But I have taken the liberty of finding you a good fellow at the university who can help out."

Poor Edward, such a strong, strong man, but despite his best intentions, he seemed almost to crumple in front of me.

"But you will still translate the field notes we bring back into our pages, will you not?"

"I will, Edward. I will."

In May, with a new assistant, he headed out again (but who was to know in advance that he would find yet another disappointment?). The usual hawks accompanied him as he descended into the Blue Water canyon. But the birds dived down toward him, as if his presence challenged them in some way, swerving only at the very end. This seemed quite strange. At least, it had never happened to him before. But it was no stranger than his arrival at the encampment. He no sooner reached the bottom of the trail than it became clear that something had changed.

The chief's house was deserted.

Edward was standing in front of it, staring up at the narrow band of blue sky, when two farmers passed by. The old

Havasupai chief was dead, they told him. There was a new chief.

"And Tasáwiche?"

"Gone."

"Gone?"

After her father's death, she had married outside of the tribe and left to live in Tuba City. When he heard the news, his chest turned to stone. He couldn't think of a worse sign that it would all come to a bad end. His new assistant set up for his filming in the canyon, but Edward's heart wasn't in the work just then.

"Eastwood," he said, "I'm going back up. I've got to ride over to Tuba City."

"Are you sure, boss?" he asked.

"As sure as I am of anything," Edward told him.

He began the climb back up to the rim and early the next afternoon arrived in Tuba City, where he wandered along the dusty main street, staring at the people lounging on the street corners.

Tasáwiche? Which of the overweight, old-at-twenty-five Indian women, with skin like parchment and many children tugging at her skirts, had his Muse become? He sauntered along, looking, looking, and though one or two of the women met his stare, no one who called herself by her name stepped forward to make herself known to him.

An hour went by, and then he saw her, a dark face in a dark serape standing just inside the doorway of a saloon.

"Tasáwiche?" The woman turned, turned away, walked in the opposite direction as he hurried toward her. "Tasáwiche! It's Curts'!" he called to her.

She stopped, turned, smiled, showed him a nearly perfect oval mouth, empty of teeth. Edward raised his hands to his temples. It couldn't be Tasáwiche, no. But it was....

"Mister?"

His time to turn away. "Yes?"

An Indian in denim, with a round face and an empty eye-socket, came walking up to him. "Why you talking to my wife?"

Edward looked down at the dusty street. "I thought she was someone else."

"You what?"

"I'm lost," Edward said.

The man's face changed, softened. "Oh," he said, "where you need to be?"

"The canyon," Edward said.

The man squinted with his good eye. "You *are* lost," he said.

"I am," Edward said. "I am."

thirty-two

jimmy fly-wing's story—10

WHEN YOU FLY HIGH, soaring, wheeling, turning, stooping sometimes to tear your prey from the face of the earth, you see for such long distances—cloud mountains and rivers of light shaded into the air itself, dust streams and other birds, in flocks, and winging on their own—you have a vision of your country that cannot be conveyed in any other way but song. And so you sing out your pleasure, in shrieks high and low, either solo, or when joined by another solitary for one of those gams in air that birds do sometimes make, especially when mating takes them over and drives their wings.

But is my country your country? Do you sing along with me or do you sing against my voice?

I see from this height the meandering rivers, the mazy plains, the realm where Sky dropped down to bless life on Earth, as it is lived. Diving down to Earth, giving my assistance where I can to the man I am pledged to follow, and then swooping back up again, to drift on currents invisible from below except when the sun in certain angles illuminates the flow of particles or birds such as us caught in the moment as images of ourselves, what we once were, what we could be, what might be true or might not.

I sense the call now and navigate my way over mountains to where the salt sea impinges on the curves of land, below volcanoes and a range that stretches to the ocean, and I become myself, necessary, at the ready, doing what I can to keep the present from running out and back and away into what we immediately call the past.

Nambe, Pombe, Ponca,

Sarsik,

Taos,

Tewa....

thirty-three

a chance meeting

SEATTLE, 1919. WIND WAS blowing the rain against the front
window and glass door. Clouds had long ago settled over the
Sound and the beautiful peaks of the Olympic range, always
snow-covered, had gone in, out of sight behind the clouds.
Rangy, Edward sat, most unlike him, stooped over a glass of
whiskey, drinking, in a First Avenue saloon. I don't think I'd ever
seen him as desperate as this, and since I had just told him news
about my own life, I believed I held some responsibility for his
current condition.

"I should be a success at my business, William," he said.
"Which I am not. I mortgaged the business and the house, and
borrowed to the hilt, three times over. And now I've lost the
house and the studio in this divorce. And Clara won't give me
back my negatives. Her revenge for all the years I spent in the
field. She's keeping the negatives, which I call theft."

He took a drink.

"I should be a success as a husband and as a father. But Clara
has kept what is mine, and the children are caught between the
two of us. I am here in my hometown but staying in a hotel, and
I can't go to the house to visit my youngest child." He downed

another drink, and took out his pocket watch and studied it. "She is late."

"She's a good girl, Edward," I said. "I'm sure she'll be along."

"I've made a damned fool of myself, searching all over the Southwest for an Indian girl I thought was some sort of amulet, a magical creature who would ensure our success. I'm rather ashamed to admit that I chased after a sophisticated New York woman who hobnobs with men richer than I can imagine. And that trip to the brothel, I am sorry that I ever set foot inside the place."

Another drink.

"And I should have been long done with my fieldwork and published the rest of the volumes in the series, which I have not. Morgan the elder is dead. Morgan the younger has cut me down to a trickle of cash. Belle da Costa Greene won't answer my letters."

He drank again, a sip, and then tossed down the rest, sighing and staring out the window, as though from sheer intensity of vision, he might halt the rain and bring the mountains back into view.

"So much work behind us now," he said, "and yet still a great deal ahead of us. I know I can raise the money somehow, somewhere, even if I have to take on work for someone else for a while. I just haven't yet figured out how and where. I am in the newspapers. I have published two books and made a motion picture. I have been celebrated, or my work has. People in the know know who I am. I have known presidents. I have known chiefs, chief after chief after chief." He picked up his empty glass and stared at it a moment. "I will find a way."

Outside the rain kept falling. He looked up over his glass, his head turned sideways, as though his very eye were a camera lens and he was positioning himself to make a portrait. "And you, married? How will you support yourself," he asked me, "while I'm off trying to make some money?"

"I'm taking a position at the university," I said.

"Where I found you," Edward said.

I lowered my gaze. "Yes." I answered, and took a drink myself. "Edward, I know my marriage is not convenient for you. I know how close we are to completing the project. But it's not that I'm going to miss another fieldtrip. As soon as you raise more money, I promise I'll come along."

"As soon as I raise more money?" Edward asked incredulously. "Yes, yes, but how will I do that? I have sold off every artifact I have ever bought from the tribes. And there is no one left to ask for money, and no one has come along to give."

"If I had a personal fortune, I would turn it over right now," I said. "But, alas, I have nothing of consequence. Except the experience of all our years in the field."

"Yes, yes, that is worth everything, and worth nothing at all."

"It has meant a great deal to me, Edward. It has been my life."

"And now that we have only a few more tribes to meet, we are packing it in?"

"When we are ready to go again, I will go," I said.

"I have to save some money first. I'm going to open a new studio. Beth has promised to help me. And I'll find other work as well, I'm sure. I should be able to find something. I have a reputation, don't I?"

"Yes," I said. But didn't add that part of it was for throwing away his life on Indians. I didn't see it that way, but others did. Look how the New York crowd treated him, like a beggar at the door.

We sat a while in silence, Edward refusing to look at me. The wind played its music on the glass of the window and door. And then the door opened and in stepped a man in a suit, glistening with rain water, his hat pulled down over his eyes.

"Damned weather here," Edward said. "Most of my life, lived here. And never liked the weather."

"It has a certain beauty," I said.

"Then you stay here, damn it. I'm leaving for the field!" And with that, he stood up and dashed his glass to the floor, where it shattered into dozens of pieces.

"Edward!"

"Go," he said. "Enjoy your life. I understand." And he then apologized to the bartender, who had come over with a broom and dustpan to clean up the broken glass. He appeared quite calm, as though what Edward had just done was quite a common occurrence.

"Allow me," Edward moved to help pick up the glass, but the man gestured that he step back. Edward bumped against a chair, and nearly knocked over the man who had just come in out of the rain. "Excuse me," Edward said, rising to his full height and looking the man in the eye.

"Nothing to apologize for," the man said in a familiar voice.

"Jimmy?" Edward said. "Jimmy Fly-Wing!" The man removed his hat and smiled at us both. Sure enough, it was our old Jimmy, looking not a day older than when I had last seen him in the field, or when Edward had last seen him in Chicago. (In fact, Edward considered, he had never looked better.)

"Jimmy, where have you been?"

"Riding around the West, reading, studying."

"And you just walked in here out of the rain, this saloon of all saloons, looking for a drink."

"I don't drink anymore, Edward," Jimmy said.

"Be that as it may," I said, "this is a dry warm place. Every man needs that." Edward gave me another of his angry looks.

"That explains it, Myers, doesn't it?"

I didn't bother to respond. And Edward didn't seem to care.

Jimmy spoke up. "I saw your musical show in Omaha," he said. "It inspired me. As I was sitting there, I saw it all. It came to me all of a sudden, something I should have understood long, long ago. I have to say, I always felt it. But I didn't understand it. I wanted to help you, Edward. I wanted to help you keep the old ways from disappearing. And now I'm back. Listen. My People aren't dying. They're not like the buffalo. They're going to go on living. But it's how they will live that troubles me. No one wants to live without knowing where he comes from, no one wants to live without a past."

Edward was quite far gone by this time. I wasn't sure that he heard everything Jimmy was saying. "What do you know?" he said, tilting his head inquisitively. "You saw the show in Omaha? You should have said hello." He turned to me, smiling, as though he had never given me that awful stare or thrown that glass. "Was I there in Omaha?" Before I could tell him yes or no, he slammed his shot glass on the table. "Jimmy has a project!"

"It sounds quite a bit like our own," I said.

"Certainly," Jimmy said. "That is my life now. That is what I have become."

Edward pulled out a chair and bade him sit. "Jimmy, I'm happy to hear that. This is fortuitous, if I must say."

"Is that right?" Jimmy said.

"Yes, I don't know what you're doing here, but we know what we're doing, don't we, William?"

"We do," I said.

"And what would that be?" Jimmy said.

"We have a secret mission," Edward said. "Waiting for my daughter Beth."

"Is that so?" Jimmy said. "Why is it secret?"

"I can't tell you," Edward said, "because it's too secret."

"I can keep a secret," Jimmy said.

"We'll tell you when the time is right," Edward said. "Meanwhile…." He called over to the bartender. "Say, this man would like a drink."

Jimmy waved the man away. "Edward, I told you; I don't drink anymore."

"Of course, of course," Edward said. "But this is rather perfect timing."

"Is that so?" Jimmy said. "I'm happy to hear that."

"Do you know that Myers is leaving me for a while so he can get married? To a schoolteacher. He likes schoolteachers. He's known this one a long time. Did you know about that?"

"No," Jimmy said, giving me a stare. "First I've heard of it."

"Because I've only just now told Edward the news," I said. "But I am not leaving the project. We just don't have the money for another field trip right now." Visions of my sweetheart, my old love, her smiling face, passed before my eyes. And I have to admit that the thought of remaining behind in Seattle when Edward set out once again, whenever that would be, gave me a hope so delicious, it nearly made me swoon. I don't know that he felt it, he certainly didn't show it, but I was ready to admit my own field fatigue and settle at home. Oh, hearth, oh, home!

"You're a courageous man," Jimmy said. "Giving up all that time from your life the way you have. I know what that's like."

"I thank you," I said, rather touched by his words, by his recognition. I glanced over at Edward, who was staring out at the rain as though completely uninterested in what I was talking about. "I'm not abandoning Edward. It's only—"

"I understand," Jimmy said. "There's no money left."

"That may be true, but that's not the reason. After many years of back and forth with a girl, long since become a woman, I popped the question to her last week."

"Congratulations," Jimmy said. "We should smoke a pipe. Down on the shore. Facing the mountains. Except that it's raining so hard out there we probably couldn't strike the match."

"We will, after the weather settles," Edward said. He fixed his gaze on our old field associate.

Jimmy came over and shook my hand. After a moment he turned to Edward, and said, "I know where you can make some money."

"You do?" Edward sat up straight at the mention of this.

"I do. I met a man who knows a man who...."

"A man who what?"

"A man who makes movies."

"You've traveled farther and wider than I imagined," Edward said, his voice turning suddenly quite serious.

"I suppose I have," Jimmy said, then explained that while traveling in Alaska he had met Robert Flaherty—"Oh yes!" Edward said—who had mentioned a producer named Halbstein, who had referred Jimmy to a director named DeMille down in Los Angeles, who said he might have some work for a cameraman on a new picture that was going into production next year.

Just then the door opened again, and we all looked in that direction.

A tall, blonde girl in her early twenties, dressed as though she were headed to church, walked hesitantly into the saloon. The umbrella she held at half-mast glistened with rain water. All our eyes lighted up.

"Beth!" Edward said.

"Dad!" she said. She glanced over at me. "Hello, Mr. Myers."

"Beth," I said, unable to avoid noticing how much she had grown.

Edward reminded her that she had already met Jimmy in the field some years ago.

"Are you visiting here?" she asked.

"More than just visiting," Jimmy said. "I've come to help."

"Dad didn't tell me that you would be helping us," Beth said.

"He wasn't aware that I was going to drop in."

Out in to the rain, streetlamps had come on, and the water of the Sound looked darker than the sky.

"Clara got the studio in the divorce," Edward explained in the motorcar on the way over to the business. "Which is where all my negative plates are stored."

"I see," Jimmy said. "And we're going to steal them back for you? There must be hundreds."

"Thousands," Edward said. "And all of them neatly filed away in the studio archives."

"But we're not going to steal them, are we, Dad?" Beth said as we drew closer to the studio. But she already knew the answer to her own question.

Beth brought the key. She led us into the dark studio, where the familiar odors nearly brought Edward, already sagging a bit from all the alcohol, to his knees. In a moment, he recovered and led us into the storeroom in the back. Only then did he turn on a lamp, which allowed us all to see each other, fellow conspirators, in a dim and somewhat sinister light. Even Beth, so dedicated in her devotion to her father, showed shadows beneath her eyes.

She had brought tools, hammers, and gloves for us to wear as we held the negative plates.

"Guard your eyes," Edward said. "I will demonstrate."

Going to the shelf, he took down a glass plate—made from his original negative, and from which the image was transferred chemically to a copper plate that he used to print the photographs for our volumes—and walked over to a row of large basins at the back of the room. (Had Beth arranged these to be here for us? How carefully had they planned this together? All he had told me was that we were going to recover some work that was his over at the studio. Certainly, it would account for his afternoon of excessive drinking. Oh, yes, it would!) He set the plate down in the basin, raised a hammer, and brought it down on the glass. The sounds of it splintering gave me a shiver, and Beth let out a cry that made it even worse.

Edward turned to her. "Can you watch us do this?"

Beth held up a hammer. "I am on your side in this, Daddy," she said, and went to a shelf, took down a plate, walked to the bin, and shattered it with one blow.

"Edward?" I raised my feeble voice.

"Don't worry," he said, "the publishers have another set in their offices. These are mine, though, and Clara has refused to return them. So…."

"Guard your eyes," Jimmy said. "Beth, gentlemen, guard your eyes."

It took us most of the evening, each of us with a hammer, smashing the plates, Achomawi, Acoma, Apache, Apsaroke (Crow), Arapaho, Arikara, shattering the plates, Flathead, Haida, Klamath, hammering, smashing, splintering, Klickitat, Mandan, Papago, shattering until nearly midnight. It was a miracle that none of us was cut or hammered each other or any part of ourselves—except for Edward (I don't know about Beth, because she never said a word to me about this incident, which her mother could only have considered as the grossest betrayal), who years later admitted to me that at one point, when the alcohol began to wear off, he felt as though he were hammering his own heart.

thirty-four

moving pictures

OREGON, 1923. THE BEACH was crowded with Egyptian soldiers and their horses and chariots, while over near the bathhouse, where the grass-line began, mobs of Israelites huddled together, eating sandwiches and smoking cigarettes. The tide was out, revealing a thick swath of dark, wet sand dotted with pebbles and seaweed and grasses, and in the middle of the swath stood a rotund man a decade or so younger than Edward, in a safari coat holding a megaphone in one hand and a cigar in the other.

"We have only a few hours, ladies and gents," he said in his amplified voice, a dignified and yet electric tone that turned everyone's head in his direction. "In a few minutes I'm going to call you back to places, and we're going to try the scene again. Remember that time and tide waits for no man, and this includes even us wonderful dancers of the silver screen. I want you Egyptians to get all of those nervous laughs out of your system—we can't afford to stand around and wait while you mull over the news that these tidal flats stink like sin and catch your slippers when you walk. Got that? Now—" He swung his megaphone around and looked straight out toward where Edward was standing at the edge of the beach. "Where the hell is that wrangler?"

He kept on gazing in Edward's direction.

"Are you the wrangler?"

"Me?" Edward called out to him.

"Yes, you. Are you?"

"No, Mr. DeMille," Edward said, with an exaggerated shake of his head. They'd been introduced for about two seconds before they left Los Angeles for Oregon and DeMille had understandably quite forgotten. "I'm the new Stills man."

"Stills? Yes, sure. But we're making a motion picture. You know how to operate a camera?" The director kept speaking directly to Edward despite the distance between them.

"Yes," Edward said with a big nod.

DeMille looked up the beach and then said, "Wait there, don't go away."

He then turned to shout some directions to a man at the other end of the beach. "You, wrangler!"

The man was hitching feedbags onto the horses' tacks, while the grooms lounged about and smoked cigarettes. Edward wandered up toward the trees, feeling a dull ache in his hip and cursing the long train ride and trip by car. It would take a few days of strolling around this beach but he knew that he would limber up a little, and more importantly, earn his money.

"Hey, you!" Edward was making a photograph of a group of actors in plumed helmets lined up in front of a row of chariots when DeMille crooked his finger at him.

"Yes, sir?" Edward said, and walked toward them.

"You say you know your way around a motion picture camera? One of my guys is stuck on the road somewhere. I need your help. The tide's coming in."

"Glad to be of assistance," Edward said, suddenly cheerful at his lucky break.

"What's your name?" DeMille asked. Edward told him. "How'd you get here?"

"A man named Halbstein? I spoke with him in LA; he told you about me."

The director wrinkled his bald brow and then rolled his face into broad smile. "Of course! He introduced us! I remember now. The Israelite! How fitting! Onward!"

And so they went to work, and just in time, too, since the tide came rolling back in with an unexpected wind to push it along. Fortunately for the Children of Israel, the film showed them escaping to the other shore—not the shores of India or China, that with a great act of imagination one could conjure up as lying there thousands and thousands of miles on the other side of the ocean, but this same shore, from which they had fled, photographed from another angle. Fortunately for the Egyptian soldiers, they would not drown that day. For that they would have to return to a stage set back in Los Angeles, and even then they would have their demise delayed until DeMille could touch up the film to show them rushing to meet their doom under tons of falling water as the Red Sea tide crashed back upon them.

After their long day of shooting, one of the assistant directors explained all this to Edward over supper in the large staff tent, as he was passing around a bottle of whiskey.

"Nobody drowns. Hardly anybody even gets wet. The magic of movies."

An actor, his plumed helmet on the table in front of him, put in, "But everybody who sees it, they're going to believe it happened just this way."

Just as in my photographs, Edward was saying to himself. He wanted to speak up, he wanted to assert himself, he wanted to make his presence known.

"They're not going to believe it ever happened," said a voice

behind his chair, "until they see it, and see it my way." Edward
turned to see the director standing there, food tray in hand. "In
the Bible, God just wrote the script," he said. "And a script isn't
anything until it's made."

"Right, C. B.," said the assistant director, and DeMille
blessed them all with that big smile of his.

"Mr. New Camera Operator," DeMille said.

The assistant director looked at Edward. "He means you."

"Yes, Mr. DeMille?"

"You think we got it today?"

"I do. I think we did."

"Good, good." He stood there, hovering, but clearly not
ready to sit down with them. "Who'd you work for before this?"

"Mostly for myself."

"What'd you make?"

"I've been working on a big project, Mr. DeMille," Edward said,
and he explained as much as he could about it in two sentences.

"Real Indians?" DeMille's face darkened in a frown. "I got
enough problems making movies about fake Israelites."
Everybody laughed, including Edward. In a softer voice,
DeMille added, "Though I put an Indian girl in one of my early
pictures. Nice girl. I still remember, her name was Red Wing. A
Winnebago, she was. I think." He paused to light a cigar. "Say,
Mr. New Camera Operator—"

"Curtis, Mr. DeMille. Edward Curtis."

"Curtis," he said. "What do you think about the ideas
going around that the Indians are really one of those lost
Israelite tribes?"

"They are, boss, really?" said one of the crew members. But
DeMille wasn't waiting for an answer and with another of his
gracious smiles moved along to another table.

It was a warm night, and after the meal Edward had nowhere

to go, so he took another slug of the whiskey and listened to the talk. Which was pretty much like all the talk of a crew in the field, touching on family left behind for those who weren't flirting and future plans for those who were. The way one of them put it was that everybody was either running from something or running toward something. Eventually the question came to him. "How about you, Mr. New Camera Operator," one of the crew said.

"Name is *Curtis*," Edward said.

"So, Curtis, are you running from something or running toward something?"

"Good question," Edward said. "I have to think about it."

"Don't think, just say it."

"Alright then. I'm running toward my paycheck," he said, getting a laugh from almost everyone at the long table.

"We're all supporting families," one of the crew said.

"I've got a lot of relatives," Edward said.

"Oh, yeah? How many you got?"

Thousands, tens of thousands, couple of hundred thousand, Edward was going to say, when just at that moment a lovely Hebrew girl walked past, her hair in a long single braid dangling behind her back, and Edward's stomach leaped into his chest. Amid all of these people, and movie people are great people to be among, he felt a sudden terrible drying up of his soul, a sinking awful miserable blast of loneliness.

And then he looked again as the girl laughed with a wide mouth, as a friend, another Daughter of Israel, made some comical remark, and both women lighted up cigarettes, as they strolled off into the night.

"Ladies?" Edward called after them.

It was so dark he couldn't see anything except the glow of the tips of their cigarettes—both of which stopped in midair a few feet ahead of him.

"Hey," one of the women said, apparently quite aware he was following.

"Hey," Edward said.

"It's so boring here, ain't it?"

Edward begged to disagree.

"The ocean is beautiful," he said.

By now he could see the two of them dimly outlined in the dark, and they had walked back toward him.

"Yeah, sure," one of them said. "I got the ocean outside my house at home."

"Sure you do," the other woman said. "Since when?"

"I moved."

"You did?"

"With Larry."

"You didn't tell me."

"You didn't ask."

"Ladies," Edward said, "the ocean is beautiful but now that we can't see it, things have become rather bleak, so—"

He didn't know what else he was going to say, when one of the girls interrupted. "You want to take a swim?"

"Why not?" the other said and began to peel off her clothes. The first girl did the same. The two of them stood naked in the darkness—the moon hidden behind the clouds—while motioning for Edward to undress.

He studied them, transfixed on the sand as if in a dream. And before he knew it, they were running toward the sound of the rushing surf—and then the moon came out from behind the clouds, showing them the ragged coastline and the darkly illuminated sand—and after a hundred yards or so he could hardly take a breath and fell behind, catching sight of their slender buttocks reflecting the moonlight as they waded into the low surf.

"Come on in!" one of them called back to him. "Before the waters part!"

The other girl bobbed up and down in the surf. "Part your own waters!" she called.

He stood there a moment, marveling at the sight of them, and then undressed and walked into the surf.

The cold shocked him into shivering, and for every step forward, his heart took a step back. By the time he was up to his chest, he had lost sight of the women, and felt like an iceberg from toes to neck.

"Yip!"

"Hey!" He could hear them crying out in pleasure from somewhere ahead of him in the rolling surf.

"Ow, ow!"

"Whoo!"

A younger man would have caught up with them already. Edward, in his early fifties, could scarcely keep up the pace. And yet if he did catch them—he was thinking, wondering, when the bottom dropped out from under him, and he began swimming hard, but even as he moved outward, their voices fell away.

Suddenly he was riding big swells, under the hard moon, like a spotlight or lens bearing down on him even as he floated upward, up. And then down, and tugged away by a sudden current.

For an instant he had the thought, perhaps not even a thought but the grain of a thought, of letting go, and letting the current and tide carry him where it would. Give himself over to it. Sail away on the rolling swells, sideways and outward, sideways and outward, toward some paradise out beyond to the west. And why not? He was ruined, wasn't he? Working for peanuts at a monkey's job?

He took a deep breath, glanced up at the moon, saw the old chief's face glowering at him, and with one great burst of attention—what might have been his last, he later decided—he turned around and like some elongated salt-water beast, hurrying toward some prehistorical transformation from ocean thing to land animal, paddled for the shore.

MEDITATION ALOUD BEFORE SLEEP

Soaked in brine, exhausted, Edward lay down his head. Everything's slowing down—me, the world—he said in the dark to the sinking moon. I have a paycheck, yes, but my heart's breaking, and still I'm not done. I'm done, and I'm not done. It's over, and it's over, and it's not done. Life, wife, children gone, and still not done. Still not. Oh, but I miss Myers! Our work together, our talks going on into the night. Where is he now? Somewhere on this coast, still in Seattle probably, wrapped in blankets next to his new wife, wrapped in the darkness of sleep. All the nights on the prairie, sleeping in tents, sleeping on bedrolls on the ground, stars above us as thick as berries in syrup, sometimes birds calling at daybreak, horses nickering in the dark, the Milky Way unscrolled, odors of bison and roasting meat, dogs whimpering and wolves howling—wolves, oh, Wisconsin wolves—and the nightbird, and the spiraling sunset, the flat white heat of desert day—

How do we cross without water? How do we drink without cups? Cup our hands, cross our hearts, strip to nothing but ourselves and smell the mingling scents before we even meet? Yes, I am Blackfeet, Chinookan, Quilcene, Osage, Brule, Blood, San Juan, Atsina, Spokan, Tewa, Tiwa, Mono, Havasupai, Umatilla…all the others known and unknown who walked the plains and burned the fields and forests, foraging, fighting, planting, uprooting, uprooted….Night fell, and we huddled together in the nearby cave, nothing more than an overhang protecting us from the tears of the night gods, while spirits spun around us, sloughed off skin of the once-living, they laughed and cried, sang and called to us, and we sang back to them, raising our voices so that we drowned out the noise of the demons who would pull us down into the earth, for we once came from there, or was it from a hole in the sky? And it would be wrong to return early to the place from which we first set forth....

And I am beyond drunk, and beyond lonely, detumescent in soul and spirit, sad at heart, undernourished. Years have gone by, and I have given everything to this, and what has come of it? No! He sat up in the dark, agitated by a spurt of acid in his chest. Foolish even to think of giving up, so close to the end!

When the God of Moses was preparing the Children of Israel to cross the Red Sea, giving them a leader and a prophet as assistance and sustenance, we huddled here at this Pacific shore, turning the stick and turning the stick and turning the stick, making sparks fall into embers, that we might create fire, and with fire create all that would come after. Flathead, Hopi, Hupa....

And Roosevelt and Morgan, and Myers, and some of my children, and Clara despising me, and where am I?

Yuki, Yukuts, Walla Walla, Washo....

And if the gods give me time, if they allow me to finish, I will go on.

And why, again?

And why not?

Myers, here is what I want to say: the hours, the days, the years. For my own people could never have given me the pleasure these thousands of early Americans here have given me. Though some did not settle. And still wander. The lost tribes. The last tribes.

They have given me pleasure, in many different ways.

And I have given them....

What?

Apache, Mono, Shoshone....

Library of Congress, Prints & Photographs Division, Edward S. Curtis Collection LC-USZ62-52209

thirty-five

the last tribes

JUNE OF 1927

AND SO IT HAPPENED that Edward Curtis, nearly sixty, with a sad and heavy heart, traveled north, with the goal of photographing the last Alaskan tribes, and found himself twelve days by steamer out of Seattle on the field trip that turned out to be his last, with his dutiful daughter Beth—who had put up the money, with the agreement of her husband, a decent man named Magnuson, for this final expedition (all the cash Edward had earned working for DeMille had been spent on earlier treks, to Northern California, to the plains again, and to Arizona, not very economical planning anymore, even when they needed it most, because their cash was so low)—and Eastwood, a new, young assistant, and an unusually silent Jimmy Fly-Wing.

Edward had not visited these waters since his trip on the *George W. Elder* many years before, and despite his melancholy—a divorced man, nearly bankrupt, who had not seen his youngest child in almost a decade—he felt quite exhilarated to be at sea. The sea, the sea! You gazed down into the waters, and the past, if not the future, swirled up into your view, and he spent many hours at the rail, gazing, dreaming, drifting.

The sky, too, was glorious. They reached Nome on an afternoon when the sky seemed so clear it was as though someone had taken the entire globe of the world and turned it upside-down so that any residue of cloud fell directly to the surface of the sea.

Nome—a collection of wooden houses and a few brick buildings, most of them spewing smoke from their chimneys from hearth-fires despite the fact it was June. These buildings sat like some child's model of a village against the vast sky and mountains of this broad and open land. The goal of Edward and his party was to charter a boat immediately and head north out into the Bering Sea, but their initial inquiries at the docks at first came to nothing. Though it was only the beginning of the summer, summers here sped briefly to a cooling conclusion—they needed to find a boat.

They checked into a small, wooden hotel, and darkness eventually fell. Beth, Jimmy, and Eastwood went out for a stroll, as Edward himself might have done years ago. But now the photographer was tired, his body felt like slabs of wood heaped up on one another, and he sought the relief of his bedroom, despite the available light. He smelled hearth-smoke all the way into his dreams, and the next morning, when he gave Beth a good-morning embrace, she told him she smelled smoke in his hair.

"What do we do now?" she said to the group after a breakfast of tea and oatmeal.

"Back to the docks," her father said.

"To the docks!" Eastwood, all boy (a trait, I suppose, Edward admired), let out a yip and a holler, and raced down to the water ahead of them. Before the others were even halfway there, he came running back toward them. "Look!" he said, pointing toward the water.

"What's that?" Beth strained to see.

"There it is," he said.

"There's what?"

A small boat lugged its way into the harbor, smoke streaming behind it like a small, dark flag.

"It's Harry-the-Fish," Eastwood said.

"A boat called 'Harry-the-Fish'?" Beth had been holding her father's arm as they walked. Now she let go and hurried along a little farther toward the pier.

"The owner is Harry-the-Fish," Eastwood said.

"The boat," Beth called back to them, "is called the *Jewel*...." She was peering out into the thin white air of the Nome summer morning.

"*Jewel Guard*," Eastwood said, at her shoulder.

"And who's Harry-the-Fish?" Edward said.

"The owner," Eastwood said, as they approached the pier together.

"How do you know that?" Edward said.

"I asked around while we were out walking last night," he said.

"So this is a man with references, eh?"

Eastwood smiled mischievously. "People told me that the only person crazy enough to charter a boat to greenhorns like us is Harry-the-Fish."

Waiting at the pier for the boat to dock, Edward wondered if this were true. And then as the *Jewel Guard* drew closer, he believed that nothing else was the case. The boat was about forty feet by twelve feet, and as it approached, it appeared to be an ideal craft for muskrat hunting in a swamp but certainly never designed for storms in the Arctic Ocean.

Whereas Harry-the-Fish lived up to his name entirely. They smelled of smoke—he reeked of the sea. Even his teeth appeared to be covered with greenish moss of the sort that you see on the rocks when the tide pulls out.

"Where will you be heading?" he asked, holding a hand to one shaggy ear. His shirt cuff was frayed and stray strands of thread spilled out from his coat sleeve, the coat itself a palette of all sorts of strains and smears and adding to the odor—the very aura of the sea—that surrounded the man.

"Nunivak Island," Edward said.

"Oh, sure, sure, just a hop, skip and a jump away, sir, yes, yes, that's it, of course."

"So you'll do it?"

"The *Jewel Guard* is my sweet, little honey," said Harry, squinting at him, and then allowing his eyes to fall on Beth. "Much as you care for your wife here—"

"My daughter," Edward said.

"Your daughter? Fine family outing to the islands, I see, I see," said Harry, pawing at his collar with a grease-stained hand.

"Research," Edward said, explaining about this being his last fieldtrip after nearly three decades of work and—not that this stranger would care, but Edward loved to hear his own words on the subject—that the final volume was in view, the end in sight. Sitting in the wooden hotel to which they'd all retired after meeting Harry's boat, Edward felt as though he were speaking not so much to a deaf man as to a fellow who spent so much time alone at sea that any human contact was something he wanted to go over and over again, the way you might pause over a favorite passage in a favorite book.

"What exactly are you going to do up there?" Harry said, turning serious. So Edward had Eastwood brief him, while he and Beth strolled back to the docks and took another look at this boat.

"Are you sure, Dad?" Beth said.

He was shaking his head, staring at the low bow, the shabby wheel-house, the tattered ropes lying about the greasy deck. "It's our only bet, so we've got to chance it," he said.

"You're sure? You don't sound so sure."

"It's summer, damn it," he said. "How much bad weather can we run into up here in the summer?"

They got their answer by midnight the next night.

Eastwood and Beth had gone below deck, trying to get some rest before the early dawning of the second day of their trip. Edward felt it incumbent on him to stay a while up top with their pilot and guide, some residual politeness, I suppose, left over from his days of running the portrait studio. And while Harry-the-Fish worked with his ropes, Edward and Jimmy had a chance to talk.

"It's all coming to a close soon," Edward said. "We're running out of tribes at the same time that we're running out of money. I never thought we'd get this close to finishing."

"There's still some ways to go," Jimmy said.

"Some distance over the water, yes," Edward said.

"Some distance, yes," Jimmy said.

"But we're getting there."

"We're almost there," Jimmy said.

It was around that time that they noticed the wind had begun to pick up, the sound of the waves slapping against the hull, making up a rough and erratic but nonetheless comprehensible rhythm of the sea, the plap, slap, the plap, slap, slap of them.

<hr />

And Harry-the-Fish bellowing into the rising wind, "Fish, fish, fish!" He asked Edward to take the wheel for a moment while he went below. And there Edward stood, with the engines growling, whining, the deck and the very timbers below and the mast and riggings above him, singing, creaking, whining, against the bap, bap, the bap, bap, slap, the slap of the waves....

Now grinding of the engine, whining, grinding....

The pap, pap, the pap, slap, pap, the slap....

Jimmy said, "I'll help Harry," and went below.

"Dad?" Beth came up just then, and even in the faint light of the wheelhouse Edward could see that she looked a bit peaked.

"Feeling it?" he said.

"I need some air," she said, turning away toward the railing. The fog was closing in, and it was all she could do to make out the railing itself. Billows and billows of fog floated in over the rail, threatening to smother her in the grayness of it all.

"You're not frightened, are you?" her father said to her when she stepped back inside the cabin.

"No, no," she said. "Just a little queasy."

"Now you know what it was like when your mother first discovered she was carrying you." He said his little joke, flicking his eyes from the compass to the sea, from the sea to the compass.

"Thank you very much, Dad," she said. "I'll have to remember that. If I ever have children, it will be just like a night on the heaving water of the Bering Sea."

"Except for one thing. And I shouldn't say it, but I will."

"What's that?"

"This isn't heaving. Not yet. This is calm."

"Oh, Dad, you shouldn't have said that." And with that, she bent over the rail, lingering there for a few moments, before standing upright again. Or as upright as she could, given the roll of the deck.

"You still feeling queasy?"

"About the same. But, Dad?"

"Yes, Beth?"

"You mentioned Mother."

"I did?"

"You did."

He thought a moment. "Just in passing. I don't want to start a quarrel with you."

"You couldn't," Beth said.

"Oh, I bet I could give it a try."

"No, Dad," she said. "I love you both. And I understand why she couldn't live with you anymore. I just wonder why it took her as long as it did to figure it out. No, I think she had figured it out, but she didn't want to admit it. Or she wasn't brave enough."

"I suppose," Edward said, "you'd have to be brave to live with me."

"I think you have to be brave to live with anyone, Dad," she said.

"Well," he said, "you're getting pretty philosophical. Pretty and philosophical."

"Oh, Dad," she said, and what a thing it was, to be steeped in such thick fog and feel herself blush. Quick as a hummingbird, she kissed him on the cheek and went below, leaving him with his regrets for his marriage and his life, and his hopes for her and the future.

"Fog?" Good old Harry stuck his head up above the hatch a few minutes after Beth had returned below.

"Thick as the cream in your coffee," Edward said.

"You have a way with words, don't you?" Harry said, hitching himself up onto the deck and coming over to take the wheel.

"There'll be ice floating free out there," he said. "I think we'd better lay to and drift with it."

Drift they did for a few hours. Even though it was frustrating that they weren't speeding toward the island, Edward was glad to be taken off any collision course with floating ice. Drifting was alright, he knew enough about life by now to say that. You could drift and drift, and if you had some luck the currents could still propel you in the proper direction, toward your desired goal. You just mustn't be in too much of a hurry. You need your patience. You need to remain calm.

Beth remained calm. Jimmy returned to the deck, his usual cool self. But Young Eastwood couldn't control his nerves. When he came on deck in the middle of the night, his voice sounded as wretched as the noise of the wind in the rigging, and his brown eyes glowed with a ghostly sort of fear.

"Drifting?" he said, waving his hands wildly. "Drifting? How can we be drifting? Isn't it dangerous not to be using power?" He rushed to the rail, as if he might have the power to see what they couldn't, the looming chunks of giant, floating ice. But they could hear them, the grinding, churning ice all around them, floating as they floated.

"I can hardly believe—all of this, my God!" he said. "Am I still asleep and having a nightmare?" He turned to look at Edward, who was leaning against the entrance to the wheel-house, poised to watch this useless protest against the elements. "Mr. Curtis, I signed up to do fieldwork in the plains! Now can you please tell me where the plains are? Out there somewhere in the howling wind and the crushing ice?"

"Howling ain't right," said Harry-the-Fish from his position at the wheel. "You ain't never heard real howling if you think this is howling. This ain't purring like a kitten, but it ain't howling by a long shot, either. You wait a little bit and you can hear some howling. If that's your pleasure."

"No, it's not," Eastwood said, looking over at Edward the way a child might look to a parent when he finds himself in a troubled situation and needs a helping hand to get out. "It's not my pleasure, not at all."

"I've been on the plains when some nights it's been worse than this," Edward said to him.

"In big snows?" Eastwood said.

"Snows, big rains. Some floods."

"But no earthquakes?"

"You're standing there on this deck worried about earthquakes?" Harry-the-Fish spoke to the lad as though he were some rare species of southern mammal.

"No earthquakes," Edward said.

"Then it couldn't ever have been worse than this," Eastwood said.

"And why's that?" Harry remained fascinated and repulsed both at the same time.

"Because," Eastwood said, looking at Edward but speaking to Harry, "there may be snow piling down on you on the plains, but you don't have to worry about the ground opening up beneath you and swallowing you."

"There ain't any ground here anyway," said Harry.

"He means the ocean," Edward said.

Harry gave him such a look as might have skewered a whale in the belly and kept it spinning about the barb. "You think I don't know that?"

"I knew you knew that," Edward said. "I don't know why I said that, Harry."

"Oh, I know why," he said, "because it's the middle of the night and the ice is singing and the wind is humming—that's humming, not howling—and the only good thing anybody can do right now is sleep or pray or both. So why don't all of you go below and try some of that, and I'll stay the watch until it gets light?"

No arguing with Harry-the-Fish on nautical matters. Jimmy went up and stood with Harry at the wheel. Eastwood went below. Edward followed and found Beth in the cabin, where she was sleeping as soundly as she ever did when she was a child.

Eastwood quickly fell asleep while Edward knelt alongside Beth's bunk, listening to her breath. A quiet sigh passed her lips, and he leaned over and kissed her on the forehead, the way that he had when she was so much younger.

"I hope you're feeling a little better," he said.

Beth opened her eyes for a moment, smiled, closed her eyes once again. "Are we home?" she said.

"If Nunivak Island is home, then we aren't home yet," he said in a whisper, certain that she was really more asleep than awake.

But Beth surprised him by speaking again. "I am feeling better. I love this, Daddy. Working with you."

"I do, too, sweetheart," he said.

"It's so exciting. Nearly finished. After all these years."

"I agree," he said. "And a good thing, because the money's run out."

"I'll dream us a bankroll," Beth said.

"You do that," he said, and kissed her again, stroking her head as if she were no more than two years old.

"This is what I missed," he said.

"What?" She raised her head up one more time, and then she was gone.

He went to his bunk and sank down onto it, shivering with fatigue, yet lying there with his eyes wide open. All these years, yes. All the traveling. All the hours on the trail, by himself or with assistants, while Clara was busy at home. It was like going to war, he decided. He had been away at war. Except he always stood on the side of peace. He never harmed anyone. He always put forward the picture of the Indian as whole and good and handsome and beautiful. As they once were, if not now. And if his photographs made them look more noble than most of them are, then at least they—all of them, like all of us—will have a glimpse of how things might have been.

The ship interrupted his thoughts with a shudder, a shudder and then a roll. And then he was thinking again, about how his life, looking back, seemed now a mess of debts and lost chances. But the work carried him along. And it was important, wasn't it? Damn Clara, too, for not possessing the understanding to stay with him! He always knew how to find the main path again, didn't he? Here, where he was now, at more than midlife—if this rising sea were a path to find, he had found it. Why couldn't she have followed?

These thoughts slapped at his mind while Beth and Eastwood slept peacefully on opposite sides of the cabin. Eventually, he closed his own eyes. But still he could not sleep, a parade of mistakes and missed opportunities marching before him. Clara, the children, the project, money, the future—all his sins piled up into a further mound of misgivings, while he stood off to the side, testifying in his mind to anyone who would listen that he had tried, oh, yes, he had tried!

At last, he was dozing off when he heard a loud noise on deck and felt the boat give a huge shudder. He climbed back up to find wind blowing large sheets of ice-fog across the bow, which for a few moments gave a good illusion of motion. But there was Harry, pounding his fists on the rail.

"The fog's back? How long did I sleep? Harry?"

But Harry couldn't seem to hear him. A giant mailed fist smashed against the boat and sent it rocking and reeling.

Library of Congress, Prints & Photographs Division, Edward S. Curtis Collection
LC-USZ62-74554

thirty-six

the storm

HOWLING WIND—SHOUTS, SCREAMS. Harry on the deck shouting into the wind, "We're aground! We're goddamned, Jesus, frank in the muck of it, run aground!"

Eastwood and Jimmy appeared alongside Edward. And then came Beth, her hair mussed by sleep and the wind, looking the way she did when she was a child and just roused from dreams. "What's happened?" Beth said.

"I knew I shouldn't have given up dry land," Eastwood said.

"We're stuck on a piece of rock," Edward said. "Even if it's just a small piece."

"And if the storm keeps up the wave's are going to use it like an anvil and beat us to small pieces," Harry said.

"Is it supposed to keep on blowing?" Edward asked him. "Maybe it will blow us off."

"Before that happens, it's going to tear us apart." Harry, a forlorn look coming over him, said, "If we sit here long enough it's going to pound us down to nothing."

"What about the dinghy?"

Harry waved off Edward's idea. "Even if we could get it over the side and board it," he said, "it'd be like going over Niagara

Falls in a breadbox."

Beth reached for her father's hand.

"Your hand is so warm," he said, trying hard not to show her what he was thinking.

"I'm alive," she said.

"And you're going to stay that way," Edward said, giving her hand a squeeze and sending her below. "Harry?"

"Yes, sir?"

"Can I see the chart?"

"You know how to read a chart?"

"I can try." He got out the sodden charts and pointed a finger at where he thought they were. "Not so far off the coast, are we?" Edward said.

"If you're thinking of swimming, forget it," Harry said. "Even if the currents weren't so fierce, you'd freeze to death before you swam a quarter of a mile."

"It's summer," Eastwood put in, coming up and looking at the chart over our shoulders.

"Summer in Hell," Harry said.

As if to prove his point, the wind surged, and a huge wave crashed over the side of the boat, leaving them soaked and shivering.

"Maybe it will knock us off the rock right away," Eastwood.

"Maybe it will tear us up while it knocks us," Harry said.

"You're an optimist," Edward said.

Harry showed him his furry teeth. "I am, I am, so let's eat breakfast."

"It doesn't feel like morning," Edward said. But even as he spoke he noticed that the light seemed to have increased a fingernail's width in brightness. This turned out to be an illusion quickly crushed by the punch of the next wave, which sent them all staggering against the wheel-house, while the deck shuddered beneath their feet.

More waves, more clouds, deeper darkness.

Hours passed, and the boat was still taking a terrible beating. Edward stood in the wheel-house, staring out into the blankness of the wind and the waves, beating at his own chest. Each time the waves slammed them and the boat shuddered like an old warrior preparing to go down, Edward slammed his fist against the wheel. Just think! Just think! Just think! Until finally, Harry-the-Fish took him by the arm. "Save your strength," he said. "You're going to need it."

The wind howled, another wave washed over them, to punctuate his words. "You say it's hopeless to try the dinghy?" Edward said.

"Mr. Curtis, I'm telling you—"

Boom! Another wave surged across the deck, smashing the glass in the side window of the wheel-house.

Boom! Slash! Another sent Edward stumbling against the door, where he slid to his knees and then crawled back to the door.

"Mr. Curtis?"

"What is it, Harry?"

"Where're you going?"

"I want to see my daughter," he said to him over the roar of the wind.

"Keep your head down," Harry said as he reached up and pulled open the door. Water surged in from the deck, knocking Edward back against the wheel-house. He struggled to his feet and pushed forward, only to find it better to crawl to the hatch for fear of being blown overboard. The wind yanked at his arms, and he flattened himself like a snake and crawled forward on his belly.

"Dad!" Beth poked her head up through the opening of the hatch.

"Stay there. I'm coming!" he called to her.

He crawled forward and wrestled himself down into the hatch. It was cold and dark below, and wet as hell. Cracks in the hull let the water surge in as the waves broke across them, so that if they'd been in the water, instead of stuck on this rock, they'd have been sinking by now.

"Beth, stay with me," he said, not knowing what he meant or what good it would do, even as he took her in his arms and held her close, as though she were a small child again.

"Mr. Curtis?"

"Eastwood...."

"Yes, sir," he said.

"How are you doing?"

"Mr. Curtis, I think I really do prefer work on the plains."

They had a good laugh, a laugh so loud it almost rivaled the noise of a huge crash up above. A moment later Harry-the-Fish and Jimmy came clattering down the hatch. "Wheel-house is about to go," he said.

Beth went instantly from laughter to tears.

"Darling, darling girl," Edward said, "your Papa's here, it's going to be alright."

"It's not," she said, in a trembling voice. "It's only in stories that things turn out alright."

"Just the opposite," Edward said, "in stories it's always melodrama, but in life things just eventually smooth themselves out."

"Not in my life," she said. "Not after you left."

"I didn't leave, Beth. I just made a lot of fieldtrips."

"My whole life you made a fieldtrip," she said, her words angry enough to carry above the growl of the wind.

All of them were huddled so close together in the hold, it was easy to mistake anyone's conversation for your own.

"When I have children," Eastwood said, "I'm going to take them with me."

"Don't do that," Beth said. "He almost killed my brother once on a fieldtrip."

"Beth!"

"And now he's definitely getting me killed."

"Beth, please."

A young woman, and she began to shake and tremble, wracked with tears and desperate laughter at the same time.

"But it's not going to be that way," he said. "It's not. You have a life to live, you have a husband waiting for you."

But he was sorry that he said this, because Beth began to weep and weep so hard that he thought she might go to pieces in his arms. The only thing that stopped her was a terrible roaring wave that smacked the stern and sent them tumbling up against each other in the dark. They huddled there a while, listening to the roar of the wind and water.

"Dad," Beth said, quieter now. "Do you pray?"

"I used to, when I was a small boy. My Pap got us all praying. I've told you about him, he was a man of the Bible. But I stopped after a while."

"Mama made us say our prayers always. Do you think it does any good?"

"You mean, could our prayers stop this storm?"

"Do you think?"

"I don't know, Beth. I don't know."

"Harry?"

"Yes, miss?"

"Do you pray?"

"Not since I was a pup."

"To whom did you pray?"

Jimmy, who had been silent to the point of near-invisibility, spoke up. "I've been praying just now to the Great Spirit, to the Sky."

"Good luck," said Harry-the-Fish. "Unless the Great Spirit walks on water."

"Sky floats above it," Jimmy said.

"It's not my territory," Harry-the-Fish said.

That's when things really began to go to pieces, waves smashing them from two directions and the wind howling so loudly that they had to stop speaking or shout themselves hoarse. Icy seawater spilled down the entrance to the hatch, and they were soon up to their ankles in wash. It was all Edward could do to stand, but he did, kissed Beth on the forehead, and moved toward the hatch.

"Dad?"

"I'm going," he said. "The dinghy?" He turned to Harry.

"Lashed to the stern, if it's still there," he said, sloshing through the water after him. "But water's probably too rough to put out in it."

"Will you help me?" Edward asked.

Harry gave a shrug. "I'll help you."

"I'll go, too," Jimmy said.

"Stay here with Beth," Edward said to Eastwood. It was all he and Jimmy could do to climb to the deck without looking back. As he crawled out of the hatch, the wind hit him in the face with the force of a blow from a baseball bat. "It's getting light!" he shouted, marveling at the pearly white luster on the undersides of the low-hanging clouds.

But the waves were still relentless, and on the deck, the boards were ripped and splintered; it looked as though a team of men had attacked it with sledgehammers.

"We're coming apart," Harry shouted to him.

"How much time do we have?"

"I'd give us an hour or two, at best."

Edward was breathing hard. "We have to do this now, while we still have a chance."

"We don't have a chance," Harry said.

"Unless the Great Spirit walks on water," Jimmy shouted to him.

Edward shrugged, and on their hands and knees they made their way to the stern. "Where's the dinghy?"

Harry pointed to a torn lashing, whipping about in the wind. "Gone."

It was ending, it was over, a finish Edward had never expected, death by drowning, but if he could convince himself that he had done mostly his best for a good, long number of years he should have few regrets. He began to mourn for all the children, but especially for his dear Beth, the young woman waiting innocently below for news that her all-knowing father had figured out how to escape their plight. Oh, Beth, with your whole life still ahead of you!

"Beth!" he cried out, slipping down to all fours on the deck and shouting into the air. "Beth, Beth, Beth, my darling girl!"

"Yeah, yeah, yeah," said Harry-the-Fish, staggering above him for a moment before the wind blew him down onto the deck, where he held on for dear life to a protruding board.

The wind blew even harder, and the waves crashed across the deck.

"If only—" Edward shouted into the wind.

"If only what?" shouted back the hard-bitten Alaskan sailor.

Edward huddled on the deck, his fingers holding onto the imperfections between the planks, his own words lost to him in the wind that whipped his body and terrorized his soul.

"If only!" He bowed his head, something he hadn't done since childhood, and said a prayer in his mind to old gods and new, hoping that they all might hope for some deliverance. His life felt like a stone cast into the sea.

"Wait!" Jimmy called over to him.

"Wait for what?" Edward raised his heavy head and called back.

"Wait, wait, wait…," came Jimmy's reply.

"Thank you, Jimmy," Edward said.

"Wait," Jimmy said again.

And over the course of the next few minutes or so, while they all lay shivering on the deck, the wind dropped off to a fierce breeze.

Fog lingered at the waterline, but above them, long horse-tail clouds trailed across the upper part of the sky and the western horizon glowed pink and orange, and then settled into a lavender that reminded Edward of more southern places. Wayward seabirds landed on their bow and called to each other and to them and to whatever unknown god was turning the lavender now to purple and then, quickly sinking in shade, to inky blue. The waves lapped gently now against the rocks, and if you stared at any part of the horizon, you had the illusion that rather than being shipwrecked on these jutting boulders, all of them, rocks and all, were steaming for some farther destination.

And here was Harry-the-Fish, his clothes drenched, shaking from the cold, making a goat-song to add to the end of their near-tragedy. "Summer weather. Fickle, fickle. We're lucky to be alive."

Eastwood crawled out from below. Jimmy looked up from where he had been clinging to a spar. "You see," he said.

"I'm not sure I do," Edward said. "But I'm happy."

And here was Beth standing next to Edward, drenched but exultant. "Look!" She pointed to the northeast, toward a thin shoreline emerging from the fog bank, like a photograph coming into view in a bath of chemicals. Scudding clouds met ropes of smoke rising from a group of wooden huts. "There! There it is! Dad! The last tribe!"

Jimmy, Eastwood, Beth, and Edward leaned over the railing, straining to see further. The fog suddenly lifted altogether. People stood on the beach near a tall totem pole depicting an eagle, a bear, and a fish, waving, waving to the boat.

Library of Congress, Prints & Photographs Division, Edward S. Curtis Collection LC-USZ62-47004

thirty-seven

the kayak

O, MY MUSE! What these next years brought! Such happiness—
we completed our final volume!—and such sorrow!

Staying in Seattle, when the rest of them had set out for the
north, made yours truly feel quite strange. My habits had been
settled for decades and decades: outward bound with Edward
and others, and returning from the field usually to repair to our
work-cabin in Montana, but now and then to other sites, rather
than home, where we sifted through our notes and organized
our recordings and made the photographs that made our work
so distinct from all the others who might have wandered into
the field. I didn't like hearing the news of this last expedition
second-hand, but it was better than not hearing it at all.

At this time I resembled something like a happy man, happy
in my home with my wife, and pleased, in a bittersweet way, to
be able to put my hand into the record of the last trip to the
field. Let critics attack us for occasionally overzealous fieldwork,
but not for heartless presentations. We could have
photographed Nunivak Island men in their everyday clothing
and photographed their spectacular masks and costumes separately. Why not put them together?

Jimmy agreed. At one of our last work sessions together, he sipped water and commented on the ferocity of the masks. "True warriors," he said. "They swell my heart."

Jimmy had been such a stalwart, especially in the final years of our work, moving to Los Angeles and standing shoulder to shoulder with Edward, while editing the pages I would send down from Seattle.

As for my own heart, oh, it was filled. My beloved, my schoolteacher, and I had, at long last, set up our household in the old Curtis waterside shack that Clara had left empty after moving into the city long ago. With help from some fishermen neighbors, we sealed it well against the winter cold and damp, and I heaped up my notes against one side of the bedroom—the same room where Edward's father had died, long before I met the man who changed my life forever. Now nearly midway to a century of life, I felt less the heroic young man than the older, wiser advisor to the young.

"Say no more about this, William," my beloved said to me when I made my lament about all the years I had put into the project, a lament that I so often heard from Clara from the other side of the sorrow created by absence.

"Say no more?"

My beloved, her dark hair now streaked here and there with a strand of gray, turned to me from the stove where she was toiling over our evening meal. "Say no more, and come here and help me clean the fish, please."

"Oh, love and death, being and disappearance!"

"Did you say something?" She turned to me, holding a scaling knife.

"Just thinking aloud."

"Come clean the fish, please, while you think."

Yes, my Muse, she had a sense of humor.

Whereas Clara had little or none of whatever feeling of loyalty to our work she once might have possessed. Fortunately, her antipathy toward her former husband (which rose considerably after the destruction of the plates) did not spill over into our relations. Now and then I stopped in at the studio, which she, aided by a number of her family members, had made into a great success, and finding her sometimes alone at the counter, I initiated conversations about the long past, and once in a while, when a cousin or brother-in-law could take the watch for customers, we even took a walk along the hilly streets downtown.

I believed it was the gallant part of me, and not the gossip, that sometimes raised the subject of Edward, so that she did not have to bring herself to ask the questions that I answered before she spoke. Nonetheless, she sometimes asked, upon hearing about some particular event in his life, some particular questions.

"And Beth went along with him?"

I felt her pain at knowing that she, the mother, did not know the full details of one of her daughters' lives. It showed in her eyes, the flatness of her stare. Never a truly pretty woman, she had not aged well, and her cheeks had sagged, and small hairs had sprouted on her reddened chin. Time, which for me and Edward seemed—and I put the accent on *seemed*—to stand still during our nearly thirty years in the field, had flowed all around and over Clara, tugging at her the way the tides might, carrying her along.

"And Magnuson?" She referred to Beth's husband, with whom she lived outside Los Angeles.

"No, he did not go."

"Another of those lonely separations," Clara said. "How sad…." She sighed, and this turned into a cough, decades of misery rumbling up out of her chest.

Where we live, traveling as often as we do over water, there is ample time for reflection on life's torments as well as its pleasures, and I had plenty to say that night at the supper table about what I had seen that day in Clara's face, and in the churning water at the stern of the ferry, as the city grew smaller behind us.

"I worry for her," I said. "She does not look well."

My beloved, dutifully pouring me a glass of our local, illegal cherry wine, stared up at the ceiling, as though some message might have been written there, and then said, "I don't know how I kept my own health while you were away."

"The children you taught gave you strength," I said. "You stayed close to youth and that kept you young. Clara's children grew up, and grew away from her over the years, except for Katherine, of course."

"He—Curtis—he hasn't seen Katherine in a long while, has he?"

"No," I said, "of all of them, she took her mother's side. Perhaps because she is the youngest."

Now a look I recognized, and worried about, came into her eyes, and I got up from the table, went to her side, and took her in my arms. "I know, I know," I said. "Life might have been different for us if—"

"Oh, hush," she said.

"No, no, I would not have stayed in the field as long as I did."

"If we had married early and had—?"

"That's right, that's right."

"So now we have only my pupils…"

So, yes, we had our sorrows, my beloved and I. But there were more sorrowful things in this world.

One cool afternoon in the autumn of that year, without any warning (and, given her fear of water, entirely surprising), after running the business, after separation and divorce, after each of the children from Hal to Beth to Florence had left home, with only Katherine remaining, Clara went for a kayak ride alone, leaving behind a simple note.

When he heard the news, Edward pictured it clearly:

The sun on the water, broken by wind into shifting fragments, the pattern of her worries, drifting. Oh, and the tide driving it. A range of shore, trees, white-capped mountains beyond, leaping into the foreground, and the vast Western ultramarine sky, against which all this propelled itself toward her burning eyes.

The water dancing! The light!

He didn't know why, why some people took this way out and others stay until the very end is thrust upon them, rather than reaching toward it with outstretched arms, something perhaps she had always longed for, the quiet upon quiet of a stillness in the dark.

She must have told herself when she set out in a fragile boat onto the frightening waters that she had to hurry to reach the city pier. Pushing off from shore. On her mind—what?—had she taken some laudanum? She had, over the years, taken laudanum for her nerves. Or a few sips of whiskey now and then to calm her frightened soul? Only Katherine still cleaved to her, but the other children? They had abandoned her! Yes, to marry, to work, and while they paid lip-service to her—a mother knows, a mother knows—they lived their own lives. She didn't begrudge them that. But nevertheless she felt alone, abandoned, defeated in her struggle to make and keep a family. Yet didn't she want him to know that after all the quarreling and the jealousy—yes, because she was in a certain way jealous, because he had a purpose beyond the family, beyond the business, and he was in a certain way selfish and blind, because he put his project before everything, before her, before the children, his business, everything—that she still wanted to meet him halfway? Yes! And so she paddled out into the current and with great determination tried to keep moving toward the farther shore.

And when the tide carried her past the point that she had in mind for mooring, she stood, and inexplicably waved her arms at the sun, at the light, and lost her balance—an accident, or something she had planned? Who could say? Who could say?—and she fell, or jumped, and struggled, the boat overturning, and she looked up a moment at the sky, seeing what? His face? The children? Her parents? The face of her God? A smile, a glimpse, perhaps even a wink? She went under, and came up again, and under and up and out again, and as she was flailing about, hoping to touch him or all or any of the children, she lost her hold on the light and the air, her dress dragging her down, and he reached out a useless hand to her, but she had already closed her eyes, and then opened them, and with her last breath felt herself pulled one way—up! toward the surface—and the other way, down! toward the bottom—just as she had to the very end felt torn, pulled apart between her life and her love...oh, never to resolve it, because it was unresolvable...drifting down and down, sinking deeper and deeper, until the seal-boy—a creature Edward had heard of in dreams of the people of the Last Tribe—swam up from below and took her by the arm and led her along, north, into the Strait. "I heard you," the seal-boy told her, "even before you knew you were coming this way," and then released her where she would be found on the shore of an island, or if not she, then something resembling her, before she could forgive Edward....

Could she forgive him? He asked this of himself—we all would—over and over, for a good long while.

And then life overtook us, all of us, from Edward and the children, growing, grown, to me and my sweet-heart, her dark hair turning grayer and grayer by the year, and the waters moving and the land under the sun. It was another country back then, when a man could know within his single lifespan the prairie, mountains, and deserts, the waters of Puget Sound, the fancies of the slender isle of Manahatta, a mogul and a President, the turmoil and glory of a family, deep friendships, few enemies, chief after chief after chief, and most of the intricate outer and inner worlds of most of the tribes. All of us disappear as air, yes, air and light, lightning and shadow, except for what images a man like Edward can capture.

As always, as in any life, except that you don't know it until you live it—and no art, neither stories nor novels nor paintings nor photographs nor statues nor dances nor poems can convince you—you find yourself closer to the end than to the beginning, and the end begins.

Library of Congress, Prints & Photographs Division, Edward S. Curtis Collection
LC-USZ62-49644

epilogue

jimmy takes charge

AND LATER, DECADES LATER, more awful news, aiee! The way such word travels! Signal flares lighted up from mountain top to mountain top! Drums resending sound from village to village! Smoke signals in clear light telling stories to be spread! A letter sent by ship! Messengers on horseback racing the news from place to place! Telegraph lines sailing the cryptic noise along the wires! The telephone rings!

Hal Curtis, now in his mid-fifties, has just arrived at his sister's farm outside Los Angeles, and he takes the call. "Hello?"

"Who is it?" Edward shouts to him from the hallway, studiously putting on his boots, ready, he thinks, to take a walk with his only son.

"Uh-huh," his son says. "Uh-huh. Oh, no. Oh, how awful!"

"What is it, Hal? Damn it!" One of his boots skids away from his hands, and he bends, aching at the hips, to retrieve it. Do you know what it is like, could you possibly know the anger in the joints and the damned irritations and inflammations!

"Pop?" Hal stands in front of him now, here in the narrow hall of Beth and her husband's farmhouse, to which Edward had retired some years before.

"What is it, son? Who was that?"

"It was William Myers's wife."

"And?"

News, news, news, the news. It was awful.

"Myers? He's gone? He's younger than I am, much younger! At least ten, twelve years!"

"I'm sorry, Pop."

"Suddenly I don't feel like taking a walk." Hal, always an affectionate boy, throws an arm around his father, helps him back into the kitchen, and offers him a chair. "How did he go?" Edward asks, sitting at the table like a boy himself, one boot on, one boot off.

"She didn't say much, Pop. She was distraught."

"Yes, I imagine she was. But how?"

"She mentioned his lungs, pneumonia."

Edward snorts hard, like one of the horses Beth and Magnuson keep in the barn. "Seattle weather. Kills a man eventually." He takes in a few breaths, as if to test his own lungs, and then closes his eyes and begins to cry.

"Pop!"

"Oh, oh," Edward says, trying to speak, though overtaken by sobs.

"Pop?"

Edward finally finds a deep breath, and his voice breaks through as he looks up at Hal. "Oh, Christ! He was a good man. I've missed him."

He sits there a while in silence, and Hal respectfully keeps his counsel. Eventually he looks around at his son. "Did she mention his notes? I had a letter from him. He was writing the story of our work. He typed up everything we did, you know? He was great with languages, but he was also the fastest typist. We used to sit up all night in our work-cabin in Montana...."

Edward pauses to clear his liquid throat.

"We'll have to get those notes. We can give them to Jimmy. Though we'll have to find him first, won't we? I haven't heard from Jimmy Fly-Wing in a very long time, not since we finished our final volume. I don't even know if he is still alive. But if he is, we'll ask him if he can finish the story." Harsh intake of breath as if at his own seeming coldness. "Myers gone....Myers gone. I can hardly believe it." But if he can believe that he is now over eighty years old, after what seemed like only minutes beyond Beth's announcement, on the deck of the *Jewel Guard*, that the last tribe was in sight, then he can accept that Meyers has died.

"Sioux and Cherokee and Comanche and Absaroke and Cayuse and Cheyenne—"

"Pop, Pop, calm down," Hal says.

"What? Why the hell should I? The day is going by, another damned day I won't be able to live over....Osage, Oto, Pima, Pomo...."

"Pop?" Hal's voice jolts him out of his reverie, and the Western light streaming in through the kitchen window strikes him full in the face

"Yes, son?" He blinks and blinks. Liquid surges in his throat. "I have to get to Brazil."

"Brazil?"

"Before all the gold disappears."

"Gold, Pop?"

"Yes, yes, I've been studying this question." Edward takes a painful breath, and then another just to test the pain that came with the first. And the pain stays with him at each inhalation. "I've been reading. I've been convinced for years. Gold drives the world. Gold caused all of the first big troubles in the West, when some damned fool discovered it in the Black Hills, and we just marched the cavalry in, or sent them in on their damned horses, I should say, and trampled on the treaty with the Sioux."

He swallows, testing the function of his throat. "You're not Sioux, are you?"

"It's me, Pop. Hal."

"Of course," Edward says, breathing again with the pain. "She died, didn't she?"

"Mother? Yes, she did, a long time ago, twenty years ago."

"I miss her," Edward says.

"I miss her, too, Pop," Hal says.

"I didn't treat her exactly right. But I had a mission, a vision, a quest, as my Indian friends say. A quest." He rests his head on the kitchen table.

Hal puts his arms around his father. "I know you did, Pop. We all knew."

"You all knew, but how many of you approved of me?" Edward doesn't look up.

"Pop," Hal says, "you are the best man I know."

Are those the last waking words that Edward hears? Quite soon, he closes his eyes. When next he looks up he sees Beth, and he follows her to the door. The sky, bone-white where the sun burns strong as it always does in this part of California in autumn, and blue at the horizon, shades into a blue as blue as the palest part of a jay's wing where you might hold it up to the same bright sun. He stares at the garden a while, listening to the chickens cackling up in the pen behind the house. His right hip throbs. In the distance he hears a few faint noises, a mechanical chafing that he takes to be the roar of a train passing through town some miles away. Once the train noise fades bird-noise dots the vast expanse of sound. And then a vast stillness. And more stillness. And a stillness beyond that.

He moves from the door to the back window to watch Beth bent over her work in the garden.

Suddenly overcome with an irrational fearfulness, he wrenches himself from the window and decides to go ahead with a scheme that he had devised while first reading about the gold rush in Brazil. He slowly climbs back up the stairs and digs through the clutter on the floor of the bedroom closet until he finds a small traveling bag. He then goes to his son-in-law's chest of drawers, as if it is his own, and pulls out socks and shirts and underwear and stuffs them into the bag.

With some effort, he climbs back down the stairs and goes straight to the room that in this small house passes for a library and study. There he stands at the bookshelves, bag in one hand, and with his other hand runs his fingers across the spines of all the volumes of his life's work, whose names and numbers and contents he knows nearly by heart.

So many tribes, Jicarilla, Nunivak, Osage, Oto, so many people, so many faces, so many songs, so many years! He couldn't begin to pack with him even a small part of it. But the volumes are worth money; he can sell them in town to raise the cash for his trip. And perhaps even bring one or two volumes along with him, to show anyone who might doubt what he had done and what he might do next. He pulls some volumes from the shelf, from the top first, so that in a few moments a mound of books piles up at his feet, and the bag, already stuffed with clothing, begins to bulge with the shape of the books. He stops to take some deep breaths, and then pulls down a few more of the heavy books, until his arm aches and a small but sharp electrical pain races between his shoulder and his jaw.

"Should I call Beth?" he asks himself, and then the ground, the walls, the roof, start to tremble, a roaring like that inside of a racing locomotive overtakes him, and as he turns away from the bookshelves, they shake the rest of their contents down onto his back, and he sinks under their weight onto the floor.

Just as suddenly as it starts, the rumbling ceases, and he lies there listening, scout-like, almost no breath at all, beneath the heap of books.

"Dad?" He hears Beth's racing footsteps—her screaming shout. "Daddy!"

The room shakes again.

"Heavy seas," he says. "But we'll get there." He gathers all his remaining strength to raise his head and look into Beth's eyes.

And the wind picks up, and in fact he feels as though his entire body, every limb and organ, has been transformed into a higher stage of its nature, as he spies a woman bundled in seal-skins, standing just forward on the bow of the *Jewel Guard*, one hand on the rigging, the other raised, her long finger crooked toward Edward.

"What is it?"

"Come here, tall man."

"Who are you?" Edward ambles across the rolling deck, possessing, he notices—marvels, really—more agility on this moving surface than he had before he had gone below.

"You don't know who I am?" the woman says, pulling the skins away from her face. It is she—the clamdigging princess of Seattle—her face a map of a thousand trails.

"How did you get here?" Edward asks, knowing there is no answer to his question even as he asks it.

She bites the tip of the pointing finger on her right hand until it bleeds and drips designs in blood upon the deck. "Listen to me," she says. "And watch." How can he take his eyes from her, except to glance down at the bloody designs? "Listen carefully. I can only tell you once. There are many worlds," she says. "Three to you, and for others of us, at least four and perhaps five. And maybe even more, the way the worlds go on. But here is how it looks to us." She motions with the finger that is dripping droplets of blood onto the deck.

upper world (she draws)

---

middle world

---

under world

"You see that? And do you know where you live?"

"In the middle world, of course," Edward says. The sun stays hidden above the fog. The wind blows harder, and, feeling a chill in his chest, he pulls his arms tightly around himself.

"But you know that there are these other worlds, too, don't you?"

"I have listened to many stories about them."

The woman shakes her head and points at him with that dripping finger, like some young schoolmarm—for she is no longer an old woman, her face is smoothed out by the powerful winds. "Stories, you listen to stories. But stories are more than that, or why else would they continue? I want you to see. I want you to see just how many stories there are."

"Worlds within worlds within worlds?"

"Or worlds outside worlds outside worlds."

"All a dream of a dream of a dream...."

As he speaks, the wind rasps against his cheeks, but he feels nowhere near the cold he should—he blinks into the draft. A dark object moves along the edge of his sight, where the white line of the water meets the white border of the fog.

"Where is everyone?"

"In another dream."

He is about to ask her where they are dreaming it, when the object he had seen in the distance suddenly comes gliding over the water and slows down just where they are standing. It's a young seal, seated in a kayak, using its flippers as paddles.

"Are you ready?" the clamdigger woman asks him.

Edward smiles, feeling a pleasant heat rise to his cheeks. "Where are we going?"

"Some new place."

The seal raises a flipper. "Get in now," he says.

Edward climbs gingerly down into the canoe, feeling it roll with his weight from side to side, the seal pilot (or boy?) righting them with his flippers. (Or was it paddles?)

Just then light bursts through the fog bank above and around them, and Edward catches a glimpse of the mountains, their snowy peaks splashed all of a sudden with morning luminescence. "Day already?" he says.

"Day is night and night is day. The light began here," says the seal.

Edward nods his head, enjoying the rising of the morning, with the hope of warmth it carries, at least in this month of June. Hearing a faint clamor above the waves, he turns around to look for the source of the sound—some walrus or seal or who knows what other sort of Arctic animal splashing about in the frigid water—and the strangest thing happens, among all these strange events of the past few hours—he hears a woman call his name.

It sounds to him like Clara. Clara? But she is gone, isn't she? How can she call out to him up here now in these icy waters if she is gone? But exactly when is he dreaming this? Did he dream it before she went under the waves, or is he dreaming it now, so much later after the fact? Or in both of these times?

They glide smoothly toward a beach, nearly free of ice on the easterly shore of an island, a stony inlet where mild waves wash ashore. Edward soon forgets about his question. When the seal motions for him to step out of the kayak, he finds himself in water up to his knees. Cold as it is, the gravelly bottom makes him feel good and welcome. It is only after he takes his first steps past the low surf that he realizes he is alone!

Time whirls away and night falls as suddenly as ice sheering off from a glacier—and the stars boil above him in the great stewpot of heaven, bubbling up around the edges of the sky in vast patches of glistening clusters. A wolf lopes across his path, and when Edward sets his eyes on the horizon again, he discerns a small spot, which becomes a hut made of ice.

A woman ducks out from the knee-high entrance, a beautiful young dark-haired woman, with familiar cheekbones and Chinese eyes. The hood of her white parka is thrown back to reveal her glistening hair; her leggings are as red as the faces of warriors he had imagined as ready for battle.

"You, Curts, must come with me," the woman says.

"Tasáwiche?" he says, feeling hope surge into his chest. "How did you get here?" Though he is wondering, who, if this beautiful creature is Tasáwiche herself and not some ghost of the worn-down Havasupai girl he had seen in Tuba City, who, who, who was he?

"I missed you so," he says, reaching for her.

"Come inside," she says.

He follows her in and finds himself in a warmer place, where children gather around him. A fire crackles in the center of a tent and the air is smoky with the scents of roasting fish and tobacco. A hunter in sealskin stands at the entrance. Men sitting around the fire begin to chant. On the far side, Myers sits with a recording machine, listening so intently that Edward chooses not to disturb him. Sparks, like fish, swim by in the air. The song rises in intensity, so that he feels it along his arms and in his chest. A long spear floats before him. He reaches for it, with his aching arm, but misses. He falls back onto a mattress of animal skins. Someone touches him, and he looks up to see Beth smiling down as she takes him in her arms.

"Dad," she says.

"What are you doing here?" he says.

"Oh, Daddy," she says.

"I'm so happy you're here. This is the last tribe. And you saw the first sign of them, their little smokes rising to the sky. You saw their totem."

"Oh, yes, yes, eagle, bear, fish…."

Beth looks up as if to catch a glimpse of said totem and whispers something that he misses. Edward rolls his eyes around and sees me just then, standing next to one of the hunters where I have been watching.

"Jimmy! Where have you been?" He tugs loose from his daughter's hold, so that he might stand and greet me.

"Loafing about," I said. "Waiting for you."

"How kind of you," he says. "You have always been a kind fellow, Jimmy," he says. "And generous, yes, giving me so much of your time." He shakes his head. "Time? Your life!"

"And from you we have gotten a fair exchange, Edward," I say. I cock my head and ask him the Great Question. "Are you ready?"

He looks around for his daughter, but she is gone, probably just out to play at the water's edge, he thinks, and Myers is gone, where did he go, just when he needed him? And Tasáwiche? And the clamdigging princess?

Gone, all gone.

What happened next was easy, effortless, the thing that always seems so difficult to contemplate actually for reasons beyond my ken, turning out to be as simple as the movement of a wrist.

—and so he allowed me to carry him up and away with me through the smoke hole to where the air turned thin and white and from which height we had our clearest view of the earth as it is, canyons and river beds, forests decking the slopes of the mountains, swathes of desert, antelope running toward the shadows of oncoming night, and beyond them herds of horses that have been racing wild since their earliest ancestors had been born and died and then rekindled in stock by the Spaniards and then again by our many Western peoples— those wild ponies, how they moved, how they flew, how we joined our bodies and souls to them in the great hunts— smoke from many camps rising to make a shallow gray stream in the air, a stream on which glided the hawks, and above them, soaring, the eagles, guardians of all who lived, beneath the clouds we rose to meet.

"Wait! Wait!" Edward gestured wildly. Oh, this place of earth, he didn't really want to leave it! The children! He wanted to stay with the children! But what choice did he have? We could hover here briefly, but only briefly.

"There! Brazil!" I pointed out to him that stretch of landmass jutting out into the ocean.

"I always wanted to go there," he said. "The gold, the gold! Please, let me stay," he said in his broken Sioux.

"Too late," I told him. "That would have been another story."

And so, upon taking a deep breath, I urged him upward, and we rose and passed through the clouds above which sky darkened to the purple of the finest feathers on a hawk's wing, and I recognized the realm I had not visited since the end of my boyhood. We soared up, past our Earth's moon and sister planets, into the dark of the desert of space, before reaching great rivers and oceans of stars, vast ribbons of lights, gigantic swatches of white-heat and—hawk, Hal had once cried out in his fever, vermilion!—dark red and high green and purple, where flowers of galaxies bloomed and died and dark holes sucked in entire eons of time, turning the very essence of knowing into embers of forgetfulness. It ran color and burned color and splashed color and the smoke of the end of things drifted out into the sparking flow, where it seemed once to all of us who lived below so seamless a stream of light that we might one day set our canoes in the liquid space and paddle forward.

Or ride our horses. Starry-maned ponies that made it across a million miles at a trot.

"Oh, oh," he said, "I have not been here before."

"Or you have," I told him, "but just don't remember."

After a cosmic while we stopped to rest the animals. Edward dismounted, and seeing a great ledge of stars just above him, leaped like heroes before!

And caught hold of it, and without any pain whatsoever pulled himself up.

And from that great promontory of light, he saw passing before us millions of buffalo, so many that they blotted out many more millions of suns and gave the center of the galaxy the appearance of darkness, from the center of which now and then shot out spears of livid flame, which made us pause before we dared to cross against the flow.

And almost as many were the People, the origin and spawn of all the tribes going back to the days of the bridge of old land crossing to the New World, every chief present, every warrior, every mother and wife and daughter—Tasáwiche! Her father, Wipai! Chief Joseph! Gosh-o-ne! so many others—every brother in arms and every child, spinning off at the ends of spokes from the molten darkness at the center to the long vastly distant ends of the universe, every one of them floating, turning there, and giving the eye the sense of seeing everything that had ever happened and would happen all at once, past, present, future. All these souls!

Ay, Edward, sepia-toned, Edward, you'd think with all these souls out here that even in this soundless space there might be noise.

Listen.

From over the hill, over the next horizon of galaxies, beyond the forest of stars, and above the glowing mountains, from beneath the scintillate water and suffusing all glorious gold-toned space, drums and song, rhythm, chanting.

Edward, a smile testing his usually dour face, released his hold on the ledge of stars and went tumbling and swerving in every direction, up and down, side to side, and soon faded to a dot on the no-horizon of space, all the while saying to himself, over and over, over and over, over and over, the names of the tribes that kept him on the earth.

Achomawi,
Acoma, Apache,
Apsaroke (Crow), Arapaho,
Arikara, Assiniboine,
Atsina (Gros Ventre),

Blackfoot, Blood,
Brule (Sioux),
Cahuilla, Comanche,
Cowichan,
Cree, Crow (Apsaroke),
Cupeno

Cayuse,
Hidatsa, Hopi,   *Chemehuevi, Cheyenne,*
Hualapai, Hupa,   *Chimakum, Chinookan,*   *Dieguenos,*
Inuit   *Chipewyan,*   *Diomede, Flathead,*
                  Chochita Pueblo   *Gros Ventre (Atsina),*
                                       Haida,

Isleta Pueblo,   *Havasupai*
Jemez Pueblo   *Jicarilla (Apache),*
                  Kainah (Blackfoot), Kalispel,
                     Karok, Kato
                                          Keres

Klamath, Klickitat,

Kosimo, Kotzebue,
Kutenai

Kwakiutl,
Laguna Pueblo,
Maidu, Mandan,
Maricopa, Miwok, Mohave,
Mono, Nakoaktok, Nambe,
Navaho,
Nespilim, Nez Percé,
Noatok,
Nootka

Nunivak,   Ogalala
(Sioux), Osage, Oto,
Papago, Paviotso, Pawnee,
Piegan, Pima, Pojoaque, Pomo,
Ponca, Puye

Qahitaka,
Quilcene (Twana),
Quilliute, Quinault, Salish,
Salishan, San Ildephonso,
San Juan,
Santa Clara,
Sarsi, Selawik,
Serrano

Shoshoni,
Skokomish, Spokan,
Taos, Tesuque,
Teton

Sioux,
Tewa, Tiwa,
Tolowa,
Tututni

Willipa,
Wintun, Wishham,
Wiyot

Shasta

Umatilla,
Wailaki,
Walapai

Walla
Walla,   Wappo,
Washo

Yanktonai (Sioux),
Wichita

Yakima

Yaqui, Yavapai
Yuma

Yurok

Zuni

IN MEMORIAM

Edward S. Curtis, 1868–1952

Edward S. Curtis, internationally known authority on the history of the North American Indian, died today at the home of a daughter, Mrs. Elizabeth Magnuson. His age was 84. Mr. Curtis devoted his life to compiling Indian history. His research was done under the patronage of the late financier, J. Pierpont Morgan. The foreword for the monumental set of Curtis books was written by President Theodore Roosevelt. Mr. Curtis was also widely known as a photographer.

Notes on the Photographs

All of the photographs in this book and the following captions come from the Library of Congress EDWARD S. CURTIS COLLECTION

Page iv (TITLE PAGE)
Canyon de Chelly--Navajo: Seven riders on horseback and dog trek against background of canyon cliffs. (1904)

Page 30 (Chapter 3)
Sunset of Muir Inlet, Glacier Bay, Alaska; Large ice formations in water; mountains in background. (1899)

Page 76 (Chapter 5)
Hopi children (1905)

Page 94 (Chapter 6)
Home of the Havasupai: Havasupai woman seated in doorway of wickiup made from small trees, brush, reeds and earth; peach orchard blooms in background, sandstone canyon wall behind. (1903)

Page 116 (Chapter 7)
The old-time warrior—Nez Percé: Nez Percé man, wearing loin cloth and moccasins, on horseback. (1910)

Page 128 (Chapter 8)
Theodore Roosevelt's Children and Home: Sagamore Hill (1904)

Page 138 (Chapter 9)
Nakoaktok warrior; Kwakiutl man, full-length portrait, standing, facing front, holding pole. (1914)

Page 158 (Chapter 10)
Joseph—Nez Percé. Chief Joseph, half-length portrait, facing front, wearing warbonnet and several necklaces. (1903)

Page 166 (Chapter 11)
Babe and parent. Half-length portrait of mother and child facing front. (1905)

Page 172 (Chapter 12)
Joseph Dead Feast Lodge—Nez Percé (1905)

Page 184 (Chapter 13)
Qahatika girl, wearing scarf, head-and-shoulders portrait, facing front. (1907)

Page 224 (Chapter 16)
Interior of Wichita grass-house (1927)

Page 230 (Chapter 17)
Atsina camp scene: Tipis on plains. (1908)

Page 246 (Chapter 19)
Black Cañon: Rear view of Crow Indian, standing, over-looking Black Cañon. (1905)

Page 252 (Chapter 20)
Giving the medicine—Navaho: Navajo shaman gives medicine to participant sitting atop blanket(?) used in sweatbath, as two others look on. (1905)

Page 258 (Chapter 21)
A smoky day at the Sugar Bowl—Hupa: Hupa man with spear, standing on rock midstream; in background, fog partially obscures trees on mountainsides. (1923)

Page 280 (Chapter 22)
A child's lodge: Piegan girl standing outside small tipi. (1910)

Page 288 (Chapter 23)
Snake dancers entering the plaza: Spectators gathered on hillside and rooftop, snake dancers below. (1905)

Page 310 (Chapter 24)
Custer monument and group: Edward S. Curtis (second from right) and four Apsaroke men on horseback at the Custer Monument. (1908)

Page 366 (Chapter 27)
Camp Curtis: Log cabin in clearing in front of a large rock formation. (1908)

Page 374 (Chapter 28)
Puget Sound baskets (1913)

Page 378 (Chapter 29)
Masked dancers in canoes [B]—Qagyuhl: During the winter ceremony, Kwakiutl dancers in masks and costumes representing (left to right) Wasp, Thunderbird, and Grizzly-bear, arrive in canoes. (1914)

Page 384 (Chapter 30)
Wedding guests: Kwakiutl people in canoes, British Columbia. (1914)

Page 396 (Chapter 31)
Canon de Chelly—Navajo. Seven riders on horseback and
dog trek against background of canyon cliffs.

Page 424 (Chapter 32)
Invocation—Sioux: Dakota man, wearing breechcloth,
holding pipe, with right hand raised skyward. (1907)

Page 428 (Chapter 33)
Pgwis—Qagyuhl: Kwakiutl person wearing mask of mythical
creature Pgwis (man of the sea). (1914)

Page 448 (Chapter 35)
A bridal group: Kwakiutl wedding party, bride in center, hired
dancers on each side, her father on far left, all standing on platform, with plank wall behind them and flanked by two totem
poles. Groom's father on the right behind man with a box-drum.
(1914)

Page 460 (Chapter 36)
Hamasilahl—Qagyuhl: Ceremonial dancer, full-length
portrait, standing, wearing mask and fur garments during the
Winter Dance ceremony. (1914)

Page 470 (Chapter 37)
Country of the Kutenai [Flathead Lake, Montana]: Kootenai
Indian standing in an elk-hide canoe which is beached on the
rocky shore of Flathead Lake, Montana. (1910)

Page 478 (Epilogue)
Watching for the signal—Nez Percé. Two Nez Percé men on
horseback, one holding a bow, with gun in holster, while the
other is holding a coup stick. (1910)

For further discussion of *To Catch the Lightning*,
please visit www.sourcebooks.com or www.alancheuse.com
for a Reading Group Guide.

About the Author

Alan Cheuse is the author of the novels *The Bohemians* (1982), *The Grandmothers' Club* (1986), and *The Light Possessed* (1990), plus three collections of short fiction, *Candace and Other Stories* (1980), *The Tennessee Waltz* (1991), and *Lost and Old Rivers* (1998), and a pair of novellas, *The Fires* (2007), as well as the nonfiction work *Fall Out of Heaven: An Autobiographical Journey* (1987). As a book commentator, Cheuse is a regular contributor to National Public Radio's *All Things Considered*. He has edited with Caroline Marshall a volume of short stories, *Listening to Ourselves* (1994), and with Nicholas Delbanco, *Talking Horse: Bernard Malamud on Life and Work* (1997). He is also the editor of *Seeing Ourselves, Great American Short Fiction* (2007) and co-editor, with Lisa Alvarez, of *Writers Workshop in a Book: The Squaw Valley Community of Writers on the Art of Fiction* (2007). His short fiction has appeared in publications such as the *New Yorker*, *Ploughshares*, the *Southern Review*, the *Antioch Review*, *Another Chicago Magazine*, and elsewhere. Visit him at www.alancheuse.com.